The Lady Gets Lucky

She exhaled and tried to steady her heartbeat. As she calmed, reality began to set in. She looked around and considered the last five minutes.

You were alone with a beautiful man wearing hardly any clothing . . . and you told him to cover up.

Oh, for heaven's sake. How stupid. How utterly foolish. No doubt he thought her mad, a silly innocent who deserved a life of spinsterhood. Most women would leap at the chance to see Kit Ward in such a position. Moreover, they'd know how to turn it to their advantage, giving him come-hither looks and inviting smiles.

And what had Alice done?

She'd told him to drape a blanket over himself. Pinching the bridge of her nose between a thumb and forefinger, she tried not to cry. She couldn't face him, not now. Perhaps not ever. These lessons were a terrible idea.

She reached into her pocket, took out the recipe for poulardes à la Portugaise, and placed it on the bed. Then she hurried for the door.

"Where are you going?"

Also by Joanna Shupe

THE Lady Gets Lucky

~ The Fifth Avenue Rebels ~

JOANNA SHUPE

AVONBOOKS

An Imprint of HarperCollinsPublishers

THE LADY GETS LUCKY. Copyright © 2021 by Joanna Shupe. All rights reserved. Printed in the United States of America. No part of this book may be used or reproduced in any manner whatsoever without written permission except in the case of brief quotations embodied in critical articles and reviews. For information, address HarperCollins Publishers, 195 Broadway, New York, NY 10007.

First Avon Books mass market printing: November 2021

Print Edition ISBN: 978-0-06-304505-7
Digital Edition ISBN: 978-0-06-304403-6

Cover design by Guido Caroti
Cover illustration by Anna Kmet

Avon, Avon & logo, and Avon Books & logo are registered trademarks of HarperCollins Publishers in the United States of America and other countries.

HarperCollins is a registered trademark of HarperCollins Publishers in the United States of America and other countries.

FIRST EDITION

21 22 23 24 25   LSC   10 9 8 7 6 5 4 3 2 1

For my grandmothers,
one Southern and one Italian/German,
who both instilled a love of food in me.

The Lady Gets Lucky

Chapter One

✺

Chateau de Falaise
Newport, 1895

$\mathcal{Y}$ou are the most adorably charming man," the older woman said as she patted Kit's arm. "This house party would be dreadfully dull without you."

Since the end of dinner service, Kit had held court in the drawing room, with no less than eight pairs of eyes on him at all times. Over coffee and port, he joked and smiled, nodded and winked. Dazzled everyone in attendance without breaking a sweat.

In fact, charm was his only strength. He'd spent a lifetime perfecting a genuine-sounding laugh, a grin to win over the hardest of hearts. He knew how to put others at ease and make them feel important. Now he did this without even thinking, the effort so rote he'd forgotten why he started doing it in the first place.

And he'd started to hate himself for it.

"While all that is undoubtedly true," he said to the small group of mothers and chaperones, "I fear it is time for me to return to my room. If you ladies will excuse me." He inclined his head and stepped back.

"But it's early yet," one of the women protested, even though most everyone had retired hours ago.

Kit let his lips curl with a hint of wicked intent. "I never said I intended to sleep."

They tittered and fanned themselves—as he knew they would—which gave him the opportunity to slip away. The corridors were blessedly empty and the farther he got from the others, the more he was able to relax.

When he finally reached his guest room, he unknotted his bow tie and splashed bourbon in a crystal tumbler, not stopping until the glass was nearly full. The silence calmed him, a soothing respite from talking for six hours straight.

You have no one to blame but yourself.

True. In the beginning, his finely honed skills were his armor, a way to ensure he was never lonely or felt out of place ever again. But the problem with armor was twofold: it was hard to shed and he was vulnerable without it. Who was he underneath? The possibilities were too terrifying to contemplate.

A quiet knock sounded on his door. A tap, actually, as if someone was trying to get his attention while not causing too much noise. It was a familiar technique, one he'd employed often—as recently as this afternoon, in fact.

He hadn't been in the house even a full day when one of the chaperones invited him to her bedchamber, asking for help with her window casing. There'd been no problem with the window, of course, but Kit had provided other kinds of help, the kind that required little clothing and a flat surface. The interlude had been enjoyable for both of them, but she'd worn him out.

Any more window-casing issues would need to wait until the morning.

A second knock, slightly louder this time, had him striding to the door. As he pulled it open, he said, "Mary, my dear—" The words died in his throat. A slight girl, looking quite nervous, stared up at him. He remembered seeing her at dinner but couldn't recall her name. Had they even been introduced?

He gave her an easy smile. "Hello. Are you lost?"

"No." She darted a glance down the corridor. "May I come in?"

Interesting. He was still confused, though. This was one of the virginal heiresses trying to catch Harrison's eye at the house party. True, Harrison had already set his eye on someone—Maddie— but the heiresses didn't know that. So, why was the girl here?

He cocked his head. "You want to visit my room? Alone, at night?"

"Yes," she said through clenched teeth. "Please. Before someone sees me."

Shrugging, Kit widened the crack until the girl was able to squeeze through. She stood in the middle of his bedchamber, head swiveling and hands wringing, as if she didn't know what to do with herself. Brown hair was elegantly styled atop her head, and she still wore her evening gown, an expensive cream silk with no embellishments or dazzle, as if she didn't need frivolity. It was a refreshing and straightforward approach to sartorial matters and he liked it. She was adorable, in a younger sister sort of way.

He closed the door quietly and found his bourbon. "Would you care for a drink?"

She blinked several times, her expression shocked. "Goodness, no. I can't drink."

Even more interesting. "Because?"

"Because . . . Well, I don't know. My mother never lets me and—"

"Your mother isn't here at the moment." He went ahead and poured her a small drink. "And I think an illicit visit requires illicit refreshment, don't you?"

She took the heavy glass from his hand and stared at the contents as if waiting for something to happen. Were all virgins this cute?

The side of his mouth hitched. "It won't bite, I promise. Go on, sip it."

Shaking her head, she placed the glass on the dresser without sampling the spirits and walked to a pair of armchairs by the fire. "May we sit? You are making me nervous standing there all . . ." She waved her hand at him, as if to indicate his general self.

"All . . . ?"

"All tall and handsome. It's quite disorienting."

Amused, he lowered himself into a chair. "I'd apologize but I fear I wouldn't mean it. I've never been handed a more flattering comment, unintentional as it may have been."

"I beg your pardon. I tend to say the wrong thing. It's a terrible habit."

"If complimenting me is a result of that terrible habit, then may you never reform." He took a sip and watched her over the rim of his glass. Her cheeks were flushed and she was breathing heavily. Embarrassment? Excitement? "A bit unusual for me to be the responsible party in this situation, but I feel I must point out the danger of what we're doing. If we're caught, it could prove incredibly awkward for you."

She didn't flinch. "We won't be caught. My mother has taken her nightly laudanum and I made sure the maids were dismissed for the evening."

"Ah. Then all that's left is for you to tell me why you're here."

Clearing her throat, she folded her hands in her lap, fingers twisted tightly. "From what I have observed, you seem to know what you are doing with women."

He pressed his lips together to avoid laughing. Something told him amusement would offend her, and he had the strangest urge to protect her feelings. "I do have a bit of experience with women, yes. Comes with the tall and handsome territory, I'm afraid."

"That's perfect," she said, looking oddly relieved. "You are exactly what I need."

Indeed, this conversation was taking an unexpected turn. "I don't understand. You are here to try to marry Harrison Archer."

The young lady waved her hand. "Oh, Mr. Archer is in love with Miss Webster. Everyone can see that."

She'd noticed as much after one dinner? Perhaps his late-night visitor was more than she seemed.

"You are very astute, aren't you? I mean, you say I'm handsome and you aren't wrong, but you also picked up on Harrison's feelings for Maddie."

She sank into the plush armchair, shrinking before his eyes. "Oh, it's merely a lucky guess. I don't know anything."

"Are you embarrassed of being called clever?" When she sighed and looked down at her hands, he had his answer. "Being smart is nothing to be ashamed of."

"Of course you'd say that," she said. "You're a man. It's not the same for women. We shouldn't aspire for intelligence."

"That's absurd. Who told you such nonsense?"

"My mother."

No spirits and an attitude of women worthy of a caveman? "I believe I don't care for your mother."

"We are losing focus."

He grinned as he sipped from his glass. This young woman was entertaining, in an unusual way. "And what focus is that?"

"I would like your help in learning how to seduce a man."

The bourbon slid down the wrong pipe and Kit choked, bending over and coughing as he struggled for air. Droplets rolled down his chin, so he wiped his face. "You *what*?"

She swallowed, her delicate throat working. "I'd like you to teach me how to seduce a man."

"Why?"

"Because I need to seduce and marry one."

Her tone indicated that the explanation was simple, like he was an idiot for not understanding. He held up a hand. "Wait a moment. We should back up and begin again." He put the heavy glass on the side table. "First things first. What is your name?"

Oh, God. He didn't even know her name.

Here she was, blathering on for almost ten minutes, and Mr. Ward hadn't a clue as to who she was. It was utterly mortifying.

Skin aflame, Alice forced out, "Miss Alice Lusk."

"Were we introduced earlier?"

"No. I was . . ." *Watching you from afar.* That sounded bizarre and off-putting, so she said, "Conversing with the other guests."

"Ah," he said, his dark eyes glittering. "Well, it is a pleasure to meet you, Miss Lusk. I am Mr. Christopher Ward, but friends call me Kit."

She knew all this, but politeness dictated that she smile and nod. "A pleasure to meet you, as well, Mr. Ward."

"You may call me Kit, as we are past formality, I think." He indicated the bedchamber and Alice's internal body temperature rose even further. "Now, what is this about seducing a man?"

"I need to learn how it's done."

"Why?"

Wasn't it obvious? Seduction, man, wedding. "So that I may marry him."

The side of his mouth kicked up, making him appear even more roguish. "Lure him into a compromising position where you're both discovered and—gasp!—you're forced to marry. Is that it?"

"No!" Goodness, that sounded Machiavellian. Her plan wasn't as crafty as all that. "I don't wish to trap a man into marrying me." That was worse than being married solely for her dowry. The last thing Alice wanted was a husband resentful of being duped for the next fifty-odd years.

"Then what is your plan?"

She bit her lip and stared at her lap. The plan occurred to her tonight during dinner. With her second season now behind her, it was apparent that the right man was not going to come along and sweep Alice off her feet. The right men were not interested in a girl like her. They flocked to the pretty, outgoing debutantes. The only men who paid Alice any attention were the desperate fortune hunters and the older widowers looking for a young biddable bride. Certainly no man who would ever love her for herself. Mama said this was expected, that Alice's dowry was her only redeeming quality.

The men won't mind your plain face when they hear the size of your dowry.

It was true. Alice hadn't the first clue as to how to attract a man with her character, rather than her father's bank account. And she couldn't change her dowry, so where did that leave her? Utterly doomed, no doubt.

Then an offhanded comment at dinner gave her an idea. Maddie caught Alice watching Kit and had tried to warn her off. "Kit is the very Devil. With one smile, he manages to turn even the shyest woman into a vixen. It never fails," Maddie had said.

The words had bounced around in Alice's brain and, even more curious, she'd continued to observe him. With black hair and dark eyes, strong jaw and elegant nose, he was wickedly handsome. The black evening wear hugged his lean body, showing off wide shoulders and long limbs. Looking at him caused hundreds of imaginary butterflies to erupt in her stomach.

But it was more than his looks. He was comfortable in his own skin, commanding a room the instant he walked inside. During the cocktail hour nearly every woman—young and old—had fought for a scrap of his attention. He'd entertained them with easy smiles and raucous stories, the group hanging on his every word.

During the soup course, he'd winked at an older woman across the table and she offered a bold stare in return, one that burned with hidden meaning. He had flirted right there at the dinner table, out in the open, which Alice found astounding. What conjurer's magic did he possess to cause women to act this way?

He manages to turn even the shyest woman into a vixen.

And Alice began to wonder about her own dilemma. Was Kit capable of such a metamorphosis . . . even with the most unlikely of pupils?

She needed more confidence, more . . . experience. No man would fall in love with an insipid, timid mouse. If she could transform herself into a girl like Maddie—fun and sociable—then perhaps she could land a handsome husband.

"Alice," he said, interrupting her thoughts. "Your plan is what?"

Was he actually going to make her say it? Uttering the words aloud to this gorgeous, charming man would be humiliating. "Is it necessary for you to know?"

"I'm afraid it is, dear Alice. I cannot aid and abet the tricking of some poor unsuspecting fellow."

"I am not tricking anyone."

He picked up his glass once more, long fingers wrapping around the heavy crystal. "That remains to be seen."

Sakes alive, he was going to force her to say it. She took a deep breath and let the air out slowly. *You can do this, Alice. You need to become a vixen, remember?* "I am quite shy around the opposite sex. That, combined with my large dowry, attracts a certain type of man, one not interested in *me*. Do you understand?"

"You are hoping to marry for love."

"Yes, or as close to love as I can get."

He studied her over the rim of his glass as he drank. She couldn't tell what he was thinking, his inscrutable gaze glittering in the gaslight. The longer his silence lasted, the more nervous she became. Why had she thought this was a good idea? Clearly, this had been a mistake. He was trying to think of a way to refuse without hurting her feelings.

She started to push out of her chair. "I should go. This was a—"

"Wait a moment." He held out his free hand, staying her. "Don't rush off. Give a man time to think, if you please."

Heart pounding, Alice sank into the plush upholstery and tried not to faint from mortification. Would he tell the other guests of her strange request? She'd become the laughingstock of the house party. Her mother would learn of it, too.

Oh, God. She'd made a terrible error in judgment in coming here.

"You're panicking. Calm down, Alice." Tapping his fingers on the glass, he cocked his head. "Why me?"

Was he actually considering it?

Hope caused her to sit straighter in her chair. "Because Miss Webster said you manage to turn even the shyest woman into a vixen."

Kit threw his head back and laughed, the muscles in his throat shifting under sun-kissed skin. "Maddie would say as much. She's always telling me to mind my manners around her friends. Still, that doesn't necessarily make it true."

"You're being humble. From what I observed tonight, I believe her."

"Well, I'm not certain I believe you're even shy. You haven't had much trouble talking to me and you've barged into my room like a general headed into battle."

Irritation swept over her skin like a hot cloth, and she lifted her chin. "I am ridiculously shy."

He nodded as his mouth twisted into a teasing grin. "Indeed, I can tell. More bourbon, Alice?"

Oh, he was annoying. "Will you help me or not?"

Standing, he went to refill his glass at the sideboard. She couldn't help but stare at the wide shoulders stretching the fabric of his fine shirt, the way the white silk vest hugged his torso. He possessed lean hips and a firm backside only achieved through vigorous activity. Kit was the finest-looking man she'd ever seen, and his appearance sent heat cascading through her belly.

Yet, he was right. She wasn't so nervous with him any longer. Why?

When he turned around, she tried to pretend as if

she hadn't been ogling him. Considering the smirk on his face, she likely failed. He leaned against the sideboard. "What does my help mean? Am I taking you to bed? Drawing you diagrams? Writing a treatise? I'm not quite sure what you expect."

She chewed the inside of her lip. "Well, I'm hardly your type of woman. It is safe to say that"— she gestured to the bed—"is impossible. I thought more like question and answer sessions, or role-playing. Insight into the male mind and what they find attractive."

A crease appeared between his brows, deepening as she spoke. "I don't have a type of woman," he said, "but if I did, how are you so certain you're not it?"

Because you're perfect and I'm . . . me.

Kit could have his pick of women at this house party. Probably already had, considering he'd believed her to be someone named Mary at the door a few moments ago. "If nothing else," she said, "I am realistic about my appeal, which is why drastic measures must be taken."

"I see." He brought the glass to his mouth for another sip. "And what will you do if I decline to share my wealth of knowledge?"

She frowned, not caring for the direction of the conversation. If he planned to refuse, she wished he'd spit it out and save her the humiliation. "Find someone else, I suppose. Mr. Archer, maybe?"

Kit made a scoffing sound. "A true waste of your time. Harrison was a bit of a late bloomer and not exactly a pillar of success in the romance department."

"Well, there must be another man willing to help me, if you won't. A footman or groom, perhaps. They are generally young and energetic."

"The prospect of you asking another man fills me with an overwhelming sense of dread. Why not ask one of the ladies? Maddie or that redhead, Miss Young? They both seem to attract male attention."

Would she actually learn the ins and outs of the male mind by discussing this with a woman? Alice doubted it. Because, really, who knew how men thought better than another man? "No, I need more than a few tips. I need a degree in seduction. From a man."

He drained his glass and set it down with a heavy sigh. "Sadly, that man cannot be me."

Alice's stomach sank, disappointment sweeping through her. *I failed and now he'll tell the entire house party of my request. Everyone will laugh at me.*

Idiot.

How could she have been so stupid? Why had she considered for a single moment that this gorgeous, charming man would waste any time on *her*? A momentary lapse of sanity, obviously.

She pushed to her feet, her only thought of escape. "Of course. Forget I asked. I'll leave you to your night."

"Wait." He blocked her path and put up his hands. "Let me explain."

Run. Get away. Go hide.

"Not necessary." She dodged around him and lunged for the doorknob. "I understand perfectly." She tried to pull the door open but it wouldn't budge.

Kit was leaning on the door to prevent it from opening. "Dash it, Alice. Let me at least explain why."

She slumped and nodded. The quicker she listened, the quicker she could return to her room and cry.

A light touch on her elbow guided her around to face him. They were close enough that she could see the light flecks in his dark irises and the evening whiskers dotting his jaw. And it was worth noting he smelled fantastic, hints of warm caramel and honey, exactly like the spirits he'd poured her earlier.

He was frowning, his gaze concerned. "I don't want you to leave here thinking this is because of *you*. It's not. I must refuse because of Maddie."

"I . . . I don't understand."

"She ordered me to stay away from the heiresses. I believe *off-limits* was the term she used. So, I must respect her wishes and not interfere with the purpose of the house party."

"Oh."

Well, that wasn't a terrible reason. And Maddie had warned Alice away from Kit at dinner, as well. Ordering him to keep his distance from the guests made sense. Except . . . "But you thought I was one of the guests at the door when I knocked."

His lips twisted into a wicked smile that she felt all the way down to her toes. "She's a guest but not one of the innocent young women, believe me."

A chaperone, then. "So you'll help me after the house party, once we're back in New York?"

Chuckling, he wagged a finger at her. "Clever,

Alice. Very clever. Will you be able to slip away as easily in the city?"

"No." Her mother paid the hotel staff handsomely and they did whatever she wished, including keep an eye on Alice. "It would be extremely difficult."

"I assumed as much."

"You . . ." Alice cleared her throat. "You won't tell anyone I was here, will you?"

"Of course not." He lifted her hand and kissed her knuckles, his eyes boring deep into hers, mesmerizing her. "I wish you luck, sweet girl. You will find the right man, I promise. You're too intelligent not to get what you want."

The press of his lips on her skin along with his intense scrutiny caused a riot in her bloodstream, a rush of tingles and warmth that traveled to every part of her. Her knees actually buckled and she sent up a prayer of gratitude for the door at her back. Otherwise, she would have collapsed into a puddle on the carpets.

It was all too much. He was overwhelming, with his delicious smell and soft mouth, and she didn't know what to do. No man had ever spoken to her so nicely or touched her in such an intimate manner. She needed time to think, to process the emotions battling inside her.

No wonder why Maddie had warned Alice away from Kit. Perhaps he *was* the very Devil.

Speech failing her, she nodded once, pulled out of his grip and hurried out into the corridor.

Chapter Two

❦

The next afternoon the guests gathered under a tent outside, and Kit wondered if he'd made a huge mistake.

First, Maddie's suitor, the Duke of Lockwood, had arrived unexpectedly and Harrison appeared a knife's edge away from punching the aristocrat in the face. Secondly, today's outing was an egg hunt, a childish game that would require Kit to engage in small talk with one of the young ladies for the better part of the afternoon.

Third—and worst of all—Alice Lusk hadn't looked at him once today.

Currently, Alice was staring at her hands, which were placed in her lap, and ignoring the conversation swirling around her. Tiny lines bracketed eyes lined with dark circles and guilt pricked at his chest. He didn't like seeing her tired and . . . withdrawn.

I am ridiculously shy.

Said the woman who'd paid him a midnight visit and asked for lessons on men. He nearly snorted.

Perhaps shy around others, but she hadn't been shy with him.

Even despite Maddie's warning to stay away from the young ladies, he'd considered helping Alice. No woman should be forced to endure an unhappy marriage. Wasn't Kit aware of the potential results of such a circumstance better than most? His father had used his mother's inheritance for mistresses and gambling, while treating Mama abominably. He'd even committed her to an asylum for a month when she wouldn't move to Staten Island, as he'd wanted. Mama had led a powerless, unhappy existence until her dying day, eight years ago. Witnessing her sadness had broken Kit's heart.

Yet, Kit had agreed to keep his distance from the unmarried girls here. Maddie was a good friend and he wouldn't break his promise to her, even if the shadows in Alice's eyes twisted something up inside him. He had the urge to go over and make Alice laugh, just so that haunted look would disappear.

They are off-limits, Christopher.

Maddie's words, uttered just before the guests arrived, echoed through his head. Perhaps he could find a way to offer Alice advice without—

Oh, for God's sake. Who was he trying to fool? Thick desire had rolled through him last night when Alice had asked so sweetly for instruction. He knew himself. That desire, combined with the nature of her request, would have him flirting, making inappropriate suggestions . . . doing anything he could to tempt adorable Alice into bed.

He really was a scoundrel.

Maddie brought out the egg hunt supplies and Kit smothered a groan. "You owe me," he muttered to Harrison, who was seated at his side. "I cannot believe I am about to go on a damn egg hunt."

"Don't let her hear you complain." Harrison tipped his head toward Maddie. "Furthermore, it's not like I forced you to come."

"You're one of my closest friends. You think I'd let you embark on wooing your lady love alone? You need all the help you can get."

"Sure, right. Just admit you like parties, Kit."

Kit frowned, annoyed at his friend's remark. Yes, he liked parties—but that wasn't why he'd come to Newport. "I'm here for you, in case I didn't make that clear. But if you don't need me, I'll return to the city. I have a thousand things to do at the moment."

Recently, Kit had realized there were careers for men like him—and not a gambler or confidence man like his waste of a father. No, this was a business well suited to a risk-taking smooth-talker who wished to keep on the right side of the law. Something different, an entertainment venue the city needed—a supper club. A classy establishment, the supper club would be part Delmonico's, part Metropolitan Opera House and a sprinkle of Tenderloin dance hall.

The endeavor excited Kit like nothing else ever had. He'd even brought work—work!—with him to this Newport house party, some preliminary estimates of up-front costs that he needed to double-check. If all went to plan, the supper club would open this autumn, and he would finally prove to everyone that he was good for more than a laugh.

So yes, he had better things to do than spend a long weekend at the ocean.

Harrison grimaced. "The supper club. How could I forget? I'm being an ass, so forgive me. Don't leave. I really do need your help."

"Of course you do. So be nice to me."

"Do you really think you can get this supper club off the ground?"

Kit shifted and tried not to react, though his ears grew hot. "You don't think I'm capable of it?"

Harrison shrugged, his eyes darting to Maddie as she walked around the tent. "Feels like a lot to take on, a lot of responsibility. Why would you bother? It can't be for the money."

No, it wasn't for the money. It was for things money couldn't buy, like self-worth and respect. Excitement. Proving to himself and everyone else that his mind wasn't as empty as they believed. A legacy that might redeem his awful branch of the Ward family tree.

You're just like your old man, his father had said to Kit on any number of occasions. *Smile to get what we want instead of thinking so hard.*

Fucking bastard. Kit hoped his father was broke and miserable.

Maddie arrived holding a hat with slips of paper inside, and Harrison and Kit each selected one. Whichever guests had the corresponding number would partner up together. "Which lucky lady has selected number four?" Kit shouted over the din of conversation and ocean breeze.

No one answered and the others began pairing up. Harrison matched with Katherine Delafield, a likable girl whose father was a real estate tycoon and unmitigated bastard. The Duke of Lockwood held up the same number as the bold Miss Young, a fellow troublemaker if Kit ever saw one. In fact, he'd purposely avoided that particular temptation in the hopes of not breaking his promise to Maddie.

As the teams moved off to the side, one young lady didn't budge from her seat. *Alice.* Ah, he understood. His would-be pupil must also have number four. If so, why hadn't she claimed him?

Standing, he adjusted his cuffs and smoothed his hair, practically preening to make himself presentable. He didn't know why it mattered, but he wanted to look his best. Or perhaps he was merely stalling. He hadn't liked disappointing her, causing her to lose the sparkle in her eye last night.

There must be another man who would be willing to help me.

Was she considering someone else? If so, Kit would need to promptly set her straight. A suggestion like hers in the wrong ear could lead to trouble.

Going over, he held up his slip of paper. "Are you my partner for the egg hunt, Miss Lusk?"

Her shoulders rose and fell on a long breath. "It appears so, Mr. Ward."

"Well, no need to look so glum. The good news is that I know the chateau grounds forward and backward, so we stand to make off like bandits. Are you ready?"

"Have I a choice?"

There was no chance to respond because Maddie began to explain the rules and prizes. Alice didn't seem interested in the jewelry offered up to the winning teams. Instead, she stared at the water, her mouth pulled into a frown. Was she so unhappy about partnering with him?

His cheeks grew hot as he stood there, being ignored as the teams departed. "Would you rather switch? I'm certain I can convince someone into giving me their number."

"No, that would be even more humiliating." She pushed away from the table and stood. "Let's get this over with."

Confused, he held out his arm and led her out of the tent. Though the sun was strong, the breeze coming off the water felt cool on his overheated skin. While everyone headed toward the gardens, Kit started for the beach.

"Wait, why are we going this way? Most everyone else is starting in the gardens."

"Exactly. Maddie likes a challenge. She won't make this easy, and hiding eggs in the gardens is too easy." Besides, they could have a private conversation down near the waves and not risk being overheard.

Kit planned to get to the bottom of why she was ignoring him.

They descended the steps leading to the Cliff Walk. "There." He pointed to an egg on the stone. "I told you."

She bent to collect it. "You care about her, don't you?"

"Maddie? Yes, she's a close friend. We spent a lot of time together after Harrison left for Paris." He took the egg and placed it in his hat. "Which is why I must uphold my promise to her."

"I understand."

"Do you?" He shielded his eyes from the sun

and stared down at her. "Because my refusal to help you has nothing to do with you."

"Yes, you already said."

"Yet I sense you don't believe me." Otherwise, why ignore him? Why the disappointment when they were partnered?

"I do."

"Really?"

"Really. Now, may we cease discussing it? I am embarrassed enough."

They began walking once more. The tide was out, the waves gentle and rolling, which allowed them to converse without shouting. "There's no reason to be embarrassed about asking for help, for trying to take control of your own life. I applaud it, actually."

"You do?"

"Yes. My parents were unhappy in their marriage, and I saw the misery inflicted on a woman with no power, no say over her life."

"I'm sorry."

He lifted a shoulder. "My father is not a nice man." An understatement, but there was no reason to scare Alice with tales of the Ward family. Those nightmares belonged to Kit and his two siblings, both of whom had moved away years ago. He hadn't seen either since his mother's funeral, and his father had skipped town before even that, as soon as Kit's mother grew ill. Four years it took her to die, and that bastard had already taken the family money and started a new life out West before she was cold in the ground.

Unfortunately, the distance hadn't kept his father from trying to get his hands on Kit's sizable trust fund. Kit's maternal grandmother had set aside money for all the grandchildren, which they could access when they turned eighteen. Kit had been the only Ward sibling smart enough to refuse their father's demand for money, and he hadn't heard from dear Papa since.

"I take it you two aren't close," Alice said as she scooped up another egg.

"That is correct." He pointed to the green egg in her hand. "That egg has more morality than my father." Alice's lips twitched, so Kit gave her an exaggerated expression of surprise. "Have I nearly made you laugh?"

The side of her mouth hitched. "You are amusing."

"Well, that is something." He dropped the second egg into his hat. "Tall, handsome *and* amusing? You'll turn my head with all that flattery, Alice Lusk."

She blushed under the rim of her hat, color decorating her cheekbones. "As if I could ever."

"Turn my head, you mean? You seriously underestimate your appeal. When you left my room last night—" Shit. He couldn't dare tell her that he'd pleasured himself to thoughts of her, while the sweet smell of her perfume or soap still lingered in the air.

"What?"

"It would hardly be a suitable conversation for a young lady."

Alice stopped to look up at him, her expression more serious than a nun in church. "But that is precisely why you *should* tell me. That is why I came to you for help in the first place."

He shoved his free hand in his trouser pocket.

This was dangerous territory indeed. The words were burning his tongue, his mind anxious to see her reaction as he told her the truth. *I pulled out my cock before you were even down the hall. I sat on my bed, smelling your lingering flowery scent, and stroked myself, my erection so hard it hurt. Twisting and pulling, I worked my shaft until I trembled and spend erupted into my hand.*

He shouldn't. He promised Maddie, and Alice deserved better. She needed a gentle soul to help her wade into the shallows before allowing her to jump into deeper, more salacious waters. Those were the depths Kit loved—the more salacious, the better, actually—but Alice was innocent. He didn't want to corrupt her.

Gesturing to the walk ahead, he said, "Shall we continue?"

WHAT HAD HE been about to say?

Mind whirring, Alice struggled to keep her hat on her head in the stiff breeze as a silent Kit led her along the path. The light, easy mood from before had shifted like the tide, and now he was polite but no longer his charming self. In fact, he'd hardly said two words since she'd prompted him to tell her about last night. Why?

She wished he'd talk again. Clearly, they needed to avoid the topic of the previous evening, which was fine with her. She'd experienced enough rejection for one weekend. But what else should they discuss? She didn't know him at all and, even if she did, she was terrible at conversation.

What did strangers of the opposite sex talk about when they were alone? Kit didn't seem enamored of his family, so best not to offend him by probing on that front. Politics and religion were often touchy subjects, not that he seemed inclined to discussing either. What was left? Hobbies and interests?

His deep voice interrupted her musings. "I can hear you thinking, Alice."

"That is ridiculous," she said automatically.

"So, you weren't thinking?"

"Of course I was thinking. I'm always thinking." She paused. "Aren't you?"

"Not if I can avoid it. Introspection is not my forte." Something in his voice sounded off. Hollow, almost.

"Thinking doesn't always mean introspection."

"I believe that is the very definition."

"Hardly. Introspection is more when—" When he grinned, his aim became glaringly obvious. She narrowed her eyes. "You were trying to get me to talk."

"Guilty. Still, isn't that better than being lost in your own head?"

Yes, though she wouldn't give him the satisfaction of admitting it. "Shall we go back?"

"Let's keep going. This will lead us to the edge of the property, behind the gardens. Look, there's another egg."

Sure enough, he was right. She added the egg to the pile in his hat. "You don't strike me as the type of man to enjoy an egg hunt, yet you are surprisingly good at it."

"See? And you were disappointed to be my partner."

Was that what he believed? "Not disappointed. Embarrassed."

"Which we already discussed. You've nothing to be embarrassed about."

She disagreed, but wasn't up to debating it at the moment. "Furthermore, I know you'd rather be paired with anyone else."

"Not true. I was already planning to get you alone to check on you. From the moment I walked into the tent you ignored me."

Her brows pulled together. "I didn't think you'd notice." *Or care.*

"Of course I noticed." He stopped and held her arm, his grip tight without causing her pain. "I saw you right away, staring at your hands and not meeting my eye. I was worried about you."

Her face slackened in surprise and she blinked several times. "Why?"

The edge of his mouth curled, and he dragged his free hand through his dark hair, making it even more unruly. "I don't know. Probably because I didn't like disappointing you last night."

"And you thought you'd broken me, was that it?"

"Broken is a harsh word," he muttered, but didn't deny it.

Before she could stop herself, she blurted, "You have an inflated sense of yourself, sir." Instantly, she covered her mouth, horrified. "Oh, that was rude. Forgive me."

He didn't appear offended, however. "No need to apologize. Has anyone ever told you how pretty you are when you're riled?"

Pretty. The word wrapped around her and sank into her flesh, deep into her bones, nourishing her like a plant starving for water. Kit thought she was pretty? Or . . . was he just trying to make her feel better? Unsure, she turned and started walking.

"Wait up." His long legs easily caught up. "Why are you hurrying away?"

She didn't know how to put it other than to tell the truth. "You needn't ply me with false flattery. You've already turned me down, remember?"

"I've never lied to you, Alice." He stepped in front of her, leaving her no choice but to stop. "And I told you why I turned you down. It has nothing to do with you."

"Fine, but may we never speak of it again? It is mortifying."

Something in her voice must have convinced him because he raised his free hand in surrender. "Consider it a forbidden topic."

"Good." Sighing, she pointed to the stone steps ahead. "Let's go up and find more eggs."

Once they were on the back part of the chateau's property, he pointed them toward an old potter's shed. "Over there."

"Are you certain?" The structure appeared one stiff breeze away from falling over.

"Trust me."

She followed him to the shed, which was hardly bigger than a coat closet. He opened the door. "After you."

Inside, he set his hat containing their eggs on a large upside-down pot. The shed was stacked with sacks of dirt and feed, rakes and other gardening equipment. There wasn't much space to move about.

She looked around. "Do you really think there are eggs in here? We are quite far from the tent."

Kit headed for a large piece of machinery in the corner. "At least two, if I were to guess. Look behind those bags over there."

Sure enough, three eggs were eventually located behind bags, pots and garden utensils. When they were back outside, Kit said, "So, what shall we discuss if not that off-limits topic?"

As if she had a clue. "No doubt you'll come up with something."

"Well, I do have excellent conversation skills with the opposite sex, but I fear pointing that out would bring us around to that off-limits topic."

She didn't know whether to laugh or grind her teeth. He was impossible. And sort of adorable. The teasing words fell from her mouth easily. "It's becoming clear that I should have tried to get to know you better before visiting your room last night."

He gasped like an actor in the third act of a murder mystery. "Are you saying you would have reconsidered had you known me? You wound me, cruel woman."

She bit her lip, feeling lighter than she had in ages. This type of natural rapport was new for her. Kit deserved most of the credit, of course. He made everything so effortless.

Joking aside, she did have a desire to learn more about him. Perhaps he wouldn't give her lessons in seduction, but she might be able to discover the secret to his confidence, the joie de vivre that ensured his appeal. "I am curious about your hobbies and your interests. What do you do with all your nonintrospection time?"

He chuckled and pleasure wound through her,

her chest ballooning with the simple delight of amusing this charming man. Hardly anyone laughed with her. Some of the hotel staff would occasionally converse with her but—other than the kitchen staff—they mostly kept a polite distance.

"If you can believe it, I am in the process of opening a supper club," he said. "I am soon to become a nighttime purveyor of good food and good times."

"Is that like a social club?"

"Sort of. A social club open at night that provides various forms of entertainment. One opened a few years ago in the Metropolitan Opera House after the fire. It's a small secret club among a certain set, but I'd like to do a bigger version."

"That . . . actually sounds perfect for you."

"Thank you. I cannot claim all the credit. My friend Preston is the other half of the venture."

"Preston Clarke, the builder?" She wasn't from New York, but she knew the name.

"You've heard of him? Oh, look in that bush. I think I see an egg."

Alice plucked the blue egg off the ground and added it to the pile that Kit carried. "Mr. Clarke came to the hotel where I'm staying. He was trying to lure the chef away."

Kit's head swiveled sharply. "You're staying at the Fifth Avenue Hotel?"

"Yes. My mother likes the rooms."

"And how do you know this—about Preston and the chef?"

"I was there."

He came to an abrupt halt and one egg tumbled from his hat down to the ground. His body went oddly still. "You were there? Where, in the kitchens?"

Alice picked the errant egg off the ground and put it back in his hat. "Yes."

"Why?"

Under no circumstances would she reveal this secret to him—or anyone else. Her mother forbade Alice's interest in cooking eons ago. Instead, she shrugged and tried not to notice how his confusion only made him more appealing. "I just go in there sometimes."

"Balderdash. An evasion, if I've ever heard one. You may confide in me." He dipped to stare into her eyes. "Do they sneak you extra cake every now and then?"

Please. She could make her own cake.

"No—and you'll laugh if I tell you. Goodness knows I already have enough to be embarrassed about with you."

"Again, there is no embarrassment and you simply must tell me. I'll chuck these eggs into the ocean if you don't."

She gestured toward the water behind them. "Go ahead. I don't need the jewelry." She had more than she'd ever wear, thanks to her father.

"I promise, I won't laugh."

He looked so sincere that her resolve weakened. "Do you swear?"

Kit used a finger to cross his heart. "If I laugh, I'll give you those lessons you asked for, promise to Maddie be damned."

How could she lose? She lifted her chin. "Angelo is a friend and he—"

"Wait." His jaw fell and he shook his head as if trying to clear it. "Angelo? Are you talking about Chef Franconi? *The* Chef Franconi?"

"Yes. He worked for my family in Boston for years before moving to New York." She'd spent her whole childhood in his kitchen asking questions and learning all she could about food.

"This is amazing. You have to help us."

"Help you with what?"

"Franconi, of course. He keeps refusing us. We've been trying to hire him."

"He won't leave the hotel." Angelo loved it there and they paid him handsomely. Furthermore, being the head chef in an established hotel such as the Fifth Avenue was a feather in the cap of any chef. Going to a new venture, like a supper club, was a step backward.

"Do you know that for certain?"

"Absolute certainty."

Kit stared off into the distance, his eyes vacant. "Damn."

"There are other chefs," she pointed out.

"Yes, but none that can cook like Franconi. He's the very best in the city, possibly the country. Do you think he'd sell us a few of his recipes? Then we could still be associated with his name without hiring him."

"I don't know. He might." An idea began to brew in the back of her mind, a devious plan where everyone came out ahead. "Out of curiosity, which recipes are you most interested in?"

"Well, the ducklings à la bigarade, of course. And the chicken dish, the one with the rice."

"Poulardes à la Portugaise," she supplied. "What else?"

"The lobster thermidor." He stroked his jaw with his free hand. "I'd have to think about it, I suppose, but six or seven main courses and a few desserts should do it." He grinned at her. "This is fantastic. I can't wait to tell Preston that we've got an in with Chef Franconi."

"I haven't agreed to help you yet."

His happiness faded as he studied her face. "And what would it take to convince you to help us?"

Alice didn't answer, instead letting the silence drag out. He was a smart man; let him figure it out.

His brows slowly rose and his lips twisted into an impressed smile. "Oh, I see. Well done, Alice. It seems you'll get those lessons, after all."

"Really? You'll do it?"

"If Franconi agrees, yes. I assume you'll need to talk to him once we're back in the city."

"Not necessary."

"Don't we need him to agree to share the recipes with us?"

"Yes, he'd need to agree, but the recipes are here." She tapped her temple.

"You've memorized Franconi's recipes?"

Yes, as she'd made most of the chef's dishes many times before, including the ones Kit wanted to buy. "Nearly all of them, actually. I will cable him this afternoon to arrange a price."

"Excellent. So, you'll spend the day tomorrow writing them down for me and, in exchange, I'll give you some tips on how to appeal to whichever man your heart desires."

That sounded . . . abrupt. She didn't want tips. She wanted to be *transformed*. After all, her future depended on it. She had to convince him to do more than jot down a few hints.

No, this wouldn't do.

Fortunately, if Alice had learned one thing from her father, it was how to negotiate. Daddy owned the second-largest transport shipping company in the world, with steamships and cargo ships all over the globe. He always said never to accept the first offer.

Lifting her chin, she tried to put some force behind her voice. "No."

"I don't understand. I am offering to help you in exchange for the recipes. It's a fair trade."

"Sharing those recipes for a few hints is hardly fair. No, you'll have to do better. Fair is a full lesson for every recipe I give you."

Chapter Three

$\mathscr{K}$it studied the slight woman at his side. For a supposedly shy person, Alice could certainly drive a hard bargain. Yet, he still didn't have a clue as to what she expected of him. "A full lesson? Like how to kiss in exchange for ducklings à la bigarade?"

Color dotted her cheeks, and her gaze grew slightly unfocused. Was she considering it? He'd love a peek inside her mind right now, just to discover if she fancied the idea of kissing him or not.

Because the more he was around Alice, the more he definitely wanted to kiss her.

"That would hardly be proper," she said. "And as I mentioned last night, questions and answers should do."

"What about role-playing?" He could think of several naughty games they could play together, like the farmhand and the milkmaid. The footman and the wealthy widow. The shopgirl and the—

She's a virgin.

Damn. He exhaled and tried to remember where

he was and with whom he was dealing. Whatever happened, he could not corrupt her.

"Perhaps," she said, clearly oblivious to the lascivious meaning behind his suggestion of role-playing. "We'll have to see. Do we have a deal?"

"Fine, I agree." What did he have to lose? Spend a few hours with this clever, unconventional girl to get several of Franconi's recipes? There was no downside. "I'll cable you once we're back in New York to set up a—"

"No, no. It must be here. This weekend."

Kit's eyes nearly popped out of his skull. "Here? But I've already explained why that's impossible. Maddie will shove me onto a spit and roast me alive."

The little minx merely lifted a shoulder and began strolling toward the tent. "Dash it," Kit muttered, and started after her. "Why can't this wait until we're in the city?"

"You said it yourself. I won't be able to slip away in the city, not like I can here."

"But . . ."

If only he didn't want those recipes so badly . . .

If only Preston had been able to convince Franconi on his own . . .

If only Maddie hadn't warned him off the young ladies . . .

Speaking of Maddie, her beau had just arrived, which doubled the number of men interested in her at this house party. Would their hostess now be too distracted to keep a tab on what Kit was doing with the guests?

He did love a good gamble.

"All right, Alice. We'll start tonight."

"Really?"

She kept her gaze on the ground as they walked, but the twin spots of color were back on her cheeks. He loved those sweet blushes of hers. "Indeed. Only four nights remain, so we must maximize our lesson time. Though daytime works, as well." He'd need to capitalize on every opportunity if he planned to get a decent number of recipes.

They approached the edge of the gardens, where a large topiary loomed. One of the Roosevelt girls had coaxed Kit behind it two summers ago and . . . well, they hadn't been discovered for hours.

Hadn't been discovered . . . Hmm.

"Let's go this way." He clasped her elbow gently. "I want to start our lessons."

"*Now?*"

"No time like the present. Follow me, Alice."

They made it about four steps before she dug in her heels. Balancing the ridiculous eggs hampered his ability to maneuver, so he stopped, as well. "Are you changing your mind already?"

"I haven't even cabled Chef Franconi yet. There's a chance you'll receive nothing in return."

Her eyes were more green than brown in the sunlight, and he was transfixed. She was lovely, with a delicate nose and flawless skin, full lips that were slightly torn, as if she'd recently been biting them. Was this from worrying about her future? He didn't like the idea of this clever girl hurting herself out of anxiety.

That was when he decided the recipes could wait.

"This lesson is free. Come along." He tugged her elbow, leaving her no choice.

When they rounded the shrub, he set the hat full of eggs on the ground. The diamond-shaped topiary would conceal them, in the unlikely event that another guest wandered by. Alice twisted her fingers into her skirts and looked around, as if they'd be caught at any moment. "Don't worry," he said. "Trust me, no one can see us back here."

"How do you know?" He merely arched a brow at her, his lips curved in a half smile. Understanding dawned on her face. "You have past experience with this location."

"That's not important. For this to work, you must trust me. I'll not tell anyone of what we're doing and I won't let us be caught."

She studied his expression, then nodded. "I believe you."

"Good. Now, we haven't much time." He held up his arm. "Our first lesson? Holding my hand."

"What? No." Alice took a step backward. "Why do I need to touch you?"

"Your reaction is precisely why, Alice. No one is around." He gestured to the sprawling emptiness of the estates surrounding them. "If I had to guess, you believe men are too different, too strange for you to understand. That you are somehow inferior. Well, despite what the politicians tell you, women are not inferior. At all. They are fascinating and beautiful and intelligent. And the right look from a woman can bring a man to his knees."

She swallowed, her eyes dipping to his hand. "Really?"

"Yes, but first I want you to hold my hand. That's all. See that I'm made up of skin and bones, just like you." Gloveless, he wiggled his bare fingers.

"How is this going to help me seduce my future husband?"

"Do not question the master as he paints a canvas. Here we are. Take my hand."

Her bottom lip disappeared between her teeth, yet he didn't rush her. He couldn't force her to take his advice to heart and he certainly couldn't do anything against her will. No, this had to be all Alice.

Slowly, she reached out, as if she were about to touch a rabid animal.

"Wait," he said. "Remove your gloves."

She gaped at him. "What? But that's . . ."

"Inappropriate? Scandalous? Shocking? Yes, I know. That is what makes life worth living, dear Alice. Come on. Remove those shackles of society and touch my hand."

She stared at her hands. Then, with a dexterity that surprised him, she undid the pearl buttons at her wrist and began pulling the glove off. He took it from her, nodding to her other glove. "Now that one."

"But—" The stern look he gave her eliminated any complaints, and Alice quickly did as he asked.

He pocketed both her gloves, then held up his hand once again. "When you're ready."

Inhaling, she squared her shoulders and wrapped her fingers around his entire hand, as if she were worried he might bolt. When he didn't move, she caught his gaze. "And?"

"That's up to you. But you can't let go, not just yet."

"Well, this is silly." She shifted on her feet. "How long are we supposed to stand here?"

"As long as it takes."

"You're not making any sense."

He tried not to smile. "I know. Humor me."

As the seconds ticked by, her body relaxed bit by bit. Kit waited patiently, standing perfectly still, as Alice grew more comfortable with him. Finally, after what felt like forever, he received his reward.

Alice's fingers began to move, shifting gingerly, testing the structure of his hand. Learning the shape of his bones. Not teasing so much as exploring, her gaze locked on where they were joined. She brushed the dark hairs on his knuckles. Examined his fingernails and studied his palm. Her soft touch and blossoming curiosity had his pulse picking up. He was more the participating type, so letting her take the lead was strangely thrilling.

He had no idea what she would do next.

Her thumb ran over the vein on the back of his hand. "You don't wear gloves much, do you?"

"Hmm? Oh, gloves. Hate the blasted things."

She traced along his index finger, lingering on his knuckle and causing him to shiver. She said, "Your fingers are long and thin. Most men have thick fingers."

Her exploration grew more specific. After cataloguing each finger and fingertip, she caressed the lines embedded in his palm. They both watched her progress, their heads bent close together. The breeze carried her scent into his nostrils and she smelled like vanilla and a hint of orange. Heat unfurled in his chest and slid south, toward his groin. He imagined licking her neck, then lower, between her breasts . . .

Pull yourself together, Christopher.

He absolutely could not return to the tent with an erection.

"I hadn't thought your skin would be so rough," she said as if this were a great discovery. "Is it because you don't wear gloves?"

"Probably," he croaked, the word scraping over his dry throat.

Sighing, she threaded their fingers together snugly, her delicate hand finally flush with his. He hadn't moved or offered up any instruction whatsoever, but it felt like the sweetest victory.

"Strange," she said, still staring at their hands.

"What is strange?"

"You were right. I was scared of touching your hand. And now I'm not." She gave a light, surprised laugh. "It's astounding."

He cleared his throat and tried to sound matter-of-fact. "Good. We should head back to the tent."

"Oh, of course." She pulled away and shook her head. "I lost track of the time."

As did I.

In moments, he returned her gloves and buttoned them for her. After picking up their eggs, he led them back to the tent. Kit tried to think logically about what happened, that it was nothing more than a few simple swipes of her fingers over his skin. After all, women had touched him far more intimately than that nearly every day for the last eight years. He should be inured to it by now.

But he wasn't. He'd wanted Alice to keep going, which was dangerous. If this was to work, he had to remember his role, that he was preparing her for another man—not seducing her himself. *Give her some advice, help build her confidence, get Franconi's recipes and move on.* That was it.

"Did that bother you?" she asked in a tight voice.

"Touching my hand? No. Why would it?"

"You're quiet. It caused me to think I did something wrong."

"Of course not," he rushed out. He tried to keep it light. "I've been touched in far worse places—but only when I ask nicely."

She didn't laugh. "If I fail at one of our lessons, then you have to tell me. Otherwise, how will I learn?"

Oh, he didn't think Alice would have trouble learning in the least. Indeed, based on the last ten minutes, he predicted she'd become a siren in hardly any time at all.

The question was whether he could survive it.

THE FILET DE boeuf melted on Alice's tongue, the meat unbelievably tender and flavorful. Sautéed chanterelle mushrooms, not usually found at this time of year, accompanied the rich sauce drizzled on top. Alice would need to ask the cook, Mrs. Berman, where those mushrooms had come from. Perhaps she could bring some back to Chef Franconi. His chanterelle soup always made her feel better when she was down in the doldrums, which was often when she was around her mother.

Tonight's dinner had been quite enjoyable thus far. Alice was seated between Katherine Delafield and one of the chaperones, with her mother placed at the other end of the long table. Maddie had done this purposely, and Alice was grateful for it. Mama tended to carry a dark cloud wherever she went.

Best of all, however, Kit sat directly across from her. It was certainly no hardship to sneak the occasional peek at his handsome features as he entertained those around him. He really was charming, with a quick wit and broad smile. Their half of the table practically hung on his every word, the jovial mood spreading to anyone in earshot.

As she savored a bite of beef, her gaze drifted to Kit's bare fingers, now wrapped around his wineglass. *I touched those.* She knew the roughness of his skin, the silkiness of the fine hair. He was strong yet delicate, with long fingers more suited to mischief than hard labor.

Katherine leaned over. "How was your afternoon, Alice?"

"Lovely, actually. Again, congratulations on winning."

Katherine, along with Mr. Archer, had won all three prizes in the afternoon's egg hunt. She'd graciously given Alice, the second-place winner, the diamond bracelet. "Thank you, though I believe my partner deserves the credit. It was as if Mr. Archer had a map with the location of every egg."

"Mr. Ward was much the same way. Hence how we came in second."

"And how was that? Did you two have fun?"

"We did. He's very easy to talk with."

"Oh." Katherine's brows rose along with the tone of her voice.

"What?"

"Nothing. I thought I caught you staring at him a moment ago."

Alice tried to laugh, but it came out more like a strangled sound. "Why would I stare at him?"

"I couldn't say, but I hope you're being careful."

"About what?"

"Not falling under his spell." Katherine tilted her head in Kit's direction. "He's quite the charmer, but certainly not the settling-down kind."

"Oh, there's nothing to worry about there. He would never be interested in someone like me."

"What do you mean, someone like you?"

"You know, boring. He's so . . ." She waved her hand, trying to come up with the right word. "Much."

"Alice." Katherine put down her fork and moved closer. "Do not for one second think he wouldn't seduce you if given the chance. You are pretty and a kind person. So take it from me, Mr. Ward and his friends are absolute scoundrels."

"His friends? You mean like Mr. Archer?" Harrison had seemed quite nice, actually.

"Harrison's not a bad sort. I meant Preston Clarke. He and Kit are . . . Well, don't get any romantic notions in your head, is all I am saying."

"Sounds like you are speaking from experience. Have you and Mr. Ward . . . ?"

"God, no. Just be on guard at all times."

Odd that Katherine hadn't offered up the same denial about Mr. Clarke.

Alice nodded once. "I will. Thank you." She couldn't help but smile. It was nice to have other women looking out for her.

There hadn't been much opportunity to make friends in Boston. Her mother rarely allowed her to socialize with girls her own age, saying they were all vapid and silly, and Alice had been tutored at home rather than a finishing school. During the season, Mama kept Alice close, saying there were too many dangers in New York to allow her any independence. Consequently, Alice spent most of her time in the hotel, either in her room alone or in the kitchen with Chef Franconi.

"You're welcome." Katherine picked up her wineglass. "Like my aunt says: know your worth. If we think so little of ourselves it becomes all too easy for others to do the same."

"That is good advice."

"It has certainly helped me through some low moments."

That was a surprising revelation. Katherine seemed put together, as far as Alice could tell. Mature, with a good head on her shoulders. She'd just returned from an extended stay in Spain, too. Alice longed to travel, but Mama wouldn't hear of it. Dining on French cuisine was as adventurous as Mama allowed. "I'm sorry to hear you struggled. Was it a scoundrel?"

"In a way." Katherine took a long swallow of wine. "So learn from my mistakes, Alice."

Alice slid her eyes toward Kit and was shocked to find him staring at her. He quirked a brow, and she could see the curiosity in his gaze. Alice had no idea what to do or say, her stomach knotted in the face of his gorgeous intensity. My goodness, he was potent.

Dinner soon ended. Everyone rose and the ladies

departed for the drawing room, while the men remained at the dining table. As Alice walked, her mother came alongside. "I do not like being separated from you at dinner," Mama said in a low, disapproving tone. "I should be close to serve as your chaperone."

"Nothing untoward will happen at the dinner table. And you were seated near the duke tonight. That is certainly an honor."

Mama sniffed. "A good thing, too. You were focused on your food instead of the other guests, as usual. At least I was able to converse with His Grace. You would have bored him silly. Now, remember to stand up straight. You want to impress him, make him think of you as a potential duchess."

Alice inwardly sighed. She'd exchanged two words with the duke since meeting him, and his interest seemed entirely concentrated on Maddie.

"And," her mother continued, "stay away from that good-for-nothing Mr. Ward. He is not the sort I want you associating with."

Alice didn't bother arguing. It never did any good and would merely exhaust her. "Shall I get you coffee before I visit the facilities?" Her mother's joints were in constant pain and she preferred when Alice handled the pouring.

"Yes, and hurry. You know I hate relying on strangers."

Indeed, Alice knew this. Soon she had her mother settled with coffee and then she was able to escape for the washroom. The chateau was large, built like a cathedral with stone buttresses and high ceilings, and it took several minutes to walk the long corridors. After she finished in the washroom, she started back, taking her time before returning to hover and wait on Mama.

"And where are you going?"

Alice jumped at the deep voice, her hand covering her heart as if to keep it from popping out of her chest. Kit stepped out of the dark room in which he'd been lurking, a smirk affixed on his face.

Tiny shocks continued along her frame, quickly followed by flutters in her stomach. "Kit, my goodness. You scared me."

His fingers wrapped around her forearm and he pulled her into the empty room. "I apologize." He released her. "I wanted to check on you."

"Oh." Was he worried she would get lost? "As you can see, I am fine. Shall we return?"

"Am I making you nervous?"

"No, why?"

"You're edging toward the door as if you want to escape."

She planted her feet. "I'm not used to having a man drag me into a dark room."

"Admittedly, the dark room bit normally goes differently for me, but I won't bore you with those sordid details. Did you hear back from Franconi?"

"I did. He's agreed to five thousand per recipe."

"Christ. That's dashed expensive, but I suppose it's worth it." He shoved his hands in his trouser pockets. "And you know each of these recipes?"

"I do. Down to the tiniest detail."

"Excellent. We'll begin tonight. I'll write Franconi a check when we return to New York."

Excitement raced through her, centering in her chest. "I'll come to your room after my mother goes to bed."

"No. I have plans, so I'll come to you."

Her shoulders deflated as questions buzzed through her mind. What were these plans? Was he leaving? Was he meeting another woman? Mary, perhaps? "All right."

"You may ask me, if you wish."

Had she been so obvious? "It's really none of my business."

"True, but we are friends now, Alice. I don't mind answering personal questions."

"Are you meeting another woman?" she blurted.

"I am not. The duke and I are headed to the casino."

The amount of relief she felt was embarrassing. Why did she care what Kit did in his free time? They were not lovers or partners. They barely knew each other. She had no right to feel proprietary over him. "If you want to meet another woman—"

"Stop right there." He held up a hand. "I don't and I won't, not during the house party. I plan to dedicate all my energies to our mutual cause."

"Thank you."

"There's no need to thank me. This is not altruism on my part. I'll get as many recipes out of you and Franconi as I can manage in the next few days."

For some reason, that promise made her shiver. *This is not seduction. He will provide you with information, that's all.*

"Actually," he said, stroking his jaw. "We should probably meet in my room. Farther away from your mother, and if your absence is noted you can say you went out for a walk."

Good point. "Fine. Just send word when you are back."

"I'll throw a pebble at your window."

"You will?"

"No." His mouth hitched. "I'll just knock softly on your door."

That made much more sense. "I'll wait up."

"Excellent." He stepped closer. Before she knew what he was doing, he lifted a hand and dragged his knuckles across her cheek. "I'll hurry."

She froze at the simple touch—which seemed anything but simple, actually. It felt intimate, like a promise of what was to come. A wave of heat followed where he'd brushed her skin and perspiration broke out on her forehead. Her lungs began to burn, and she realized she wasn't breathing. She forced air into her throat, gulping like a fish, grateful that she hadn't passed out in front of him.

Then she realized she was alone.

Sweet mercy, how was she going to keep from fawning at this man's feet every time they were together?

Chapter Four

❧

$\mathcal{K}$it whistled softly to himself as he made his way through the upstairs corridor. He'd just knocked on Alice's door, which meant their first real lesson would soon get under way.

He could hardly wait.

Throughout the night he'd watched the time, anxious to leave the casino behind and return to the chateau. He hadn't cared a bit about gambling, but taking the duke out on the town had been for Harrison's benefit, to give his friend more time alone with Maddie before all hell broke loose. Because Kit had a feeling the duke was not here for a simple visit. Engagement rumors were rarely wrong in circumstances such as this, and Lockwood's sudden appearance meant Maddie would soon receive a proposal.

And if she said yes, God help them all.

Once inside his bedchamber, Kit removed his topcoat and tossed it on the bed. Then he unknotted his bow tie and removed his collar. Alice might not appreciate his state of undress, but he couldn't help himself. He'd been in these clothes all damn night and was itching to get out of them. If Alice didn't like it, that was too bad.

He'd just finished putting away his budgets and notes on the supper club when the door opened. Alice slid inside, still dressed in her evening gown. Her hair was slightly askew, as if she'd been lying down while waiting on him. Had she imagined being his willing pupil? He couldn't stop thinking of it, like how she'd hang on his every word, rapt with attention, eager for instruction and guidance. With her big, doe-eyed gaze focused on him, watching and waiting, while her brain absorbed his expertise on men and women. Perhaps she'd ask for more personal instruction at the end of the lesson as a way to get in the teacher's good graces . . .

Damn. There he went again, off on a prurient tangent and forgetting with whom he was dealing.

Exhaling, he poured them each a glass of bourbon. "Shall we sit?"

She nodded and followed him to the armchairs near the fire. When they were settled, he stretched his legs and took a long drink. "So, what would you like to know about men?"

"Wait, before we begin." She held out a piece of paper. "That is the recipe for lobster thermidor."

"Thank you." He took the recipe and slid it into his trouser pocket. "It's one of my favorites."

"Mine, too."

"Considering Franconi was your family's chef, you've probably had it many times."

A tiny smile emerged and she sat straighter. "I can still remember the first time Angelo served lobster thermidor. He returned from Paris, where he'd visited Chef Mourier and learned of the dish. Knowing how much I like lobster à la Newburg, he prepared lobster thermidor as a surprise for my sixteenth birthday."

"How lovely. I actually ate it in Paris when I visited Harrison a year ago. We dined at Maison Maire."

Brows rising, she leaned in. "Oh, I am so envious. Tell me everything. Was the food as delicious as I've heard? Did you meet Chef Mourier? And did he melt Gruyère on top? I've seen other chefs use various cheeses, but Angelo and I agree Gruyère works best."

Kit drank his bourbon and studied her in fascination. She'd come alive discussing lobster thermidor, of all things, her face now radiant and her eyes sparkling. Who would've guessed it? This was a very different person than the girl who'd clung to her mother's side after dinner, not speaking to anyone. This Alice was intelligent and passionate, brimming with excitement.

When he didn't answer, she shrank in her chair and shook her head. "I must be making a fool of myself. Ignore me. Please, go on with the lesson."

"You are not making a fool of yourself," he rushed out. "I am merely admiring your enthusiasm. I had no idea you were so passionate about food."

"I'm not. I like to eat." Her hand shook as she brought the crystal tumbler to her lips. She took a small sip of the spirits, then grimaced. "Oh, that's terrible."

"Give it time. The taste will grow on you—sort of like Gruyère."

She snorted a laugh, and then covered her mouth. "That was unladylike. Forgive me."

Had she any idea of how adorable she was? Warmth slid through him, a heat unrelated to the bourbon. "It was genuine. I liked it."

"My mother would be horrified. She hates the way I laugh."

"Considering the circumstances"—he gestured to the two of them—"I think that would be the least of her concerns."

"True." She attempted the bourbon again, but didn't appear to like it any better the second time. "May I ask you questions now?"

"I am at your disposal, Miss Lusk. Ask away."

Drawing in a deep breath, she held out another piece of paper. "Here they are."

"You wrote your questions down?" He put his glass on the table and accepted the paper. "Were you worried you'd forget them?"

Spots of color dotted her cheeks and high on her chest. He tried—unsuccessfully—not to stare at her décolletage, which promised perfect apple-shaped breasts. Not that she noticed, considering her gaze was fixed firmly on her lap. "I thought it might be easier."

He found her embarrassment charming, but it was cruel to prolong her torture. "We may proceed in whichever manner you prefer. Tonight I'll read your questions."

There were four questions, the penmanship incredibly neat. He could almost imagine her laboring over the words, wondering over his answers. He cleared his throat. *"How are you able to converse with people so easily?"* The side of his mouth hitched. "I've never thought about this before. Do you mean with women?"

"Men or women." She clutched her crystal tumbler. "Just people in general."

"For the most part, people like to talk about themselves. Whenever I am at a loss for words, I inquire about them, what they did that day or what they plan to do that night. Their likes and dislikes. Hopes and dreams."

"And they don't feel as if you're prying? My mother says invading someone's privacy is rude."

"There's no law forcing them to answer. However, I find most people are self-centered. They will leap at any opportunity to discuss themselves."

"Even you?"

"Oh, especially me. I am more self-involved than nearly anyone on earth." After all, wasn't that what Father had said, that Kit's thoughts centered only on himself and nothing else?

You're as shallow as a saucer, Christopher.

It had been a frequent refrain in the Ward household, like any time Kit smoothed his hair in a mirror or took pride in his clothing. When he bounced from activity to activity, eschewing church and schoolwork to make the girls laugh instead. His father never failed to comment on it, and Kit came to hate him.

Mostly because he feared his father's words might hold some truth.

Kit threw back the rest of the bourbon in his glass and stood to refill it. "One question down. This is going well, I think." When he returned to his seat, he glanced at her paper. "Next question. *What do men find attractive about women?* Well, that varies with each man you ask."

"In general," she blurted, her color rising once more. "Or you. We can use you as an example."

"Me?" He rubbed his jaw. "Well, there is the obvious, like breasts. Any size, any shape, will do." She opened her mouth, probably to complain about his banal but true answer, so he held up a hand. "Beyond that, I like eyes. There's nothing more powerful than when a woman stares at you from across the room like you are the only person who matters."

Alice quirked a brow like she didn't believe him and he felt his skin grow warm. Was she disappointed in his answer? "Is that all? Bosoms and eyes?"

Yes, definitely disappointed. The old humiliation, the feeling that he wasn't smart enough in the things that mattered, crawled along his neck. *Show her you are more than a thoughtless clod.*

Leaning forward, he put his elbows on his knees and stared at the drink in his hand. The liquid was nearly the color of Alice's eyes. He dropped his guard and let his thoughts run free. "I like a woman's smile. Her laugh. Someone who makes me laugh, as well. A sense of confidence, that she is competent and interested in more than just gossip and fashion." He took a breath. "I like . . . kindness. To see that she's worried about others, not just herself. She must be able to hold a conversation. And I'd want her to be smart, smarter than me. Which isn't difficult, granted—" He snapped his jaw shut.

His throat tingled with irritation, an overwhelming panic that he'd exposed too much.

Alice stared at him in a way he couldn't decipher, but it seemed like a mixture of pity and fascination. *Definitely exposed too much.*

After taking a long drink, he offered her his best seductive grin. "Did I mention long legs? And breasts definitely bear repeating."

She took another small sip from her glass, then licked her lips with a provocative swipe of her tongue. No grimace this time, which felt like a minor victory. She tapped her finger on the side of the crystal. "Your expectations seem very high. Is that why you haven't yet married?"

"I am a scoundrel, dear Alice. That is why I haven't married."

"So, no need to limit yourself to merely one."

"Indeed." He crossed his legs and settled deeper into the chair. "There is a whole world full of beautiful women out there—and I have no need of a dowry."

There was that look in her eye again, the one he didn't care for. "What about companionship?"

Why was the little innocent intent on turning this around on him? Kit's fingers tightened around his glass. "I have companionship any time I want. I can *companionship* every damn night, if I feel like it."

She cocked her head and he could practically hear her thinking. This first lesson had taken an unexpected turn—and he wasn't sure he liked it. He stood. "That's enough for tonight. We'll pick this up tomorrow."

He half expected her to argue, but she merely nodded and set down her glass. "I will see you in the morning, then."

They walked to the door. He peeked into the corridor to ensure it was safe. "Completely empty. Off you go."

She started to leave, but then paused. "Kit, forgive me. I have no right to question how you live your life."

The apology stunned him. For a supposedly shy woman, she had no trouble speaking her mind. And now he felt even worse, like he'd ruined the night with his prickly insecurities. "You have nothing for which to apologize. It's been a long day and I am unnecessarily irritable. I am sorry."

"You've been very insightful and I appreciate your honesty."

The ache between his shoulders eased somewhat. "I'm glad. I hope you found tonight useful."

"Oh, I did. It was utterly fascinating."

She slipped through the crack in the door and disappeared into the corridor. Kit quietly closed the door and stood there a moment, wondering if he hadn't made a terrible mistake by agreeing to this bargain.

THE NEXT MORNING, Alice had just finished eating when Kit, wearing his tennis whites, strolled into the dining room. The clothes fit him perfectly, each stitch caressing his lithe frame, the light color a stark contrast to his dark hair. Her stomach jumped, her skin coming alive with awareness as she tracked his movements. He filled a plate at the sideboard, then sat next to Mr. Archer at the opposite end of the dining table.

The two of them began speaking in low tones, their heads close together, and Alice was left to watch Kit's face. Light played off the sharp angles, illuminating his cheekbones and strong jaw. Full lips that promised sinful delight and wicked pleasure. Goodness, he was attractive.

There's nothing more powerful than when a woman stares at you from across the room like you are the only person who matters.

Was that what he wished? To feel like he mattered?

While it was clear he'd been embarrassed by his answers last night, she found them fascinating. Christopher Ward was more than the society charmer he played so well, and she liked the real version of the man much better. His answer for what he liked in a woman had been genuine and off-the-cuff, and she could fall hard for a thoughtful man such as that.

"Alice," her mother hissed. "Stop staring. It's rude."

She quickly transferred her gaze to her near-empty plate. The scrambled eggs were creamy and well seasoned, sprinkled with fresh thyme. They were every bit as good as Angelo's eggs at the hotel, which were nothing short of heaven on a plate. After she took the last bite, she started to get up for another helping.

Mama's hand grabbed her arm. "Where are you going?"

"To get more eggs."

"Alice," her mother scolded in a harsh whisper.

"Do not dare. What will everyone think if you are shoving food in your face all the time?"

"That I am hungry?"

Mama's lips flattened, her gaze hard and cold. "Do not get fresh with me. We discussed your preoccupation with eating in front of men and how it will ruin your chances at marriage." Turning, she waved to the footman. "Please, take our plates."

Alice watched as her opportunity for more eggs walked out of the dining room. She closed her eyes and tried not to scream. *I will be married soon and then I can eat all the eggs I wish.*

"I am off to visit with my cousin Jane this morning," her mother was saying. "Perhaps you should come with me. I'd hate for you to wander about here by yourself."

Alice's pulse leapt. With her mother out of the chateau, perhaps she could convince Kit to give her another lesson. Two of the questions from last evening still remained unanswered. "I have a touch of a headache. I didn't sleep well last night. I think I'll spend the morning in my room."

"I told you not to have that second cup of coffee after dinner." Her mother looked down her nose sharply. "Alice, we need you at your best during this house party. How will you ever land a decent husband if you—"

"Miss Lusk, I didn't see you when I arrived," Kit said smoothly from the end of the table. "Forgive my rudeness in not greeting you earlier. I trust you are well this morning."

Her mother made a strangled noise in her throat at the interruption, but Alice ignored her. "Good morning, Mr. Ward. Mr. Archer," she said.

"Miss Lusk," Harrison said with a polite nod. "Good morning."

The other occupants at the table—two heiresses, three chaperones and Mr. Webster—all looked up at this exchange, the dining room so quiet one could hear the coffee getting cold. Grateful that Kit had interrupted her mother's tirade, Alice gave him a small smile.

He winked at her.

Winked, like they were co-conspirators . . . or lovers.

Her chest expanded, an unexpected heat blooming in her lower half. She pressed her lips together as her mind tripped over the possibility of that small gesture. Before she could react, however, the moment passed. He went back to his quiet conversation with Harrison and everyone else continued their breakfast.

"How incredibly rude," her mother said under her breath. "If the duke hadn't arrived, I swear I would have taken you back to New York already. I'm not certain these people are a good influence on you. Not dressing properly for breakfast, interrupting our conversation . . . the lack of manners is staggering."

Alice said nothing. She knew better than to argue with her mother. If Mama wanted to leave, there would be nothing Alice could do to stop it.

I must make the most of my time here.

The house party would end in a few days, and the goal was to leave Newport a much different woman than the one who'd arrived. She needed to speed things along. Hopefully, Kit hadn't made other plans this morning.

Moments later, Mama pushed back from the table. Alice followed her upstairs, silent, as her mother kept up a steady stream of commentary. Instead of listening, Alice wondered over that wink and what it had meant.

They stopped outside her mother's door. "How long will you stay at Jane's?" Alice asked abruptly.

"I will eat luncheon there and return." Mama pointed in the direction of Alice's room. "Go lie down. There is an afternoon of croquet planned today and we cannot have you looking tired."

"Yes, Mama."

They parted and Alice slipped inside her room. She pressed her ear to the door and waited, barely breathing, until she heard her mother leave ten minutes later. Then she waited some more, giving Mama ample time to depart.

When certain it was safe, she hurried through the corridors toward the opposite end of the chateau where the men's rooms were located, far away from the unmarried ladies. No one was about, thankfully, and she soon arrived at Kit's door. Was he here, or still downstairs?

She knocked, glancing up and down the hallway, praying he answered quickly.

The oak door swung open and a bare throat greeted her.

Blinking, she dragged her gaze higher and met Kit's amused stare. "Hello."

He stepped back and motioned her in. "Hello, Alice." It was then she noticed that he was clad in only a silk dressing gown, his hair wet from a bath.

She couldn't force her feet to work, her legs frozen. There was too much to see, too much to take in. The bare skin, the dark hair, the bones and tendons creating ridges and angles . . . and she didn't dare look below his waist. "I—I should come back later. When you're . . ."

"Stop. Get in here before someone sees you out there."

She slipped through the door, trying to maintain a proper distance from his scantily clothed form. But really? Was there any distance proper enough for this situation? "I apologize. I should have warned you I was coming."

"Nonsense." He closed the door and turned the lock. "I was going to seek you out, so you saved me the trouble. Your mother called for a carriage, I heard. How long will she be gone?"

"Until after luncheon."

The side of his mouth hitched. "Indeed, that does give us quite a lot of time."

Her heart galloped in her chest, a frantic rhythm that echoed throughout her body. How was he able to take the simplest of sentences and turn them sexual?

He charms as natural as breathing. It is not aimed at you.

Instead of moving to another room to get dressed, he crossed to the chairs by the fire and settled himself. The dressing gown covered him from shoulders to shin, but the bare feet and throat were enough to weaken her knees. This was the closest she'd ever been to a man in such dishabille and it was disconcerting.

How could she possibly concentrate now, when her mind was fixated on picturing what he looked like under the dressing gown?

A wool blanket rested at the foot of the bed, so she gathered the cloth in her hands and shook it out. "Here," she said, taking the blanket to him. "Use this to cover yourself."

He took the wool from her. "Why?"

"Because this is improper. I can see your toes."

He wiggled the appendages in question. "Not a fan of feet, then?"

"I like feet just fine." Her skin burned, like she'd stood in front of a hot oven for an hour. "But I shouldn't see you like this."

His brown eyes searched her face, then he stood. "Forgive me. Allow me a moment, please." In half a dozen steps, he crossed the floor and disappeared into a dressing room, closing the door behind him.

She exhaled and tried to steady her heartbeat. As she calmed, reality began to set in. She looked around and considered the last five minutes.

You were alone with a beautiful man wearing hardly any clothing . . . and you told him to cover up.

Oh, for heaven's sake. How stupid. How utterly foolish. No doubt he thought her mad, a silly innocent who deserved a life of spinsterhood. Most women would leap at the chance to see Kit Ward in such a position. Moreover, they'd know how to turn it to their advantage, giving him come-hither looks and inviting smiles.

And what had Alice done?

She'd told him to drape a blanket over himself.

Pinching the bridge of her nose between a thumb and forefinger, she tried not to cry. She couldn't face him, not now. Perhaps not ever. These lessons were a terrible idea.

She reached into her pocket, took out the recipe

for poulardes à la Portugaise, and placed it on the bed. Then she hurried for the door.

"Where are you going?"

Startled, she spun around, her back hugging the wood. Kit now wore navy trousers and a white shirt, and he was affixing a cuff link. She was both relieved and disappointed. "I should go."

"Alice, wait." He held up his hands. "Please, allow me to apologize. I made you uncomfortable and that was not my intention."

She dropped her head onto the wood, feeling even more foolish. "I overreacted."

"No, you didn't. What I did was horribly inappropriate. I am entirely in the wrong."

"Then why do I feel ridiculous?"

"I haven't a clue, but let's call this one a draw. I feel like a masher and you feel ridiculous."

"Nonsense. You never touched me against my will."

"True, but I was attempting to flirt and caused you discomfort instead. It qualifies in my book."

She blinked several times, waiting for the rest of the joke, but it never came. Was he serious? "You were flirting? With me?"

"Of course." He shook his head and put his hands on his hips. "A beautiful girl arrives to my room and I'm not yet dressed? Adding clothing to the equation is generally the last thing I'm considering."

Ah. It wasn't *her*. Any woman would qualify. "I see. Well, perhaps you'll have better luck with the next girl who comes along."

"Shit." Frowning, he dragged a hand through his damp hair. "That wasn't what I meant. I'm not flirting with anything in skirts, Alice. I meant you. Only you."

"No need to spare my feelings." She pushed off from the door, determined to put their relationship back to rights. Lessons, recipes, that was all. Anything else was impossible.

Kit darted in front of her, not touching her but still making it impossible to pass. "I am not sparing your feelings. How many more times must I mention your appeal before you believe me?"

"I assumed you were being charming, lying to make me feel better."

"Then let me quickly dissuade you of that notion. I was not lying and I do find you attractive."

Chapter Five

❦

$\mathcal{K}$it watched Alice's face as she absorbed his words. She really had no idea of her appeal—and after watching her interact with her mother, he was beginning to understand why.

Mrs. Lusk didn't let Alice get a word in edgewise. She rolled over her daughter, as if Alice was of no consequence, treating her little better than a dog. Kit had seen the way Alice shrank in her chair this morning when her mother started talking. Hence why he'd interrupted their conversation, because he'd been desperate to see a little joie de vivre return to Alice's expression.

He did feel badly about the dressing gown business. Alice was innocent and not up for his usual tricks. By teasing her in such a fashion, he'd disrespected her. Not wearing a collar was one thing; inviting her in while nearly naked was quite another.

More than anything else, he didn't want to scare her away.

Finally, Alice's shoulders relaxed and she gave him a tiny smile. "Shall we begin our lesson?"

Thank God. Relief cascaded through him and he gestured to the chairs. "After you."

When they were settled across from each other, she pointed to the bed. "I put the recipe for poulardes à la Portugaise on the coverlet."

"Excellent. That is Preston's favorite."

"I agree, it is delicious. However, tell your chef not to rush the steps. Time is required for the flavors to develop."

He arched a brow. "It almost sounds as if you've prepared the dish yourself."

"Me? No, of course not. But I have watched Angelo make it many times."

She was lying. Memorizing the recipes? Offering tips on the preparation? When he combined that with her excitement over lobster thermidor, he was certain Alice did more than observe Angelo. He smoothed his trousers and affected a casual tone. "You must be a quick study. When I was in Paris, I tried to learn how to make a béchamel sauce and I ended up scalding the milk every time. By the fifth batch, they told me to give up."

She chuckled. "The first time I attempted a béarnaise, the bain-marie was too hot—"

Horror filled her expression, and they stared at each other for a long moment. While he felt victorious, he sensed there was a reason Alice had lied. So if she wasn't ready to confide in him, he wouldn't press.

She seemed to collect herself, bit by bit, her armor rebuilding as the seconds ticked by. "Angelo tries to teach me every now and again, though I am terrible at everything."

He doubted it. She was smart, observant and clearly loved food. If he had to guess, he would say she was probably quite competent in the kitchen. However, he'd already pushed her enough today by answering the door in his dressing gown. He needed these lessons to continue as much as she did, and offending her was not the way to collect Franconi's recipes.

He adopted his most charming grin. "It is nice to have friends who are willing to teach you."

"Yes, it certainly is." Her eyes flicked to his mouth for the briefest of seconds before returning to meet his gaze.

Well, well. That couldn't have been more obvious. Was his pupil considering another type of lesson, one that involved lips, teeth and tongues?

That suited him just fine. Last night had been altogether too personal from his point of view. He was not interested in spilling secrets or having his choices dissected again.

Your expectations seem very high.

Resting his elbows on the armrests, he steepled his fingers. "Let's skip the questions today. I think we should focus on practical examples, rather than theoretical."

"Meaning?"

"Meaning real-world experience. Not merely information."

"Like the hand-holding?"

"Exactly." The possibilities were endless, but they should start with the basics. "I assume you know how to dance, so what about flirting?"

Her brows lowered, her gaze suspicious. "You can teach me to flirt?"

In his sleep. "Of course. I am quite proficient at it—and a woman or two has flirted with me over the years."

"I bet. Does it work?"

"Depends on what you consider success, but generally yes." He edged forward, more eager than he cared to admit. "So, would you like to learn how to flirt with a man?"

"I suppose I should, if I want to attract the right husband."

"That's the spirit. First things first, flirting begins with the eyes. Watch." He stared directly into her eyes for a shade longer than polite, then looked away. Then he did it again, talking her through. "Meet his gaze and hold it so there can be no mistake. He needs to know you are looking just at him. Then before it becomes impolite, shift your eyes elsewhere."

"Won't it bother him, thinking that I am staring at him?"

"No, and if it does, you certainly don't want to marry him."

"Good point."

"Now you try." He encouraged her with a flick of his fingers.

She focused on the wall, then exhaled and cleared her throat. Turning her head, she locked eyes with him for a long minute before looking away.

"Perfect," he said. "Now, the next step is to angle your body in the direction of the person with whom you are flirting."

"Like, move toward them?"

"No, not necessarily." He shifted to the right and looked at her from over his shoulder. "Instead of staring like this, turn your body"—he slid until he directly faced her—"to give him every bit of your attention."

She adjusted her limbs and angled closer to him.

"You may also lean in," he said. "Ever so slightly. Like you want to get closer, but you don't know if you should."

She bent nearer and he caught a hint of vanilla and spice. Very nice. "Excellent. The last bit is a tad advanced, for when you know you have the right man in mind. Ready?"

She nodded. "Definitely."

"Do everything I've mentioned and before you look away bite your lip." He demonstrated once. "Now put it all together and show me."

Taking a deep breath, she shook out her shoulders, like a prizefighter loosening up before a fight. She was adorable and he had to struggle to keep from smiling.

First, she angled toward him, then found his gaze and held it, luring him into the soft chestnut depths. He held perfectly still, not minding this experiment in the least. Had he ever noticed how unique her eyes were? Her irises were light and dark, greenish gold and brown, now shining in the midmorning light. She eased in a tiny bit closer and there was that scent again, as if she'd just come from baking in the kitchen. Was that a perfume? If so, he needed to purchase it for all his future mistresses.

When the stare lingered a shade longer than normal, she slipped her bottom lip between her teeth and bit down on the plump flesh, drawing attention to her mouth. He knew she was merely following directions, that this was not for his benefit, but a spark raced along his spine all the same. Now he was thinking about kissing her, wondering what that mouth would taste like on his own and if her lips were as soft as they appeared. If he moved a tiny bit closer to her . . .

She looked down at her hands and the moment passed. Kit blinked a few times to clear his head. Arousal simmered in his gut, his mind racing with prurient possibilities.

Christ, she was a quick study. And he was in trouble.

Throat dry, he stood and crossed to the sideboard, intending to pour himself a drink despite the early hour. He needn't be sober for an afternoon of croquet.

"How did I do?" she asked, a tremble of uncertainty in her voice.

He couldn't lie, not about this. Not to her. "I think you've mastered it. If that had been real, I would have dragged you off to a secluded spot and kissed you already."

"Really?"

Carrying his drink back to his chair, he toasted her with his glass as he sat. "Indeed. Well done, Alice."

As if she'd never heard a compliment before, her lips twisted into a stunning smile, transforming her into an enchantress. A siren. A goddess among lowly mortals. Men would wage wars for a smile like that. In fact, Kit was tempted to continue praising her just to keep that look on her face.

"Thank you," she said. "I am curious, though. How do men do it?"

Wait, what were they talking about? Her smile had derailed him. "Do what?"

"Flirt with women."

He rubbed the back of his neck and tried to gather his wits. "You want me to show you how I flirt?"

"Yes, please. That way, I'll know when a man is doing it to me—that is, *if* it ever happens."

"You may already check that box. I have flirted with you many times."

"The dressing gown."

"That, and other things." He'd touched her cheek and dragged her behind a bush to hold her hand. Ruined a perfectly good pair of shoes in that blasted egg hunt so she would win one of the prizes.

"Prove it. Flirt with me so I know what it looks like."

"I don't attend society events, so I'm not certain my skills are applicable." He was more likely to flirt with an actress or chorus girl, encounters which tended to skew toward direct.

"Fine, I'll play. You see a woman at a nonsociety party. What do you do?"

Stubborn woman. She wanted to see him at his best? Fine. He smirked and said, "Just remember, I'm not responsible for whatever happens after this demonstration." He put his drink on the side table and rubbed his hands together.

Offering up a lazy smile, he pitched his voice low. "Hello, miss. Have we been introduced? My friends call me Kit."

She folded her arms across her chest, expression unchanged. "My name is Alice."

"Hello, Alice." Her name rolled off his tongue in

a sensuous caress. He slowly dragged his gaze over her neck, her chest, then back to her eyes. "May I get you a drink? Some champagne, perhaps."

"No, thank you."

He leaned in. "Your eyes are beautiful. I've never seen any quite like them, with the hints of green and gold between the dark brown." All true, but she did not seem impressed.

"Hmm," was all she said.

This wasn't going as it usually did, so he picked up his drink and took a long sip, watching her over the rim the whole time. When he finished, he licked his lips while staring at her mouth.

She arched a single brow, her mouth flat. Unwilling to concede defeat just yet, he barely brushed her arm with his fingertips. "Have you seen the gardens? I hear they're quite lovely at this time of year."

Instead of blushing or giggling, she sighed.

Sitting back, he frowned. This made no sense. These methods were tried and true, honed over years of engaging with the opposite sex. One or two had worked countless times. Putting all of them together was almost a guarantee—yet Alice had practically yawned. Where had he gone wrong?

"Is there more?" she asked. "Or is that it?"

HE TRULY USED these tricks to get women into bed? Alice shook her head. Perhaps Kit didn't know as much about women as he thought.

"I don't understand," he muttered, rubbing his jaw. "You didn't like any of that?"

"To be honest, no. It made me uncomfortable."

His eyes widened. "Uncomfortable? How?"

This was hard to put into words. But it was clear the real Kit hadn't been flirting with her, not the man she'd come to know over the past two days. She wanted him, the sensitive one who hid his true feelings underneath all that charm. "Just everything. It was too . . . invasive. And artificial."

"Artificial? Invasive? I was complimenting you and offering to fetch you a drink."

She lifted her shoulders. "I didn't care for it."

"How was any of that artificial? You do have beautiful eyes and the gardens are probably lovely right now."

"I don't know. I just . . . That wasn't you. That was some other man, one who didn't care about getting to know me. You stared at me like a piece of meat."

A strangled noise escaped his throat and his skin turned a dull red. Had she embarrassed him? "I'll have you know," he snapped, "that some women like to be stared at intently, as if a man is undressing her with his eyes."

"A woman you just met? How unpleasant." She covered her mouth. Had she really just said that?

Now he'll never give you another lesson. Brava, Alice.

"I can't believe this." He shot up out of his chair and returned to the sideboard for a refill. "You are lecturing me? *Me?* I am not the one who needed lessons in flirting. I have flirted with countless women since the age of fourteen!"

Now she'd stepped in it.

Before he could kick her out and never speak to her again, she rushed to explain. "Kit, it's me. I'm certain your . . . skills are quite successful with every other woman on earth. I already told you, I'm defective in this area. Don't listen to my opinion."

His glass was full when he sat back down. "Tell me, then. What does work with you? If I wanted to flirt with Alice Lusk, what must I do to succeed?"

She shifted in her chair and contemplated an answer. *Why didn't I fake a reaction?* Then she could have avoided this embarrassing conversation. "I suppose I know you too well. I'm not fooled by this false flattery and adopted charm. Honestly, I find you most attractive when you are being honest."

"I have never lied to you, Alice."

Didn't he see the difference? "No, but you don't reveal much of your real self, do you? Not like when you told me what you find attractive in a woman."

He took a long swallow of the light brown spirits. "Why are we dissecting me once again? This is supposed to be about you."

Indeed, he was right. For some reason, she kept digging and poking, trying to understand him better. But to what end? He was helping her in exchange for recipes. They weren't friends—or potential lovers—so she needed to be more respectful. Needed to keep her thoughts to herself, as she did with her mother. "I apologize. I shouldn't have said any of that. Thank you for the lesson today."

When she started to rise, he held out a hand. "Wait. Let's go back to what would work with you."

"Why?" He honestly wished to flirt with her? And needed her advice on how to do it?

"Call it a challenge to my skills. I'd like the chance to redeem myself."

"I don't understand."

"What do you find attractive about me? If I wanted you to kiss me, what would compel you to do it?"

She held her breath, her mind tripping over his request. Was he serious? Hadn't they already established her lack of expertise on this subject? Still, he seemed curious, his gaze eager. She had to say something. "Kit, this is highly improper—"

"Fuck proper. Everything we are doing is improper." His lips tightened, his jaw turning hard. "Please, just answer. What do you find appealing about me?"

"Your looks, obviously." She gestured to his face and body.

His head turned and he stared at the wall, a muscle jumping in his cheek. She sensed her answer upset him, but hadn't a clue as to why. Was he ashamed of his appearance? No, that didn't make any sense. They had discussed his handsomeness before and he hadn't minded.

"That's it?" he asked. "Nothing other than how I look?"

Oh, he wished for her to elucidate.

Wouldn't you hate to be nothing more than a pretty face?

Yes, she would. No one, save Kit, had ever complimented her looks, but Alice could sympathize with being judged for what was on the surface. After all, most people took one glance at her and decided she was shy and boring. Not many had tried to actually get to know her.

He watched her carefully and she realized this mattered to him. So she cleared her throat and scooted closer, their knees almost touching, her eyes squarely on his chest. "I like how you put people at ease. You make everyone around you feel important, as if they matter, because they have your attention. You're observant. Not only do you listen and ask questions, but you remember the answers." He didn't move or speak, so she dragged in a breath and kept going. "You're kind. You could have ditched me for the egg hunt, but you didn't, and I've seen you assist the older chaperones when you didn't have to. And no doubt you had far more exciting places to be this weekend, but you came to support Maddie and Mr. Archer. That tells me you are loyal to those you care about."

His shoulders rose and fell with his breath, but he still didn't react, his gaze remaining on the wall. Did he hate her answers? She kept talking, hoping to prove her point. "In order for me to kiss you, I would want more of the man from last night, the truthful one who told me what he likes without shame, without artifice. The man who showed his genuine self for a moment. I would rather kiss him than the scoundrel who doesn't mean a word of what he says."

The clock chimed the half hour and she tried not to fidget as she awaited his reaction. Had she offended him? This was why Mama always told her to be seen and not heard. She was terrible at conversation, especially with the opposite sex.

"Kit, I apologize—"

His head finally swiveled toward her—and her words died in her throat. Dark, hooded eyes stared at her, his expression intense and a little wild. A little dangerous. A thrill ran down her spine and her heart began racing inside her chest.

She didn't know what he was thinking, but somehow she knew her words hadn't upset him. In the least.

He liked what I said.

"Alice, I . . ." He dropped his gaze to her mouth. "I really, really want to kiss you right now."

He seemed perfectly serious and rational, suffering no delusions of any kind that she could tell. Nevertheless, this could not be happening. Men like Kit did not find Alice appealing. "You do?"

"More than any damn thing in the world."

"Because of what I said?"

"Because of who you are."

Her breath lodged in her throat but she didn't move, uncertainty twisting in her belly. Could she do this? Of course she *wanted* to kiss Kit—what sane person wouldn't?—but this wasn't part of what he owed her for the recipes. "You don't need to kiss me as part of the lessons."

"I am aware, and this has nothing to do with our bargain. This is because you have me tangled up in knots. I can't explain it, but it's like you're this clever, fascinating puzzle and I need to dig deeper." He exhaled and leaned closer. "Please let me show you. It'll be so good, I swear. Better than good, actually." He placed a hand on her armrest, his body angled toward her. "It'll be perfection."

He hovered close but didn't push her, as if he were waiting for her to meet him halfway, and she was ready. More than ready, in fact. Her blood thickened, heated, with a slow roll of desire unlike anything she'd ever experienced. It was as if a line tethered the two of them together and she had no choice but to close the gap. Still, she did it carefully, so he could revoke the offer if he changed his mind. To her surprise, however, he didn't speak or pull away.

Indeed, it seemed this was happening.

When their mouths were almost touching, she paused to linger, breathing him in. Anticipating the moment when she would learn what it felt like to be kissed. She licked her lips. "Show me, Kit. Please."

"It would be my pleasure."

He bent forward and his mouth met hers with a simple brush of his lips. Fascinated, she watched as he tilted his head and returned for another swipe. He cupped her jaw in his palm. "Close your eyes, Alice. Feel what I am telling you with my mouth— and tell me what you are feeling with yours."

Oh. So, kissing was like communicating without words.

She let her lids fall shut and sank into the sensations, like the soft press of his flesh against hers, the smell of his soap. The way his exhales gusted over her skin. How his fingers tightened, as if to hold her close. *He's telling me he wants to discover more.*

So did she.

Without overthinking the recklessness of what they were doing, she began kissing him back, matching his movements and capturing his mouth in an even exchange. He grunted softly, and she took that to mean she was doing something right.

Then he deepened the kiss, with more suction and pressure, commanding their pace, and she could feel him in every part of her body, from the roots of her hair down to her toes. Tingles slid along her legs, in her core, and her pulse throbbed in time with her heartbeat.

He pulled back slightly. "Stop?"

She shook her head once, then returned her mouth to his, not ready for this lesson to end. Kit did not disappoint, kissing her thoroughly, again and again, his lips coaxing and demanding, and her hands drifted to his shoulders, then up to his hair. The strands were soft, like silk, and she was shocked when a faint moan escaped her throat.

The sound must have excited him because he flicked his tongue against the seam of her lips, and she parted them, surprised. He slipped his tongue in her mouth and rubbed it across hers, and she marveled at the intimacy of it. *Kit's tongue is in my mouth.* While unbelievable, it felt divine as he stroked and twisted, twining with hers until she did the same. The second she teased his tongue, turning the slightest bit aggressive, he groaned.

"Yes," he murmured. "More of that, please."

She complied, needing to explore his mouth as he had explored hers. The kiss went on and she soon forgot where she was and who she was with. She became this wanton creature, a woman chasing her own pleasure and offering pleasure in return, as if they were of the same mind, the same goal. Her skin crackled, excitement humming just under the surface, and she wished he would kiss her everywhere.

When he pulled back, her fingers unintentionally tightened in his hair. Was that it? She panted and tried to drag air into her lungs. "Are we done?"

His mouth twitched. "Do you want to be done?"

"No, not really."

"Good, because neither do I. May I bring you over here to sit in my lap? It'll make it easier on my back, but I don't wish to frighten you."

"Oh, I'm sorry." She had no idea he was uncomfortable. "Of course, if it's easier for you."

With a seductive smile, he reached over, plucked her from her seat and placed her on his lap. "There. That's better." With a hand on the back of her head, he brought her face closer. "Now, kiss me again."

Chapter Six

❧

𝒦it paused and waited to see what his little vixen would do. Alice had surprised him time and time again today, so he tried not to move when she inched forward and touched her lips to his once more. *God, yes.* He relaxed and kissed her back, doing nothing more than enjoying the feeling of having her on his lap, within such easy reach.

She's a virgin.

He reminded himself of this for what seemed like the hundredth time since they started kissing, like whenever he wanted to whisper dirty words in her ear or slide his hand under her skirts. Which was often. He longed to do all manner of wicked things to this woman, to see how deep her passion ran, to discover what it would take to drive her wild. She'd placed a shell around herself, insisting she was shy, and Kit loved a challenge.

There was nothing shy about her kiss. Her lips were eager, her tongue demanding, and that hint of aggression made him impossibly hard. He kept it as chaste as he could manage, however, telling her how much he wanted her with just his mouth. That, and the erection digging into her backside. She couldn't be so innocent as to not understand *that* particular message.

He let his lips drift over her jaw, down her throat, giving her soft kisses and gentle licks. This lesson was certainly more enjoyable than last night's invasive question and answer session. She tasted sweet and delicate, a forbidden treat he hardly deserved but would savor all the same. To prove it, he lightly sank his teeth into the velvety skin of her throat.

Alice gasped and threw her head back. *"Oh."*

"Like that, do you?" He moved to a different spot and bit her gently once more.

Her fingernails sank into his scalp. "Is this what people do? Bite each other?"

"Only if you're very lucky."

"I'm serious, Christopher."

Christopher. Hardly anyone called him that anymore. But the word sounded different coming out of Alice's mouth, a breathy rush of syllables that nearly blended together to become something new. A secret shared between the two of them.

He wanted to hear it again.

Putting his lips near her ear, he asked, "Who is kissing you?"

"You are."

"Say my name, Alice."

"Kit," she said quietly, almost shyly.

"Wrong. The other one."

"Christopher," she breathed.

A sizzle raced along his nerve endings and gathered in his groin. When his cock twitched, she froze. "Was that . . . ?"

"You wanted lessons," he said, "so now you've learned how you affect me. I cannot hide it. You should feel free to ignore it, however."

"Not certain how that is possible. It feels like a tree trunk."

He dropped his head onto her shoulder and suppressed a laugh. This woman and his vanity were a match made in heaven.

"Are you laughing at me?"

Sobering, he cleared his throat. "Not at you, per se. More like your descriptions. They are certainly creative."

"May we return to my question about biting?"

"I am always happy to return to biting." He demonstrated, nibbling on the skin behind her ear.

She clutched his arm and swayed against him. "Why does that feel so delicious?"

"It does, doesn't it?" He did it again lower, careful not to mark her. She wriggled on his lap, torturing him with a bit of friction to his poor neglected cock.

"Do you like it, as well?"

He released her and leaned back, offering her his throat. "Try it and find out."

"Really?" She sounded eager and he bit off a grin.

"Of course. I am at your disposal."

"Again, this isn't necessary as part of our bargain."

This again? He sighed and cupped her nape with his hand to bring her closer. "Will you bite me already?"

She hesitated, even in the face of his encouragement, so he waited. He couldn't cajole her into doing what he wanted. Victory was much sweeter when earned and not taken.

And Alice was brave—much braver than she believed, in fact. She claimed she was shy, but a shy person did not come looking for help in seducing a husband. A shy person did not speak her mind so freely, or argue with him when she did not agree. She was no doormat, except in the presence of her mother, and someday Kit would get to the bottom of that mystery.

Just when he'd about given up, humid breath drifted over his neck. Her lips touched his skin first, a soft kiss that sent goose bumps darting across his body, and then her tongue followed with a firm swipe. Closing his eyes, he tried not to react. It wasn't easy, not when lust careened through his veins like a locomotive. He'd been with many partners over the years and never had to employ so much patience. In any other circumstance, he would have carried her over to the bed and begun shedding clothing by now.

But Alice was not a bed partner, and this was not an affair. It would never go beyond this. He would help her with some tips and simple experience in exchange for Franconi's recipes. Once back in New York, they would never see each other again.

Her mouth stopped right above his collar and the scrape of teeth caused him to shiver. Then she clamped down, biting him harder than he'd expected, and he grunted. The resulting sting sent a jolt through his limbs, straight to his erection. *Christ.* Then she sucked on his skin as if trying to draw out poison, and his eyes nearly rolled back in his head. Who'd taught her to do *that*?

Oh, God. It was torture. Panting, he gripped the armrests of the chair and tried not to thrust his hips as she continued to suck. The pressure of her mouth was exquisite and unrelenting, and he had forgotten how pleasurable this felt. It had been ages since a woman had marked him in such a possessive manner, as if she wanted the world to know he belonged to her. He should stop this, as a bruise on the side of his throat would only invite questions, but no one would ever suspect Alice responsible.

And Kit liked the idea of seeing her stamp on his body for days to come. Next time, he'd have her mark him where no one else could see it.

Next time? He was losing his mind. This could go no further, even if he desperately wanted it to.

She released him and eased back to admire her handiwork. "The skin is very red. Did I hurt you?"

"No," he wheezed, his body buzzing with craving and need. "Quite the opposite."

"You enjoyed it."

"Indeed. Any more enjoyment and I would require a new set of trousers."

"What? Why?" Her brows pinched in the most adorable way, and he had to remind himself this was all new to her.

"Never mind. Suffice it to say either I am a fabulous teacher or you are a quick study." He kissed her cheek. "Or both, perhaps."

"For the record, you are quite good at kissing yourself."

"Thank you. I am offering up my services any time you'd care to practice."

"Any time?"

He nipped her jaw with his teeth. "Any time, my dear Alice."

The offer was a legitimate one. He'd kiss her day or night, in any location she preferred. With other women, there wasn't opportunity to linger and enjoy their kisses, as he was too busy trying to get them into bed. Kissing had felt like a nuisance, a distraction from more important goals.

Not so when it came to Alice. He could kiss her for hours, sink inside her mouth and drink in her sighs until he was delirious with it. With so much to discover and explore, she would never bore him.

He wasn't sure what that meant and he didn't care. At least not right now, with this sweet creature still sitting on his lap.

The clock on the mantel chimed the hour and Alice started. "Oh, no. I must hurry to luncheon. If I am not there and my mother returns . . ."

She didn't finish the sentence, as if Kit could draw his own conclusions. Yet he didn't understand the mother-daughter relationship between these two. "If you are not there, then what?"

Alice slid off his lap and smoothed her skirts. He instantly felt the loss of her warm, soft curves. "She'll assume I am up to no good. Which means she will never let me out of her sight again during this house party."

"But you *are* up to no good," he couldn't help but point out, his mouth fixed with a smirk.

"Stop annoying me, you devil. Now, do I look a mess?"

She looked fetching and utterly delectable, but

her skirts were slightly rumpled and wisps of hair fell in her face. He would be remiss as a clandestine lover if he didn't point them out. "Come."

Rising, he brought her into his washroom. Wetting his hands, he smoothed her hair back in place, then used a tiny touch of pomade to hold it. "Better. Let me fix your skirts."

"Why? Are they horribly creased?" She tried to spin and look over her shoulder, like a dog trying to chase its own tail.

"Stop. I'll do it." Dropping to one knee, he reached for her skirts . . . then paused. "I'll need to start with the petticoats, Alice."

She shook her head and started tugging fabric. "No, merely pull the outer skirt down."

He didn't wish to tell her how much experience he had with ladies' clothing, but he was absolutely certain her idea wouldn't work. Stilling her hands, he asked, "Do you trust me?"

Though her eyes were wild with panic, she nodded. "Of course. Would I be standing in your washroom if I didn't?"

Fair point. "Then let me help you."

She bit her lip and released her skirts. "All right."

He reached under the layers of silk and cotton, trying to avoid touching her stocking-covered leg. As much as he'd like to learn every detail of what Alice hid under her skirts, he wouldn't disrespect her with an uninvited grope. When he found the petticoat, he held it and lifted the other layers up to her. "Here, hold these."

A blush covered her face and throat, but she didn't speak as she took the cloth.

Kit worked quickly, smoothing and evening out the plain cotton. When he finished, he took the next layer, a stiffer and fancier petticoat, out of her hands, and evened it out. This was what would give her dress the bell-shaped curve that was all the rage nowadays. Then he straightened the outer skirt. "There. Almost as good as new."

"Am I still wrinkled?"

He rose and took her face in his hands. "Alice, you're perfect. Stop worrying." Unable to help himself, he kissed her again, taking her lips greedily, as if he needed the memory of her mouth to survive the afternoon. She relaxed into him, clutching his wrists and slipping her tongue past his lips. He took it, wasting no time in twining their tongues together, relishing the warm, slick taste of her.

She finally pulled away, both of them gasping for breath. "I need to go."

Clasping her hand, he led her to the door of his bedchamber and peeked into the corridor. It was empty. "No one is around. It's safe for you to go."

"Goodbye," she whispered, then slipped through the crack and disappeared.

He closed the door and exhaled. All of that had been unexpected . . . and wonderful. Too wonderful, actually. Thank fuck he had time to find his own release before the afternoon's festivities.

As he locked the door and unfastened his trousers, a thought suddenly occurred. That kiss in his washroom had felt as natural as breathing. He'd looked down at her pretty face and upturned lips and needed to taste them, plain and simple.

So, what on earth did that mean?

AN HOUR LATER, the guests gathered on the lawn beyond the tennis court. Croquet teams were quickly formed, with the Duke of Lockwood and Mr. Archer each leading a team. Alice wasn't playing the first round, so she sat near the other young ladies, far away from the chaperones. Far away from her mother.

Kit had opted out of croquet, and he lounged in a chair at the opposite end of the table where he sipped a glass of lemonade. There was a red mark on his neck, just above his collar. She'd left a *mark* on his skin. A love bite. It was depraved and forbidden, and she found herself smiling every time she thought of that patch of red.

Was it obvious he'd been kissed and bitten there? Would anyone know she'd sucked on his skin until it changed color? Would anyone know that her lower half still throbbed with delicious need?

While the answer was likely no, Alice still avoided her mother's eye, worried Mama would suspect something just from looking at her. She felt positively transformed by what happened in his bedchamber, like she'd discovered she could play the piano after never once taking a lesson. Like she'd baked a perfect soufflé without ever reading the recipe first.

I kissed Kit in his bedchamber, she wanted to yell. Moreover, he had enjoyed it. Perhaps not as much as she, but his reaction had been real. *Very* real. Impossibly big and real.

She almost snickered. She, Alice Lusk, thinking lewd thoughts. Who would have guessed such a thing were possible?

I am offering up my services any time you'd care to practice.

Warmth cascaded through her veins, the promise of more kisses from Kit like a fever in her blood. She snuck a glance at him and was surprised to find him staring at her. Blinking, she frowned and moved her gaze to the table. Was he mad? They needed to avoid looking at each other so as to not arouse suspicion.

The risk of getting caught was already high enough, and there were just three days left before she returned to New York. To her life of dancing and balls and small talk. To finding a husband who might possibly want her for *her*. She wasn't ready, not yet. Hence why these lessons with Kit were so important.

"Anyone know how Maddie is feeling?" Lydia Hartwell, a young woman from out West, leaned in. "It's too bad she couldn't join us."

Katherine Delafield sat next to Alice, which was how Alice noted the worry on the other woman's face. "She seemed fine before lunch. I cannot understand what would have happened to make her miss this."

A noise sounded from Kit's end of the table. "Oh, can't you?" The edge of his mouth quirked, making him look mischievous. "No guesses at all, Miss Delafield?"

Katherine chewed her lip. "Absolutely none."

Why was Katherine concerned about Maddie? And what did Kit know about it?

Oh, Katherine was supposed to have her picnic with Mr. Archer today. What with all the kissing in

Kit's room, Alice had forgotten about it. She angled closer to Katherine. "How was your picnic lunch?"

"I didn't go," Katherine whispered. "Nellie and I thought . . . well, I backed out at the last minute and left Maddie alone with Mr. Archer."

"I see. You were matchmaking."

"Exactly. Everyone can see they are perfect for one another."

Hadn't Alice said as much to Kit? "I suspect the duke's arrival might muck up the works."

"True, but I have faith that destiny will prevail. Which means, dear Alice, a duke will soon be up for grabs." Katherine elbowed Alice's arm meaningfully.

"You and Lockwood would make a striking couple," she said.

"I meant *you*. I have no interest in Lockwood."

"You don't?"

"Goodness, no. I spent enough time traveling around England to know I'd never want to live there. And being a duchess would be so . . . restrictive. I like my freedom, thank you very much." As if she'd revealed too much, she added, "But you shouldn't let my feelings color your future. One can hardly do better than a duke—and a handsome duke, at that. I think you should pursue him, once Maddie and Mr. Archer are official."

"I wouldn't even know how." While Kit was trying to teach her how to seduce a man into marrying her, those lessons hadn't been intended for a duke. For heaven's sake, every young woman in New York City had set her cap for Lockwood this spring. Alice couldn't compete with *that*.

"Do what Maddie did," Katherine said. "You attend the events he's attending and use every opportunity possible to talk to him. Throw yourself in his path at every turn."

"And that works?"

"It did for Maddie. Not to mention that you are here together at this house party. You have the chance to get to know him now, before the rest of society descend like locusts once we're back in the city."

Katherine made it sound so easy, but Alice was not Maddie. She wasn't bubbly or fun, with plenty of friends and activities. If the duke courted someone like Maddie, why would he ever look twice at Alice? It seemed silly to point this out, however, so Alice merely said, "I'll think about it."

"Oh, the enthusiasm is overwhelming," Katherine said dryly. "Look at him out there. Wouldn't you rather marry a man who looks like Lockwood than some boring American fortune hunter?"

They both angled toward the croquet match. The Duke of Lockwood was leaning against his mallet, ankles crossed, his back straight and proud. The wind ruffled his brown hair while the sun kissed his skin and turned it into a warm gold. He really was appealing, in a stiff and proper sort of way.

"Look at those shoulders and tell me I am wrong," Katherine said out of the side of her mouth. "And you'd become a duchess."

"His Grace would never be interested in a woman like me."

"Are we back to this tedious tune? Alice, remember what I said: know your worth."

Without meaning to, Alice's eyes darted toward

Kit—only to find him staring at her once again. An emotion she could not place swirled in his brown depths, but it was fierce and disconcerting. Perhaps a little bit thrilling. She couldn't look away, caught in the murky tide pools hiding his thoughts. The desire to kiss the frown off his face rose up in her chest.

"Finally, the first match is over," Lydia was saying, and Alice dragged her attention off Kit to see the players leaving the court and heading for the tent.

"Who won?" Alice asked.

"Lockwood's team," Katherine said. "If I had to guess, judging by Mr. Archer's expression."

The duke, a fresh grass stain now marring his pristine trousers, stalked to the refreshment table. Mr. Archer dropped into the chair beside Kit, then said something under his breath that caused Kit to laugh, making him appear even more handsome. More captivating. More *alive* than anyone else around them. Alice's stomach dipped and she thought about his mouth and tongue and how much she had liked having them against hers. And how very necessary it was to feel them again. Soon.

Nellie Young, daughter of the financier Cornelius Young, had been on Mr. Archer's team. She dropped into the chair next to Katherine and leaned in. "Those two should just jump into a boxing ring and be done with it," Nellie murmured. "I hope Maddie knows what she's doing. Neither of them seems like the concede quietly type."

"Definitely not," Katherine agreed. "I hope I didn't ruin things by leaving Maddie alone with Mr. Archer for the picnic today."

Nellie shook her head. "Based on his swagger and Maddie's absence, I'd say you did exactly the right thing." She glanced over at Alice and winked. "We're a matchmaking lot, Miss Lusk. Be careful you don't get caught up in our shenanigans."

"I've already begun," Katherine said proudly. "I'm going to push her toward Lockwood when Maddie throws him over."

"Which is ridiculous," Alice put in. "The duke would never be interested in me."

A strange expression crossed Nellie's beautiful face as she stared out at the empty croquet court. "Oh, I think you'd be surprised by what interests His Grace."

"What does that mean?" Katherine tapped Nellie's arm. "What are you hiding?"

"Absolutely nothing. Excuse me, I need to fetch a stiff drink."

"Only lemonade over there, I'm afraid," Katherine said.

"Which is why I'm headed back to the house." Nellie stood and pushed her chair in. "See you ladies at dinner. Have fun in the second game." She strolled away in the direction of the chateau.

Teams for the second game were organized. When Katherine saw that Alice had drawn Mr. Archer's team, she quickly switched their sticks to put Alice on Lockwood's team. "What are you doing?" Alice hissed.

"Helping you. Now, don't waste your chance."

The duke approached the table and gave them a wide smile that didn't quite reach his eyes. "Ladies, who is partnering with me for the second game?" Lydia and Alice raised their hands, and Lockwood clapped his hands together once. "Excellent. Let's select mallets, shall we?"

"Perhaps I should take your place, Lockwood." Kit came to his feet and shoved his hands in his trouser pockets. "You're probably tired from the first game."

"That's not necessary," Mr. Archer said, staring directly at the duke. "His Grace and I are perfectly happy to go again, aren't we, Lockwood?"

"More than happy, actually," Lockwood drawled, his jaw tight.

Alice exchanged a worried glance with Katherine. Nellie had been right—these two men were not about to back down. Whatever happened during this house party, it was not going to end well.

"Have a seat, Kit." Harrison slapped Kit on the back. "No need to wear yourself out on our account."

Kit's attention turned to Alice as he sat, his face blank but his eyes burning intensely, as if he were trying to see under her skin. Into her brain. Was he upset that his request to play had been shrugged off? If so, what had that to do with her?

Chapter Seven

$\mathcal{K}$it was in a foul goddamn mood.

Everything was going terribly. After today's glorious lesson, Alice had ignored him—again—and though Kit knew the reasons behind her mask of indifference in regards to him, it rankled. Instead, she'd stared at the duke with stars in her dashed eyes, as if that prig was the only glass of water left in a desert.

As if that weren't bad enough, Maddie was now showing off her betrothal ring. The guests had gathered in the salon for a drink before dinner when Maddie removed her glove to display a diamond and emerald monstrosity on her left ring finger. The ladies had squealed and expressed their delight at the match, as if Maddie had just won some sort of prize.

Throwing back the rest of his champagne, he swapped the empty coupe for a full one on his way over to Harrison. His friend looked ready to tear the furniture apart with his bare hands. "Now what?" he murmured once at Harrison's side.

"I don't know," Harrison said tightly. "I hadn't thought that bastard would propose. I thought I had more time."

They both glanced at the duke, leaning against the mantel as if he hadn't a care in the world.

"God, I hate him," Harrison said.

After watching Alice study Lockwood all afternoon, Kit had to agree. "Impossible to avoid a scandal now. You have to proceed cautiously."

"There's no time for caution," Harrison snapped. "Or else I'll lose her. For good, this time."

Kit studied Alice, who sat stiffly beside her mother on the far sofa. His prized pupil subtly watched the duke from under her lashes, and Kit's blood boiled. "We have to get rid of him."

"Get rid of who?" Nellie appeared on Kit's right side, champagne glass in her hand.

"The duke," Harrison said.

"Ah. Bet you're wishing you hadn't stayed away so long, Harrison."

Harrison didn't answer, though his lips pressed together in a flat line.

"I understand why he's upset," Nellie said to Kit. "But why are your drawers in a twist?"

"Solidarity," he lied.

The felicitations continued in the middle of the room, as did Alice's surreptitious observation of Lockwood. Was she actually interested in the duke? Kit took another a gulp of champagne. Alice had better taste than that, hadn't she?

Nellie angled toward Kit and Harrison instead of the other guests. "You know, Katherine was angling to match the fair Miss Lusk with the duke. It appears that was a wasted effort."

Kit sucked in a breath. Had the Delafield girl really been trying to pair Alice off with that oaf? *Wasn't that the point of the lessons?* Yes, but not now. Not here. And what happened when Maddie threw the duke over, as she most assuredly would before the house party ended? Would Alice use the tricks Kit taught her to woo a duke?

The pit of his stomach hollowed out, leaving an empty cavern despite all the champagne. He hated the idea of Alice and Lockwood. She deserved better than a drafty manor house in the English countryside, surrounded by servants and a husband who ignored her. She needed laughter and friends—

"Oh, Kit," Nellie said on a chuckle. "You are as transparent as a window."

He deliberately moved his gaze off Alice. "I have no idea what you are talking about."

This got Harrison's attention. "Transparent? About what?"

Nellie lifted a brow and elbowed Kit. "Go on. Tell him."

"There is nothing to tell."

"Really?" She leaned in. "I saw her leave your room earlier, you know."

Harrison shifted to glower at Kit. "Who was it? Was she responsible for that love bite?"

Kit dragged a hand down his face. "Quiet, both of you. It's not what you think."

"I'd say it's exactly what I think," Nellie put in.

"And what were you doing on our side of the chateau?" Kit asked, turning it around on her. "Whose room were you visiting?"

"I wasn't. I was out for a walk."

An obvious lie. "In the corridors?"

"Kit," Harrison said under his breath. "Maddie expressly warned you away from the young ladies. There will be hell to pay if she learns of this."

"She won't—and it's innocent." Mostly. "There is nothing to worry about."

"That purplish mark on your throat would imply otherwise. Do not ruin this house party, Kit, not until I win her back."

"You have my word." He didn't dare look in Alice's direction. "I have it under control."

"And to think," Nellie drawled, toasting Kit and Harrison with her coupe. "I almost didn't come. What a shame it would have been to miss all these scandals."

Kit liked this girl. No surprise, as their personalities were similar, but he was glad he'd found Alice first. It turned out that corrupting an innocent woman, coaxing her out of her shell, was far more enjoyable than he'd ever imagined. "From what I hear, you normally start one or two of your own. So catch up, if you would, Miss Young."

"Already did, Mr. Ward." Her mouth twisted into a devilish smirk. "Some of us know how to keep ours private, however."

The duke started toward them and Nellie excused herself, drifting to the other young ladies. Smart of her. No doubt Lockwood was coming to gloat. Kit braced himself, ready to break up a fistfight, if necessary. God knew it wouldn't be the first time—he, Forrest, Harrison and Preston all had their share of scrapes while in college.

Gleeful satisfaction danced in Lockwood's gaze, confirming what Kit had suspected. The duke wanted to rub Harrison's nose in the engagement. "Ward, if you don't mind, I'd like a private word with Archer."

The tone brooked no argument, but Kit wasn't about to desert his friend. "I think I'll stay, actually."

Lockwood sipped his champagne and focused on Harrison. "No felicitations, Archer? It must sting to lose to me thrice in one day."

"Jesus," Kit muttered under his breath. Was Lockwood mad? Taunting Harrison was dangerous.

"Enjoy it for now, Lockwood. Kit, I'm headed outside for some air. See you at dinner." Harrison stalked in the direction of the door.

"Not sure stirring him up is the wisest course of action," Kit said when they were alone.

"I am responding merely in kind. The cleverness that you Americans credit yourselves with." He shook his head. "It's quite sad."

Kit very rarely argued. His attitude was devil-may-care with a dash of live-and-let-live. But he really was coming to loathe the Duke of Lockwood.

And they were trying to push sweet Alice toward this unbearable snob? Absolutely not. Kit would never allow it.

Leaning in, he lowered his voice, "Listen here, Lockwood—"

"Good evening, Your Grace. Mr. Ward." Alice had joined them, her brown gaze bouncing between the two men. "May I offer Your Grace congratulations on the betrothal?"

Lockwood inclined his head a fraction, as if displays of real emotion were beneath him. "Thank you, Miss Lusk. I could not be happier."

"Indeed." She bit her lip, seemingly at a loss for words. Lockwood said nothing more, content to let the silence stretch, but the longer it went on, the redder Alice's face became.

As much as Kit did not wish to converse with Lockwood, he couldn't bear to see Alice struggle. Her newfound confidence had been hard won, and he didn't want her to doubt herself. "And how was your game of croquet this afternoon, Miss Lusk? Were you victorious?" Kit had departed as soon as the second match began, heading back into the chateau instead of watching Alice watch the duke.

She offered him a grateful smile. "We were, thanks in large part to the duke's skill in the game."

"You showed remarkable skill yourself," the duke said. "I believe a bloodthirsty competitor lurks inside you."

Alice beamed as if Lockwood had showered her with compliments. "Your Grace is clearly teasing, but I did have fun. I haven't played croquet in ages."

Lockwood said nothing, his eyes affixed proudly on Maddie across the room, and Kit couldn't take one minute more. "Miss Lusk, care to walk with me?"

She cast a look over her shoulder toward her mother, who was conversing with another chaperone. "I cannot leave. It wouldn't be proper."

"Just around the room, then?"

"I suppose that would be all right, if my mother agrees."

When she started to turn in her mother's direction, Kit grabbed her wrist. "Let's live a little, shall we? After all, it's always better to beg for forgiveness than to ask permission." Especially when Mrs.

Lusk would surely say no. Alice's mother used every available opportunity to stare daggers at Kit, as if he were dirt on the bottom of her slipper.

"Go on, Miss Lusk," Lockwood said. "I'll keep an eye on you, should Mr. Ward try anything improper."

Fuck off, Kit told Lockwood with his gaze. The duke smirked and sipped his champagne, but Kit didn't bother giving him a set down. Instead, he held out his arm to Alice. "Come with me."

She excused herself to Lockwood, then took Kit's arm, and he led her to the far side of the room, near the piano. At least here they would still be in clear view but out of earshot.

"Are you certain this is wise? We could arouse suspicion." Folding her hands, she kept a proper distance. Kit set his coupe on the smooth surface of the piano and crossed his arms.

"Are you setting your cap for the duke?" The words tumbled out of his mouth before he could stop them, and she blinked a few times, her dark lashes kissing the tops of her cheeks.

"You don't care for him, do you?"

"No, but it hardly matters what I think. It's what you think that matters."

"He's betrothed to Maddie. I don't think anything about him beyond that."

"So you aren't interested in him? In becoming a duchess?"

Her brows drew together. "Where is this coming from?"

How could he explain it without sounding as if he'd been obsessing over her? *You were staring at him, and then I saw you switch sticks to join his team for croquet. And now, you came up to chat with him out of nowhere.*

Kit's shoulders sank. He was acting ridiculous. Worse, he was acting *jealous*. He didn't do jealousy. Ever. Lovers were temporary and no one had a right to put a claim on anyone else. What had come over him?

It was time to return to the purpose of his association with Alice. "Forget it. When is our next lesson?"

"Do you think Lockwood could ever be interested in me?"

He dragged a hand down his jaw and tried to gather the scattered shards of his sanity. "Of course. As well, I heard Miss Delafield was attempting to matchmake."

"True, but it hardly matters now." She gestured to the small group admiring Maddie's ring. "Seeing as how he's spoken for."

"The engagement will not last. So, if you are interested in marrying Lockwood, you still have a fighting chance."

"Along with every other debutante on the East Coast."

"Not every debutante has me helping her, however. I'd say that gives you an advantage." If Alice put her clever brain—and his lessons—toward winning the duke, nothing could stop her. Lockwood would be a fool not to take notice.

"Hmm." She turned to study Lockwood in a way that set Kit's teeth on edge. "Living an ocean away from my mother would have its perks."

"Yes, but what about your friends? The rest of your family?"

"I don't really have friends, not close ones, anyway. There aren't any siblings or cousins. And my father travels all the time for business, so I'd still see him."

Kit wasn't ready to give up yet. "He'd probably ship you off to some drafty old manor house in the middle of nowhere."

"I wouldn't mind that. It would be fun to explore. Perhaps have a ghost or two for company."

Had she an answer for everything? "He's terrible at cards." Kit had witnessed this firsthand at the casino. "No doubt he'd gamble your money away the first chance he got."

"I'm very good at managing money. My father saw to that. Besides, why are you trying to talk me out of pursuing someone? It's the whole reason you are giving me lessons."

He had no idea. Perhaps he'd truly lost his mind.

"I am not trying to talk you out of the duke. Pursue him all you like when Maddie throws him over." The only thing left to do was retreat. "I'll find you after dinner." With that, he quit the room and went searching for Harrison.

ALICE FOLLOWED THE faint smell of roasted meat down to the chateau's kitchen. Dinner had long finished and her mother had turned in for the night. Which meant Alice was free to do as she wished without being followed.

Originally, she planned to find Kit and embark on more lessons, but something about their conversation during cocktails bothered her. He'd actively tried to talk her out of pursuing the Duke of

Lockwood, offering up excuses on why the match was unsuitable. Why? Wasn't Kit eager to wash his hands of her?

It made no sense. Kit was a certified scoundrel. A first-rate bounder with no intention of marrying. And even if he did plan to take a wife, he wouldn't want Alice.

Christopher is not the marrying kind.

Maddie knew it. Katherine had warned her away, too. Entertaining romantic thoughts about Kit was foolish and impossible, like wishing on rainbows. Alice was much too practical for that nonsense, and she needed to find a suitable husband instead.

So, she would work harder to ignore the fluttering in her stomach when they were together. To forget the racing of her heart, or the heavy pulse between her legs when Kit kissed her. It was temporary. She needed to build up distance between them—literally and figuratively.

Which was why she went to the chateau's kitchen that night.

The kitchen was huge, a big open space where multiple staff members could move about freely. A long table stood in the middle, which was where the Websters' cook, Mrs. Berman, waited. "Forgive my tardiness," Alice said as she entered. "I had to see my mother settled first."

Mrs. Berman had dark brown hair with a touch of gray at the temples. Though she was probably tired, she gave Alice a smile and held up an apron. "No apologies necessary, miss. There's always plenty to do around here. I've kept busy, believe me."

Alice tied the fresh apron over her clothing. After dinner, she had changed out of her silk evening gown and into a more casual dress. "You are kind to show me how to bake this bread. I am eager to see the magic that makes it so delicious."

"It's an honor. Not many ladies are interested in cooking or baking."

"My mother often reminds me of that—which is why it's easier for me to sneak down here at night."

"I understand. It'll be our secret."

Alice relaxed, relieved. "Thank you. Now, tell me about this bread." There had been a unique cinnamon bread at afternoon tea the past two days, unlike anything she'd ever tasted. The texture was similar to a brioche, but different. So Alice had asked Mrs. Berman to let her assist in making it.

Mrs. Berman motioned to the table, where ingredients and jars waited. "It is called babka, which in Polish means 'grandmother.'"

"Are you from Poland, then?"

"My mother grew up there. I was young when we moved to America, but she taught me to make this, among many other traditional Jewish dishes. Let's start with the yeast."

Mrs. Berman had Alice repeat every step as they went along, from mixing the ingredients and heating up the milk, to beating the eggs, until they had the dough formed. They kneaded and talked, with Mrs. Berman sharing stories of her mother and the meals their family enjoyed together growing up. It sounded lovely, warm and inviting, so different from Alice's holidays at the interminable table in the Lusk dining room. This was what Alice liked best about cooking and food: the stories and the sharing. The feeling that generations before and generations after would create the same dishes with love, just as this one had.

When the dough was ready, they set it aside to rise. Mrs. Berman said, "You're very competent in the kitchen. I can tell when someone has never kneaded dough before."

"Thank you. I find baking soothing."

"Indeed, I do, too. Something about pounding the dough to work out all your frustrations."

"Exactly," Alice said with a chuckle.

They prepared a simple sugar syrup while they waited, then Alice washed the utensils and pans so Mrs. Berman could get off her feet for a few minutes. After the first rise finished, they rolled out the dough. The filling was a simple sugar and cinnamon mix, which they spread on the dough and then formed into logs.

"Now, watch." Mrs. Berman cut the log down the middle, then layered and twisted the dough around itself. "You do it."

Alice matched the cook's movements. "How is that?" The twist was a bit sloppy, but not far off.

"Good for your first time. We must put them in the pans and let them rise once more." She heated the oven as Alice went back to the sink to clean up.

"Good evening, sir," she heard Mrs. Berman say.

Curious, Alice glanced over her shoulder—then froze. *No, it couldn't be.*

Why was *he* here?

She lunged for the tap to shut off the water as Kit wandered into the kitchen, the hint of a grin on his face.

"May I help you?" Mrs. Berman asked politely.

"I was searching for Miss Lusk, actually."

"Ah."

Alice dried her hands on a towel and came toward the table. "Mrs. Berman, this is Mr. Ward. He's a friend. Another guest at the party."

"I see."

Awkwardness descended, the three of them quiet, and Alice had no idea what to do next. She stared at Kit's handsome face as he glanced around the kitchen. Mrs. Berman took matters into her own hands by asking, "Miss, would you like a moment alone with Mr. Ward or . . . ?"

Alice was grateful for the choice. It was unusual for a guest, let alone two guests, to wander belowstairs, and Mrs. Berman seemed like the protective sort. "Yes, if you don't mind. Actually, we could bake the loaves, if you like. That way, you needn't stay up and wait."

The cook showed Alice how to turn off the heat when they were done with baking. "Otherwise, you'll burn the whole place down," Mrs. Berman warned.

"I won't forget. You have my word," Alice said.

"Good. Bake them for thirty minutes, then apply two layers of syrup with the brush. That will give them a nice shine and help them last."

"Understood. Thank you, Mrs. Berman. This has been a wonderful lesson and I appreciate your time."

"Of course, miss." Mrs. Berman patted Alice's hand, then she leaned in to say quietly, "If you need me, I am at the end of the hall."

Alice bit her lip and nodded. Kit posed no danger

to her, but the sweet cook didn't know that. "Mr. Ward will help me clean up."

Mrs. Berman nodded and they all exchanged good-nights. When they were alone, Kit approached the worktable. His shoulders seemed impossibly wide, his expression ridiculously charming. He was overwhelming in the best way possible, the sort that set her belly afire with longing.

Too bad he wasn't the marrying type.

Distance, Alice. Keep up those walls.

He leaned a hip against the table and dragged a fingertip over her cheek. It came away with cinnamon on it. "Well, well. Why am I not surprised to find you down here?"

She swallowed, pushed her inconvenient feelings aside and tried to unglue her tongue from the roof of her mouth. "I was watching Mrs. Berman make bread."

"I can see that. Do you do this often?"

"No. Just tonight. Why?"

"Always off getting lessons, aren't you?" He cocked his head. "Franconi, Mrs. Berman, me. You're forever learning, trying to soak up knowledge."

"Is that not the point of life? To try and learn as much as we can while we're here? Besides, women don't have as many opportunities for learning as men do."

"Most women your age don't concern themselves with learning. They're worried about parties and invitations and dresses."

"I think if given the opportunity, more women would choose learning first. It's hard to win a race when you're always starting from behind." She put the loaf pans in the oven, then cleaned her hands on the apron. "Thirty minutes and then we brush them."

"You look at home here in the kitchen. Happy. Confident."

Did he suspect just how deep her passion for cooking ran? "I like spending time in a kitchen. Food makes memories and creates stories, and each of those stories brings people joy. It's like love on a plate."

Looking down at the worktable, he evened up the utensils on the surface. "Speaking of joy, I was worried you were skipping our lesson tonight."

Not skipping, per se, but postponing until she'd shored up her defenses against his potent magnetism. "No. I just needed to do this first. I didn't wish to keep Mrs. Berman up too late."

"Had you planned on telling me?"

"I . . ." Had he been waiting on her? They hadn't spoken after dinner and she assumed he'd fill his evening with Harrison or the casino. Drinks and merriment. Not watching the clock for when she'd arrive. "I was going to find you later."

"Were you?" He searched her face. "Or were you upset that I disparaged the Duke of Lockwood before dinner?"

Not exactly upset. More like confused. "It's clear you do not like him."

"You should make up your own mind. So, forgive me if I put you off in any way."

An apology. How unexpected. She liked this thoughtful and sensitive version of Kit Ward. A lot.

Christopher is not the marrying kind.

It was imperative to keep repeating those words, to keep a lock around her heart that prevented scoundrels—no matter how charming—from stealing it. She wanted to seduce a man who would return her affections and actually marry her. Kit was not that man.

There was only one thing to do. She handed him a dry towel. "Help me finish the dishes."

Chapter Eight

Alice rinsed another ceramic bowl and handed it to Kit. He hadn't complained once about drying dishes; instead, he merely removed his jacket, rolled up his sleeves and got to work. If this was his first time helping in the kitchen, she couldn't tell.

Working side by side with him was easier than expected. He didn't chatter on to fill the silence, as many people did. Instead, she washed and he dried, with the smell of baking bread and cinnamon filling the kitchen.

"How did you find me?" she asked as she handed him the last utensil for drying.

"I asked several footmen, one of whom saw you come down the stairs."

"What if we are seen?"

"In the kitchen?" He huffed a laugh. "Not a soul would believe I was here, drying dishes."

"Not manly enough for you?"

"Not scandalous enough for me."

She drained the water in the sink. "Perhaps it's a

different sort of scandalous. Think what the gossip columns would say."

"One shudders to consider it. I'd never be able to show my face in the Union Club again."

Now it was her turn to chuckle. "Your secret is safe with me." She dried her hands and went to the oven. "Will you help me glaze the loaves?"

He finished drying the last spoon. "It would be my pleasure."

She took the loaf pans out of the oven, making sure to turn the heat off, and pointed to the sugar syrup. "Bring that here along with a brush." When he tried to hand her the syrup and brush, she pointed to the loaves. "You may have the honor, Mr. Ward."

He frowned at the items in his hands. "What do I do?"

"Brush the top of each loaf with syrup."

"How?"

Alice's lips twitched but she managed to keep a neutral expression. He was adorable. Taking his hand, she dipped the brush into the syrup and moved to the piping hot bread. "Now brush all over the top, really coating it." She released him and nudged his shoulder with hers.

He lightly touched the brush to the bread, almost as if he were afraid of tearing it. "How much should I brush on?"

"We'll go with what feels right, but we need to brush two coats on each. Don't worry about hurting the bread. Give it a good soak."

Growing bolder, he applied more glaze to the loaf. "You're laughing at me."

"I am not. The only way to learn is by doing."

"Sort of like kissing," he said, his voice deepening.

She could feel her skin heat in a way that had nothing to do with being near the warm oven. "Exactly. No one is perfect at first."

"Well, I was . . . but I'm preternaturally skilled in that department."

His arrogance drew a laugh out of her. "I can hardly argue, considering. So, who taught you how to kiss?"

He switched to the other loaf. "A milliner's daughter when I was eleven. She was fourteen."

Goodness, eleven! How different his experience had been from hers. "How did you meet her?"

"I went to buy my mother a hat for her birthday. It was before she grew ill, but I noticed she was sad. I had the foolish idea that a new hat might cheer her up."

"Why foolish?"

He sighed and put the syrup down, but he didn't move away, the two of them not even an arm's length apart. "She needed a new husband, not a new hat. Except I was too young to know as much."

Clearly, his mother had meant a lot to him. And she undoubtedly had adored Kit, a sweet son who wished to make her feel better. "I bet she loved that hat."

A soft, affectionate smile emerged. "She asked to be buried in it."

"Oh, Kit."

His shoulders rose and fell with the force of a deep breath. "I hadn't thought of that in a long time. It is a rare nice memory, one of only a handful from my childhood."

Shadows darkened his whiskey-colored gaze, a

flicker of sadness in a man who leaned toward the perpetually cheerful. An ache blossomed in her chest and, without thinking, she rose up on her toes and pressed a kiss to his cheek. "I am sorry."

A deep chasm formed between his brows. "For what?"

She cocked her head, surprised. Had no one ever sympathized with him? Had no one ever told him that no child should have to endure hundreds of terrible memories? "For a boy who deserved better."

Blinking, he stared at her. She couldn't tell what he was thinking, his expression revealing little as they stood together. Had she overstepped? She'd merely wished to offer some comfort, a small comment to ease his mind.

Just as she opened her mouth to apologize, Kit spoke. "Shall we continue with our lessons?"

Right, the lessons. For a moment, she'd forgotten. They had seemed like two friends, talking and sharing, getting to know one another better, but that had been an illusion. She and Kit weren't friends. They were friendly, yes, but he was helping her in exchange for recipes.

Stepping back, she wrapped a towel around her hand and lifted one of the hot loaf tins. "Of course. Let me move these so they cool down for tomorrow." Soon she had both loaves in the larder, where they would remain until tea the following afternoon. When she returned to the kitchen, Kit held the bowl with the sugar syrup in his hands.

"Oh, I suppose we should wash that." She tried to take it from him . . . but he didn't let go.

"Wait a moment," he said. "We'll use this for our

lesson. I want to demonstrate that anything can be used to flirt. Even food."

Was he serious? "How on earth can one use food to flirt?"

"Think about it. You use your mouth to eat food, and anything that calls attention to a woman's mouth has the potential to drive men wild."

She considered this. "Because it brings to mind kissing?"

"And other things," he said cryptically.

"What other things?"

"Things your husband will show you. Now, watch me." He dipped a finger into the syrup and brought it to his lips, where he licked the liquid off before slipping his finger into his mouth. Lids falling closed, he gave a tiny moan.

Good God.

While only a performance on Kit's part, the move caused a riot inside her, waves of wanting that had her gripping the workbench to keep from crumbling. His masculine appeal was almost painful, almost overwhelming in its intensity, with a face she could stare at for hours. From the full lips and cleft in his chin, to the sharp jaw and angular cheekbones, Kit was a superior specimen of manhood.

Finally, he dropped his hand, his gaze clearing as if he hadn't just sent the temperature in the room soaring. "Now, you."

Put the syrup on her finger like he had? No, no, no. She couldn't possibly do that. Her attempt would appear ridiculous compared to Kit's debauched version. "Oh, no. I would look foolish."

"No, you won't. Besides, it's just me, and I am the perfect man with whom to practice."

Because we have no future together.

Because we won't see each other again after this house party ends.

Indeed, how could she have forgotten?

"Please, Alice," he whispered, his voice as seductive as fine wine. "I want to see it."

Before she could talk herself out of it, she dipped her finger into the syrup and put it to her lips. Then she remembered his advice on eye contact, so she locked gazes with him before sliding her index finger into her mouth, slowly. Carefully, as if she had all the time in the world. He fixated on her lips, and his mouth parted slightly on a small gust of air.

Emboldened by his tiny but immediate reaction, she slid her finger deeper, rubbing it against her tongue, then withdrew slightly before returning. In and out. Then again. She sawed her finger past her lips while groaning as if enjoying the taste. Kit's pupils were wide, his skin flushed as he observed quietly, intently, his chest expanding and contracting.

After one final flick of her tongue she took her finger out of her mouth, and Kit swallowed loudly. They didn't move or speak, the moment stretching in tense silence, and goose bumps raced along her arms, across the back of her neck. The air thickened and each lungful felt like a chore, a struggle, as if the room was filled with smoke. A craving was building deep inside her, growing and twisting, urging her closer to him. Even if her mind would never allow her to admit it, her body desired this man.

And based on the way he was looking at her—like a slice of Baked Alaska—he might desire her, as well.

Could it be true?

I want to kiss him again.

"Kit . . ." she whispered, her voice trailing as her body swayed in his direction. How did one ask such a gorgeous man to kiss her, to ravage her? To ease this terrible craving?

Without warning, he took a step back. His mouth curved into a bright smile that didn't reach his eyes. "Well done. Fair to say you've mastered that." He hooked a thumb in the direction of the doorway. "I'm supposed to meet Harrison, so I'll see you tomorrow."

Their lesson was over? Her shoulders deflated ever so slightly. "Oh. Then I'll bid you good night."

He dipped his chin and quickly strode from the room.

Almost as if he was running away from her.

ONCE OUT OF the kitchen, Kit hurried through the corridors as if the fires of Hell were nipping at his heels.

He didn't bother going up the stairs. Instead, he went straight outside, desperate for air. For space. For distance. From Alice, from the other guests. From himself, even.

Perhaps a dip in the cold Atlantic was exactly what he needed.

"And where are you going in such a hurry?"

Kit came to an abrupt halt and found the source

of the familiar deep voice on the terrace above him. Harrison was leaning over the balustrade, a lit cigar in his fingers. Kit dragged a hand through his hair. "I feel as if I am losing my fucking mind."

"Yes, I am having a similar night. Drink?" Harrison held up a half-empty bottle.

"God, yes." Taking the steps two at a time, Kit soon found himself on the terrace. "Give me whatever is in there."

Harrison passed over the bottle and Kit took a long swig of what ended up to be scotch. The burn in his throat distracted him from the partial erection he was sporting after watching Alice suck on her finger.

Christ almighty.

That mental image would fuel his masturbatory fantasies for months to come.

And she had worried she would look foolish? Hardly. Instead, she'd looked innocent while acting naughty—a combination he suddenly found incredibly arousing. Who would have guessed?

After another long drink, he tried to give the bottle back to his friend, who was now watching him with a thoughtful expression. Harrison held up his hand. "Keep it for a few minutes. You look as if you could use it."

"Thank you."

"Besides, I've already drunk half." Harrison puffed on his cigar. "Want to talk about it?"

"No." Another drink. "You?"

"No. I haven't had enough scotch. Damn, I wish Preston and Forrest were here. I missed you all while I was in Paris."

"Preston said he would try, but he must have

been tied up in the city. And no one's heard from Forrest for weeks." Forrest had been drowning himself in liquor for years and Kit wasn't certain what to do about it any longer. Every attempt to help his friend had failed. He'd deal with it after the house party—if he survived Alice and her lessons, of course.

For a boy who deserved better.

After another sip, Kit dangled the bottle from his fingers. "Is it a terrible idea to contemplate seducing one of the heiresses?"

"Jesus, Kit. You know the answer to that question."

"I do. The trouble is, I think she's seducing me."

"Which young lady are we discussing?"

"I shouldn't tell you."

"I won't say anything. God knows you've stored many a secret of mine over the years."

Kit gulped a mouthful of scotch for courage. "Alice Lusk."

Harrison shook his head, as if trying to clear it. "You must be joking. That quiet girl with the terrible mother?"

"Yes. She's . . . surprising."

His friend let out a low whistle. "High praise coming from the man who has seen and done just about everything—and everyone."

"Har. I'm serious. This girl has turned me inside out in a matter of days."

"Wait, what do you mean? Were you just with her?" Dawning realization washed over his expression. "This is who gave you the love bite. Well, good for Alice. I never would've guessed."

"It's not like that. I'm . . . tutoring her in exchange for recipes. For the supper club."

"Tutoring her? In what, how to give love bites?"

Kit didn't answer. He merely drank and let Harrison's joke fall flat. When his friend realized it was the truth, he gaped at Kit. "Are you serious? She actually approached and asked you to teach her how to kiss?"

"Not in so many words." He gave a shortened version of the lessons-for-recipes bargain he struck with Alice. "She wants to marry for love and is convinced no man will ever want her except for her dowry."

"This is like some erotic fairy tale young men share around the campfire. And it's actually happened to you." Harrison's mouth twisted. "You are absolutely fizzing, my friend."

"Stop. It was supposed to be innocent, not sordid. Flirting and advice on men. It wasn't supposed to turn physical."

"Yet it obviously did."

"I didn't pressure her, if that is what you're worried about. All of it has been her choice."

"Still, you must know this is unwise. If you're caught you'll have to marry her, Kit."

"We won't be caught. Sneaking around and secret indiscretions are second nature to me."

"So, what is the problem?"

Kit downed more scotch and contemplated his answer. "I don't know. I'm not used to wanting someone I cannot have, I suppose."

Harrison snorted. "We can form some sort of club, then. Shall I come up with the secret handshake?"

"Shit, sorry." Harrison had been pining for Maddie forever, and now she was betrothed to another man. "Is that why you're out here?"

"Maddie disappeared after dinner to meet with her father and Lockwood."

"Ah. Discussing details of the wedding, perhaps?"

"Doubtful. No, that goddamn duke is up to something. I need to find out what."

Kit leaned over the railing and closed his eyes against the ocean breeze. "He's worried. I think that is why he proposed now, instead of waiting until the guests departed."

"Hmm." Harrison matched Kit's posture. "You might be right."

"It'll resolve itself. Maddie's in love with you. She's just too stubborn to admit it."

"Yes, well. Her admission won't mean anything when she's walking down the aisle to marry another man."

"So you think she needs a nudge?"

"Perhaps. What will you do about Alice?"

"Nothing." Kit dragged a hand across his nape. "I only have to last two more days. Then we'll return to the city and I won't see her again."

"She really has you tied up in knots, doesn't she?"

An understatement. He'd nearly pounced on her in the kitchen a little bit ago. Considered putting her up on the worktable and lifting her skirts, where he could hear her whimpers and taste her moans while he brought her to orgasm once or twice. "It's fine. I can control myself for two more days."

"There are simple solutions," Harrison offered. "You could tell her you have enough recipes. Or you could visit one of the houses in—"

"No," Kit said, his tone sharp.

Harrison chuckled. "All right."

"Do not infer anything from that answer. I want as many of Franconi's recipes as I can get."

"Oh, indeed," Harrison drawled. "The recipes."

"Fuck you."

Harrison threw his head back and laughed. "This is refreshing. I like having a partner in misery."

"Enjoy it, then, because my misery will only last for the next two days. And I really do need those recipes."

They stood in companionable silence for several minutes while the waves crashed below in the darkness. The wind continued, a steady and bracing sting on Kit's skin. He wondered if Alice had gone to her room, if she had undressed for bed. He pictured a prim white nightgown that covered her from head to toe, her luscious little body hidden from prying eyes, even at night. Would she crawl under the covers, lift that nightgown and touch herself? Slide the pads of her fingers over her clitoris—

Damn it. He gritted his teeth against the wave of lust cramping in his belly. He couldn't think about Alice pleasuring herself now. Or ever.

"I can hear your mind spinning," Harrison said, blowing out smoke. "So, what are you going to do about her?"

"Keep it platonic. Just talking and no more . . . other things."

"Good luck," Harrison said, his tone full of skepticism. "It's not as easy as it sounds. I should know, considering I've been resisting the impulse for other things for years."

"I can do it. I resisted punching my father in the face my entire life. I can remain strictly friends with an innocent shipping heiress from Boston."

Harrison made a scoffing sound in his throat. "You act as if you're thinking with your brain in these moments. I predict you won't even last a day."

"Wrong." Kit took another drink. "I can do it. It's just two days." If he kept repeating his positive affirmation, he would succeed.

Hopefully.

Chapter Nine

❦

Alice paced in Kit's bedroom. It was late but he still wasn't here. He had to seek his bed soon, didn't he?

Perhaps she should return to her own chambers. It was wildly inappropriate for her to be here at this late hour, and she would be ruined if discovered. Yet, he'd fled the kitchen earlier in a state of panic. She didn't understand it. Had she done something wrong?

The clock on the mantel chimed two, which meant she had been here for over an hour. The recipe she'd written, along with a slice of the cinnamon babka, sat on his nightstand. There was no reason for her to wait.

Except this tiny feeling in the pit of her stomach, one that hadn't abated ever since he left the kitchen.

I merely want to ensure he's all right, that we're all right.

Besides, she owed him the recipe, Franconi's ducklings à la bigarade. And he sort of helped with the babka, so it seemed only fair to bring him the first slice.

Lies. You wanted to see him. You wanted more of what happened in the kitchen.

Fine, yes. Maybe that, too.

Regardless, she could not wait until the morning— or the afternoon—to find out why he'd departed so abruptly. They might not be friends, but they were friendly—and wouldn't anyone check on the welfare of another in such a circumstance?

Just a few days remained in Newport. She certainly felt more confident with Kit, but would that confidence translate to a potential suitor? Alice wasn't certain. Better to keep up these lessons with Kit before she returned to New York. To Mama's watchful gaze.

To finding a husband.

Sighing, she pushed that worry off for another day. The house party afforded too many opportunities to waste with future worries.

The one small table in his room was littered with papers. She didn't wish to pry, but they appeared to be tallies and estimates of some kind. For his supper club? A pair of eyeglasses rested near a pencil and she smiled as tenderness expanded in her chest. She could picture him here, working hard on his ideas.

The latch clicked and she spun toward the door. Fear gripped her for a brief second when she considered it might be Kit's valet, but that disappeared when Kit stumbled into the room. He nearly tripped over his feet, his body loose and uncoordinated, while his black evening jacket dangled from his fingertips. "Fucking hell," he whispered as he struggled for balance.

He hadn't seen her yet, so she took a step forward. "Do you need help?"

Sucking in a harsh breath, his head snapped up. "Alice." He took two steps toward her. "You—Is that indeed you?"

"It is indeed me."

The door stood open and he seemed in no hurry to close it. Alice walked toward him, intent on shutting it, and was surprised when he quickly staggered away from her in the opposite direction. She closed them in and chewed on her lip. So, it *was* her. Clearly, she had done something to upset him. "Kit, is there something wrong?"

He threw his jacket onto a chair, then swept his hand out like an Elizabethan courtier. "I'm drunk."

"I can see that. I meant—"

"What is that?" He strode unevenly to the nightstand. "Is that the bread you were making? Goddamn, that looks fucking delicious." Picking it up, he lifted the slice of babka to his mouth.

"Yes, I thought you should have the first piece, since you helped me—good Lord. Did you just put that entire thing in your mouth?"

Cheeks bulging, he chewed and let out a groan. "Mmm. Delicious," he managed to garble. After he swallowed, he said, "You are an amazing cook, Alice."

Perhaps, but she wasn't supposed to be.

Ladies don't sweat in a kitchen. Ladies sip tea and let others sweat in a kitchen.

She could almost hear her mother's voice. Mama

had forbade Alice's culinary pursuits eons ago. That didn't mean Alice didn't still sneak into the kitchen every chance she got, though. When she married and had her own household, Alice would cook and bake as much as she pleased.

Another reason why she needed Kit's lessons. The sooner she found a husband, the sooner she could have said kitchen.

Kit unbuttoned his vest, pushed it off his shoulders and let the silk fall to the floor. Then he removed his bow tie and collar. Alice was too fascinated to complain. Was he planning on disrobing right in front of her?

You should say something. You are taking advantage of his inebriation.

"Kit, perhaps—"

"Help me with these damn cuff links, will you?" He held out his wrists.

"I should go and let you rest," she said, though her feet didn't move.

He began struggling with the silver at his wrist. "You're a good person, Alice. Do you know that?"

She couldn't stave off the small grin. Drunk Kit was adorable. "As are you."

"No." He shook his head, his tousled hair going in all directions. "I am most definitely not." One cuff link hit the carpet and he began working on the other.

Taking pity, she went to assist him. "Here. Give me your hand."

His mouth hitched as he presented his wrist. "See? Good person. Even though I am thinking very dangerous things about you, here you are, trying to help me."

"Dangerous things?" Picking up the discarded cuff link, she set both on the dresser. "What does that mean? Are you upset about what happened in the kitchen?"

He sat heavily on the bed. "Upset? Fuck, no. I don't get upset. Ever."

He didn't?

Also, it was worth noting that Kit's language leaned toward the crude after he'd been drinking. No idea why she found that bit of knowledge entertaining, but she did.

He toed off a dress shoe and kicked it, where it thumped against the wall. With jerky movements, he lowered his suspenders and started on his shirt.

"Kit, wait. Before you get undressed, I need to talk to you."

"No time for that, Alice, my dear. My head is swimming and I am far too drunk for talking." The shirt obscured her view of his face and he seemed to get stymied in removing it. "Help."

Trying not to laugh, she went over and tugged his shirt over his head, down his arms. "There."

"What's this?" He peered at the piece of paper she'd left next to the babka plate.

"Franconi's duckling recipe. I owed you. For earlier."

"Thank you, but I hardly think teaching you to suck on your finger is worth those delicious ducks."

"No?"

He flopped back on the bed and closed his eyes. A lock of dark hair fell over his brow. Between that and his evening whiskers, he appeared quite the rogue. "God, Alice. I have never wanted to fuck anyone more than I do you. I cannot stop thinking about it, no matter how hard I try."

Alice froze. Did he just say . . . ? *Her?*

No, that had to be the alcohol talking.

He chuckled darkly. "And it is very hard. All the time."

"Kit—"

"I meant my cock. In case that wasn't clear. My cock is hard all the time for you."

She couldn't help it; her gaze flew to his crotch. Was it hard now? She couldn't see anything but a normal bulge. Though it was quite a nice bulge, she supposed.

Stop. You should leave.

"I'll just . . . get you a glass of water before I go."

Going into the washroom, she found a glass on the sink, which she filled and brought out to Kit. He was pushing his trousers off his hips and down his thighs, and Alice thought her skin might go up in flames.

She covered her eyes with her palm and tried to edge her way to the nightstand.

"You don't have to hide your eyes. Consider this another one of our lessons. This is what a man looks like in just his undergarment."

"This is not a good idea." She already had more than friendly feelings for him. Seeing him nearly undressed would tip her into serious "like" territory.

"Ah, so you'd rather see me naked? That can be arranged. Give me a minute."

"Kit!" She dropped her hand and put the glass on the nightstand. He was sitting on the bed, long limbs covered in a thin cotton that only empha-sized every ridge and valley. A shadow of dark hair rested on his chest, while wide, sculpted shoulders pushed against the cloth. She didn't dare look lower.

Even still, he was beautiful.

Inhaling deeply, she said, "Stop. I don't wish to see you naked."

A deep crease formed between his brows. "You don't?"

"No." Not like this. Sober, yes. But he was not in his right mind and would only regret this tomorrow. "You need to drink some water and go to sleep."

The half grin he gave her, along with the affection in his gaze, made her chest ache. "This is what I am talking about," he said. "You are a good person. Kind to everyone, even your mother—who definitely does not deserve it. You've put aside your interest in cooking just to make her happy. You treat everyone the same, no matter their class or profession. Or reputation. Look at me, for example."

She blinked a few times, stunned. Were these drunken ramblings . . . or was this really what he believed? No one had ever spoken so favorably about her before. Also, no one had ever seen past the shyness or the wall she'd built up to keep out the loneliness before. Her insides melted on a wave of tenderness and longing.

Stepping closer, she bent to remove his other shoe. "And just what is wrong with you?"

His shoulders rose and fell with a shrug before he dropped back on the bed once more. "I'm a fool. A pretty but dim bulb. It's why I'm so good at being a scoundrel."

"That is not true," she said quickly.

"It most definitely is. As shallow as a saucer, my father used to say."

What an awful thing to say to a child. "You said your father was a terrible man."

"He is definitely that. I know I shouldn't care but insults sink inside and fester, especially when they come from parents."

Indeed, they did. Hadn't Alice discovered that better than almost anyone?

Kit continued. "But you, my dear Alice, you are the opposite of me. You are deep and complicated, like the ocean. I could study you for years and never learn all I wished to know."

Her hands refused to work, her brain trying to absorb his compliment. While she was flattered, it hurt that he had such a low opinion of himself. Kit radiated confidence, an easy swagger that drew attention no matter where he went. Was that all an act? Did he really believe he was nothing more than a pretty face?

The idea that he might nearly broke her heart. Just because he was handsome and popular did not mean he was shallow or dim. Kit was smart. He knew how to read people, how to interact with them. Which was precisely the reason why his supper club would undoubtedly become wildly successful.

She opened her mouth to tell him all of this and realized his eyes had closed. His chest expanded rhythmically, his breathing regular, while his arms were relaxed at his sides. Indeed, though his pants were halfway down his thighs, it seemed he'd fallen asleep. Her heart twisted, then squeezed, brimming with something far more meaningful than she was willing to admit.

After removing his trousers and covering him with a blanket, Alice tiptoed from the bedroom and into the corridor. The house was deathly quiet, leaving her alone with her thoughts. Which mostly centered around Kit and everything he'd said tonight.

Had he meant any of it?

THE NEXT AFTERNOON, Kit pulled his hat lower as he strode toward the tent outside. Why was it so dashed bright out here? His head throbbed, as if an ice pick repeatedly stabbed his temple. Jesus, why did he drink so much last night?

No telling how long he stood with Harrison on the terrace, sharing not one but two bottles of scotch. Everything that followed was hazy, but he recalled Alice in his room. She'd brought him a slice of the bread she helped bake earlier . . . and he couldn't remember anything else. What had he said? He'd been naked when he awoke this morning. Had she undressed him?

Worse, had he undressed in front of her?

God, he hoped not. She'd never talk to him again, if that were the case. No doubt he horrified her enough with his inebriation and ramblings; adding his cock to the mix would prove disastrous.

The back of his neck heated with a rare bout of embarrassment. He dreaded facing her today. Rarely did he drink so much these days, but she wouldn't know that. She must think him a terrible lush.

"You look about as miserable as I feel," Nellie said as she came alongside.

"Thanks," he grumbled. "Did you drink too much scotch last night, as well?"

"No, but this is the last place I want to be at the moment." They started along the path, gravel crunching beneath their shoes. "I wish Harrison would hurry up already so we can go home."

"I thought you were having a good time." Kit studied her profile. "You know, strolling near the male guest chambers."

"Hardly." She put a hand on his arm and drew to a halt. "Kit, I wanted to say something. About Alice."

"There's no need to—"

"Stop. I know your type, which means there is every need." She exhaled slowly. "Not many young women my age are kind to me. Yet, Alice is. Always. She's a good person. Decent. She doesn't deserve to be toyed with or—God forbid—ruined. Do you understand what I am saying?"

Kit's hands clenched into fists, so he shoved them in his trouser pockets. Really, he couldn't blame Nellie, who was only looking out for Alice's best interests—and Kit was not in Alice's best interest. Anyone could see that. Which was why he'd decided to keep their interactions strictly platonic from now on. "I understand. There is nothing to be worried about. We have a business relationship of sorts, not a romantic one."

"I am happy to hear it. Because if you hurt her, I will find you in your sleep and relieve you of a body part. Can you guess which one?" With one last pointed glare, she strolled away, whistling on her way to the tent.

Kit shook his head, then winced. Damn hangover. Still, Nellie's warning was a necessary reminder. Whatever was happening between him and Alice—the kissing, the love bites, the flirting—needed to end, and their association must remain aboveboard. He would treat her politely, if not distantly, and they would exchange information at the end of the day. And definitely not in his bedroom.

He entered the back of the tent and purposely did not look in the direction of the young ladies. Lockwood stood near the refreshment table, so Kit headed there, intent on finding something to settle his stomach. "Afternoon, Lockwood," he mumbled as he arrived.

Then he spotted the cinnamon babka on the table, and his brain began tripping over the memories. They were all centered on Alice, sucking sugar off her finger, rubbing the digit over her tongue, working her lips up and down . . .

Swallowing hard, he reached for a slice of lemon pound cake and tried to forget how aroused he'd been in the kitchen last night.

"Ward," Lockwood greeted. "I noticed you and Archer were absent from luncheon. I do hope no one has grown ill."

Please. Lockwood would wish a plague on Harrison, if it were possible. "No need for concern. Just a bit too much scotch. Did you spend another night at the casino?"

"No. I enjoyed a quiet evening with my fiancée."

Kit hoped Harrison hadn't heard that news. "Any clue what is planned for this afternoon?"

"Another game. Just the unattached ladies and Harrison this time, so we are off the hook."

"That's a relief. I don't think I could take another hike around the property at the moment."

"You are looking a bit green, if I am honest."

"I'll be fine." Unable to stop himself, his gaze traveled the room until he found Alice. She was staring at him from under her lashes, her brows pinched in concern.

Kit, is there something wrong?

He jerked his eyes away and gave her his back. She'd asked that question last night . . . but why? Blast, he hated not remembering. When he was that drunk, he was prone to talk about his family, his father, and how he had disappointed them all. Preston said the more Kit drank, the more morose he became. Had Alice seen him wallowing in self-pity?

Sighing, he rubbed his eyes.

"Certainly no one would care if you went back to bed," the duke said.

Not sure why, but the comment stung. "And deprive the ladies of the most handsome and charming man here? I couldn't possibly. No, as you Brits say, stiff upper lip and all that."

A familiar brown-haired woman appeared on Lockwood's other side. The duke, being absurdly polite, turned so as to not give her his back. "Miss Lusk," he said, with a tip of his straw hat.

"Your Grace," she returned with a small smile. "I trust you are well this fine afternoon."

"Indeed. It is a lovely day and I cannot complain about the company."

Alice didn't bother greeting Kit. She acted as if he weren't even there, instead studying the treats on the table.

"May I fetch you a slice of cake, Miss Lusk?" The duke gestured to the food. "Or a macaron?"

"Have you tried that sweet bread, Your Grace?

That one there?" She pointed to the babka. "I think it looks divine."

"No, I haven't. Shall we try it together?"

Kit ground his teeth, wishing he could boast of Alice's skills in helping to make the cinnamon bread.

"I'd like that."

Lockwood cut two slices and dished them up, handing the first plate to Alice. She waited for the duke to have his own before lifting the bread with her fingers. "Three, two, one . . ."

At the same time, they both took a bite, and Kit ripped his gaze away from Alice's mouth. *Damn it all to hell.* Had she done that purposely, knowing he'd be watching?

"Alice!" Mrs. Lusk rushed over and snatched the plate from Alice's hands. "There's no need for gluttony. We must leave some of the bread for others," she hissed, then presented the duke with a saccharine-sweet smile. "Please forgive her rudeness, Your Grace."

"There is naught to forgive, Mrs. Lusk. I've been known to have quite the sweet tooth myself."

With one last sharp look in Alice's direction, Mrs. Lusk carried the plate away and returned to her seat. Alice shrank, her eyes fixed on the grass under their feet, and Kit had the strangest urge to bundle her up in his arms and take her anywhere but here.

"Would you like the rest of mine?" Lockwood held his plate out to Alice. "I won't let her see, I promise."

"Your Grace is very kind, but that is not necessary." Alice's voice was small, defeated, and Kit wanted to flip the refreshment table in fury. How dare Mrs. Lusk crush Alice's confidence like that? Alice motioned to the chairs. "I should return to my seat, anyway." She hurried toward the unmarried ladies and sat, her eyes downcast.

Kit's hands trembled with the need to comfort her, so he shoved them in his trouser pockets instead.

Keep your distance. It's for the best.

Maddie walked to the front of the tent, where she explained the rules of the game. Kit left the refreshment table and went to sit next to Harrison, who wasn't paying a bit of attention to the words coming out of Maddie's mouth. When the game started, Harrison didn't move.

Kit lifted a brow at his friend. "Weren't listening, were you?"

"No. What are we doing?"

"Oh, not *we*. You."

Harrison's gaze darted at the faces in the tent, everyone watching him closely. "What am I supposed to do?"

"Sardines. You're to hide and the ladies will find you."

A game Kit was more than glad to sit out. Hangover or not, he didn't feel up to an adult game of hide-and-seek. Unless he could hide with Alice in a very dark, very secluded spot.

Shit. He rubbed his forehead. This had to stop.

With some not-so-subtle maneuvering, Harrison convinced Maddie to hide first, which meant he and all the ladies quickly departed. Kit and Lockwood were left with the chaperones.

Alice didn't even look back as she hurried from the tent.

Chapter Ten

❧

"Alice, wait up."

Alice didn't slow at the feminine voice. Instead, she kept moving away from the tent, away from the scene of her latest humiliation.

We must leave some of the bread for others.

How mortifying. What must Kit think of Alice now? She couldn't face him again, not ever. The duke had been kind, but Kit hadn't said a word. Just observed the entire scene, probably pitying her. And she wouldn't blame him for it one bit.

Every day with her mother was a struggle. Alice tried to stay positive, to keep from drowning in the shame Mama heaped on her shoulders, but there were days when it all felt like too much. Today was one of those days. Mama had been irritable since waking up and learning that Alice had overslept. This had led to biting comments and spiteful accusations during the morning and early afternoon. Now this scene in front of Kit? Alice wanted to die.

This is why I need lessons from you, she wanted

to shout. Yet her voice, along with her confidence, had disappeared after her mother's words.

"Alice." Nellie appeared and forced Alice to stop. "Where are you going?"

Alice looked up. Goodness, she was headed toward the beach, to the wide expanse of ocean and sky. Maddie clearly wasn't hiding in a conch shell, so it probably seemed like a silly choice. But when Alice left the tent, she hadn't been thinking of anything other than escaping. "I don't know. I wasn't really thinking."

Nellie's expression softened. "I can tell." She linked their arms together and continued toward the water. "Did the duke say something to upset you?"

"No!" Alice shook her head. "He was very kind."

"Mr. Ward, then. I should have known—"

"No, no." Alice stopped and heaved a sigh. "It was my mother. She can be . . . overbearing at times."

"That is putting it politely. She makes dragons seem cuddly. I bet you will be glad to get out from under her thumb."

An understatement. "Yes, and if I weren't so terrible with men, it would have already happened."

"Oh, Alice. That's not true. You aren't intimidated by the duke, certainly. I've seen you walk up and speak to him several times." She led Alice toward the water again, the ocean breeze rustling their skirts. "And you and Kit have formed a certain friendship."

The words and the way Nellie said them gave Alice pause. "What do you mean?"

"Well, it's obvious the two of you are friendly."

"It is?" Her cheeks grew hot. Had the other ladies noticed? Had her *mother* noticed? Oh, goodness. Was she making an utter fool of herself at every turn?

"Calm down," Nellie said in a soothing voice. "I meant it is obvious to me. No one else has noticed a thing. I promise."

"Katherine caught me staring at him. Maddie, as well. Everyone must think I am ridiculous, thinking myself capable of a man like that."

"Whoa. I think you and I had better have a chat. This sounds more complicated than I assumed."

They continued to the stone steps that led down to the ocean and sat. Alice arranged her skirts, hoping to minimize the damage to her pleats. Nellie unpinned her hat and turned her face up to the sun. "God, that feels good. I hate wearing hats."

Alice studied this bold and unique woman at her side. How she wished she could be more like Nellie. "Is it true you spiked the punch at your debutante ball?"

"With brandy." Nellie smiled. "Three of the girls vomited into the shrubbery."

Alice couldn't help but chuckle. "Aren't you ever worried about what people will think?"

"Never." Nellie grimaced. "At least, not anymore. I learned what I think of myself matters much more. I promised my mother before she died that I would live every day like it's my last and I intend to never break my promise."

"I'm sorry." Alice knew Mrs. Young had died when Nellie was a girl.

"Thank you. Incidentally, this is why I feel entitled to tell you that you don't owe your mother a thing, Alice."

"I beg your pardon?"

"Your mother." Nellie looked over. "You see, my mother died when I was eight and I would give almost anything to get her back. But as much as I wish I had a mother—and believe me, I have spent many nights crying over it—I would not want *yours*. Do you understand what I am saying?"

"That your mother was not like mine?"

"Not all mothers belittle their daughters and make them feel small. You might not realize as much, but many mothers are loving and nurturing. Supportive. Friendly. Which is why you should not feel badly for cutting her out of your life when you marry. At all."

"Cutting her—" Alice sucked in a breath. "I could never. She is family."

Nellie reached over and clasped Alice's hand. "Even a strong family can have a rotten branch or two. It's better to cut those branches off for the tree to remain healthy."

Alice considered this. Cut her mother out of her life? She hadn't thought such a thing possible. "I would feel terrible."

"Because you are a kind and decent person. But one thing I've learned over the years is that sometimes you must put your own happiness first—and women rarely have the opportunity to do so. Don't squander your chance."

Alice stared at her feet. Nellie *understood*. She understood the longing and frustration, the little ways that a person shoved their dreams aside because they were told they weren't good enough. Or that it wasn't proper. The thousand tiny cuts that shredded a person's will until there was nothing left but blind obedience and surrender.

Alice said softly, "I dream of moving as far away as possible. Leaving New York and starting a family on another continent."

"That would certainly be possible with Lockwood. But I suspect your interest lies elsewhere." Nellie bumped her shoulder against Alice's. "By the way, I saw you leave his room yesterday."

Alice sat up, panic flooding her bloodstream and making it impossible to draw a breath. "What?"

"Don't worry. I haven't said anything to anyone. Save Kit, of course."

"You did? What did he say?"

"That the two of you are merely friends. Business associates of a sort. Do you have feelings for him?"

"No," Alice blurted. "Of course not. That would be absurd."

"Why absurd? Has he hurt you?"

"No, absolutely not. I merely meant he is not the marrying kind."

Nellie picked up a pebble and rolled it down the stairs. "In my experience, men aren't the marrying kind until they are the marrying kind."

"What does that mean?"

"It means they don't consider marriage until it's staring them in the face. Moreover, marriage is easier for men. They get the creature comforts of home along with regular bed sport. From what I've seen, women do all the hard work in a marriage."

A myopic view, in Alice's opinion. "Women get security, both financial and emotional, in a marriage. Children. A home of our own. It cannot be all bad."

"For some women, perhaps." Nellie brushed dirt from her hands. "But let's not get philosophical. We need to know how you feel about Kit."

"I'm fond of him, certainly, but it isn't anything serious. We are helping each other. An even exchange of favors."

"Was one of those favors that love bite on his neck?"

Alice dropped her head into her hands, heat enveloping her. "Oh, sweet heavens."

Nellie bumped their shoulders once more. "I am joking, Alice. I don't care if you kissed him up and down the beach at midday. But I do suspect kissing and love bites are out of the ordinary for you."

Alice figured she might as well confess the truth behind her arrangement with Kit. Nellie would assume the worst, otherwise. "At dinner the first night, Maddie said Kit could turn even the shyest woman into a vixen. That gave me an idea. I went to him and asked . . ."

Nellie's hand covered her mouth, her eyes dancing. "No, you did not! You asked Kit to turn you into a vixen!" She grinned. "Oh, this is too delicious."

"You mustn't tell anyone!" Alice clutched the other woman's forearm. "I would be ruined and my mother would never forgive me."

"I won't tell a soul." Nellie made a locking motion over her lips, as if she were turning a key. "I don't believe in gossip and Lord knows society already punishes women enough. I would never add to it by curbing anyone's fun."

"Thank you." Alice relaxed. "You are very easy to talk to. I wish I had your confidence and insight."

"Both are hard won, I'm afraid. Which means anyone is capable of it. You just have to want it badly enough."

Alice thought about that. Was such an attitude truly mind over matter? Nellie made it seem simple, but she hadn't lived with Alice's mother for twenty years. Even Daddy avoided Mama these days, spending more and more time at his office.

"Is he a good kisser?"

Nellie's question startled Alice. "What?"

"Kit. Is he a good kisser? I bet he's very, very good."

Alice's lower half clenched as the back of her neck crawled with heat. "Indeed, he's very, very good."

"Bully for you!" Nellie knocked her knee against Alice's. "I like this. I think you might be exactly what Kit needs."

Alice thought back to last night, with Kit sprawled on the bed.

My cock is hard all the time for you.

She still couldn't believe he'd said it, drunk or not. Was it true? Did he desire her in that fashion, or had it been the alcohol talking?

"The question for you, dear Alice," Nellie continued, "is whether he is what you need. A scoundrel is not an easy undertaking, not unless you've broken him first."

"Broken him?"

Nellie stood and took Alice's hand, pulling her upright. "We should head toward the house," Nellie said. "Maddie is inside somewhere and the sooner we find them, the sooner this ridiculous game ends."

Alice straightened her skirts and the two of them set off across the lawn. "Should we take the path instead?"

Nellie shook her head. "Cutting across the grass is more expeditious and I am feeling lazy."

More like Nellie was anxious for the afternoon's activity to finish. "What did you mean by breaking him first?"

"A man like Kit never has to work for female companionship. Everything comes easily for him, especially women. He needs to crawl through fire to earn the love of a good woman. I suspect you might be that woman."

"That is ludicrous—"

All of a sudden Alice's foot dropped out from underneath her and she crumpled to the ground, using her hands to break her fall. Sharp pain shot up from her ankle through her leg. "Ow!"

"Oh, no. What's happened?" Nellie knelt at Alice's side, her brows lowered. "Did you trip?"

Alice screwed her eyes shut as the stabbing ache in her ankle grew worse, stealing her breath. All she could do was nod.

Nellie shifted Alice's skirts to see her foot. "You've fallen in quite a large hole. I am going to get help, Alice. I'll be right back."

Alice didn't want the other woman to leave but she couldn't force the words past her throat. She was too focused on not crying or writhing in pain. Digging her fingers into the soft grass, she held on and tried to keep breathing.

KIT TAPPED THE table with two fingertips, irritated beyond measure. Lockwood was charming the chaperones and his future mother-in-law, leaving Kit alone with his thoughts—which was never a good thing.

He couldn't shake the memory of Alice engaging Lockwood in conversation a few moments ago, just as she'd done last night. Was she hoping to make a favorable impression on the duke? Was that why her mother's comments had seemingly deflated Alice's confidence?

Kit shouldn't care. Once Harrison lured Maddie away from Lockwood, there would be nothing preventing Alice's pursuit. And shouldn't Kit encourage it? Then Lockwood could take Alice over to England, away from her mother, and start a new generation of ducal progeny. Hooray.

Yet the idea burned like acid in his mouth. She deserved better. Not him, of course—no, he'd make a terrible husband for any woman—but someone not so stiff and boring. A marriage between Alice and Lockwood would give *mundane* an entirely new meaning.

Movement just beyond the edge of the tent caught his attention. Nellie Young was there, motioning to him. That was odd. Then she put her finger to her lips, telling him to be quiet. Was something wrong?

Curious, he went out to see her. She stood behind the tent flap, clearly hiding from the chaperones. "What is it?"

"Come with me." She tugged his sleeve. "Alice has fallen and hurt herself."

Goddamn it. "Where?"

"The edge of the back lawn, near the stone steps to the Cliff Walk."

Without waiting on Nellie, Kit broke into a run, his stomach in his throat. What had Alice been doing near the steps? Everyone else had gone toward the carriage house and the chateau. The beach was the last place Maddie would hide.

A crumpled figure lay in the grass. *Alice.* He sprinted toward her, not even caring that he'd lost his hat somewhere along the way. She raised her head and groaned, misery etched in her expression.

He knelt at her side and tried to see how badly she was injured. "Alice, sweetheart," he said gently, and swept a lock of hair off her face. "Tell me what happened."

"Ankle," she gritted out.

Her legs rested near a giant gopher hole, and one foot was already swollen inside her slipper. No doubt the injury would worsen over the next few hours. "Let me carry you back to the tent."

"No, Kit. My mother."

Kit didn't give a damn about Mrs. Lusk. "You cannot walk on it, Alice. The rules must be bent in extreme circumstances."

"And I am here," Nellie put in, slightly out of breath. "So it's not as if you two are alone. Kit is right, Alice. You cannot walk on your ankle. Let him help you."

Alice closed her eyes and grimaced. "Fine. Goodness knows this day cannot get any worse."

Kit slipped one hand under Alice's knees and one under her arms. Ever so slowly, he lifted her and cradled her against his chest. She wrapped her arms around his shoulders and exhaled. A quick peek at her face revealed tears building on her lashes. "Am I hurting you?" he asked, trying not to jostle her as he moved.

"No."

"Then what is it? Why are you on the verge of crying?"

She shook her head. "Just the pain in my ankle. Don't worry about me."

"I *am* worried about you," he said. "I don't like seeing you hurt."

She dropped her head onto her arm, her face near his throat. "I'm an idiot. If I had been watching where I was walking, none of this would have happened."

"It was my fault," Nellie said. "I should have led us to the path instead of cutting across the grass."

"Alice," he said, turning his head toward her. "It was an accident. That's all. Nothing to be embarrassed or upset about."

"But—"

"I won't hear anything more about it. If you won't believe yourself, then believe me. I would never lie to you."

She remained quiet as they approached the tent. Mrs. Lusk was the first to rush out, coming to stand directly in their path. "Alice," she said with a frown, her gaze raking over Kit as if he'd deflowered her daughter in the middle of Fifth Avenue. "You stupid girl. What have you done?"

"She tripped, Mrs. Lusk," he said. "Merely turned her ankle."

Mrs. Lusk cast a brief glance over her shoulder at the other matrons. "I demand that you put her down. This is unseemly."

"I'll do no such thing, not until she's settled comfortably."

"Mr. Ward, as her mother I must insist you let her walk—"

"Mrs. Lusk," he snapped, his voice like a whip in the breeze. "Kindly get out of my way, or I will carry her into the house and put her directly on my bed."

The threat of Alice in Kit's bedroom did the trick. Mrs. Lusk moved aside and Kit was able to get Alice under the tent and settled in a chair. The chaperones converged on Alice, offering up sympathy and remedies, and with reluctance he backed away, relinquishing her to the others. Instead, he went to fetch her lemonade.

It wasn't much, but he needed to do *something*.

"Nicely done with Mrs. Lusk," Nellie murmured out of the side of her mouth at the refreshment table. "I was prepared to tackle her, if necessary."

"I do not care for that woman," he said.

"Neither do I. Now, which of us is going to find Maddie and the rest of the guests?"

Kit snuck a peek at Alice, who was currently being besieged by the chaperones. Was she still in terrible pain? He hated that he couldn't do more. Carrying the glass, he turned and took a step toward Alice.

"I'll go," Lockwood offered, and Kit stopped in his tracks.

Apparently the duke had overheard them. Nellie and Kit exchanged a look, and it was clear they were thinking along the same lines. No telling what the duke would find if Harrison and Maddie were alone in a dark place together. No, it was better if Kit went searching instead. "I have an idea of where Maddie planned to hide. I'll go and send everyone back to the tent."

Nellie inclined her head. "I'll make sure Mrs. Webster has sent for a doctor."

Needing to reassure himself that she was all right, Kit looked over at Alice. Her mother frowned disapprovingly at her daughter's side, while the chaperones fussed and fluttered. Alice appeared miserable. A second later, she glanced up and met his eyes. *I'm sorry*, she mouthed.

She was apologizing to him? Whatever for? He should apologize to her for dashing out of the kitchen last night, for getting drunk and saying God knows what in his room. For agreeing to help her in the first place. The list was endless. Alice had done nothing wrong whatsoever.

He stared at the lemonade in his hand. What was he doing? Fetching her lemonade like some pimply-faced lad with a single hair on his balls? This was ridiculous. He was not a "fetch refreshment for the virgin" sort of man, and hovering around Alice would bring both of them undue attention.

Thrusting the glass in Lockwood's direction, he muttered, "Here. In case Alice is thirsty."

The duke appeared confused but didn't argue. "Good idea. Might take her mind off the injury."

Lockwood strode toward Alice, so Kit hurried in the opposite direction. It took no time at all to find the group in the pool's changing room, and ten minutes later everyone had returned to the tent. The young ladies made more of a fuss over Alice than the chaperones, and it soon became clear that

Alice was mortified. She stared at her lap and kept offering apologies. It was quickly decided that Alice should be carried up to her chambers, so Kit, Harrison and Lockwood each stripped off their coats and lifted a side of Alice's chair. Slowly, they carried her inside the house and up the stairs.

The progress was tedious, made more so by Mrs. Lusk's unnecessary and relentless commentary throughout. Kit couldn't see Alice's face, as he was positioned at the back of the chair, but her tense shoulders suggested her mother was compounding Alice's humiliation.

"Mrs. Lusk," he interrupted as they turned a corner. "With all due respect, what will make this go faster is silence."

Harrison pressed his lips together, clearly trying not to laugh, but Kit ignored him. The only reaction that mattered was Alice's, and he was relieved to see her shoulders relax ever so slightly.

Good.

When they arrived at Alice's chambers, Mrs. Lusk preceded them and held open the door. They carried Alice inside and set the chair on the floor. Kit moved to scoop Alice up so he could place her on the bed—and Lockwood put a hand on his arm.

"As the only attached man here," the duke drawled, "it stands to reason that I should be the one to lift her."

"Thank you, Your Grace," Mrs. Lusk said as she looked down her nose at Kit. "We would not want anyone to get the wrong impression."

Palms up in surrender, Kit backed away and let Lockwood settle Alice on her bed. Her mother placed a pillow under Alice's ankle and then shooed the men from the room. Though Kit had to clench his jaw to keep from protesting, he knew it was for the best.

Besides, nothing would keep him from coming back later tonight to check on her.

Chapter Eleven

*N*ight had descended and Alice was reclined on her bed. With nothing else to do, she savored the delicious jambon à la gelée sent up by Mrs. Berman. The doctor had already come and gone, proclaiming the injury a sprain and telling her to keep off her feet for a few days. Many of the young ladies had visited, as well, sitting and keeping her entertained. Nellie apologized again for cutting across the lawn, which was unnecessary. The injury was no one's fault but Alice's, because she hadn't been looking at where she was walking.

The only bright spot of the day had been when Kit carried her across the lawn. Though it was impossible, she could still feel the imprint of his hands on her body, the shift of his shoulders as he moved. He was quite strong and . . . fit.

He needs to crawl through fire to earn the love of a good woman. I suspect you might be that woman.

Nellie was wrong. Kit would never be interested in anything serious with her. He might find her attractive—which was, frankly, head spinning in itself—but marry her? Absolutely not. She had a better chance of finding and marrying a unicorn.

Moreover, now that he'd witnessed Alice's humiliation—multiple times today, in fact—he would no doubt keep his distance. She was clumsy and pathetic, a social disaster. After this weekend, she'd be lucky to marry anyone, even an older fortune hunter who sweated through his collars before noon.

A lump formed in her throat. How foolish she'd been to think she could ever have *more*.

More was for women like Maddie and Nellie. Women who spoke their minds and were unafraid of consequences. Women without mothers like Alice's, who never stopped criticizing and analyzing her daughter's every move.

After a brisk knock, a maid came in and motioned to the dinner tray. "Were you finished, miss?"

"I'm not that hungry. You may take it downstairs, Ida. But please tell Mrs. Berman the gelée was divine. I loved the touch of Madeira in there."

"I will, miss."

Ida departed and Alice was alone with her thoughts again, her eyes staring at the ceiling. Were the rest of the guests enjoying dinner? Was Kit entertaining those seated around him, as he usually did?

Her mother had nearly skipped the meal, insisting she needed to keep watch over Alice instead. Desperate to prevent that from happening, Alice claimed fatigue and promised to use the time to sleep. Thankfully, Mama relented and dressed for dinner, which had provided Alice with a brief respite.

She reached for one of the books Maddie delivered earlier. This one was about bees, a subject Alice found fascinating. Not only did they produce delicious honey, they pollinated plants and flowers, fruits and vegetables. They were like a cook's best friend.

Before long, dinner ended and her mother returned, frowning when she entered Alice's room. "I had hoped to find you asleep. Instead, you are awake and reading—at night, no less. Your eyes will be ruined. Your dowry can only compensate for so much, Alice."

Never mind that there was adequate lighting in the room, thanks to the lamps. "I slept a little," she lied. "Did you have a nice time at dinner?"

"These friends of Miss Webster's," Mama sneered as she took the book out of Alice's hands. "I swear, if I had known those gentlemen were attending, we never would have come. And Miss Young, as well. You must steer clear of her. A good thing the duke is here or the whole guest list would be thrown into question."

There was no use arguing so Alice didn't bother to try. Instead, she changed subjects. "Have you spoken to Daddy?"

"What on earth for?"

To let him know I'm injured.

Alice was close with her father and she missed him while she and her mother were away. "I'd like to telephone him tomorrow, if you don't mind."

"Alice, he is a busy man. He does not have time to come to the telephone to engage in frivolous small talk with you."

Frivolous? Daddy always seemed happy whenever she rang him up. "I'll keep it brief, Mama."

"See that you do. I am off to bathe. I'll sit with you before I go to bed."

"That's not necessary. I know your joints were hurting you earlier. You should rest."

"Nonsense. I will wait to take my medicine so that I may keep you company." Mama's medicine was laudanum, which she used nightly to help her sleep.

Mama disappeared into the corridor and Alice closed her eyes, wishing she possessed the ability to reason with her mother. Not even Daddy tried any longer, however.

Mrs. Lusk, with all due respect, what will make this go faster is silence.

Kit's sharply spoken directive had nearly caused Alice to swoon. No one stood up to Mama like that. Even more surprising, Mama didn't usually acquiesce that easily, either. Yet she had listened to Kit. The whole exchange had been absolutely remarkable.

The door cracked slowly, hardly making a sound. Kit's handsome face appeared as he peeked into the room. Alice gaped at him and pulled the coverlet up to her chin. "What are you doing?" she whispered. "You shouldn't be in here."

"Are you alone?"

"For the moment, but my mother will return shortly. You need to go."

Instead of obeying, he slipped into the room and closed the door behind him. "I had to check on you. How are you feeling?"

"Kit. You must leave. If we are caught . . ."

"Stop worrying. I heard your mother go into her room and I assume she is getting dressed for bed. Tell me how you are doing."

Despite her panic, Alice couldn't help but melt at his concern. Her toes curled under the bedclothes. "I'm fine. Bored, but fine."

He peeked at the spine of the book on the side table. "Bees? Really, Alice?" He put his hands on his hips. "A good thing I arrived when I did so that I may save you from yourself."

"That book is interesting! Did you know bees have five eyes?"

"And yet all of them would be bored stiff from reading that terrible book." When she chuckled, he grinned down at her. "See? That's better."

"I don't care what you say. I plan to keep reading it tonight."

"Then I suppose I'll need to return later and entertain you."

She bit her lip. Was he serious? It seemed impossible that he wished to spend time with her after she'd made such a fool of herself. "I'm certain you have better things to do."

"I don't, actually. But if you'd rather I didn't, I understand." A shadow passed through his eyes, an uncertainty so unlike him that she frowned.

"It's not that I don't want you here. I do. It's just . . . what if we are caught?"

"No one will find out." He put a hand over his heart. "This is my area of expertise. I'll wait until your mother goes to sleep and then I'll come back. All right?"

"All right." Excitement bubbled inside her, light

and heavy at the same time. It was the happiest she'd felt all day.

"Excellent. I'll return when everyone settles." He started to leave and then paused. "Alice, I just wanted to apologize for anything I said last night that might have been . . . crass. I don't remember much from when you were in my room, but I hope I didn't scare you."

She struggled to keep her face from betraying her as she recalled his words from last night.

My cock is hard all the time for you.

No, she hadn't found that scary. Not a bit. More like thrilling. Unbelievable and flattering.

He was studying her carefully, so she answered honestly. "No, you were a perfect gentleman."

"Oh." His shoulders relaxed, his expression softening. "Well, let's not spread that around, shall we? I do have a reputation to maintain."

"Your secret is safe with me."

The side of his mouth hitched and they stared at each other for a long second. It was a companionable silence, not awkward in the least, and she was probably blushing, but who cared? He was gorgeous and charming and she could stare at him for eons and never tire of it.

Finally, he blinked and started for the door. "Until later, queen bee."

He disappeared and she tried not to sigh like a lovesick maiden. Kit was certainly hard to resist—and it was becoming increasingly difficult to remember why she needed to resist him in the first place.

THE NIGHT CRAWLED along at a snail's pace. Kit and Harrison sat smoking cigars and talking for a few hours until Harrison left for his midnight rendezvous with Maddie. Kit worried over the illicit meeting, but considering he had one of his own planned, he couldn't throw stones.

A knock sounded on his door around one o'clock in the morning. The footman he'd engaged for information stood in the corridor. "Sir, her maid's just gone to bed. Said the madam has gone to bed, as well."

Thank Christ. Mrs. Lusk had finally retired. Kit had worried the woman was part vampire and would stay up all night drinking the blood of her enemies.

Pulling a sawbuck out from his vest pocket, he handed it to the footman. "Thank you, Henry. Much obliged."

Turning, Kit collected the basket of emergency "entertain Alice" items. Then he set off for the other side of the chateau.

The corridors were dim, with long shadows and dark corners. No one was about, the rooms quiet. Kit's feet made no noise whatsoever on the carpets, the faint sound of the ocean covering his breathing. It really was the perfect house for sneaking about.

He didn't bother to knock on Alice's door. After carefully turning the latch, he let himself in. She was wearing a heavy dressing gown but covered with a thick blanket. Her hair was down, probably brushed out by a maid, and he nearly tripped at the sight of all those long chestnut locks falling over her shoulders. God, she was lovely, with her big eyes and creamy skin, along with the pureness that shone from within her. It was as if her sweetness was a tangible, visible feature, making her even more appealing.

Warmth spread through him and all he could think about was kissing her again.

Platonic, Christopher. Remember?

He approached the bed. "Are you tired? Or would you like to see what I have in the basket?"

"The basket, of course." She sat up straighter. "What did you bring?"

He put the basket on the floor, then went to drag an armchair over to the bed. Once he sat, he lifted the lid on the basket and began removing his stash. "First, wine." He lifted the bottle of Bordeaux and put it on the nightstand. "It'll help you sleep."

"Or pass out."

"True, but we'll limit ourselves to one glass, I swear. Next, I found this downstairs in the kitchen." He handed her a plate containing different meats, cheeses and olives. He hadn't found the provisions as much as paid someone to put them together. "And lastly"—he took out a deck of playing cards—"entertainment."

She wrinkled her nose at the cards. "I don't know how to play."

"Fortunate for you, I do. I can teach you any game you'd like to learn. Now, isn't that better than bees?"

"Only slightly," she answered with a small smile, and popped an olive into her mouth. Her mouth moved as she chewed, her tongue darting out to lick her plump lips, and his stomach clenched. It reminded him of their lesson in the kitchen yesterday, when she'd nearly had him panting from licking a bit of sugar off her finger.

Why must she be so annoyingly good at all these tips he'd given her?

Clearing his throat, he opened the wine and poured two glasses. When he handed her a glass, she took a sip and blinked. "Oh, I like that. I hadn't thought I would, but I do."

"I'm glad. Wine is essential when one is laid up in bed with an injury."

"And I suppose you know this from firsthand experience?"

"No, but I have been laid up in bed before. Does that count?"

Reaching for another olive, she asked, "Was that innuendo?"

"Of course. Though I must try harder if you couldn't tell."

Instead of eating the olive in her hand, she playfully chucked it at his head. "Not necessary. I am a fast learner."

"I am perfectly aware," he muttered under his breath as he picked the olive up off the floor.

"What was that?"

"Nothing." He took the deck of cards and began shuffling. Like any scoundrel, his card skills were finely honed. With one hand, he separated portions of the deck with his fingers, flipped a section, then reinserted it into the stack of cards.

Alice whistled. "Can you teach me to do that?"

"It just takes lots of practice. Not certain it's the best skill to lure a proper husband, however."

"Because proper husbands don't play cards?"

"No, because proper husbands do not want their wives playing cards."

Taking a piece of cheese off the plate, she said, "Maybe I don't want a proper husband."

There was a dangerous statement. "Of course you do. You cannot marry a rogue or a gambler."

"That's the problem. My aunt didn't learn of my uncle's gambling proclivities until they were married and he nearly put them in the poorhouse. My father had to step in and clear their debts. So, how may a woman tell whether a man is a rogue or a gambler before she marries him?"

Kit thought back to his own parents. His father had wooed their wealthy mother quickly, pressing her to marry him with false promises and bogus credentials. She hadn't known the truth until it was too late, and then tried to "fix" him.

But Franklin Ward had been unfixable. He was a terrible gambler and cruel husband, concerned with having control of his wife's money and mind, and to hell with anyone who got in his way. The entire family had paid the price for that bastard's greed, emotionally and financially, but especially Kit's mother, who grew ill and withered away for years. Sad and heartbroken, she was a shell of her former self, becoming a woman with her future stripped away and a husband who deserted her. But no matter how hard Kit pushed, she had refused to divorce Franklin.

"I don't know," he told Alice with a shrug. "I would advise not to rush into a marriage, that you should get to know him first. Do a little digging. Ask his friends, his staff. Habits are hard to break. If he has any that are hard to live with up front, they'll only get worse as the marriage drags on."

"Once a scoundrel, always a scoundrel?"

"Precisely."

She picked at the embroidery on the comforter. "Nellie said a scoundrel is not an easy undertaking, that he must be broken first."

Kit chuckled, leaned back in the chair and put his feet up on the edge of Alice's mattress. "She is not wrong, though I'm not certain how she arrived at that conclusion."

"Experience?"

"I do not doubt it."

He reached for his glass of wine and was surprised to see how quickly the night was passing. He'd already been here twenty minutes. When had he last spent this much time fully clothed with a woman in a bedroom late at night? Not that he didn't wish to see Alice naked—he definitely, absolutely did—but he liked just being with her, too. Talking about bees and scoundrels, drinking wine and laughing together. It felt . . . nice.

Alice made it easy to be with her. He could relax, not worry about whether he was impressive or smart enough. Whether he possessed enough ambition or wealth. She accepted him, yet challenged him when it was required.

And he really liked kissing her.

Another olive bounced off his shoulder. "Are we going to play or not?" she asked.

Smirking, he pointed at the floor. "I am not picking that one up. Enjoy explaining its presence to your mother."

"Kit!" she hissed. "You must pick it up."

"Maybe, if you are nice to me."

"I am always nice to you. It's you who—"

She closed her mouth abruptly, color dotting her cheeks, and he held perfectly still, waiting to see how she would finish that sentence. Was she implying he hadn't been nice? When she remained silent, he said, "It's me who . . . ? What were you going to say?"

"Forget it." Busy fingers adjusted the coverlet, her gaze anywhere but on him. "So, cards?"

He pressed his lips together. There was a card game they'd played during the long nights at boarding school, before they'd discovered alcohol and women, and it forced the loser to confess a secret. Many a nickname had been crafted during those late-night sessions. "I have a simple game," he said, shuffling anew. "It will take no time at all to learn."

"Perfect," she said, and reached for her wine. "I am ready."

Giving them each half the deck, he explained. "We both flip over one card at a time. High card wins and that person may ask a question of the loser. The question must be answered truthfully, however."

Alice's brows shot up, her lips parting in surprise. "You are making this up."

"I am not. It's how I learned that my friend Forrest is scared of butterflies and moths."

"Perhaps if I could talk to him about bees, he might change his mind about flying insects."

He grinned. "If the opportunity ever arises, I just might have you do that. So, what do you say?"

"What if I don't want to tell the truth?"

"Then you must take both cards. The person who gets rid of their cards first wins, though."

"Fine, I'll play."

"Flip a card over. Let's see who has the highest one."

Kit's card was a four of spades, while hers was a

jack of diamonds. She inhaled sharply and rubbed her hands together, like some sort of mad genius in a laboratory. "That means I get to ask you a question."

"Yes, it does. I'm ready. Ask away."

The pause she took in composing her question should have given him a clue, yet he was still taken aback when she asked, "Why did you leave the kitchen so abruptly last night?"

His muscles locked, his entire body frozen with dread. He couldn't tell her the truth, that seeing her suck on her finger had nearly caused him to lose his mind. Lust had overtaken his body and stolen his wits, with an ironclad grip he hadn't experienced in years. It had been embarrassing, frankly. Women had done all manner of depraved acts in front of him, yet this one innocent woman licked sugar from her finger and he almost spent in his trousers.

No, he couldn't tell her the truth.

Scowling at her, he snatched up both cards and put them in his deck. "Next hand."

When the cards were flipped Kit had the higher value. While he stared at her and contemplated his question, she reached for her wine. Though she appeared calm, he could see the pulse pounding in the slim column of her throat.

The question fell out of his mouth. "Did I say anything inappropriate to you last night when I was drunk?"

After a healthy sip of wine, she swallowed. "Yes."

He closed his eyes briefly. *Goddamn it.* Of course he had. "What did I say?"

She set her glass on the nightstand. "That is another question, I'm afraid. You'll have to wait until you win again to ask it."

Chapter Twelve

❧

$\mathcal{A}$lice nearly chuckled at the outrage on Kit's face. He was adorable when he didn't get his way. She suspected it was a rare occurrence.

He wagged a finger at her. "You think you are clever, but I will just ask it in my next turn. Here." He placed a card on the bed. "Flip."

She had the higher card once more, which caused his scowl to deepen. The urge to poke at him, to tease him, danced in her chest, but it was cruel to make light of his frustration. She wouldn't like it if the tables were turned. So, she decided to take it easy on him. "What is your favorite word?"

"Fuck."

Blinking, she let out a strangled noise at his immediate and crude answer. "Really?"

"It's the perfect addition to any sentence. Plus, it happens to be my favorite pastime."

Fire coasted over every inch of her skin, flames licking everywhere and undoubtedly turning her a bright shade of red. Good God, did he say these things merely to embarrass her?

They dealt another hand and Alice won a third time. He drummed his fingers on the armrest. "Damn it. All right, toss me another easy one."

Well, she certainly wasn't going to do that *now*, not after the last answer. She took another sip of wine, liking the warm, relaxed feeling rolling through her veins. It was like a hug from the inside. Cradling the glass in her hands, she studied him, from the deep brown eyes and sharp nose, to his perfectly formed cheekbones and a jaw that could have been carved from stone. Dark evening whiskers covered the lower half of his face, which only enhanced his appeal in her opinion.

Handsome was an understatement when it came to Kit, but he was more than a tall Adonis. There was a magnetism, a charm that drew people to him, yet he made those around him feel included. He didn't act snooty or above anyone else, even if his looks were extraordinary.

And despite his compelling personality, he was surprisingly private, which only made her greedy to know more. Perhaps this was the ideal game for the two of them.

Inhaling for courage, she asked, "How many women have you been with?"

His mouth twisted in apparent amusement. "Are you truly broaching that topic with just your third question?"

"That is a question, Kit, not an answer."

Shaking his head, he let out a deep chuckle. "I see. Indeed, I would ask what you mean by 'been with,' but since I am not allowed to ask a question then I must assume you mean taken to bed." Long fingers stroked along his jaw, rasping over the whiskers, and she longed to feel that scratchy skin for herself. When they'd kissed, he had been freshly shaven. What would the stubble feel like on her neck or chest? On her breasts?

Biting her lip, she tried to rein in her wayward thoughts. She had to keep reminding herself that Kit was not the marrying kind. Losing her heart— and possibly more—to him could never happen.

Just as she was about to prompt him for an answer, he reached forward, took both cards and placed them in his deck. *He doesn't want to answer.* Her stomach sank. No doubt it was a ridiculously high number, one that would only depress her and cause her to feel inadequate.

I can have companionship any time I want.

Of course he could. And the instant the house party ended, he would return to New York and his women and parties and clubs. Soon he'd forget all about silly Alice Lusk and her inability to watch where she was walking and her embarrassingly cruel mother.

"Alice, look at me," Kit said quietly. When she dragged her eyes up to his, he said, "I don't believe in keeping track, like it's a contest or something to brag about. Women are a gift, a treasure. I am honored when they trust me in such an intimate way, and it feels wrong to break that trust by turning them into a cheap tally."

"Oh." She swallowed around the thickness in her throat. "That's a very good reason for not answering."

"You assumed it was because the number was high."

"I did."

"Would it matter if it was?"

"Not to me. I mean, we're just friends. As you said, once a scoundrel, always a scoundrel."

Expression serious, he said, "I don't hold women to a different standard, either. If I did marry and my bride was not a virgin, I wouldn't care. As a society, we place too much importance on a woman's innocence. Let me assure you, there are plenty of women who enjoy what happens in the bedroom. To suggest that women must remain pure, that only men should enjoy the act, is pure garbage."

The intelligence and practicality of the answer stunned her. He was more progressive than any man she'd encountered—and many of the women, too. "And you think you are a dim bulb," she chided. "Nothing could be further from the truth, Kit."

He grew very still, his gaze sharpening, hardening, as he studied her with an intensity that made her squirm. What had she said? She had merely wished to compliment him—

Oh.

He clearly didn't remember that particular drunken confession.

"I said that last night, didn't I? In my bedroom?" When she nodded, he rubbed his forehead. "I always complain about my family when I'm that drunk. Don't pay any attention to those inebriated ramblings."

"I didn't." She certainly didn't agree with any of the horrible things he'd said about himself.

But if those had been inebriated ramblings, then what about the compliments he'd paid her? The desire he'd confessed? Were those also forgettable drunken ramblings?

"I said more, didn't I? God, Alice. Please tell me. I hate not remembering and I am panicked over the possibilities."

She took pity on him. How could she withhold this when he was so tortured by the lack of knowledge? "You paid me some very nice compliments. You offered to remove your clothing, which I declined. And you told me your father said you are as shallow as a saucer."

"Is that all?"

My cock is hard all the time for you.

The words floated through her mind again, as they had many times since last night, and the effect was the same, the statement causing a barrage of tingles in her bloodstream. Chaos in her lower half. She felt both hot and cold at the same time, the area between her legs throbbing.

"You are blushing, sweet Alice." Angling in, he rested an arm on the edge of the mattress. "What did I say to cause such a reaction?"

No, she could never repeat it. If she did, she would combust and disappear in a cloud of ash and cinder. "The compliments, they were very graphic."

"That does not assuage my concerns, actually. Perhaps you could elaborate."

"I'd really rather not."

"You are embarrassed to repeat it."

"Yes."

His brow wrinkled. "Did I offend you?"

Quite the opposite. The revelation was both flattering and arousing, but there was every possibility he hadn't meant a word of it. "Not at all. As you said, I shouldn't pay attention to those ramblings."

"Hmm." Sitting back, he sipped his wine. "I never said I lied when I was drunk. If I paid you compliments, they were undoubtedly true."

Alice choked on the piece of cheese in her mouth. After several coughs and a long drink, she got her breath back. "I see."

Kit flipped another card. "Let's keep playing. I intend to get it out of you one way or another."

"And if I refuse?"

"Then you'll keep collecting cards and lose the game."

A clever strategy, but one she could employ, as well. "Then I will keep asking why you left the kitchen so abruptly."

"Damn it, Alice," he said on a huff that sounded part exasperation and part amusement. "Fine. During the card game, no questions about the kitchen and no questions about last night. Deal?"

"Agreed."

When the cards were revealed Kit's was higher in value. "My turn. Do you want to continue our bargain once we return to New York?"

More lessons for recipes. The thought of not seeing him, of never talking with him again, sat like a boulder on her chest, pressing down and robbing her of breath. She'd grown fond of him in such a short amount of time, and besides, she wasn't yet transformed into a vixen capable of luring the man she wished to marry.

However, there were practical issues to consider, like how she would dodge her mother and avoid the many pairs of prying eyes at the hotel. "I would like to, but I cannot see how. Besides, you have your life there. Your parties and friends."

"I could make time."

Yes, between his many assignations and planning his supper club. Her throat burned with irrational jealousy—which was ridiculous. She had no hold on Kit. They were barely friends. Definitely not lovers. So, why would she care where he spent his nights?

Yet, she did.

And the more time she was in his presence, the stronger the attachment to him grew. Right now, it was a giddiness in the bottom of her stomach when she thought of him, a shiver coasting down her spine when he approached. The longer this went on, though, those reactions would deepen. Soon, she'd find herself heartbroken and miserable because he didn't return her regard.

It was best to stick to their original plan, which was to confine this bargain to the length of the house party. "It would be impossible."

A muscle jumped in his jaw but he inclined his head. "I understand. It was silly of me to ask."

"No, it wasn't silly. I—" As she talked, she sat up straighter and her injured foot slid off the pillow and thumped onto the bed. Pain exploded in her ankle and she gasped, her eyes screwing shut.

"Shh, it's all right." He was there, gently repositioning her foot onto the pillow. "Deep breaths, Alice. In and out. Try to relax."

"Ow, ow, ow," she said through gritted teeth.

Gentle fingers clasped her hand. "Squeeze as

hard as you can. Breathe and squeeze my hand, Alice. Listen to me and try not to think about your foot. Just breathe and squeeze."

Using all her strength, she crushed his hand and tried not to cry.

"Breathe, sweetheart."

The reminder worked, and she dragged air into her lungs. Without letting up on the pressure on his hand, she forced deep breaths. Soon her heart rate began to slow and the pain ebbed slightly. Time stretched and she began to relax, bit by bit, and she became aware that she was still holding on to him as if he were saving her from falling off a cliff.

But she wasn't ready to let go, not when his free hand was lightly brushing the crown of her head. The long sweeps of his palm soaked into her skin and filled her with tenderness. She'd never had anyone show her this much kindness before. Her mother wasn't fond of hugs and Daddy wasn't one for sickbeds.

Just a few more minutes so I can store this feeling up. A pleasant memory for when the house party ended and they left this little bubble of happiness.

"Better?" he finally whispered, his hand stilling on her hair.

She couldn't lie, so she nodded. "Thank you."

Neither of them let go.

She kept her eyes closed, unwilling to break whatever spell was happening in the room. "That was surprisingly effective. Where did you learn that trick?"

"My mother. I used to sit at her bedside when

she was ill. She was in a fair amount of pain near the end and hated laudanum."

Alice's heart twisted for the little boy who had tried to take his mother's pain away. God, this man was so easy to love. It almost wasn't fair. "I'm sure she appreciated it."

"I hope so. It was awful for me at the time, but looking back I am glad I did it." Clothing rustled and she felt his lips press to the top of her head. "I should let you get some sleep. It's late."

Please, stay. Don't ever leave.

Stupid, stupid Alice. Hadn't she just convinced herself of the need for space, that she couldn't allow herself to feel anything more than she already did?

He started to release her. "Wait," she heard herself say as she clutched his hand harder. "It still hurts."

His gaze turned speculative as he scrutinized her face. "Does it?"

"Yes," she lied.

The clock softly chimed the late hour, but she wasn't tired. It was as if electricity had been injected into her veins, rushing through her blood and giving her power. Her pulse pounded, a steady drumbeat deep inside, and she was slipping, falling, the world disappearing as she stared into his dark brown depths.

Slowly, he bent toward her. "Perhaps a kiss will distract you."

KISSING HER WAS madness, but Kit couldn't seem to help himself. Her lips were these perfectly plump, bow-shaped temptations just begging for his mouth. He'd been trying to resist her all night, since the moment he entered her room and saw her luscious hair spread out over her shoulders. Up until now, he'd been doing a fine job.

But then she'd been in pain, and the sight had wrecked him. He'd crumbled, rushing over to make her feel better. The more he touched her, however, the more he seemed to crave it. To need it. Then his reason departed the instant her big eyes met his, beseeching him not to leave.

Christ, he was a fool for those eyes.

He paused just before their lips met. "Or would you rather I left?"

She pulled on his hand, doing her best to bring him closer, so he gave up fighting it and pressed his mouth to hers, kissing her hard. This was different from their earlier explorations. Those had been lessons, a guided descent into vigorous kissing. Now she was on equal footing, giving as good as she got from the start, and the result set his insides ablaze. All the desire he'd been storing the last few days came out in this kiss, his tongue slipping into her mouth almost immediately, twining and stroking with hers.

His hand cupped the back of her head, holding her as he devoured her. Delicate fingers slid up his chest and over his jaw, exploring, and blood pooled in his groin in sweet pulses. God, he wanted her too badly. It was all he could think about lately, ever since she sucked on her finger in the kitchen.

She's a virgin, not a mistress.

And yet his body hadn't received the message, apparently, because his cock was already hard, pushing against his clothing in a desperate bid for friction. That would have to wait until he returned to his room, however. Kissing was as far as he could take this tonight.

So he continued, making the most of what he could. He changed the angle, deepened the kiss, loving the way she softened to accommodate him and bring him closer. Her mouth was wet and lush, her tongue slick and greedy. If only he could stretch out next to her, feel the length of her alongside every part of him. Wrap his arms around her, sink inside and just stay there for days.

She let go of his other hand and shifted to put her arms around his shoulders. His free hand drifted to her waist, then higher, where he caressed her ribs through a few layers of flimsy cloth. More wasn't possible with Alice, but it didn't stop him from wanting it, from contemplating sliding his hand under her dressing gown and finding her breast, tugging on her nipple.

As if reading his mind, she arched her back and thrust her breasts higher in offering. His thumb swept over the plump side, and she moaned in her throat. *Yes.* He could live on that sound for the next fifty years. It was honest yet bewildered, as if she couldn't believe what he was doing to her and never wanted him to stop.

She didn't pull away. Instead, she whispered, "Please," against his mouth.

He didn't tease her. If she was bold enough to demand it, then he would deliver. His palm covered her breast over the dressing gown, the supple weight filling his hand. Her nipple was hard, begging for his lips and teeth—

A nearby door closed, the sound penetrating the fog in his brain.

He drew back, panting. "Who—?"

Alice slapped her hand over his mouth. She put up a finger, telling him to wait, her head cocked toward the sound of the noise.

A few seconds later, she turned to him, her face pale. *You have to go*, she mouthed.

Had it been her mother? He wasn't certain who slept in the nearby rooms. It could have been Nellie, for all he knew. He kept his voice barely a whisper. "Who was it?"

"I'm not certain, but you need to go. Hurry, before someone catches us."

He tried to ignore the disappointment crawling through his gut like a spoiled egg. There was nothing to do but pack up and sneak out, hoping like hell they avoided discovery. Being found in Alice's room would ruin her and he would hate for that to happen.

He soon had the wine and food all hidden away in the basket. He returned the chair across the room and then stood at her bedside, unsure what to say but reluctant to leave.

Go, she mouthed, and waved her hands toward the door. "Hurry."

Now was not the time to press his case. Tomorrow. They would discuss this tomorrow with clear heads and no one listening. Then he could give her another lesson, possibly two, and convince her that finding time in New York wouldn't be as difficult as she believed. They could make this work, at least for a little while.

Nodding once, he lifted the basket and crept to

the door, watching for loose floorboards. The latch opened silently and then he was in the corridor. He gave her one last look before he eased the door closed. Her lips were swollen, the silken strands of her hair mussed from his hands. The swell of her breasts pushed against the dressing gown as her chest rose and fell with the rapid pace of her breathing. She was deliciously rumpled and absolutely gorgeous.

Yes, they would definitely speak tomorrow.

Alice might be stubborn, but so was he. They got along and there was no harm in kissing, was there? He wouldn't take it further and between kisses he could answer all her questions about men. She would provide him with a few more of Franconi's recipes and they would go their separate ways. It was a perfect plan, actually.

The corridors were empty, no sound he could discern. Whoever had been walking about was settled inside their room. Still, when he arrived at the other end of the chateau, he exhaled in relief. He and Alice escaped discovery, just as he had promised.

Good to know I haven't lost my touch.

Chapter Thirteen

❧

Chaos descended the next morning.

An hour after the household began stirring, Mama burst into Alice's room. Alice was still in bed, miserable after a terrible night's sleep, her ankle throbbing in pain. Clearly, she wouldn't be able to participate in the sailing excursion today, an outing she'd been looking forward to.

"Mama." Alice put down her teacup. "You're up early."

"I've directed your maid to begin packing your things. We are leaving."

Alice's jaw fell open, dread slithering along her spine. Had her mother learned of Kit's late-night visit? That had to be the reason for the hasty departure. "I can explain—"

"I saw that . . . harlot coming in out of the rain last night with another man. He kissed her on the mouth."

Mind racing, Alice tried to piece this together. The rain? "Who, Mama?"

"The Webster girl and the Archer boy. It was

absolutely disgusting and I won't have you in this house a moment longer. As soon as I speak with Mr. Webster, we will be on the first train back to New York City."

Maddie and Harrison had been out last night, kissing? Seemed Alice and Kit weren't the only two busy with clandestine activities while the rest of the house slept.

Still, Alice didn't want Mama to ruin the house party. There might be a simple explanation for what she'd seen. "Perhaps you shouldn't involve yourself. After all, Miss Webster and Mr. Archer have been friends for many years."

"Don't be ridiculous," her mother snapped. "I know what I saw, and your reputation will be ruined if we don't leave immediately."

There would be no talking her mother out of it. Years of experience had taught Alice this, so there was no choice but to go along. They would leave today, period.

"Furthermore," Mama continued, "it was my duty to notify the other chaperones of this behavior first thing this morning. Rest assured that everyone else will depart today, as well."

Mortification crawled through Alice's belly. Every young lady would blame Alice and her mother for ruining the house party, not to mention how Maddie and Harrison would feel. Or Kit.

God, Kit. He would learn of this, too. Her mother was embarrassing his close friends, ruining Maddie's reputation. Alice wouldn't blame him if he never spoke to her again.

He wasn't going to speak to you after the party ended, anyway.

That stung, and something twisted in her chest. They were supposed to have more time together— another day, at least. Now she'd never see him again.

Her throat began to ache. She tried swallowing, but the feeling wouldn't go away. Their time together had been cut short and there wasn't anything she could do about it.

You'll learn to live with it, just like you learn to live with everything else.

She was no stranger to disappointment. Kit would become another one of those longings tucked away, buried deep, that she rarely allowed herself to think about. He would move on, charming and bedding women up and down the island of Manhattan, while she would marry a man and start her own life, far away from her mother.

Alice's maid arrived and the next hour was spent listening to Mama issue orders while overseeing their departure. Alice could do nothing but sit and wait, and with each second her sadness mounted. She dreaded hobbling downstairs and coming across any of the houseguests or Maddie. Or, God forbid, Kit. Everyone must hate her.

It won't be any different from before the house party, before you made friends.

"Alice." Mama poked her head into Alice's room. "I am going downstairs to meet with Mr. Webster. Be ready to depart when I return."

Clasping her hands together tightly, Alice nodded. Her maid had already helped her to dress, which had been nothing short of torture with a hurt ankle. The doctor seemed certain Alice would recover within a week's time, but it didn't feel as though that were possible at the moment. Instead, her leg and foot were throbbing like she'd been run over by a carriage wheel.

A knock on the door startled her. "Yes?"

Nellie appeared. "How are you—?" Her jaw snapped shut as she took in the trunk on the floor. "What's going on? Are you leaving?"

She might as well confess to Nellie. "Yes. Come in and close the door."

"Is this because of your ankle?" Nellie drew closer to Alice's chair. "Has it worsened?"

"No. This is because my mother caught Maddie and Harrison kissing last night."

Nellie gasped and covered her mouth with her hand. "Are you serious?"

"Entirely. My mother is meeting with Mr. Webster right now to tell him everything."

"Oh, shit." Nellie's eyes grew huge and she glanced at the door. "I have to wake Maddie. I have to warn her. Thank you, Alice."

"You shouldn't thank me, not when I ruined the house party. All the chaperones have already been notified."

"You haven't ruined anything," Nellie said vehemently. "Do you hear me? Not you. This is your mother's doing."

Alice grimaced. People never viewed it as such. All her life she had been judged alongside her mother, disregarded because her mother was overbearing and rude. No one wanted to befriend a girl who lived under such a dark cloud.

"I'm serious," Nellie said when Alice remained

quiet. "And don't forget about what else I said. Cut off those rotten branches so that you may thrive, Alice."

"Thank you. I'm glad I got to know you these past few days."

Nellie's mouth hitched as her eyes softened. "Me, too. But you're not rid of me so easily, Alice Lusk. I'll see you back in New York."

"Really?" Alice cleared her throat against a sudden rush of emotion. "I mean, you still wish to be friends even after what happened?"

"Of course. Why would I hold your mother's actions against you?"

Because people did. All the time.

Like the few men who'd come to call on Alice but never returned after Mama talked over them the entire visit. Or Miss Wilson, who now avoided Alice because Mama did nothing but brag about the Lusk yacht during dinner one night. Carrie Astor had invited them to tea but cut the afternoon short when Alice's mother snapped at a maid for spilling a tiny drop of cream on her skirts. Not a single member of the Astor family had acknowledged Alice since.

Nellie waved her hand. "I don't have time to dive into this subject, so we'll table it for now. Just know you are nothing like your mother—and thank God for that. Now, I must go find Maddie. See you back in New York."

She disappeared and Alice was left alone with a tiny kernel of hope in her chest.

KIT KNEW SOMETHING was wrong the second he awoke.

His bedroom overlooked the front of the house and he could hear carriages and staff, a general hustle and bustle that was unusual at this time of day. Unless guests were arriving or departing—

Bolting out of bed, he hurried to the window. Sure enough, footmen were loading trunks atop the line of carriages waiting in the drive. This wasn't one or two departures.

This was everyone.

Goddamn it. What had happened?

He dressed quickly, shaving himself to save time. His valet turned even the simplest tasks into a production, which Kit normally appreciated, but he had to hurry this particular morning. If Alice was one of those departures . . .

Throwing open his door, he shrugged into his coat on the way down the hall. Harrison's room was empty, so Kit continued in the direction of the stairs. When he reached the landing, he found Nellie Young at the railing, observing the chaos below. All the chaperones and young ladies were gathered in the front hall, milling about and chattering, the din worse than the betting window at the racetrack.

He stopped alongside Nellie. "What in the hell is going on?"

"Oh, just a tiny little scandal. You see, Alice's mother caught Harrison and Maddie kissing last night after they were outside in the rain together."

"Jesus." He dragged a hand through his wet hair. "Then what?"

"First she told Maddie's father, who subsequently had a long chat with Lockwood and Harrison. And Mrs. Lusk told all the chaperones, which resulted in the exodus you are currently witnessing below."

How could Harrison have been so stupid? Had Kit taught him nothing over the years?

"Where's Maddie?"

"In her rooms. Her father is forcing her to marry Harrison this afternoon."

Kit threw his head back and laughed. "The bastard actually did it. I can't believe it."

"Amazing, isn't it?"

"What about Lockwood?"

"The duke has already departed. Ordered his things packed and drove off about fifteen minutes after leaving Mr. Webster's office."

"Boy, I really missed all the excitement today."

"Not all of it. I assume you are staying for the wedding."

"Wouldn't miss it. Are you?"

"Yes. Maddie asked me to attend, even though my aunt is having a fit about staying. I keep telling her my reputation is already ruined, so what difference does another scandal make?"

Kit searched the faces below, looking for one in particular. "Have you seen Miss Lusk?"

"Hoping to arrange for another lesson in New York?"

His head swung toward her. "She told you?"

"Yes, she did. And while she claims it isn't serious, I have to wonder about that."

"I would never hurt her—and we can discuss this later. Right now, I'd like to find her."

Nellie tilted her head toward the drawing room. "She's sitting on the sofa in there. She can't walk or stand easily with her sore ankle."

Right. He should have guessed. Moving around Nellie, he started for the main stairs. She put a hand on his arm. "Take the servants' stairs. You'll be able to sneak in there without this lot"—she gestured to the crowd below—"seeing you."

"Thanks."

He practically ran to the back stairs, which were empty at the moment. Once on the ground floor, he traveled through the rooms, not the hallways, and ended up at the entrance to the drawing room. A quick check revealed that Alice was alone with Katherine Delafield, their chaperones nowhere to be seen.

When he came in, Alice's head flew up. She didn't say anything, just watched him approach from her seat on the couch.

"Hello," Miss Delafield said. "You've heard the news, I suppose."

"I have," Kit confirmed. "Cannot say I'm surprised."

"Me neither. Harrison must be overjoyed."

"I would imagine so. I haven't seen him yet."

Alice said nothing, merely fingered a button on her jacket. An awkward silence descended, and Katherine pointed to the entryway. "I should find my aunt. Alice, we'll catch up in the city. Goodbye, Mr. Ward."

"Goodbye, Miss Delafield."

She left and Kit walked over to Alice. "How is your ankle?"

"Still hurts."

He lowered himself to the other end of the sofa. "I sense that you're upset. Have I done something wrong?"

She looked at him as if he'd grown two heads. "All of this is my fault."

"Your mother's fault, from what I hear."

"I suppose, but everyone will be talking about her. About me."

"Let them talk. In the end it won't matter because Harrison and Maddie were destined to end up together. The scandal was bound to happen at some point before she married the duke."

"She is so embarrassing," Alice whispered, her expression miserable, and Kit didn't pretend to misunderstand the person they were discussing.

"I know how that feels," he said quietly. "My father is a well-dressed confidence man. While he didn't peddle phony medicinal tonic, he fleeced everyone in sight for years. Spent my mother's fortune, then drained the trust funds of my brother and sister. He has no moral compass, no conscience and no limit to his depravity."

"I'm sorry."

He gave her a rueful smile. "He left my mother when she started to grow ill. Started a new family out West with her money before she was even in the ground. So yes, I know a little about embarrassing parents."

Her fingers reached for his hand, and she squeezed. "Thank you for sharing that."

Blowing out a long breath, he shook off those terrible memories. "What I'm trying to say is forget about her. You are not your mother, Alice. No one could ever confuse the two of you. Not in a million years."

"You are very kind."

"I am only telling the truth. Remember, I said I'd never lie to you?"

"I remember. Thank you. For everything."

That sounded ominous. "Listen, Alice. I know you said it would be impossible to continue our bargain in New York, but I have some ideas on how—"

"Kit, no."

He blinked at her immediate refusal to hear him out. "Just like that? You don't even wish to hear what I have to say?"

"It's pointless. There are too many barriers and I think it's for the best."

Disappointment sank in his stomach. "Why?"

"We'll be caught. It's just too difficult."

She didn't meet his eyes, her hands fidgeting once more. "You're not telling me the truth."

"Yes, I am. You just don't believe me."

"You're right, I don't. There is another reason you don't want to see me. Is it . . . ? Have I pushed you too far?" Christ, he'd massaged her breast last night. Had he horrified her? He'd been so certain she was enjoying it, but he hadn't *asked*. "Last night, did I—?"

"No, nothing like that," she rushed out, and he relaxed a small fraction.

"Then what?"

"Kit, you should leave. My mother will return any minute. She's quite anxious to make the train for New York."

"Not until you tell me the truth."

"Fine." She closed her eyes and pressed her lips together. "I'm not like you. I cannot do what we are doing and not feel anything. It's becoming . . . challenging."

Oh. He slumped against the back of the couch. That was unexpected. "I am not the kind of man who is interested in settling down."

"I know, which is why I think it's best if we leave our bargain here. You've helped me tremendously and I am grateful. You are funny and smart, and you gave me more confidence than I ever thought possible. Please do not think this is about you. This is about me."

"And finding a husband?"

"Yes. I must take that endeavor seriously."

He opened his mouth but promptly closed it. There wasn't anything else to be said. To argue was churlish and selfish, and it would not change the circumstances. As much as he wanted to bed Alice, he couldn't have her. She would marry and live a happy—albeit boring—scoundrel-free life. As was fitting. After all, it was the entire reason she'd sought him out in the first place.

He just hadn't expected to like her this much, damn it.

Standing, he thrust his hands in his trouser pockets. "I understand. I wish you safe travels and best of luck in your search."

"Thank you, Kit. I know your supper club will be a smashing success."

"In no small part due to your assistance. I'm very grateful."

She bit her lip and cast a furtive glance at the doorway. "They have started to leave. You'd best disappear before—"

"Alice!" Mrs. Lusk rushed into the room, her

glare cutting Kit down where he stood before turning on her daughter. "I leave you for five minutes and you entertain this scoundrel alone like a—"

"Madam," Kit snapped. "Seeing as how Miss Lusk is unable to walk unassisted, I thought I might help her into your carriage."

The older woman frowned. "We can make do, Mr. Ward. You may run along. We don't need your kind of help."

"Mama, please. You are being unkind. Would you rather a footman assisted me?"

Kit could tell Mrs. Lusk didn't like that suggestion, either. He decided to use reason to press his case. "Seeing as how I already carried her yesterday, no one is likely to notice."

"Fine," Mrs. Lusk said, reluctantly, after a long beat. "But we had better hurry. I do not want to miss our train." Spinning, she marched off in the direction of the front door.

He knelt by the sofa and slid his arms under Alice, taking care not to jostle her ankle, then stood. She wrapped her arms around his neck, not even pretending to put space between them, as he crossed the floor. "If you change your mind or need me for any reason, I'm easy to find," he said softly.

"Thank you, Kit. For that and everything else. This has been the best four days of my life."

His chest tightened and for once words deserted him.

Chapter Fourteen

～⚬～

The Duke of Lockwood looked lonely.

Sitting in the box her father had rented at the Metropolitan Opera House, Alice stared at the handsome duke, whose attention seemed miles away from the action on the stage. He hardly moved, his gaze fixed forward, but there was something about the set of his shoulders, the dark circles under his eyes, that suggested desolation. A gloominess perhaps more pronounced because of the jocularity in the seats around him.

The performance was a comedy, but the duke hadn't smiled once.

The scandal at the Websters' Newport chateau had died down somewhat in the past two weeks' time. Maddie and Harrison were married and Lockwood was now back out in society. In a month or so, it would seem as if the whole thing never happened.

Indeed, why was he so glum? Had he loved Maddie very much? It hadn't appeared that way in Newport, but then she'd been distracted, hadn't she? Nearly every waking thought had been consumed by Kit, so perhaps she'd missed quite a bit during those four days.

Kit still inhabited many of her thoughts, unfortunately. It was quite hard to concentrate when she kept reliving their conversations and interactions, the games and the kisses. She lost count of the number of times she had reached for a pen and paper to write to him since returning to New York, even locating his address, a town house on East Seventy-Fourth Street. Thank goodness common sense had prevailed, however, before she contacted him.

I am not the kind of man who is interested in settling down.

She mustn't forget it. Marriage had to remain Alice's priority, not mind-altering kisses and unrequited infatuation. Kit was everything she wanted in a man, except he would never marry, and Alice could not allow herself anything less.

Know your worth. Wasn't that what Katherine had said? It was good advice, especially for unmarried girls who craved nothing more than kisses from a certain dark-haired scoundrel.

The curtain fell for the first intermission and her gaze drifted back to Lockwood. He sat perfectly still, while the guests in his box stood and departed for drinks or a smoke. That left the duke all alone and Alice decided to pay him a visit. They hadn't spoken since Newport, and she didn't want him to think that she judged him for what had happened.

Stop making excuses for going over there. Just go and talk to him.

Rising, she glanced at her mother. "Mama, I must visit the ladies' salon."

"Again?" Her mother frowned. "I told you to stop drinking so much lemonade. Do not take too long."

"I won't, I promise."

Because her mother's long-distance vision was poor, Alice was safe to visit Lockwood in full view of the opera house. Once in the corridor behind the boxes, she hurried through the crowd toward the duke's box. Part of her marveled at this impetuous decision—something she never would have done a month ago—but this version of Alice was a tiny bit bolder.

You have Kit to thank for that.

Indeed, and she'd remain grateful for everything he taught her, even if the memories were painful at the moment. Painful because she missed him, which was odd as she'd only known him a short time. But feelings didn't base their strength on minutes and hours, apparently.

She slipped through the curtain at the rear of the duke's box. He faced the stage, his jaw stiff. A brief flash of panic caused her to hesitate—and he chose that exact moment to glance over his shoulder. Blinking, he instantly came to his feet. "Miss Lusk. I hadn't heard you enter."

Dropping into an elegant curtsy, she said, "Your Grace, forgive my intrusion."

"Nonsense. There is nothing to forgive. Might I offer you a drink?"

"No, thank you. I just wished to say hello and inquire after your well-being."

"Indeed, that is kind of you." He gestured to the seats. "Please, sit."

She lowered herself onto the plush seat beside

him and tried to remember Kit's advice. *Meet his gaze and hold it so there can be no mistake. People like to talk about themselves.*

Angling toward the duke, she stared directly into his eyes. "Are you enjoying the production this evening?"

"Not particularly." The side of his mouth hitched slightly. "I've seen this play many times over the years. I fear it's lost its appeal for me. You?"

Instead of answering, she kept the focus of the conversation on him. "Do you attend the theater often?"

"Quite a bit, yes. I mostly live in London, so I regularly attend the opera and the theater. You are from Boston, if I am not mistaken. Have you theater there?"

"You must miss London, I would imagine. What is the city like?"

"Dirty. There's soot in the air, as thick as fog some days. Other than Mayfair, the streets are muddy and full of filth. It's a shocking contrast to your city. I understand there are parts of New York that are dirty and crowded but I haven't seen them. Still, I am anxious to return home."

"Just as soon as you marry?"

His lips pressed together as if the topic was an unwelcome one. "Yes, well," he said. "That hasn't gone to plan thus far."

There was no use pretending to misunderstand. She'd been at the house party, after all. "A lifelong childhood friendship is hard to compete with, Your Grace."

He cocked his head, studying her. "True. That does not make it any less embarrassing, however."

"Perhaps, but think of the unmarried women who now wish to console you and lift your spirits. I'd say you are quite the sympathetic hero."

"Is that why you came over, to lift my spirits?"

"I wouldn't presume to possess such powers, but I did notice that you weren't overly engaged with those around you."

"Oh, I hardly know them. A state politician, his wife and their friends."

"Then why accept the invitation?"

"It was time. I cannot spend forever in America, and as we know, I must find a bride."

"Well, I have noted no fewer than four young ladies unable to tear their eyes away from you tonight, so I'd say your dance card will be filled in no time."

"Four? I must be slipping. Normally it's about seven or eight."

A snort escaped as she laughed—and she froze. Good God, she'd just snorted in front of a duke. Casting her eyes downward, she tried not to expire from mortification.

This was a bad idea. She never should have come over here—

"Forgive me, but was that an actual snort I heard?"

She winced and slammed her eyelids shut. "Is it too much to hope that we might not discuss it?"

"I am afraid we must. I cannot think of the last time I caused someone to laugh so hard they snorted, if ever."

"It is a first for me. Snorting in front of a duke, that is."

He put a hand over his heart. "I am honored."

"Your Grace is kind to humor me, but I am no stranger to embarrassment."

"Perhaps you can offer some tips on coping with it, then. If not for inciting more gossip, I would have left already."

"A very wise woman recently told me that what you think of yourself matters much more than what others think."

"A bit naive, perhaps, but a nice goal for most people."

A duke was not most people, she supposed. "Then my suggestion would be to drink until you no longer care."

Lockwood threw his head back and laughed, showing off the strong column of his throat. "I approve of that advice, actually. How had I not realized that you possess a sense of humor, Miss Lusk?"

Alice bit her lip and tried to suppress a smile. "I haven't a clue, Your Grace."

THEY WERE LAUGHING.

Alice and the damn duke were laughing in his box as if they were the best of friends. Kit ground his teeth and lingered in the back of Preston's box, cloaked in the shadows, and watched her flirt—flirt!—with Lockwood using all the tricks he had taught her. Tricks like leaning toward the duke, looking him in the eyes and asking questions instead of monopolizing the conversation.

Then Kit saw her bite her lip and smile, and he thought he might jump out of his skin.

Goddamn it.

"Is something wrong?" A delicate hand swept over his knee. It belonged to Lottie, his companion this evening. She was a friend of Preston's mistress, Arabella, who was currently sitting with Preston in front of Kit and Lottie. The outing had been Preston's idea to force Kit "to stop moping and get out of the house," but Kit's heart hadn't been in it. Even less so after seeing Alice here with her mother at the other end of the tier.

"No," he lied, keeping his gaze fixed on Alice. "Did you enjoy the first—?"

Alice stood and prepared to leave Lockwood's box. Before Kit knew what he was doing, he shot out of his chair and glanced down at Lottie. "Would you like champagne? Why don't I fetch us all some champagne?"

Without waiting on an answer, he darted up the aisle, through the back of the box and into the corridor. Throngs of people were milling about, so he weaved through the bodies and closed the distance to Lockwood's box. Music began playing from the orchestra pit, a signal that the second half was about to start. He didn't stop, just kept a brisk pace until he spotted the back of Alice's head.

People poured out of the smoking and retiring rooms, which made keeping up that much harder. No doubt he appeared like a man possessed as he trailed her, but he soon caught up. She was lovely, wearing a cream silk brocade gown with full sleeves and a faint floral pattern on the skirt. Wrapping his fingers around her gloved wrist, he dragged her to the side.

She gasped and turned, trying to pull her wrist from his grip. When she saw it was him, she gave a nervous glance around them, as if she didn't wish to be seen with him. "Oh, Mr. Ward. Hello."

"Mr. Ward, is it?" He tugged her into the nearly empty salon.

"That is your name." She twisted her arm to free herself and he let her go. "What are we doing in here?"

"Retrieving champagne." He tilted his head toward the attendant pouring in the corner. "Let's stand in line."

Her brows pinched but she didn't argue. There were about ten people in line for refreshments, so he positioned himself behind her and spoke to the back of her head. "Having a nice time?"

She angled to the side ever so slightly. "I suppose. I hadn't realized you were here. Do you have a box?"

That she'd spotted Lockwood and not Kit grated across his nerves. "I'm with my friend Preston in his box. Fourth beyond Lockwood on this tier."

"Oh." She worried her lip between her teeth. "Just the two of you, then?"

"No." He didn't elaborate. There was no reason to tell her of Arabella and Lottie. "You and Lockwood looked cozy."

She lifted a shoulder as the line progressed a tiny bit. "I thought he seemed lonely so I went over to visit him."

"Lonely? That is ridiculous."

"It's not." She shot him a frown. "He's embroiled in a scandal not of his making. And I know better than most what it's like to suffer a public humiliation. It's nice to be offered an unexpected kindness every now and again."

Dash it, why must she be such a good person? "Hard to feel sorry for Lockwood when he taunted Harrison at every turn."

"You men." She shook her head as if disgusted with his entire gender. "Everything is a contest, even marriage."

Kit crossed his arms over his chest. "Speaking of marriage, how goes your search? Any progress since I last saw you?" *Please say no.*

"No. My ankle hadn't healed well enough to attend events until yesterday."

Damn, he'd forgotten about her ankle. *Because you were jealous and let it cloud your thinking.* This was unlike him. He should be charming that beautiful actress back in Preston's box, yet he'd raced after Alice like a hound to a fox. And why? Because she was doing what she set out to do—finding a husband?

Shame coated his skin like needles. "Forgive me. I hadn't even inquired after your injury. Are you feeling better?"

"I am, thank you. How are your supper club plans coming along?"

"Better, now that we have those recipes. Thank you for that, by the way. I've sent a check to Franconi."

"Yes, he mentioned it."

"You've seen him, then?"

"Once or twice. You know me, always curious."

The line went more quickly, with the second act now underway onstage. "We plan to credit Franconi on the menu. I think his food will be a nice draw."

Alice stepped up to the counter and moved aside, motioning to Kit. "How many?" she asked.

"Four," he told the attendant.

As the glasses were poured, Alice asked, "Is she pretty?"

"Who?"

"The woman you are with tonight."

Not as pretty as you. "I suppose, yes. She's an actress, a friend of Preston's . . . friend."

"Ah." She stared at the wall. "I should get back to my mother before she starts worrying."

"Wait." He didn't want her to go yet. "Just another minute."

"No, I should return to my seat. And you have your friends waiting for you. It was nice to see you again, Mr. Ward." In a swirl of silk she departed, her steps measured and quick, as if she couldn't wait to get away from him.

He pinched the bridge of his nose. That hadn't gone well. Why hadn't he charmed her instead of acting like a jealous fool? It was as if he'd forgotten all of his own lessons.

This would not do. He needed to stop focusing on Alice and recalling her greedy kisses and innocent smiles. She was better off finding a husband of substance, one who would love and cherish her, give her children. Kit was a short-term winner, not a long-term investment. Besides, he'd soon be running a supper club, which was one shallow step above a dance hall in the eyes of society. No proper family would approve of him as a son-in-law.

She deserved the wedding, the big house, a passel of doe-eyed children with chestnut hair. None of that interested Kit. So, better to purge Alice from his mind now before he ruined her chances at a good match.

Cradling the four glasses of champagne, he returned to the other end of the tier. He edged aside the curtain at the back of Preston's box and slipped inside the salon—then drew up short.

Preston waited there, arms crossed, and a scowl on his face. Kit immediately asked, "What's wrong?"

"That is what I'd like to know," his friend said. "You rushed out of here like the place was on fire. So, what happened?"

"I went for champagne." He held up both hands. "Just as I said."

Preston stepped closer and lowered his tone. "Do you not wish to be here? I realize I pushed you into coming and brought Lottie along, but you're normally not this . . . remote. Usually by now I've scolded you once or twice about public indecency, which always prompts you to leave with your companion at intermission. Tonight, you're actually minding your manners."

This was the problem with good friends. They knew you at your best . . . and your worst.

"I will apologize to Lottie. My attention is hers from here on out."

"Good. See that it stays that way."

Preston plucked two of the glasses from Kit's hands and went into the front of the box. The two women were whispering but quieted as the men approached. Kit handed a glass to Lottie and retook his seat. He allowed himself one last look at Alice, who watched the play as if memorizing it, before he turned to his companion for the evening.

Edging closer, he put his lips near Lottie's ear. "Forgive me. I was a bit out of sorts this evening, but that was not a good excuse for ignoring you."

"You are forgiven." Lottie smirked as she placed a hand on Kit's thigh. "But you'll have to make it up to me during the second half."

He forced a smile and dropped his voice to a deep rasp. "I do love a challenge."

Chapter Fifteen

The best time to sneak into the Fifth Avenue Hotel's kitchen was around ten o'clock in the evening. Supper service had dwindled by that hour and the staff generally had more free moments to spare. Besides, Alice's mother took her laudanum at eight, so by ten Mama was sleeping like the dead.

Angelo knew to expect Alice almost every night, unless she had a social engagement, and he usually had a plate of food waiting. Either an old favorite or something new he wanted her to try. She loved talking about the flavors and ingredients, trying to guess what he'd included in the recipe.

It was the one place where she could relax and be herself. And in the three days since she'd run into Kit at the opera, the kitchen was the only place she found respite from her misery.

At first, seeing him had caused her heart to swell, as if the organ had shriveled like a raisin in his absence. But he hadn't attended alone. And once she learned where he was sitting, she hadn't been able to stop staring as he flirted with the beautiful woman at his side. Watching had seemed like a necessary torture, one that would finally convince her heart that any feelings for him were absurd. Ridiculous. Unrequited and pathetic.

And when he left with his companion midway through the second act, Alice felt like said heart had been ripped out of her chest and stomped on by a heavy boot.

Forget him. Know your worth.

It had become her mantra. Someday it would sink in and make her feel better.

She pushed through the door at the back stairs and entered the kitchen.

"Buonasera, signorina!" Angelo called when he spotted her. In his early fifties, Angelo was shorter than most men but had more energy than anyone she'd ever met. His hair had started to gray at the temples since he moved away from Boston, so she liked to tease him that New York was making him old.

He was at the stove, shaking a pan over the flame. "Come see, come see."

"Hello, Angelo. I see you've not stopped yet tonight."

"This is for you and me. Look." He pointed at the pan where vegetables and chicken livers sautéed in a brown sauce. "I visited Mon Lay Won in Chinatown and had this dish. They call it chop suey."

She had heard of this restaurant. It was referred to as the Chinese Delmonico's, but her mother refused to allow her to travel to that neighborhood. Someday, Alice would find a way to go. "It smells delicious. What's in it?"

"Fungi, buds of the bamboo, bean sprouts, some chicken livers and pigs' tripe, celery and onion. And the spices, of course."

"I cannot wait to try it."

"The rice is there." He pointed to a pot on the stove. "Use those plates and dish up the rice. The chop suey is ready." When she had rice on both plates, he brought over the skillet and poured some of the mixture out. "Now we sit," he said.

They took their plates to a tiny table in the corner. During the day, it was where Angelo worked, reviewing the evening's menu. Waiting there was a bottle of red wine for him and a glass of water for her. She sat down and smelled the dish first. "Is there vinegar or wine in there?"

"Yes, it is a Chinese wine." He tapped his nose. "I knew you would smell it."

She picked up her fork and tasted it. "This is fantastic. There's garlic and ginger root, too."

"Fast and simple, yet has a lot of flavor. This is not quite as good, though. I must go back and watch the chef make it once more."

His eagerness to learn was one of the many things she loved and respected about Angelo. "I wish I could go with you."

"Someday, lucciola," he said, calling her "firefly" in Italian. "You will marry soon and become one of those independent women with their bicycles and pantaloons."

"Bloomers," she corrected with a fond smile. "They are called bloomers."

He waved his hand. "I prefer dresses, but what do I know? I am an old man. Tell me, how goes the search for a husband?"

"Fine." She sighed. "No serious suitor, though."

"Some not serious suitors, perhaps?"

She thought of Kit and her lips twitched. Definitely not serious, but she didn't regret it; those memories were some of the best she had. "Perhaps," she hedged.

Though he grinned, Angelo wagged his finger at her. "You had best be careful. Your mother is a hawk."

"Chef Franconi!"

The booming voice from the direction of the alley startled her. She turned as Preston Clarke strode into the kitchen. Tall and intense like a thunderstorm, Mr. Clarke could not be missed in a crowd. He also happened to be Kit's close friend.

She peeked around Mr. Clarke but no one else was there. Her chest contracted with what she suspected was disappointment.

Angelo rose and the two men shook hands. "Mr. Clarke, this is a surprise. Did we have an appointment?"

"No, so please forgive my intrusion." Shifting toward Alice, there was something akin to amusement simmering in his gaze. He took her hand and kissed the back of it. "Miss Lusk, a pleasure to see you in Chef Franconi's kitchen once more."

"Mr. Clarke." Pushing her chair back, she started to stand. "I'll leave you two to your meeting."

"No, please, stay. I'm glad you're here. Chef, may I have a moment with Miss Lusk?"

Angelo tilted his head in her direction. "Only if the lady agrees."

"Of course," she said. "Shall we move to the dining room?"

"No, no." Angelo removed his plate and wine-glass and set them aside. Then he brought a clean glass and poured Mr. Clarke wine. "I insist. This is the best red wine from Barolo. Enjoy." The chef moved to the stove, where his assistants were finishing the last orders of the night.

"Chef said you often come right before closing." Mr. Clarke sipped the wine and his eyes widened as he examined the bottle. "That is nice. I might have to order a case. Anyway, I stopped by in the hopes of seeing you."

"Me?"

"I did need to speak with Chef, but yes, I had hoped to run into you. I never had the chance to thank you for your help."

With the recipes. "Oh, you are welcome. I hope you find them useful."

"We have, although it has been difficult to sample them. But I'm sure we'll figure it out."

"What do you mean? I wrote the instructions clearly."

"Yes, you did, and we are very grateful, of course. It has been impossible to locate a chef who can execute them properly, unfortunately. But I won't bore you with our silly problems. Had you a nice time in Newport?"

He stared at her intently over the rim of his glass but she couldn't tell what he was thinking. Had Kit mentioned anything about the lessons? Was Mr. Clarke secretly laughing at her? "I did. How are Mr. Archer and Maddie?"

"Still honeymooning. And you were at the opera two nights ago, I believe? My apologies for not saying hello. Did you speak to Kit?"

"I did, but only briefly."

Mr. Clarke's lips curved as if this confirmed something he already knew. "I am worried about him. He's been uncharacteristically out of sorts since returning from the chateau. I wish I knew what happened at that house party."

Out of sorts? He'd seemed a bit curt at the opera, peppering her with questions and commenting snidely about the Duke of Lockwood. But she had been so distracted by the idea of his female companion that she hadn't given it much thought. "Well, he's Kit, so no doubt he'll bounce back soon."

"Yes, he is rather like a rubber ball, our Kit. No doubt it's our troubles in hiring a chef that has him twisted in knots. You know how much the success of the supper club means to him." He took a long drink and rested his empty glass on the table. "I should allow you to return to your meal. Take care, Miss Lusk."

Her head was spinning with all the information Mr. Clarke had relayed in such a short amount of time. As he started to stand, she said, "Wait." Pausing, she struggled to put her thoughts into words. "Your problems, the ones with the recipes. You said you cannot find a chef who can execute them?"

"Indeed. That is why I am here to speak with Franconi. I had hoped to hire one of his assistants for a night or two to prepare these dishes. We'd like to host a preview of what we plan to offer as a way to generate excitement for the club."

"Chef will never allow that." Angelo was currently giving his assistant instructions on how to properly trim a large cut of beef. "He's very protective of his staff."

Mr. Clarke sighed loudly. "Then I haven't a clue as to what to do. We've approached three top chefs in the city and they've all refused, saying Franconi's techniques are too complicated."

"That's rot. Even the greenest chef should be able to follow the instructions I wrote down."

He lifted his hands and shrugged. "I don't really understand food. That is more Kit's area of expertise—and yours, I suppose."

"Perhaps I could help."

"Oh?"

"I might be able to find time."

"How? I understand you are heavily chaperoned here in the city."

Had Kit or Angelo shared that information? "I am. It would require some creative maneuvering." Perhaps Daddy could help? Alice hadn't asked him for anything recently, and he was aware at how grating Mama could be at times. It was one of the reasons he hardly spent any time at home anymore.

Yes, she would call him tomorrow. All she needed was for Mama to be preoccupied for two or three days.

"It appears that you are crafting a plan, Miss Lusk."

"Perhaps. May I ring you and let you know?"

"That would be wonderful." Reaching into his coat pocket, he withdrew a card and presented it. "I look forward to hearing from you."

After Preston left, Angelo slid into the chair across from her. "Well? What did you decide?"

"You heard?"

"Of course. Nothing happens in my kitchen that I do not know about. So, will you help them?"

Alice tapped the vellum card against her fingers. Could she do it? She had never directed a kitchen or prepared food for so many people at once. Yes, she had watched Franconi do it over the years, but there was a big difference between observing and doing. "It's a massive undertaking. You should lend him a sous chef or two."

"No. As you said, I am protective of them. They work hard in my kitchen and it is unfair to ask them for more, even if they are being paid handsomely. Furthermore, I think you should do it."

"I do want to help. But I've never cooked for that many people. And it's more than cooking one dish—it's timing an entire meal."

He shrugged. "That is a matter of planning. A dinner service is like a symphony. You are the conductor. The pieces are prepared ahead of time and you put them together at the last minute."

"You make it sound easy."

"Bella, if it were easy, everyone would be a chef. It requires skill and organization. Intuition, too. But you have all these things. You are ready."

"How do you know that?"

"Because, lucciola, I know *you*. I have watched you become a smart and capable woman. And it is time for you to flap your wings a bit, before you settle down."

Looking at the table, she tried to hide her smile. She appreciated his confidence in her. Perhaps someday she would believe it.

Do this and maybe you will.

Did she dare? With Franconi's help—and her father's intervention—perhaps Alice could pull this off. For Kit. "Will you help me with figuring out how much food to order and what needs to be made first?"

The side of his mouth hitched. "Shall I grab a pencil?"

DRUMMING HIS FINGERS on the table, Kit tried not to interrupt the awful attempt at singing occurring onstage. It had already gone on far too long, but Preston had asked Kit to audition one of Arabella's friends for the supper club. While pleasing to the eye, the woman was terrible, both off-key and off-tempo. Still, he waited until the blasted song was over before rising.

"Thank you, Helena. I don't think—"

"I don't think we've ever heard anything quite as beautiful," Preston said loudly, drowning out Kit's words. He strode toward the stage and helped Helena down. "I appreciate you coming. Mr. Ward and I will make decisions soon and we'll be in touch. Paul, will you help Miss Langley to her carriage?"

Their doorman and security guard, Paul, came forward to collect Helena. Preston returned to where Kit was brooding over a glass of scotch. Kit frowned at his friend. "She was terrible."

"That is an understatement, but I cannot send her out of here in tears. I can't believe I am the one to say this, but there are better ways to finesse these things, Kit."

Kit downed the rest of his drink and poured another. "More like you are terrified that Arabella will yell at you."

"Exactly. The point of having a mistress is to keep her happy. If she's happy, I'm happy."

"Whether you are happy or not doesn't really fucking matter to me, Preston."

"Clearly."

"I mean it. This is a business, not a place for Arabella to procure jobs for her friends."

"Is that what you think?" Preston's expression darkened, his mouth flattening. "That I'd allow that to happen?"

Kit didn't know what to think anymore. He was floundering with this supper club. They couldn't find a chef, and they had one reliable singer plus a handful of staff wondering when the hell they were opening.

He dragged a hand down his face. This place could not fail. *He* could not fail. A supper club was the only thing he was remotely qualified to do. If he couldn't do this, he really was pathetic.

You're not cut out for deep thinking, Christopher. As shallow as a saucer.

God, would the old man's voice never leave his head?

This was not about Preston or Arabella, either. This was about his insecurities and mounting panic. Perhaps this had been a horrible mistake. Exhaling, he met Preston's furious gaze. "Forgive me. I'm just . . . I don't know if I can do this."

Preston's brow furrowed. "Fellows," he shouted to the occupants of the room. "Can you give us a minute?" Preston's carpenters and the club workers all departed, leaving the two men alone. Preston leaned back in his chair. "Talk to me."

"What is there to say? It's clear we've wasted our money and our time on this place."

Preston removed the glass from Kit's hand, setting it and the bottle well out of Kit's reach. "That's enough of that, obviously. Now, I have known you a long time. In fact, some days it feels like forever. So, I can say with absolute certainty that this is the perfect venture for you to oversee. No one is more suited to this than you. Furthermore, it's too late to quit."

"We could sell it off. Or give it to—"

"No. You are going to stop moping or whatever you've been doing since returning from Newport and get your head right. Why don't I ring Lottie for you?"

"Don't." The word came out sharply, definitively. "Don't do that."

Even though Lottie made it perfectly clear that she wanted to get Kit into bed, he hadn't slept with her after the opera four nights ago. Instead of taking her to his house, he'd taken her home and dropped her off. Once in his bedroom, he'd tugged on his cock while thinking of Alice until he came all over his stomach. It was becoming a nightly— and daily—ritual.

"If not Lottie, someone else," Preston urged. "I am worried about you."

"And I can't believe I am the one to say this, but not every problem can be solved with fucking."

"Bite your tongue." Preston appeared horrified. "And you're a fine one to talk. What about when you were failing economics at Harvard and you found the professor's wife, then 'convinced' her to intervene on your behalf. I wonder how you persuaded her?"

Kit pushed away from the table and stood. "May

we focus on the club? Because that is what actually matters."

"It doesn't. Neither of us need the money, and who cares if it fails?"

"The people we've hired, for starters. Furthermore, this isn't about money for me. I—"

"Hello?"

No. It couldn't be.

Kit's head jerked toward the entrance. Alice Lusk was there, standing in the club. How on earth . . . ?

"Miss Lusk," Preston said as if he'd been expecting her. He rose and went to greet her. "Thank you for coming down. Would you like a tour?" They shook hands and Kit could only blink.

"Unfortunately, I haven't the time." She walked with Preston toward Kit's table. Kit drank in the sight of her, dressed in a lovely blue day dress with a matching hat. Her hair was pulled back, which emphasized her big eyes. "Hello, Mr. Ward."

"Alice." Screw propriety. Forgoing her hand, he kissed her cheek. "What are you doing here?"

She flicked a glance at Preston. "I am here to help."

"I don't understand."

"Surprise," Preston said to Kit. "I approached Alice about our little problem. You know, with finding a chef? She has agreed to help."

"What?" He shook his head as if trying to clear it. "Help, how?"

Preston slapped Kit on the back. "She'll explain. I have to go. I have a meeting with a concrete supplier. Miss Lusk, always a pleasure." His long legs carried him out of the room in a few steps and then Kit was alone with Alice.

"Shall we sit?" He pulled out a chair for her.

She lowered herself down, and Kit got a whiff of her familiar scent, vanilla and a hint of orange. Heat shot through him, a jolt of longing that echoed in every part of him, like his body was flooded with the want of her. He dragged in a breath and tried to remember that she was a virgin and a debutante and not his willing pupil any longer.

When he sat, she said, "I apologize. I thought Mr. Clarke informed you of my offer."

"He did not. What he said was the chef issue was handled and I should stop searching. Did you have someone in mind?"

"Yes." She folded her hands atop the table. "Me."

"You? You are going to act as the chef for our preview dinner."

"Again, yes."

This was madness. He gave her a bland look. "Will your mother be a waiter? Because I know she will not let you out of her sight."

Her lips twisted into a devious smile he'd never seen before. "I called my father and asked for a favor. He is prepared to call my mother home to Boston for three days at my request."

"How did you sneak out this afternoon?" He couldn't believe Mrs. Lusk would ever allow it.

"She went shopping and I claimed a headache. I am supposed to be at the hotel. She made me promise and will be checking in with the staff to ensure I am there."

"Then how will you get away with it?"

"My mother is not the only person with friends inside the hotel."

He chuckled. "I see. So you will sneak out during

those three days and come here. What if you're caught?"

"I won't be."

He appreciated her confidence, but she could suffer real consequences if anything went wrong. Young girls had been shipped off to convents for less. Not to mention that just two weeks ago she had proclaimed sneaking out too risky. "Thank you, but no. We'll find someone else."

She cocked her head. "I don't understand. Mr. Clarke said you were desperate."

"Not desperate enough to land you in trouble with your parents. They would not approve, Alice."

"I don't care. A friend recently told me to live each day like it's my last. So here I am."

"While I appreciate your newly adopted carpe diem attitude, this is a bit more than visiting the hotel kitchen or baking bread. This is many hours of work here at the club. Never mind that your mother might refuse to go to Boston. Worse, what if she insists on taking you with her?"

"She won't refuse Daddy, not if he tells her to return. And she's left me for days at a time before. Usually I stay in the hotel room with my maid and no one ever knows."

"This is madness," he repeated, this time aloud.

"No, this is a solution to your dilemma. I can prepare Angelo's food. You'd be hard-pressed to find anyone who could do it better. And I'm able to ask him for advice, if necessary."

Was he seriously considering this? He didn't wish to see her reputation ruined, but she knew the risks, perhaps better than he. So if she was willing to help, then who was he to stop her? And they were desperate. No chef seemed capable of the undertaking on such short notice, and Kit had seen Alice in the kitchen firsthand. She loved cooking and knew food, and he trusted her.

Those big eyes watched him carefully, her chest rising and falling quickly. Nerves? Or excitement? Was she experiencing the same giddy exuberance he currently felt in her presence?

He couldn't turn her down. Hadn't a hope of it, actually. Perhaps it was the scoundrel in him but he liked encouraging both her independence and interest in cooking. But if she was going to do this, he had to keep her safe.

And that included from him.

"If you are certain," he said, "then we would be grateful for your help. I will, however, be hiring a driver to ferry you to and from the hotel."

"If you feel it's necessary."

"I do. As far as the menu, do you feel comfortable setting the evening's courses? Or would you like my input?"

She reached into her handbag and withdrew a few pieces of paper, which she slid across the small table. "Here."

"What is this?" The papers listed various dishes and ingredients. "You came prepared. What if I'd said no?"

"Mr. Clarke said you might, in which case I should keep arguing until I wore you down."

Preston certainly had organized this neatly. What was he up to? Kit would deal with his friend later. Holding up the paper, he asked her, "So this is the order list?"

"Yes. It's for fifty people, which Mr. Clarke said was the number you're expecting."

"It is. Would next week work for you, or do you need more time?"

He half expected her to say it was too soon, but she nodded. "Of course. Wednesday, Thursday, Friday?"

"Perfect. I'll send out the invitations." He paused. "Part of the appeal of a supper club is who is preparing the supper. I had planned on mentioning Franconi. It would be helpful to list the chef, as well."

"You cannot possibly think to list my name. No one would come if they saw you'd hired a woman. And an inexperienced one at that. You'd be a laughingstock."

"You are not inexperienced."

"You know what I mean."

"More importantly, listing your name would ruin your reputation."

"Yes, so let's make up a name. Say that I am Franconi's apprentice, which is sort of true."

"That works. What name shall we use?"

She traced a seam on the wooden table with her fingertip, and he allowed himself to be distracted by the thought of those fingers tracing his skin. Having her here, in his space, for three days would be glorious torture. She straightened, her face alight with recognition. "Chef Lucciola."

"Pretty. What does it mean?"

"Firefly. It's what Angelo calls me."

The name suited her. A small package that burned bright, shining joy and happiness to everyone around her. He wished he'd thought of it himself. "Chef Lucciola, then."

She pushed her chair back, so Kit rose and went to help. He moved closer than he needed to, merely enjoying the sight and smell of her once more. When she was on her feet the air in the room stilled, time slowing as they both paused, inches away from each other. There were so many things he wanted to say, to ask . . . but he was tongue-tied. It was imperative that he keep his distance. She had a life to lead and so did he, and it wasn't fair to flirt with her when his intentions were far from serious. Nevertheless, he couldn't force himself to edge aside.

Finally, she decided for him and stepped away, her hands twisting in the fabric of her skirts, smoothing and fluffing. "I've written instructions for some of the items needed, such as the oysters and the lobster. You'll buy them Friday morning from the vendors I specified."

"Very good. Do you need me to hire any staff to assist you in the kitchen?"

"I already have someone to help me."

Irrational jealousy streaked through his nerves to tighten his muscles. "Oh? Who?"

"You." Spinning on her heel, she started for the door. "Until next week, Kit."

Chapter Sixteen

❧

Alice flipped through the pages of the *Ladies' Home Journal* on Tuesday afternoon, not really seeing the words or pictures. Her mother was on the telephone to Daddy, which was the critical part of Alice's plan. She wasn't terribly worried, however. Mama never denied him, not when he put his foot down about something. Then Alice would be free, sort of, to help Kit and Mr. Clarke with their event.

It would require dodging her maid as well as the hotel staff at the front desk. But she could give her maid the days off and sneak out through the kitchen. No one would ever believe she was breaking the rules or lying. Alice Lusk never did anything scandalous or shocking. She played by the rules and did what she was told, end of story.

A lifetime of compliance would earn her a few days of rebellion.

She could hardly wait. She and Kit would spend three days together in the club's kitchen and, though there could never be anything more, she was looking forward to every second.

When she thought of seeing him again, she could hardly breathe, her palms dampening with anticipation. Those intense brown eyes, his wicked smile . . . as well as his sharp wit and easygoing manner. He was the most interesting person in any room, and she could stand next to him and listen to him talk for eons.

Which could never happen, of course. But she would have him for three days, and that would be enough.

The door to her suite opened and Mama came in, her mouth pinched. Not a hair was out of place, as usual. Her mother was tightly cinched and battle-ready at all times. "You and your father are going to be the death of me," she said sharply. "Apparently there is a problem with the staff in Boston and he refuses to handle it himself. Says I must return immediately to deal with it, and additionally there is a dinner I must attend with him on Friday."

As her parents hardly spent any time together these days, Alice knew the interaction would be a chore for both of them. "That sounds like fun. Too bad I am not feeling well enough to travel." She pointed at her abdomen, as if she had her monthly.

"Your father also suggested leaving you here, which makes no sense. I don't like leaving you in a hotel by yourself. It's not safe."

"You've done it twice before, Mama. Remember? Last year, you had to return to Boston and I stayed here."

"That's true. But that was before that awful house party in Newport. Just by association you are a hairbreadth away from a scandal, thanks to that tennis-playing strumpet. We cannot risk any whisper of impropriety or else your chances at a good match are ruined. It's been hard enough to marry you off with just your personality and looks to contend with. Imagine if you lost your reputation."

The barb barely scratched the surface of Alice's pride. After all these years she was used to comments such as this. "I promise not to leave the hotel. It'll be just like last year." She put her magazine down and groaned in faux agony. "Oh, I think this talking is making it worse."

"I keep telling you laudanum will help with those monthly pains."

"No, it's not quite as bad as that." Alice hated the dreamy feeling that came with opiates. "I just need to sleep."

"I will instruct Mary to keep a close eye on you," Mama said, referring to Alice's maid. "In case your condition worsens."

"Don't worry about me. Just go and I'll see you upon your return."

"I shall leave first thing in the morning and return on Saturday." She heaved a sigh. "You will learn this if you marry, Alice, but wives must sacrifice to keep their husbands happy. It's the only way a marriage works."

If you marry. Alice resisted the urge to wrinkle her nose. "Daddy adores you," she said, though she doubted it was true. "He's probably missing you."

Mama said nothing in response. Instead, she went to the door. "I'll have Chef Franconi send dinner up to my room. Seeing as how you're not feeling well, you'll eat some broth and go straight to bed."

"Of course."

When the door closed behind her mother, Alice exhaled in relief. It almost seemed too easy, but her mother had no reason to distrust her. Other than sneaking out at the house party and the occasional trip to Franconi's kitchen, Alice had done everything her parents had ever asked of her. She was not a rebel or a troublemaker; she attended the parties and danced the dances. She smiled and nodded, kept her thoughts and wishes to herself and never complained.

So she had more than earned a few days in a supper club kitchen.

Hard to say what excited her more—time away from her mother, acting as a proper chef in a real kitchen, or spending three days with Kit.

Don't be silly. You know the answer.

Yes, she did—and it terrified her. Because if she were willing to go to these lengths for such a short stint with him, what would she do to prolong it?

Kit was unpacking produce in the club's small kitchen Wednesday morning when Preston walked in. His friend's gaze swept the room. "Is she here yet?"

"No, not yet." Kit slid a box of onions toward the other man. "Put that on the far counter, will you?"

Preston frowned but did as asked. "I didn't come here to work. I came to watch *you* work."

"Why?"

"Because I cannot believe you actually agreed to act as her sous chef."

Neither could Kit, but he had a hard time refusing Alice anything. Furthermore, if he said no, she might get another man in here . . . and that was unacceptable. So he could suffer through a few hours of chopping and dicing at Alice's side. "We want Friday night to succeed, don't we?"

"Indeed, we do." Preston popped a grape into his mouth. "Which is why you should be focused on other things instead of hiding out in this kitchen for the next three days."

"I will do those things when she's not here. The supper is the most important part of a supper club."

Preston chuckled. "God, you are so transparent. And I literally never thought I'd see the day."

"I have no idea what you're talking about."

"Don't you?"

"No, so if you'd spit it out and get on with your day, I'd appreciate it."

"You and Miss Lusk."

"Fuck, no," Kit instantly said. "You are entirely wrong."

"I've known you since we were boys, Kit. I'm not wrong, and Harrison confirmed it, as well. You gave her *lessons*."

Damn it. Harrison had no right to share that bit of news. Unwilling to give Preston the satisfaction, he lifted a shoulder. "In exchange for recipes. You're welcome, by the way."

"There are hundreds of chefs out there with thousands of recipes at our disposal. You didn't do this for the *recipes*. Do I seem like some sort of rube?"

Preston was so far from a rube that it was laughable. He was city bred, tough as nails and smart as a whip. Still, Kit did not want anyone to get the wrong impression. "Alice and I are friends. Nothing more. She's on the hunt for a husband and I am focused on this." He gestured to the kitchen.

"Then why didn't you sleep with Lottie after the opera the other night?"

A tomato fell out of Kit's hands and dropped to the floor. Shit. How had Preston learned that piece of information? "Perhaps I didn't feel up to it."

"Oh, I have no doubt that was true. You definitely were not 'up' for it—and now I know why."

"Do not tempt me to chuck a tomato at your head. It would be a shame to ruin your suit."

Preston smirked. "I dare you."

Kit cocked his arm—and the swinging door opened. Alice's eyes darted from him to Preston. "Kit, what are you doing? That's a perfectly good tomato."

He straightened. "You're right. I shouldn't insult the tomato by throwing it at this piece of sh—"

"Kit!"

Pressing his lips together, he turned and gave the produce his attention. Preston was wrong. The recipes were necessary to the club's success. When the invitations for Friday night were delivered, not a single guest declined. In fact, Kit had received more than a dozen requests from men not on the list begging to attend.

When they started selling memberships, Franconi's food would be a major draw—as would the entertainment. And Kit had called in a personal favor to secure the singer for Friday night's preview.

"Hello, Miss Lusk," Preston said as he went over to kiss her hand. "Forgive my friend over there. He has terrible manners."

"Good morning, Mr. Clarke."

"Call me Preston, please," he said in a sugary, flirtatious voice that had Kit fingering another tomato. "Mr. Clarke sounds like my father and I loathe my father."

Ready to get down to business, Kit hoisted a crate of apples. "Alice, where should I put all these?"

"Keep those out, actually. We're going to prepare the desserts first." From the depths of her handbag, she withdrew a white apron and proceeded to tie it around her waist. "Are you here to help, Preston?"

"God, no. I came to laugh at Kit."

"Which you've done already," Kit said. "So run along. We wouldn't wish to keep you from your skyscrapers."

Preston shook his head, though his eyes danced with mirth. "This is going to be fun. I am definitely looking forward to Friday. Thank you for your help, Miss Lusk. Kit, try not to stab yourself with a knife." He strode out of the kitchen, whistling the entire way.

"I like him," Alice said as she inspected the crates on the counter.

"That makes one of us."

"Oh, you're not serious. You have been friends a long time."

True, but Kit still wished to punch Preston every now and then.

Speaking of, the kitchen door swung open again.

Preston's expression was more serious this time. "Forgive me for interrupting, but, Kit, I forgot to tell you that Forrest is back from Chicago."

He forgot? How could Preston have let that information slip his mind? The last time Forrest was in New York, he'd nearly drank himself to death. "Where?"

"A boardinghouse over on West Twenty-Eighth Street."

Not a great neighborhood, then. A far cry from Forrest's Fifth Avenue upbringing. "You have the boys on it?" he asked, referring to the guards Preston had hired to tail their friend.

"I do. Wouldn't hurt for you to stop by and check in, though. I would, but my day is packed."

Kit nodded. "I'll go tonight."

"Good—117 is the street number." He tipped his hat at Alice. "Farewell, again."

"Farewell," she said.

When Kit didn't say anything, Alice leaned forward to catch his gaze. "A friend of yours?"

"Yes. He's not doing well, I'm afraid."

"I'm sorry. Do you want to go visit him now?"

Even though there was a mountain of work to do and no one to help her but him, she was still thinking of others before herself. She was absolutely remarkable. "No, I'll go tonight." Rubbing his hands together, he gestured to the mountain of food on the counters and floors. "What should we do first?"

"Anything we aren't using today needs to go into a cooler."

"It's back there." He pointed to the wooden door in the far corner.

"Then let's get busy." Picking up a crate of Bibb lettuce, she held it out. "Here you go."

"I see how it is." He took the crate from her hands. "You just want me here for my muscles."

She didn't laugh, as he'd expected. Instead, she put her fingers on his upper arm and squeezed. "You are more than a pretty face, Christopher."

The comment struck him as odd, but his tongue thickened all the same, his mouth suddenly cotton. He couldn't handle the way she was looking at him, as if she *understood*. "You won't be saying that after you see me in the kitchen," he joked.

"Yes, I will. Now, get moving. I don't have all day."

His brows shot up, but he didn't argue. He liked this bossy side of her. A lot.

ALICE STUDIED THE menu once more. They clearly needed more hands in the kitchen. She and Kit had been busy—rolling crust, coring apples, making custard, whipping cream, and tens of other tasks—for six straight hours. And they hadn't accomplished nearly enough.

"I am starving," Kit said as he finished the layers on another charlotte russe. "And working with all this food is making it worse."

"We're almost done for the day. I must return to the hotel, so I'll eat there."

"John is waiting for you outside. He'll see you safely returned."

True to his word, Kit had hired a driver to take her to and from the hotel each day. It seemed extravagant, but she wasn't about to argue. The luxury would save her the time of finding a hack. "Thank you for that, by the way."

"You are doing us an enormous favor. It's the least Preston and I can do." He smoothed the top of the dessert with a frosting spatula. "How does this look?"

"Perfect. Much better than your first five attempts."

"Why, thank you. Glad to hear I'm not completely hopeless." He lifted the platter and headed for the cooler. "I'll put this away and then see you off."

Frowning, she watched his retreating back and thought about his disparaging comment. If not for his drunken ramblings that night in his bedroom, she might have laughed it off as harmless. But she knew his insecurities now, knew how he thought of himself as unintelligent.

I'm a fool. A pretty but dim bulb.

She didn't like it. He was smart and charming, absolutely gorgeous . . . what more could anyone want in a person? Why couldn't he recognize any of his good qualities, besides being good with women?

When he returned, she pointed to her list. "We are behind. Though we finished most of the two desserts, I had also hoped to get some work done on the vegetables, as well."

He perused the menu and ingredients. "Shall I hire more hands?"

"Can you find some kitchen staff on such short notice?"

"Of course." He flicked his finger over her cheek and came away with a tiny bit of custard. "I won't let you down." Holding his finger to his mouth, he slowly cleaned the thick cream off with his tongue.

Her reaction was instant. Tingles rippled down her legs, along her spine, while heat wrapped around her insides, stealing her breath and causing her nipples to stiffen. How did he manage it? In one second he turned her entire body liquid. "Kit," she whispered, not even sure if she was pleading with him to stop . . . or keep going.

Suddenly, he blinked, his expression wiping clean of any passion, any teasing. It was as if the entire thing never happened. "Sorry. Old habit." He thrust his hands into his trouser pockets and leaned against the counter. "Shall we get you in the carriage?"

She couldn't answer, her body still buzzing. Every cell inside her remembered him and craved more. There was no pretending they hadn't kissed, hadn't tasted each other's skin in Newport. They had, and she desperately wanted to again. It was practically all she could think about.

I know I said we shouldn't but it's killing me to resist him.

They were alone in the kitchen. Carpenters had been in and out of the main room throughout the day, but they'd left almost an hour ago.

No one was in the building save her and Kit.

He watched her carefully, his gaze wary. Desire had darkened his eyes and his cheeks were slightly flushed. He held himself stiffly, hands in his pockets, as if he was afraid of what would happen if he didn't keep them hidden away.

My cock is hard all the time for you.

He wanted her.

She didn't know why or even how, but this beautiful man wanted her. It defied logic, but she wasn't about to complain. And the reasons for keeping her distance from him no longer seemed important.

I'll find a husband when this is over. Starting Saturday, I swear.

Lifting her hand, she placed it on his chest, right over his heart. The muscle pounded beneath her fingertips, strong and true, with the heat coming off him like a jolt of electricity to her core.

He didn't move. "Alice, what are you doing?"

"I think you owe me for my services today." The words came out in a teasing, flirtatious voice that hardly sounded like her own.

His lips parted on a quick intake of breath. "And what do you want in exchange?"

"I'm not certain. Perhaps something old. Perhaps something new."

The edge of his hip nearly touched her stomach as he shifted closer, his shoe scraping on the tile floor. "I have fond memories of old, but I'd love to explore this idea of new. Care to elaborate?"

She shook her head, incapable of putting any of her thoughts into words, not when her skin crawled with anticipation and need and wanting, so much so that she could nearly taste it.

"Does this mean you leave it up to me?" His mouth hitched. "Always a dangerous proposition, sweetheart."

The endearment sank inside her bones, melting them, and she clutched his vest in her fingers. "Will you kiss me already?"

"Still bossy." He slid a hand onto her hip and up her rib cage. When he cupped the back of her neck, he closed the distance between them. "I like it."

His mouth descended slowly, carefully, as if he

sensed how desperately she wanted the kiss and derived a perverse pleasure in denying her. Unfortunately, she didn't have much time.

This kissing business needed to get underway, now.

Rising up on her toes, she met him the rest of the way, her mouth covering his, and a resulting tremor went through him. Then he kissed her back, taking over and pushing her toward the counter. Her heartbeat pounded in her ears as she dug in, clinging to him like a raft in a churning sea. His tongue plunged into her mouth, seeking and stroking, their soft grunts and pants melding together in a frenzy. He surrounded her, hands roaming her back as her arms wound around his neck, their bodies nearly flush.

He kissed her like he couldn't get enough. Like air was overrated and unnecessary. Like he was starving for her. This was no practiced seduction or flirting. This was Kit wild with passion. Wild for *her*.

And she loved it.

Breaking off, he kissed her jaw, her neck, then bit her earlobe. She gasped, the pain like an electric shock that ran to her nipples and between her legs. He licked the flesh, as if to soothe it. "How much time do you have?"

"How much time do you need?"

He chuckled darkly. "I'll keep you all night, if you let me."

She shivered. *If only.* The clock showed almost four o'clock. Her maid would return at five. "Thirty minutes, I think."

His teeth scraped over her throat. "Perfect. I only need ten, perhaps fifteen."

"For what?"

"You'll see. Come with me." Taking her hand, he led her into the main room, where they dodged the tables and chairs until they reached a door. Kit turned the knob and held it open for her.

It was an office, with a desk, two chairs, a sideboard and sofa. "Sit," he said, and pointed to the sofa. Then he shut the door, locking it behind him.

Oh.

Stomach fluttering, she lowered herself onto the sofa and watched as Kit stripped out of his coat. After tossing it onto an armchair, he removed his cuff links. Then he began rolling his sleeves up, never taking his eyes off her. His lids were heavy, his gaze dark. "Do you trust me?"

Why did he keep asking her that question?

"Of course. Would I be here otherwise?"

"I want to make you feel good. And I promise, it will leave your innocence intact."

"Kissing, then."

He pursed his lips and raked her body with a hot look. "Definitely kissing, but not on your mouth."

Where, her neck? Her chest? Her *breasts*?

She swallowed. *He wants you to agree. He wants you willing.* Really, it was an easy decision. Another chance like this might not come around again, not with Kit. Tomorrow, the kitchen would be full of assistants and too many tasks to name. Friday, as well. Then the event was over and she wouldn't see him again. She'd return to her boring parties in a quest for a husband.

Refusing this opportunity would be unforgivable. "All right."

Relief flashed over his face before he approached the sofa. "I was truly hoping you'd say that." He slid next to her and quickly took her mouth once more. She relaxed into him, meeting the bold strokes of his tongue with her own, her lips and hands greedy for everything he gave her.

When they were both panting minutes later, he cupped her jaw and studied her face. "I want to lift your skirts and touch between your legs."

She blinked. Was this how his liaisons went, with him telegraphing every move in explicit detail?

No. He's doing this so he doesn't scare you.

Oh. Of course. "All right."

He bent to touch his forehead to hers. "I am rushing you. I just . . . God, Alice. I want to give you everything, show you everything, but I know I haven't the right."

"Kit." She wrapped her fingers around his wrists. "You're wasting time."

He sucked in a breath, surprised. "So I'm not rushing you?"

"Actually," she said with a small, albeit nervous laugh, "I am rushing you because I need to leave in a few minutes."

His knuckles brushed the underside of her jaw. "Clever, inquisitive Alice. You are going to be the death of me." Without awaiting a response, he kissed her again, fiercer this time, and her nerves disappeared like a block of ice on a hot day.

She could do this for hours, just lose herself in

this man. An elevated train could rush through the room, clacking over its iron rails, and she wouldn't budge. Kit was all she could see and feel, her entire world at the moment, and she loved it. There were no parents or future husbands right now, no dicing or chopping or mixing. Just the two of them and these kisses.

"Have you ever made yourself come?"

"I . . ." She couldn't think when he was nibbling on the sensitive skin behind her ear, his hand nearly brushing the underside of her breast. "Hmm?"

"Do you pleasure yourself?"

Closing her eyes, she gave him the truth. "Yes."

"Thank God. That will make this easier." He reached down and began lifting the front of her skirts, while continuing to lick and kiss her throat. She dropped her head onto the sofa back with a small moan. The place between her legs pulsed in time with her heartbeat and she craved attention there. Needed it. If she'd been alone, she would have lifted her skirts, as well.

When he got the fabric high enough, he slipped his hand underneath and found the center of her through her drawers. Two fingers traced the feminine folds and she eased her legs apart as best she could. He groaned and sank his teeth into her skin. "You are so wet. So hot. God, Alice."

He skimmed her flesh with his fingertips, teasing her with long sweeps determined to drive her out of her skin. Clearly, he was in no hurry whatsoever to move things along. "Kit," she breathed, her body restless under his attentions.

"I know. I'm getting there. Kiss me," he demanded, and shifted his mouth to hers, where their lips collided in a maelstrom of teeth and tongues, hunger and longing. Then his fingers rubbed that tiny knot atop her sex, the one where every nerve seemed to be centered, and she jumped.

"Is this all right?" His voice was silk and sin. "If you don't like it, just tell me." He did it again, then paused. "So do you like it?"

Her eyes nearly rolled back in her head. "I would like it more if you kept going."

Chapter Seventeen

❧

What he was doing was reckless and unwise, but Kit couldn't seem to stop. Alice's mouth was warm and plush, her tongue smooth and eager, and his fingers were exploring the slickness between her thighs. In short, he was in heaven.

He loved the way she responded to him. There was no artifice; Alice wasn't experienced enough to fake her reactions. She clawed and mewled and strained to get closer, her hips seeking his hand as he stroked her clitoris. It was the most arousing thing he'd ever witnessed.

He wanted to give her this. Needed to give her this. Her first orgasm by a hand that wasn't her own, and he would watch as she fell apart. Only one thing could make this better.

Breaking from her mouth, he eased off the couch and knelt on the floor. She tracked him with wild eyes now bright with desire. "What are you doing?"

"I am replacing my hand with my mouth."

When her thighs instinctively closed, he shifted her legs apart and slipped between them. Her knees hugged his ribs but she didn't try to cover herself. "I don't understand."

"You will understand in a few seconds. If you don't like it, I'll stop." Not once had a woman rejected Kit's tongue on her pussy, but it could happen. And Alice was a virgin. Kit had no experience with innocents other than Alice. Women of her class were taught that sexual relations were dirty and base, that only men should ever find pleasure in the act. So, this could be more than she was ready for.

But he didn't think so. No, he had a strong suspicion his pupil would love it.

He pushed her skirts higher, up toward her waist, revealing drawers of plain cream cotton with only light blue silk ribbons for embellishment. The slit in the cloth revealed her sex, now glistening with her arousal, and the sight and smell nearly caused him to spend in his trousers. He was so hard it felt as if the skin surrounding his cock might split open. "You're beautiful," he whispered.

He reached under her thighs and pulled her forward, closer to his mouth, then studied her face. Her eyes were glazed but unafraid. Bending closer to her pussy, he said, "Put your hand on the back of my head."

"Why?" Her voice was thin and breathy, and it sent more lust cascading through him.

"If you don't like it, push me away or tell me to stop. If you like it, however, do the exact opposite." Fuck, the idea of Alice holding on to him, smashing his face closer to her quim, was almost too much to bear.

Her hand touched the crown of his head and

delicate fingers threaded his hair. When he was certain she was ready, he angled forward and nuzzled her, inhaling and letting the rich feminine scent fill his lungs. *Goddamn.* He wanted to coat his face and tongue, drown in her until they were both holding on for dear life.

Then he dedicated himself to the task. There wasn't much time, and having her orgasm on his tongue felt essential to his mental well-being. He kissed her gently, getting her used to the feel of his lips on her intimate flesh. She twitched, her fingers flexing atop his head as if she wasn't quite sure yet what to make of it. Increasing the pressure, he gave her deeper kisses, worshipping her, not leaving any bit of her unexplored. Her lips parted as she panted, the sound of her breath mixing with the lewd smacks of Kit's mouth.

Had she any clue as to how enticing she was? She was the perfect combination of innocent and daring, pure and sinful. Alice made a man want to protect her, even as he was wrecking her for all other men.

Kit wished to corrupt her, draw out her inner siren, while still leaving her an angel.

Groaning, he spread her thighs farther apart and licked her opening, the moisture coating his tongue. He savored it, shutting his eyes and feasting on her as if this were his last meal on earth. She was delicious, warm and slippery, and he couldn't resist thrusting his tongue inside her channel, spearing her. Alice gasped, so he did it again and again until she rocked her hips to meet him.

Aware of the time, he swept his tongue along her seam and began laving her swollen clitoris. After a few swipes, her muscles clenched and her fingers clutched his hair, tugging ever so slightly. He reveled in the reaction, his fearless pupil demanding her pleasure, and he rewarded her by sucking the tiny bud into his mouth, focusing all his efforts on that one spot.

"Oh, my God," she wheezed. "Oh, Kit."

The words were almost his undoing, but he ignored the pounding lust in his groin that demanded release. He could come later, just as soon as he'd put her in the carriage. For now, he licked and sucked using this teeth, tongue and mouth until her thighs began shaking. His gaze shot up to her face, not wanting to miss her reaction, so he saw the instant the pleasure overtook her. Never had he beheld a more beautiful sight. Her body seized, lids flying open as she stared at him in a mixture of shock and astonishment, as a long moan rumbled out of her chest. Limbs trembling, she held on to his hair, not letting go for a second as the release went on and on.

When she relaxed, he eased off her clit and allowed himself one more swirl of the slick gathered at her entrance. This final taste would need to last him for the rest of his days, a pleasant memory he would relive over and over when Alice soon married someone else.

Pressing a kiss to her mound, he straightened. The need to free his cock and stroke himself was so raw, so consuming, that he almost gave in to it. Yet, scaring Alice hadn't been his goal. Pleasing her was all that mattered.

"I . . ." She swallowed hard. "I had no idea."

"Was it all right?"

"Could you not tell?"

He could, but he wanted her to express her reaction, share more of what was inside that gorgeous head of hers. "I have an idea but I'd rather hear what you think."

"That was amazing. Like nothing I could have imagined. If men are capable of *that*, how do wives ever get any work done?"

He threw his head back and barked a laugh. Christ, this woman. "They return the favor," he said.

"Oh." Her tongue darted out to swipe across her lips. "Do you . . . ?"

God, how he wished they had the time. He'd give almost anything to see Alice's lips wrapped around his cock. "That's not necessary. Let's get you in a carriage and back to the hotel."

He started to rise, but she put a hand on his arm. "Kit, thank you."

The gratitude in her voice caused something to unfurl in his chest, like his heart was plumping up, doubling in size. If it were possible, he'd shower her with affection every day to receive such sincere appreciation. He leaned in and pressed a soft kiss to her mouth, which she returned in kind, apparently not minding that he smelled and tasted like her.

When they broke apart, he checked the clock. "It's half past four. Time to go, sweetheart."

Within seconds she smoothed her skirts and tucked her hair back in place. He took her hand and led her out of his office and into the club. After she visited the washroom to freshen up, they crossed the floor. The workers had departed, the finishing touches almost complete, so there was no one to see as he gave Alice a leisurely kiss at the door. They were both breathing heavily when he pulled away. "There. That's a proper goodbye."

Her fingers caressed his jaw. "I'll see you in the morning."

Yes, she would, but they wouldn't be alone. This was the last time that would happen, and he already regretted sharing her tomorrow and Friday. Part of him wanted to keep this competent and clever creature his secret. But she wasn't for him. She would marry a proper husband from a good family and settle into a life of monotony and monogamy—two nouns that would never apply to Kit.

Lifting her hand, he ignored the ache in his chest and kissed her knuckles. "Come on. Let me help you inside the carriage."

IT WAS HIGHLY likely that Alice was infatuated with Christopher Ward.

She couldn't believe her stupidity. All along, she knew having feelings for Kit was a terrible idea. His position on marriage had been made perfectly clear and, even if he was interested in marriage, he could have any woman in New York. Why would he ever settle for *her*?

She had to snap out of this, shake some sense into herself before it was too late. The goal was to find a suitable husband, fast. Enduring another season with her mother at her side was as appealing as week-old bread. The first two had been bad enough. A third would sink her.

Shifting on the carriage seat, she marveled at what happened in the club's tiny office moments ago. Heat washed across her skin like bathwater, and she bit her lip, remembering. It had felt unlike anything she could have dreamed, much more intense than any of her own explorations, as if Kit had thrown a switch to electrify her entire body, with all the pleasure centered in that one spot.

She would never forget it. There was every chance she would blush for the entire day tomorrow, but the embarrassment was worth it. Not every debutante received such an education from a master.

With one smile, he manages to turn even the shyest woman into a vixen.

Was there any doubt left as to why?

However, allowing more lessons only meant allowing her feelings for him to deepen and solidify. Soon she'd drown in feelings, unable to climb out of the emotional chasm before heartbreak wrecked her life. That could not happen. She needed to remain practical about these things, keep her eye on the future—*her* future—and bear in mind her two priorities: to find a husband who wanted her, not merely her dowry, and to start a new life to please herself—instead of pleasing her mother.

An obsession with Kit would place all those goals in jeopardy.

Keep pushing forward. Put yourself first.

The carriage pulled up to the hotel, across the street from Madison Square. There was the usual late-afternoon hustle and bustle out front as guests arrived and departed. The hotel was one of the best known in the city, popular with dignitaries from around the world and local politicians.

After she disembarked, she snuck into the kitchen,

which was busy in anticipation of dinner service. No one paid her a bit of attention, and she soon was climbing the staff stairs to the fifth floor. Her maid would return any minute, so Alice needed to get into her room and make it appear as if she'd been there all day.

The corridor was quiet, so she lifted her skirts and hurried to her room. When she turned the corner, she skidded to a halt.

The Duke of Lockwood was outside her door.

At the sound, he turned and blinked at the sight of her. "Miss Lusk. I knocked on your door." He gestured to the wood as if to illustrate his point. "They told me downstairs that you were here."

"I was. I mean, I am." She took several steps forward and tried to calm her racing heart. "I went to the kitchen to fetch tea."

Frowning, he glanced at her empty hands and then looked behind her. "I would have assumed your maid would take care of tasks such as that."

"I gave her the day off. She wanted to visit the Central Park Menagerie, and there was no need for both of us to sit in a boring hotel room all day." Lord, what was he doing here? She twisted her fingers in her skirts, hoping to hide her nerves.

"Then my visit is well-timed, I hope. Would you care to take a drive in the park with me?"

"Now?"

"Yes—or any other day. I realize this is a bit forward of me, springing it on you like this but—"

"Yes," she blurted. This was her chance. To forget Kit, to pursue a husband. To know her own worth. "I mean, I'd be honored, Your Grace."

Lockwood smiled, his handsome face easing.

"Excellent. Do you need to fetch anything before we set off?"

She must look a rumpled mess. "I'll just need a moment to fetch a hat."

Five minutes later, she emerged, more put together and ready to depart. "There, now I am ready."

The duke pushed off the wall where he'd been waiting and strode toward her, all athletic grace and male confidence. Lockwood was stalwart and steadfast, with hundreds of years of breeding and expectation heaped on those perfectly square shoulders. He was a lion . . . whereas Kit was more like a panther. A very enticing panther that would lead you—

She forced those thoughts aside. This was about an outing with a duke, a man who actually wanted a wife, not a confirmed bachelor. She would not think of Kit any more today.

Lockwood called the elevator and folded his hands behind his back as they waited. "Did you enjoy the rest of the opera the other night?"

"I did. You?"

"A bit more than the first half, I admit. It was very kind of you to visit me. The whispers and stares had grown quite tedious."

Because of the broken engagement. "Society will recover. Another scandal will undoubtedly soon take its place."

The passenger elevator arrived and the iron door slid open to reveal an empty car, except for the operator. "Good evening," the older man said as she and Lockwood boarded. "Oh, Miss Lusk. Nice to see you."

"Hello, Charlie."

"Where are you off to today?"

"Ground floor," Lockwood said. With a nod, Charlie closed the door and turned the switch. The elevator began its descent.

"How is your wife?" she asked the operator. "Not still fighting a cold, I hope."

"No, she's all better, miss. Thank you for inquiring."

They arrived at the lobby and Charlie opened the doors. Lockwood gestured for her to exit, and as she passed, Charlie whispered, "You be careful now, miss."

She smiled. "I will. Thank you, Charlie."

Lockwood presented his arm. As they crossed the white-and-red marble floor, many heads swiveled their way. She waved to the manager, Mr. McMahon, who was behind the counter. "They look out for you, don't they?" the duke asked.

"I suppose so. I've stayed here many times. They're used to me."

"I have been staying here since February and I haven't learned their names."

He had? Why hadn't she seen him here? "What floor?"

"My suites are on the first floor. The Twenty-Third Street side."

The porter held open the door, and she and Lockwood descended the steps to the walk. "The carriage is there." He pointed to a sleek black open-air carriage at the curb. Nerves bubbled in her belly as he guided her over. There was no hiding while traveling in this conveyance. This outing was almost as if . . .

As if Lockwood wished to court her.

She drew in a deep breath. Could this really be happening? The duke was a constant topic of discussion in drawing rooms all across the city, which meant news of this drive would travel quickly. Even if he wasn't intending to court her, Alice's social stock would climb several points just from being seen with him.

Which sounded callous, yet that was the way of these things. Society judged a woman by the company she kept, hence the bevy of callers at Mrs. Astor's house each afternoon. They were all clamoring for the right attention from the right people as a way to guarantee acceptance. Alice had never breached this upper echelon of High Society. Her mother wasn't well liked and Alice hadn't fallen in with the right crowd of debutantes. Instead, she'd remained on the outskirts, biding her time and waiting for someone to notice her.

Perhaps someone finally had.

She cast a surreptitious glance at Lockwood as he handed her up into the carriage. Classically handsome, people said about him. One of the houseguests in Newport suggested he had a face that belonged on coins. Alice didn't care about looks as much as finding a man who was kind. Thoughtful and caring. Someone who made her laugh. A cruel husband would be worse than none at all. So, what kind of man was the Duke of Lockwood?

They settled on the seat, with Lockwood pressed tight to her right side. The June air was warm but not stifling and there was a soft breeze. The wheels began turning, taking them uptown toward the park.

"How is your mother?" he asked. "I trust she is well."

"She's in Boston. My father asked her to come home for a few days."

"And she left you alone?" His voice sharpened with disapproval. "That hardly seems appropriate. Or safe."

"As you saw, everyone in the hotel watches out for me. I'm in no danger."

"That is ridiculous. An elevator operator or domestic won't protect you in the corridors or, God forbid, if someone breaks into your room."

He genuinely seemed concerned about her safety, which touched her. "I keep my door locked at all times and never open it to a stranger. And my maid is there, of course."

"She wasn't around today, and I found you wandering the halls."

Was he worried she was engaged in scandalous behavior? Of course, she had been an hour ago . . . but that was a rarity. Alice wasn't like Maddie—or worse, Nellie Young. She wasn't a rule-breaker. Propriety was of the utmost importance to a duke, so she must impress on him her understanding of the conventions. "Your Grace, I am not one to spit in the eye of etiquette. I would never risk my safety—or my reputation."

"I should hope not," he said, his gaze fixed on the street. "Will your mother be angry you went on a drive with me without her supervision?"

Alice couldn't help it. She laughed. "No. I daresay she'll jump for joy when she learns of it."

"Fair enough. I am surprised she left, though. By all accounts, she is quite protective of you."

"My father needed her and she never refuses him. He rarely asks her for anything."

"My mother was much the same way." His expression turned wistful. "When my father was alive, they were practically inseparable."

"Is she still with us?"

"Indeed, she is. Living in London and haranguing me about grandchildren."

She smiled, imagining this poor man enduring a mother anxious for grandbabies. "I suppose every mother of an unmarried duke feels the same."

"Perhaps, but mine is especially concerned, seeing as how I am an only child."

"Ah. The heir and all that."

His mouth tightened ever so slightly. "Exactly."

"Does it bother you? The pressure, I mean. The weight of the title and carrying on the legacy?"

He blew out a long breath. "I'd be lying if I said no. I certainly wouldn't be in America otherwise. There are a hundred tasks awaiting me back in England, not the least of which is a leaky roof on the estate in Yorkshire."

Which was why he needed to quickly marry an heiress.

And unless Alice managed to screw things up on this outing, there was a chance that heiress might be her.

Chapter Eighteen

❧

The shabby boardinghouse was hardly a high-end residence. Men loitered on the stoop as night approached, their clothes tattered, bottles in hand, while they argued with one another and cussed at the pedestrians on the walk. Kit frowned. Forrest Ripley had more money than most men in the city. Why on earth was he staying here?

Kit hadn't seen his friend since their dinner in April, little more than two months ago. Forrest arrived drunk and finished three whiskeys before the first course was even served. The night had gone downhill from there. At the end of the meal, a waiter helped Kit carry Forrest to the carriage, and Kit drove his friend home. Not long after, Preston took Forrest to the Adirondacks to dry him out, but Forrest escaped and ran off to Chicago.

They all had demons—Kit, Harrison, Preston and Forrest. None of them had families to brag about, and some scars never healed. It was what drew the four of them together in college, made them such close friends. However, Forrest had taken a turn in the last six months, going from a man who liked to drink to a man who insisted on staying drunk. Kit was worried.

He bounded up the steps, ignoring the jeers and comments from the ne'er-do-wells as he crossed into the dim vestibule. The attendant behind the counter looked asleep, his head resting on the wood. Something crawled on the floor near Kit's foot. Yelping, he jumped out of the way, which startled the man awake. The attendant dragged bleary eyes over Kit's frame. "We're all booked up."

"I don't need a room. I am trying to find Mr. Forrest Ripley." He slid a few bills across the desk.

"Don't get a lotta names around here. He the fancy gent?"

Kit wasn't certain, but odds were against another man on the premises possessing anything close to Forrest's wealth. "Yes."

"Number 208."

With a nod, Kit went up the thin stairs, taking care to avoid the steps with fresh stains. Loud moans wafted out from behind door 202, and a bed frame slapped the wall rhythmically inside 206. A heated argument was taking place on the floor above. Kit put his ear to the door of 208 but couldn't hear any noise from within. He knocked loudly.

Nothing.

Pounding with his fist, he called, "Forrest, open up. It's Kit." When another minute went by, Kit tried again. "Open this damn door, Ripley, or I'm going to break it down."

Metal springs squeaked and a few seconds later the lock disengaged. The door cracked open and

Forrest's gaunt face appeared. "What do you want, Kit?"

His friend looked . . . terrible. Utterly wrecked. Like he'd aged ten years in two months. His skin was wrinkled and dry, with a yellow tint to it—unless that was the gaslight playing tricks on Kit's eyes. The smell of body odor and whiskey hit Kit's nose like a punch and sent him reeling back a step.

He breathed through his mouth and pointed to the small room. "May I come in?"

With a shrug, Forrest retreated and left the door open. Kit entered, immediately went to the window and threw up the sash to let in air. The small room was dirty, with empty bottles everywhere, even on the floor. A few slices of moldy bread rested on the wooden table.

Forrest dropped onto the bed and stretched out. "I was napping. So just say whatever you need to say and get out."

Where was this hostility coming from? There hadn't been any animosity during their last dinner. Kit dragged the rickety wooden chair in the corner closer to the bed. "I see you are back in town."

His friend's eyes were closed. "Yep."

"Were you going to let us know?"

A horrible rattling sound echoed in Forrest's chest, and he coughed for a long minute. "There's no need, not when Preston is having me followed."

Ah, so Forrest knew about the Pinkertons. "What else were we supposed to do? You snuck out of Preston's lodge in the middle of the night last month. We had no idea where you were."

"All I recall is waking up there and he'd taken the liquor out of the house."

"Why did you go to Chicago?"

He yawned. "Can't remember."

Jesus. "Well, then why did you come back to New York?"

"What difference does it make? I'm here now, so you can stop badgering me and leave me alone."

"I can't do that. Not until you tell me what is going on. Why are you staying in this shithole?"

Forrest struggled to a sitting position, his eyes suddenly more alert. "What's with all the questions? Fuck, let's open a bottle, Kit. You were always good for a party."

"I'd rather talk to you and find out what is wrong. This isn't like you."

"Of course it is. You and me, we both like to drink. We screwed women and drank bourbon almost every night during college, remember? Those were good times."

Yes, but they weren't in college any longer. And Forrest's drinking had accelerated far beyond the point of a casual night out with friends. "Forrest, help me understand. Because I'm struggling not to load you into a carriage and take you home."

"Home," he sneered. "That isn't my home anymore. They don't want me there, they never have. I'll never go back to that house."

Forrest hadn't shared much in recent years about his family, but he and his father never got along. As the only boy, Forrest had shouldered quite a bit of responsibility from an early age. When one of his sisters died in her early teens, everything at home had worsened. Mr. Ripley had pressured Forrest to go into law and take over the family business, but

Forrest hated the idea. He'd gone for a philosophy degree instead and his father never forgave him.

"A hospital, then."

"Jesus Christ, not you, too? You sound like Preston. I don't need a goddamn hospital."

"Then let me take you to the Fifth Avenue Hotel. The staff is first rate."

"I'm perfectly fine here. I like it. There's always someone to keep me company."

In other words, there was always someone with whom to drink. Kit shook his head. "It's not safe. And you need a bath."

Forrest fell back on the bed and threw an arm over his eyes. "When did you become such a nag? Where has fun Kit gone, the one who likes a party and entertaining a willing woman?"

He still liked those things. Just not all the time. "I'm still fun, but some of us have responsibilities. We cannot drink ourselves stupid in seedy boardinghouses."

Instead of being offended, Forrest laughed. "You, responsibilities? Like what?"

"I'm opening a supper club with Preston, for one."

"What is that, like a restaurant?"

"Sort of."

A dismissive grunt emerged from Forrest's throat. "You don't have a head for business. You would have failed economics in school if you hadn't fucked the professor's wife."

Kit hadn't fucked Mrs. Boswell. He might have flirted with her, but he generally didn't sleep with married women. However, that wasn't the part of

Forrest's reaction that bothered Kit the most. "I might not have a head for business, but Preston does. I'm handling everything else."

"And how long's that going to last before you get bored and move on? You've never stayed with anything for longer than a month or two."

The barb struck home, especially when Kit recalled how he'd panicked on Preston earlier today, insisting they sell the supper club or give it away. The shame of that, combined with frustration toward the man lying on the bed, transformed into white-hot anger. "Fuck you, Forrest. Thanks for having confidence in me."

"Like you've always had in me? You're the one here telling me I cannot look after myself. So fuck *you*, Kit."

"If you could see yourself at the moment, you'd be worried, too. When was the last time you ate something?"

"Today? Yesterday? And don't act like you care. I've hardly seen you this year. You and Preston both think you're too good for me."

Where was this coming from? They had seen each other at least once a month until Forrest disappeared. "Forrest, that isn't true. I apologize if I haven't been a good friend to you lately, but I'll do better. Why don't we get you cleaned up and I'll take you out to dinner?"

"Sounds like a fine idea. I'm too tired today. How about tomorrow?"

"All right. I'll come by around seven o'clock. We'll go to Sherry's. You always liked their steak."

Forrest smiled as he rolled onto his side, his eyes still closed. "Thanks, Kit. You're a gem."

Kit sighed and took another glance around. He'd have some food delivered in the meantime, and perhaps some clothing. This situation was beyond grim. In fact, Kit was reluctant to leave.

He looked down at his friend, who appeared to be sleeping. Kit stroked his jaw and decided he and Preston would have a very serious conversation with Forrest tomorrow. Something had to be done.

THE CLUB'S KITCHEN was already bursting with activity by the time Alice arrived. As promised, Kit had found assistants for the preparatory work they'd discussed last night before she left. Unfortunately, he was nowhere to be found, so she wrapped an apron around herself and went to check on everyone's work.

"Hello," she said to an older woman dicing onions. "I'm Alice Lusk."

The woman looked up from her work. She wore a purple day dress with an apron tied over it. "A pleasure to meet you, Miss Lusk. I'm Mrs. Henry, Mr. Ward's cook."

Kit had brought his own cook? That clever man. She smiled at Mrs. Henry. "Thank you for coming. I'm grateful you're here to help. You undoubtedly know more about food than I do."

"Well, that's kind of you to say, but I've never worked in a fancy restaurant. My cooking's for a family, not High Society."

"I haven't worked in a fancy restaurant, either, so we'll muddle through together as best we can. How long have you been in Mr. Ward's employ?"

Mrs. Henry put down her knife and wiped her

hands on a towel. "Let's see. Four years now this past May. Mr. Ward hired me from his parents' house, and I was there six."

"You've known him a long time, then."

"I have, indeed. A rascal, that one. Like a Labrador. He's got a lot of energy but he's loyal, you know?"

Alice's lips twitched. "I do know. Thank you for coming today. I never would have been able to do this alone."

"Oh, I'd do anything for Mr. Ward. Besides, this is a nice change of pace. I normally just cook for him and the other staff. And my children, of course." She pointed to the other two occupants of the kitchen. "Over there is my fourteen-year-old daughter, Opal." She pointed to a young girl peeling potatoes. "And that is my seventeen-year-old boy, Sam." At the sink stood a young man rinsing lettuce.

"You brought your family," Alice said. "I'm honored. Thank you, Opal and Sam." They smiled at her and nodded.

"They know their way around a kitchen," Mrs. Henry said. "They've been helping me out since they could walk. You just tell us what to do. Mr. Ward said you were quite accomplished."

Kit, always the charmer. "Well, I won't distract you from dicing the onions. Will you mince some, as well, please?"

"I will, miss."

The three of them got to work. Mrs. Henry hadn't lied—Opal and Sam were extremely competent assistants. Sam deboned chicken and made stock, while Opal washed and chopped vegetables. Alice and Mrs. Henry tackled some of the more complicated sauces and compotes. Kit poked his head in once or twice, checking in on everyone, and he brought them all a lunch of meats, cheeses and bread from a German restaurant down the block.

Alice could hardly look him in the eye. She kept recalling what happened in the tiny office yesterday, how he'd licked between her legs . . . sucking and kissing her . . . and her stomach flipped. Who would have dreamed such a thing existed between lovers? And that both of them would enjoy it as much as they had?

It didn't mean anything, however. Just another lesson. She couldn't read more into it.

The kitchen door swung open as Alice kneaded dough for the dinner rolls. "Miss Lusk, a moment?" Kit asked.

Her stomach went flying once more, but she tried to keep her composure. "Opal, would you mind taking over the kneading? About five more minutes should do it."

Opal came over and Alice shook out her arms as she walked out of the kitchen. Kneading bread was hard work. Kit was standing near the bar. "Yes?"

Without speaking, he took her hand and led her to the tiny office. When the door closed, he pushed her against the door, his long body caging her in. Dark eyes studied her face. "I cannot stand it. I am trying to stay out of your way but having you so close is driving me mad."

She bit her lip. "You may come into the kitchen and help."

"If I do, I won't be able to keep my hands off you. There's something about you in a kitchen, in command and so dashed smart, that gets me hard."

"Kit!"

"I can't help it, Alice. Are you flattered or embarrassed?"

She wasn't certain. "Both, I think, but I must return. I cannot leave Mrs. Henry and her children to do all the work. Incidentally, you are compensating them, I hope."

"Of course. With money for all three and time off for Mrs. Henry next week. Kiss me, Alice."

"We shouldn't." Though she wanted to. More than anything. "Later. When we're finished."

"I have a dinner tonight, so I'm leaving shortly."

"Oh." Her stomach deflated. He was taking someone out for dinner. Of course he was seeing other women, like the woman at the opera, so this shouldn't surprise or bother her. Yet, it did.

"A friend, Alice." He slid a finger under her chin and lifted her face. His gaze was earnest, unflinching. "A male friend. Forrest Ripley. I've known him forever."

"I assumed it was the woman from the opera."

Stepping back, he dragged a hand through his dark hair. "No. I didn't . . . that is, I am not seeing anyone."

This made no sense. During the house party, she'd asked him not to, but they weren't in Newport any longer. "Why?"

"Do you want me to?"

"It's not up to me. I assumed you would return to your life once we were back in New York."

"Alice, answer the question. Do you want me to?"

"I . . . don't know." A bit hypocritical of her to demand his attention when she'd gone driving with Lockwood yesterday afternoon. "I want you to be happy."

Putting a hand on the door above her head, he leaned in. "I am happy. I'm especially happy when you let me drag you in here so that I may lick your pussy."

"That happened once," she whispered, staring at his collar stud as her skin went up in flames. "And you shouldn't say such things aloud. Someone might overhear you."

He tucked a strand of hair behind her ear. "Will you let me do it again? It's all I can think about."

It's all I can think about, as well.

"Kit . . ." Her heart pounded in a frantic rhythm as blood rushed to her lower half. "We shouldn't."

"And when has that ever stopped you, my star pupil?" He dragged a fingertip over her shirtwaist, along her collarbone, over the edge of her corset, her sternum, until he reached her stomach. "I need to taste you again."

She was panting, boneless against the wood at her back. "I have to go."

"Think about it. Tomorrow night, after the dinner."

"Won't you be celebrating with Preston and your staff?"

"I want to celebrate with you. In here. Just you and me."

"You know I cannot stay out all night. My maid—"

"Will be told that you are ill and do not wish to be bothered until Saturday morning."

"Oh, is that so?"

"Please, Alice." He bent and kissed her throat,

then put his lips by her ear. "I want to thank you properly after everyone leaves."

She shivered, sensation nearly overwhelming her. "What if tomorrow night is a failure?"

"Then we'll commiserate together." He pressed a quick kiss to her lips and walked to the desk. "Now, I have a meeting with Preston and the club's manager. So unless you plan to be found here, blushing like a schoolgirl—"

Alice lunged for the latch and hurried out the door. Patting her cheeks, she tried to regain her composure before returning to the kitchen. No need for everyone to know she'd nearly allowed herself to be ravished in Kit's office.

You should not stay late tomorrow. Kit will break your heart if you let him.

Logically, she knew this. But the desire coursing through her veins was telling a different story, one that spoke of limited opportunity and life-long memories. Her mother returned on Saturday. Another chance like this would not present itself again.

One more time with Kit wouldn't hurt. Would it? She could have fun with him tomorrow night and keep her heart intact.

Yes, she definitely could.

Chapter Nineteen

✑

In his office, Kit went over the plan for tomorrow night's event once more. "To summarize, cocktails begin at seven. We have two attendants taking hats and canes as the gentlemen arrive, then four waiters for drinks. Everyone will sit at eight, when the dinner service starts. Madame Durham will begin performing while the men are eating, around half past eight. No plates will be cleared until Madame Durham finishes. Then dessert is served."

"Understood," said Louis, the club's manager. "I'll ensure the waiters are prepared."

Preston stubbed out his cigarette in the crystal dish on Kit's desk. "I still cannot believe you convinced Madame Durham to sing." He shook his head. "She is practically American operatic royalty."

Kit was well aware. The first Black singer to headline at Carnegie Hall two years ago, Madame Durham had also performed for European princes and queens, as well as American politicians. Though she lived in Boston, she was in New York preparing for a performance at Madison Square

Garden. When Kit heard this, he'd used a former lover's connection to Andrew Carnegie to arrange a meeting with the famous soprano. Through charm, begging and offering a hefty fee, he convinced the singer to appear in the supper club for thirty minutes tomorrow night. "Yes, and I think her performance sets a tone about the egalitarian type of entertainment we intend to showcase with the club. Between Franconi's food and her singing, I think we will sell out our memberships."

"Here's hoping," Louis said. "Was there anything else, sir? Otherwise, I need to see about the wine changes we discussed."

"That's all. Thank you, Louis."

"You are welcome. Things certainly seem to be shaping up. Whatever was happening in the kitchen today smelled delicious."

"Indeed, it did."

Mrs. Henry and her children had left already, departing just a few minutes after Alice. The group had worked all afternoon, and Alice said they were caught up and tomorrow would go as expected. He had complete faith in her and Mrs. Henry.

"I have to say," Preston continued when they were alone. "I've known you for a long time and I am impressed. You've worked unbelievably hard on this."

"You act as if I've never worked hard on anything before."

One of Preston's brows arched. "Getting women into bed doesn't count."

"Please. I've never worked hard on that."

"Hmm. Speaking of working hard to get a woman into bed, how are things with the lovely Miss Lusk?"

"I am not trying to get her into bed."

Preston had the gall to laugh. "Sure."

"I cannot fuck her. She's a virgin and on a desperate hunt for a husband."

"Yes, and from what I've heard she may have found one."

"What does that mean?"

"Oh, haven't you heard the latest? You're usually up on all the society tittle-tattle."

There was gossip about Alice? "Tell me."

"Your dear little virgin went on a ride in the park yesterday with the duke."

The pencil in Kit's hand snapped in half. "Lockwood?"

"Yes."

Fuck. That arrogant bastard. How dare Lockwood try to woo Alice? Kit couldn't blame the duke—Alice was amazing in every way—but that didn't mean Kit had to like it. Lockwood and Alice had seemed quite chummy at the opera. Had they anything in common? Was the duke aware that she liked to cook and was very good at cards, at least Kit's version of cards?

"I see that news is sitting well," Preston said wryly. "What are you going to do about it?"

Pressing his palms deep into his eye sockets, Kit considered the question. Alice needed a husband and she wanted to marry for love. Was Lockwood a possibility? He'd have no problem finding a rich wife—nearly every unmarried girl in the city would swoon at the chance to become a duchess—

which meant Lockwood *liked* Alice. That something about her appealed to him.

So, what was Kit prepared to do? He couldn't marry her, that was clear, and preventing Lockwood from courting her was beyond cruel. If he wished the best for Alice—and he most definitely did—then he had to stop kissing and touching her. He had to let her go.

It was what he'd promised after the house party, yet he'd slid into familiar patterns the instant she reappeared in his life. He must show more resolve, more willpower. Stop dragging her into his office. Stop flirting. Stop thinking about her all the damn time. She deserved someone like Lockwood, as much as Kit hated to admit it. Alice deserved the world—a title, children, a doting husband. If Lockwood was willing, then Kit couldn't stand in the way.

"Nothing," he told Preston, and lowered his hands. "I'd be happy for her, if that's what she wants."

"Indeed." Preston cocked his head thoughtfully. "Wasn't the reaction I expected, but it's awfully noble of you."

"I am not the courting type. She needs to marry to get away from her mother, and England is a fine choice."

"You're not ready to settle down, even if it means losing her?"

Kit drummed his fingers on the desk. "I don't *have* her, so there is nothing to lose. And no, I have no interest in marriage. Just because Harrison is married doesn't mean I'm next. Why don't you marry?"

Preston's expression darkened, his brows pulling together. "My father already tried that, remember? Didn't work out for him."

"You never told me how you wiggled your way out of that."

"It's not important. I won't have him manipulating me ever again."

"Which is why you flaunt Arabella around town every chance you get. To drive a stake through the old man's heart."

Preston leaned back, his face clearing. "Revenge is only part of it. Mostly, I like Arabella's company."

"And her presence keeps the debutantes away."

Preston tapped his temple. "Now you're getting it." He pushed out of his chair. "Let's go round up Forrest. I'm anxious to knock some sense into him."

They left the office, their footsteps loud on the club's tile floor. Kit asked, "Did you go inside that boardinghouse? Did you see his room?"

"Yes, but he didn't answer the door. Did he answer for you?"

"He did, but only because I threatened to knock the door down if he didn't. You wouldn't believe what I saw in there. He looks terrible. Like he's aged ten years in two months."

"That's the drink. What else?"

"Smelled terrible, too, like he hadn't bathed in weeks. Clothes were dirty. The only food in the room was a few slices of moldy bread. Bottles everywhere. Nearly broke my heart."

"Jesus." Preston jammed a derby atop his head. "What did he say?"

"Argued with me. Accused me of not caring about him. Tried to get me to drink with him."

They went out the door and Kit locked up. Preston's carriage waited at the curb, so they piled inside and the wheels began to turn. Preston studied the silver knob atop his cane. "And he agreed to go to dinner with us?"

"It was his idea, in fact."

"We'll take him to your house and get him cleaned up. The two of you are roughly the same size, so he can borrow one of your evening suits."

They traveled south on Broadway to Twenty-Eighth Street, then started west. When they pulled up to the boardinghouse, the same men were out on the stoop, harassing the pedestrians again. Kit ignored them and went inside.

Preston ducked through the doorway, the tall bastard, and followed Kit up the stairs. Other than some murmuring, the hallway was quiet. Kit knocked on the door of 208. "Forrest, open up. It's Kit and Preston."

Nothing.

Preston pounded on the wood loudly. "Get up, man. Let's go. I'm starving."

There was no sound, no movement from the other side.

Kit turned the knob and was surprised to find the door unlocked. He peered inside . . . and found the room completely empty. No Forrest, no bottles. No moldy bread. The entire room had been cleared out. "What the hell?"

"Are you sure this is the right room?"

"Of course." He glanced at the other doors. "This was where he was staying."

"Did he switch rooms?"

"Let's go find out."

They asked some of the other tenants on the floor but no one claimed to have seen Forrest. Then they went downstairs and rang the bell on the counter until the attendant shuffled out from a back room. "What do you want?" the older man snarled, his eyes rimmed with red.

"The man in room 208," Kit asked. "Did he switch rooms?"

"No. Left in the middle of the night and hasn't come back."

"What do you mean left?" Preston snapped.

"Left, left. Moved out. Took off. Skipped out on his charges, too." The man spit onto the floor.

"You're sure he's not hiding out in another room?" Kit asked. "A friend, perhaps."

"People that live here don't have friends. Plus, the boys on the stoop said they saw him sneak out around two o'clock."

"How much does he owe you?" Preston reached into his inner coat pocket.

"Four dollars."

Preston dropped a sawbuck on the counter, along with his card. "There. Keep that, and if he returns, please call me. Day or night."

Kit produced a card, as well. "Or you can reach me. Either one of us."

The attendant pocketed the money and the cards. "This fellow important?"

"He's our friend," Kit answered, "and he might be in trouble."

Preston nudged Kit's shoulder. "Let's go outside." When they were on the walk, Preston searched up and down the street. "Where are they?"

A whistle pierced through the noise. Looking up,

Kit saw a man in a dark suit leaning out of a window across the street. He waved at Preston, who nodded and pointed to the walk. In a few seconds, the man was walking across the street to where Kit and Preston waited.

"Mr. Clarke," the man said. "All's quiet inside. Nothing out of the ordinary."

Preston folded his arms across his chest. "Who was watching overnight, Al?"

"Tom. He should be here in a few hours to relieve me. Why?"

"Because Mr. Ripley snuck out around two o'clock and yet Tom didn't follow him."

"Damn," Al said, grimacing. "Things were quiet today, but he usually keeps to his room. We don't hardly see him on the street."

"You need to find him. Get more men, if you need. I want him found, Al."

"Don't worry, Mr. Clarke. We'll track him down." Tipping his hat, he ran back to the house on the other side of the street.

Kit pinched the bridge of his nose between his thumb and forefinger. "Fuck. He could be anywhere."

"The Pinkertons will find him. Hopefully sooner rather than later, but they will find him."

"So, we do nothing?" Kit's shoulders sank, his stomach hollow. He hated feeling powerless. Shouldn't they be out searching, as well?

"We stay out of their way and let the detectives work. They know their business and this is why I am paying them a damn fortune." As usual, Preston was cool in a crisis, with no outward display of emotion of any kind. While anger burned in Kit's blood, Preston didn't even look perturbed. The influence of his father, no doubt, who was as cold and detached a man as Kit had ever seen.

"I'm worried." Kit thrust his hands in his pockets. Forrest had looked terrible. Did he even have cash? More clothes?

Preston gripped Kit's shoulder. "Me, too. But we can't do anything at the moment. Come on. I'll drive you home."

The ache in Kit's stomach compounded at the idea. The last thing he needed was to go home and brood about Forrest and Alice. Nothing could be done about either situation at the moment, and Kit needed a distraction from the hopelessness burning inside his chest. "Take me back to the club." At least there he could bury himself in work.

THE NEXT DAY, Alice was too busy to be nervous. If she stopped to think about how important the evening was to Kit, then she would never finish everything that still needed to be done. He'd hardly visited the kitchen, leaving Alice, Mrs. Henry and her children alone to work. No doubt he had many tasks awaiting him, as well, but Alice would have liked a little bit of his time. A minute or two, at least. But it almost seemed as if he was avoiding her.

Which was ridiculous. Kit wasn't like that. He was honest to a fault, a man without guile. Perhaps he was nervous about tonight. She'd speak to him after the evening ended, just to make certain.

In his office? Alone, just the two of you?

She bit her lip and continued to watch over the

lobsters steaming on the range. If they overcooked, the meat would turn tough and the lobster thermidor would be ruined. *No more thinking about Kit.*

The kitchen was hot and noisy. Dinner service would begin in three hours. In addition to the five waiters that would serve tonight, Kit had hired two people to help plate the food. Sam was currently shucking oysters and Opal was preparing the consommé. Mrs. Henry was searing duck breasts for the ducklings à la bigarade.

Everything was going well. Alice merely needed to keep breathing and keep moving forward, from one task to the next.

"Buonasera, Chef!"

Starting, she turned to the sound of the booming voice. Angelo Franconi was coming in the back door. "Chef." She blinked at him. "What are you doing here?"

"I cannot come north ten blocks to see how you are faring? This is your big night, no?"

"Yes, but . . . haven't you a dinner service to prepare?"

"My assistants can handle it without me for a short time. I wanted to see how you were doing." He drew closer and peered inside the lobster pot. "Come va?" he asked in Italian,

"Va bene. Are you here to help?" she asked hopefully.

"No, lucciola. This is your performance. I am merely a spectator. Introduce me?"

"That is Mrs. Henry and her children, Opal and Sam. Everyone, this is Chef Franconi."

Angelo walked around the kitchen and talked to each of them, all the while watching what they were doing. Spectator, indeed. He didn't fool Alice. This was his food, his recipes, and he wanted to see that Alice and her team were doing them justice.

Mrs. Henry brought out a spoon and dipped it in the bigarade sauce. She held it out to Angelo, who tasted the sauce. His eyes widened and he nodded. The two of them then began a discussion about various ways to improve upon the taste.

When he finally returned to the range, he said to Alice, "Mrs. Henry is very skilled. She has soaked the orange zest overnight in cognac and it gives the flavor a nice punch. I will have to try it in my next batch."

"I'm glad you are happy. I was worried we could never prepare your brilliant dishes half as well as you do."

"I had faith in you, Alice. You just needed to have faith in yourself. You don't need my recipes. You can create your own."

She glanced up and met his eyes. "Oh, I could never—"

"Watch those lobsters. We can discuss this later. I do not wish to distract you. The lobster meat will toughen if they steam too long."

"I know, I know. Remember in Boston when I was younger and I cried every time you put a lobster in the pot?"

He patted her shoulder. "Always a soft heart, even then. Allora, I must go. Stop by the kitchen on your way in tonight and tell me the results of your dinner."

"I will, unless it's terribly late." Which it would be, because she planned to stay here with Kit. She kept her gaze on the lobster pot, hoping he'd attribute her blush to the steam.

"Be safe. I am not certain your mother would approve of you here, alone."

Alice shot him a worried look. "You won't tell her, will you?"

"I never saw a thing." He held up his hands. "Ciao, Chef Lucciola."

"Ciao, Chef."

Angelo left and Mrs. Henry came over to where Alice was removing the batch of steamed lobsters. "He is a nice man," Mrs. Henry said. "Not as intimidating as I'd assumed, considering his reputation."

"He is a teddy bear," Alice said. "Tough on his staff, but he has a good heart. He is a perfectionist about food."

"I think he is probably just a teddy bear with you. He asked me about Mr. Ward, you know."

Alice paused and nearly dropped a lobster. Mrs. Henry reached out with a towel and helped put the hot crustacean on the platter. "Thank you. I haven't a lobster to spare. What did Angelo want to know in regards to Kit?"

"How well we were acquainted, whether he was a good person. Was he a danger to you or would he keep you safe? Was he a masca . . . mascalzini or something. It was an Italian word."

"Mascalzone. It means 'rascal.'" She returned her attention to the lobsters. "What did you say?"

"That I have known Mr. Ward for a long time, almost half his life. That he is a good man." She took another lobster from Alice and put it with the others. "That I have never seen him this smitten."

"Oh?" Had Kit been seeing someone? The woman from the opera, perhaps. "I hadn't realized."

"With you, Miss Lusk. With you."

Alice dropped the tongs this time, and they fell into the lobster pot. Mrs. Henry retrieved them and dried them off with the towel. "He cannot stop watching you whenever you are close by. And you should have heard the way he bragged about you when begging me to come and help this week. He would have promised me the moon to gain my cooperation, if only to make you happy."

"You are very sweet, but Kit is not serious about me. He's told me many times that he will never marry."

"Take it from me," Mrs. Henry said, lowering her voice. "Sometimes a man's brain needs time to catch up to his other parts."

A strangled half laugh, half gasp emerged from Alice's throat. "Mrs. Henry!"

"It's the truth—and trust me, a man always catches up when the right woman comes along."

It was similar to what Nellie had said, but Alice still didn't believe this applied to Kit. "Well, even if that were true, I cannot wait around on the possibility that a man might catch up. I have to live my life, and that includes finding a husband who actually wants me. Now, not later."

"I like you," Mrs. Henry said with an approving nod. "He'd be lucky to have you."

A month ago Alice never would have agreed, but much had changed both during and after the house party. Kit was a large reason for the shift, yet it wasn't just his lessons. In the last few weeks, it was like she'd woken up after a long sleep to find the world had rearranged itself. That nothing was the same.

Only it wasn't the world; it was her. *She* was no longer the same.

She proved she could make friends, that she could defy her mother. She could cook. Excelled at it, even. And yes, she could attract a man. Had kissed one, too. A duke had asked her to go driving with him.

While she might not be as popular as Maddie or as rebellious as Nellie, she was finally fitting into her own skin. Growing and changing. Getting stronger. Indeed, any man would be lucky to have her.

Mrs. Henry went back to her tasks and Alice returned her attention to the lobsters. There was no time for introspection at the moment. An elegant dinner for fifty gentlemen required all her focus for the next three hours.

The door pushed open, but Alice was too busy cracking lobster claws to notice. "Look at you, madam chef!" a familiar female voice said.

She looked over her shoulder and found Nellie there, her hands on her hips. Wait, Nellie was in the kitchen?

Alice's mouth fell open. "What are you doing here?"

The other woman took an apron off a peg on the wall and tied it over her dress. "Helping. Put me to work."

"Wait. How did you know I was here?"

"Kit told me." She removed the small hat from her head and smoothed her red hair. Then she came over and kissed Alice's cheek. "My father was invited tonight. He will be one of the guests eating your food."

"Well, it's not my food. And I'm not the only one preparing it." She gestured to the others and quickly introduced Nellie to Mrs. Henry and her children.

"Nice to meet all of you." Nellie clapped her hands together. "Now, what may I do to help?"

Momentarily overwhelmed, Alice looked at Mrs. Henry. The older woman said, "If she finishes breaking those lobsters apart, you could start on the filling."

"Yes, of course. Nellie, do you know anything about lobsters?"

"Spent a summer in Bar Harbor. You bet I do. Scoot." She nudged Alice out of the way and started cracking claws.

Turning, Alice went to gather the ingredients for the filling and brought them back to the counter. Standing next to Nellie again, she leaned in and lowered her voice. "I imagine you have better things to do on a Friday night. Thank you for coming."

"Actually, I don't. Shockingly, a woman with my reputation is not invited to all that many events. Second, you are my friend and friends drop everything whenever one is in need. In fact, I'm hurt you didn't ask me to come earlier in the week."

"Oh, forgive me. I didn't actually think—"

"Alice, I'm teasing. I'm not hurt. I understand why you wouldn't ask, I do. And Kit tried to talk me out of it. He said I'd only be in your way."

"Nonsense. I am glad you're here." It was surreal, actually. Alice hadn't even considered reaching out to Katherine or Nellie for assistance. She was so used to doing everything on her own, with no one in her corner. But now she had *friends*. It would take some getting used to. "Won't your father be worried about you?"

A lobster shell cracked as Nellie squeezed the metal tool around the claw. "I told him I was coming to help you. Honestly, he's probably thrilled. My nighttime activities and his do not normally cross paths like this."

"I can imagine."

"And things with Kit? How goes it?"

How could Alice begin to answer? Their circumstances were the same, but the other night had been . . . astounding. Like he'd flipped her inside out and then righted her again. And if all went according to plan tonight, she would stay late and celebrate with him. Together.

"I see," Nellie said. "That blush tells me all I need to know."

"Stop. It's warm in here."

"Oh, indeed. And the Devil sells ice cream in Hell."

"I am serious. Kit is not interested in anything meaningful."

"As long as you keep that in mind and don't fall in love with him, then enjoy it. I hope you turn those lessons back around on him and make him beg."

I want to give you everything, show you everything, but I know I haven't the right.

"In a way, yes," she said. "That is exactly what I am planning."

"Good for you! I want every salacious detail after we finish the dinner service."

Chapter Twenty

❧

*E*verything was perfect.

The table settings, the waiters, the food . . . the evening was moving like clockwork, with precision and efficiency. The guests were happy, laughing and drinking, raving about Alice's food. They had been chosen carefully this evening. Fifty of New York's most influential men were here, including Hearst and Pulitzer, newspaper magnates that would hopefully write about the club in their papers. Carnegie had come—probably just to see Madame Durham—and the Scotsman was holding court and entertaining the other gents at his table. Jack Astor and Governor Morton were laughing together at another table, while Stanford White and Teddy Roosevelt looked to be in a heated conversation near the wall. Nellie's father, Cornelius Young, was here, sitting with Stuyvesant Fish, president of the Illinois Central Railroad.

Bursting with pride and gratitude, Kit even allowed a tiny bit of hope to blossom in his chest. If the performance went well, then the night would be considered a smashing success.

He strode to the side room where the performers could rest. Knocking on the door, he waited until he heard a male voice call, "Enter!"

On the other side of the door, Madame Durham was in the middle of the room, warming up her voice, while her husband sat at the small piano, playing scales. She held up a finger toward Kit until she finished her vocal exercise, then paused.

"Pardon the interruption, Madame Durham," he said. "It is almost time. Is there anything else you need at the moment?"

"No. I will be ready in ten minutes," the opera singer said. "Will that suffice?"

"Perfect," Kit said. "I'll let everyone know."

She nodded and went back to her exercises, and Kit smiled as he closed the door. Her voice was magnificent, even in warm-ups.

He was tempted to peek into the kitchen to check on Alice, but he'd restrained himself all day. Hovering over her wouldn't do either of them any good and he'd promised not to corrupt her any further. Even if it killed him.

So yes, distance. That was his new goal. Alice would marry Lockwood and have little dukes somewhere in England, away from her family.

Ignoring the sourness in the pit of his stomach, he leaned against the doorframe to the dining room and thrust his hands in his pockets. Preston arrived with a glass of champagne for Kit. "Quite a night. Is it time to celebrate your success yet?"

"Our success—and not yet." Kit sipped from the

coupe and watched the crowd. "Though everyone seems happy with the food."

"Happy? They are raving about the lobster thermidor and the duck. Everyone is dying to know who this Chef Lucciola is."

Kit smiled. They would never find out. A tiny general in crinoline, Alice had done a magnificent job of overseeing all the preparation and plating. He'd overheard her giving orders in there and the confidence in her voice heated his blood, nearly giving him an erection right in the dining room. Bossiness hadn't appealed to him in the past, but Alice was different. For some reason, when she expressed herself in such definitive terms, he enjoyed it. Too much, it seemed.

"Any chance we could hire Alice permanently?" Preston asked.

The glass paused midway to Kit's mouth as his body locked up. He hadn't considered it. After tonight's preview, he had planned to hire a chef, but that depended on how many memberships sold first. Call Kit superstitious, but he didn't wish to hire permanent staff before they knew if this idea would take. "I cannot imagine she'd be willing—or that her mother would allow it."

"What if her husband allowed it because he owned the club?"

Kit looked over sharply. "You know that's not going to happen."

"Do I?" Amusement tugged at Preston's lips. "I think you've avoided her all day for a reason, but I see your eyes drifting that way every few minutes and how you've hesitated by the door to listen to her."

"Do not ruin this night for me," he warned. "You're overstepping, Pres."

"Never seen you this touchy over a woman before, either."

"Goddamn it. Did you not hear me?"

Preston raised a hand in surrender. "I'll stop. For now."

Downing the rest of his champagne, Kit handed the empty coupe to Preston. "Watch it, or I'll tell Arabella the name of the woman your father tried to force you to marry."

His friend's face darkened, anger rushing in quick. "Don't you dare."

Kit lifted a brow, telling Preston without words that he most definitely would, before turning to fetch Madame Durham. The singer was ready, so Kit led her and her husband to the side of the stage, then went up and made the introductions. The men clapped politely and Madame Durham took the stage. Her husband sat at the piano, ready to play accompaniment.

From the first note of Giuseppe Verdi's "Sempre Libera," the crowd was riveted. Madame Durham's soprano filled the room, which had been designed to amplify sound. No one moved. The waiters stopped working and watched from the back, and the kitchen staff all peeked out from a crack in the door. Her voice was beautiful, the kind that filled one's chest with love and hope, like air infused with pure joy. Kit's eyes welled, emotion overcoming him as she sang piece after piece, showing the range of her voice.

When she finally finished, the crowd leapt to their feet and broke out into thunderous applause.

Madame Durham curtsied gracefully, barely lifting her emerald-colored skirts as she dipped. Mr. Durham also took a bow, then allowed his wife to walk forward and accept more accolades.

Finally, Kit led the couple back to the retiring room. "Thank you. That was absolutely tremendous. You are incredibly gifted, Madame Durham."

She dabbed the perspiration off her forehead with a handkerchief. "Thank you. Nights such as this make the hours of training and practice worth it. I do love to perform."

"It's not as prestigious as Carnegie Hall, but you are welcome here anytime. I'd be honored."

"As long as you stick to your promise, Mr. Ward," she said.

Kit nodded, remembering their negotiation when she agreed to perform. Kit promised to host a yearly benefit for the company she recently created, the Black Durham Troubadours. The benefit would raise money to help sustain the troupe between performances. "I've signed the contract. Your lawyer will have it tomorrow."

"Excellent. Will you make sure my driver is ready out front?" She reached for the teapot from earlier.

"I will. In the meantime, I'll bring you fresh hot water. Would either of you care for dinner? We have lobster and duck."

Madame Durham nodded. "That is kind of you. Yes, if it's not too much trouble."

Kit hurried to the kitchen, where he found Alice and Mrs. Henry wiping their eyes. Suppressing the urge to pull Alice into his arms, he leaned against the counter and folded his hands. "Did you enjoy Madame Durham's performance?"

"I've never heard anything so beautiful," Alice whispered.

"Me neither," Mrs. Henry said as a fresh tear emerged. "I'm overcome with it."

"Would you both like to meet her?"

Mrs. Henry smoothed her hair. "Oh, I couldn't. I must look a fright."

"You look beautiful," Alice told her. "And I'll come with you. I'd like to tell her how much I loved her singing."

"She and her husband would like a dinner plate," Kit said. "So if you'll fix those up, I'll take you back."

Soon, they carried plates and a fresh teapot to Madame Durham and her husband. Alice chatted with the couple about Boston, then moved over to Kit's side while Mrs. Henry continued to talk to the Durhams. Alice bumped his shoulder with her own. "How did the food go over?"

He leaned in and kept his voice low. "You were a smash. I cannot ever thank you enough."

"Nonsense. You organized all of this, so you get the glory. I hope you're quite proud."

"I called in some favors." He shrugged. "It was hardly saving lives."

"Do not diminish your talents, Christopher Ward. You are remarkable. Enjoy this moment of satisfaction because you've earned it."

His father's voice still echoed in his brain.

You're as shallow as a saucer, Christopher.

Don't worry your pretty head over such important things, Kit.

You're just like your old man, son.

It was hard to drown out the doubts and insecurities that lingered from childhood, but perhaps Alice was right. Perhaps it was time for him to stop diminishing his talents—or at least try to stop. "Thank you," he told her honestly. "I am really going to miss you."

She cocked her head and studied his eyes. "Where am I going?"

"Your mother returns tomorrow."

"Oh, right."

Nothing more needed to be said. Alice would continue her parties and balls, the drives in the park. There was no room for lessons, cooking or Kit. "I suppose your mother will faint dead away with happiness when she hears of your outing with Lockwood."

Alice gave a tiny gasp of breath. "How did you—?" She shook her head and straightened her shoulders a touch. "It doesn't mean anything. It was one drive."

"In full view of New York society. He might as well have pissed on you."

"Christopher!"

"Come on, Alice. You know how these things work. Besides, I'm happy for you."

Biting her lip, she stared up at him through her lashes. "Are you?"

No, he wanted to say. *I hate the idea of you with another man. I hate the idea that someone else will have the right to touch you whenever he wishes.* But he couldn't say any of that. Instead, he said, "Of course. He's everything you want in a husband—boring, decent looking and lives far away."

"Lockwood is not boring. Furthermore, he's exceedingly handsome."

A dark bitterness twisted in Kit's belly, something poisonous and rotten. He hadn't encountered it before, this feeling, and he didn't like it one bit. "Bully for you, then. I wish you luck." He pushed off the wall. "If you'll excuse me, I should see to Madame Durham's carriage."

AFTER HUGGING OPAL and Sam, Alice hugged Mrs. Henry one more time. "Thank you for your help—and thank you for your patience with me. I never could have done this without you."

"Nonsense. You could cook circles around any of those fancy hotel chefs any day of the week. This was truly my pleasure, miss."

"Keep taking good care of him," she whispered, and there was no doubt as to whom she referred.

"I will—though I am fairly certain this isn't the last we'll see of each other, miss." With a nod of her head, she ushered her children out of the kitchen and into the night, leaving Alice to wonder over that comment.

She bid farewell to the other kitchen staff, as well, until only she and Nellie remained. Sitting on a stool, she stretched her back. "Goodness, I am exhausted. Feels as though I've just completed a three-day race."

Nellie plucked a fresh raspberry off her dessert plate and popped it in her mouth. "Because you have. You should consider opening your own restaurant. Charles Ranhofer has nothing on you."

Alice rolled her eyes, though she couldn't prevent the grin from stretching her face. "Besides loads of experience and training."

"And a penis."

Alice's skin went up in flames at the word, but

she nodded. "Yes, that, too. Women do not work in restaurant or hotel kitchens. No one would ever take me seriously."

"Well, you impressed the hell out of me." Nellie scooped up the last of her charlotte russe and ate it. "God, this is divine."

The kitchen door swung open and an older man with white hair and matching beard peeked inside. "Nellie, my dear. Time to go."

"Oh, hello, Daddy." Nellie went over and tugged on his arm, bringing him into the kitchen. "Come in and meet my friend."

Goodness, this must be Mr. Cornelius Young. Nellie's father was something of a legend on Wall Street, and he had more money than nearly anyone, save Carnegie and Morgan. Alice wiped her hands on her apron and held one out. "Hello, Mr. Young. It's nice to meet you."

He shook her hand, his blue eyes twinkling. "The pleasure is mine, Miss Lusk. Nellie has told me much about you since returning from Newport."

She had? Alice snuck a quick glance at Nellie before responding to her father. "Your daughter is an incredible woman. I'm proud to call her my friend. Thank you for letting her come and help me tonight."

Smiling fondly at his daughter, he said, "As if I could ever stop her from doing something when she puts her mind to it. She's just like her mother."

Nellie leaned up and kissed her father's cheek. "Time to get you home, Daddy. Mrs. Paulson will be very cross if I keep you out too late." She looked at Alice and whispered behind her hand, "His mistress."

"Eleanor Young," he chastised as his cheeks reddened. "Do not go telling everyone my business."

"It's almost the twentieth century, Daddy. We're much more open-minded about these things nowadays. Besides, you're a widower. You're allowed to have fun."

Turning to Alice, he said, "It was lovely to meet you, Miss Lusk. I wish you luck with your future endeavors—which I hear might include the Duke of Lockwood."

"What?" Nellie asked sharply, the smile falling from her face. "The duke?"

Alice shrugged, feeling conflicted about Lockwood after Kit's comments earlier. "He took me for a drive. It's nothing serious."

"Oh. I had no idea," Nellie said. "Good for you. Well, we should get going, Daddy."

With final wave, Nellie left the kitchen with her father and Alice was alone. A quick glance out the door showed the club had nearly cleared out, too. The tables were empty, the dishes washed and the waiters dismissed. Kit was shaking hands and thanking the remaining guests, making them laugh and grin. He really was good at making others feel comfortable, for knowing what people wanted to hear. Everyone liked him. Including her.

I am really going to miss you.

Indeed, she was going to miss him, too. The notion of never seeing him again like this, where they could be alone, gutted her. Why had she gone and fallen for a man who would never love her back? Stupid, stupid Alice.

They still had tonight, though.

She was not about to give him up, not until tomor-

row. Then she could deal with her heartache and regrets. She could sit and ponder all of the ways she
could have acted differently, choices that would have
protected her heart. But that was not for right now.

Because if this was the last time, she planned on
making it count.

Leaving the kitchen, she found the washroom
and freshened up. There was no time for a bath, so
she did her best to wash off the sweat and grime
of the evening. She likely smelled of duck fat and
garlic, but there was no help for it now. When she
emerged, only Kit and Preston were left in the
dining room, sitting at a table and smoking cigars.

Preston saw her first. "Alice! Come over and
celebrate with us."

She lowered herself into a chair as Kit poured
her a glass of champagne. "I thought you'd left," he
said, and placed the bottle on the table.

Was that relief or unhappiness in his voice? She
couldn't tell. "I wanted to see everyone else off
before I departed." *And I wanted to see you alone.*

Preston lifted his glass. "I predict memberships
will sell out tomorrow. To a job well done!"

"To a job well done," Kit said, and touched his
glass to Preston's.

They waited for Alice to do the same. She felt a
bit like one of the Three Musketeers as she added,
"To a job well done."

They all drank, and Preston finished his champagne in two swallows. "Alice, you were dashed
fantastic in there. I hope he offers you a full-time
position." He stood and clapped Kit on the shoulder. "Must run. I'm expected elsewhere."

"Wait, don't leave yet," Kit said, a little desperately.

"Sorry, pal. You are on your own." With a wink at Alice, Preston started across the tiled floor.

"You'll let me know if the Pinkertons find Forrest?" Kit called.

"Of course. Good night, Alice!" Preston said, and disappeared.

Was Kit uninterested in being alone with her?

I want to give you everything, show you everything, but I know I haven't the right.

Hardly uninterested. If she had to guess, he was being cautious. Because he didn't trust himself alone with her?

That was promising. She slid a glance at him and found him staring at the unlit candle on the table.

My cock is hard all the time for you.

Was it still the case?

He spoke quietly, not looking at her. "You should go, before someone notices you are missing. You've been here since one o'clock and it is almost eleven."

She wasn't worried. She'd purchased her maid's silence today by allowing Mary the night off to go to Staten Island to visit family. No one would notice the hour of Alice's return. "Do you want me to leave?"

Throwing back the rest of the champagne, he grimaced. "I don't want you in trouble for helping me."

"I won't be. Do you have plans tonight?"

"No."

"Kit." She waited until he finally met her gaze. His brown depths were swirling with emotion, as tortured as she'd ever seen. For a man who had organized such a triumphant evening, this turmoil surprised her. "Would you prefer it if I left?"

"Alice." He sighed and rubbed his eyes. "It's not about what I prefer. It's about what is right."

"You've never worried about society and its conventions before now."

"Because I've never cared about anyone before. I *care* about you, Alice. I don't want to see you hurt by an association with me. We should stop before something happens that we cannot take back, especially now when you have a real chance at attaining the future you've always wanted."

He cared about her.

Kit *cared* about her.

Elation filled her, expanding in her chest like dough in a warm oven. Perhaps he didn't wish to marry her, but he cared about her . . . so she could hold on to that for now.

Whatever happened, she would never regret it. And if this was the last time she saw him, then it was better to make the most of their final moments together.

With a confidence she felt in her bones, she rose and walked over to him. His wary gaze tracked her approach, his hand tightening on the table. Leaning down, she put her lips by his ear. "I'd like to see you in your office, Professor Ward." Then she nipped his earlobe with her teeth. A satisfying gasp fell from his mouth, but she didn't tease him further.

No, she needed to see what he'd do. Needed to see if he was willing to meet her halfway, if he wanted to continue their games together. Turning, she started for the back of the dining room, toward the door that led to his office.

What would he do now?

Chapter Twenty-One

❧

Damn it.

Kit rubbed his brow, responsibility and craving at war in his head. The need for Alice was burning through him, a fire spreading through every cell—yet he shouldn't. She would regret it later. After she married, she would regret giving Kit these firsts that should belong to her husband.

You never do the right thing. Why start now?

Because this was Alice and she deserved better than a little slap and tickle in the back office of his supper club. It had all been a lark at the house party, lessons in exchange for recipes, and he'd been so confident of his abilities. Never one to get attached or worry about anyone other than himself. The life of every party, the man no one took seriously.

But now, not even a month later, everything had changed and he was on the verge of madness, torn in two directions. Part of him longed to go back there, strip her out of those boring clothes and fuck her until she came on his cock. Yet, he could not live with himself afterward if he took something so precious from her.

I'm not like you. I cannot do what we are doing and not feel anything.

She had been right. It was selfish of him to lead her down the path to ruin without offering her marriage in return. Alice was not Lottie or Arabella, a woman who could separate feelings from sexual activity. Alice had a big heart and felt deeply for those around her. She had been raised to expect marriage to a decent man, one accepted in society. A man like Lockwood.

So, Kit had no right to defile her. But God, he longed to.

I'd like to see you in your office, Professor Ward.

Fuck.

His cock thickening, he stared at where she'd disappeared. What if he kept his clothes on and pleasured her one more time? They'd already crossed that line. Where was the harm in crossing it once more before he sent her back to her life of dukes and drives in the park?

You're rationalizing.

Yes, without question. Yet the logic made sense. And he was losing the will to fight. If Alice wanted more pleasure from Kit's hands and mouth, then who was he to deny her?

Clothes remain on. Give her an orgasm and load her into the carriage.

He could do that.

Within seconds, he reached the office. Turning the latch, he walked in—and froze. Alice had removed her dress and petticoats, and was stretched out on his sofa in just a corset, chemise, drawers and stockings. *Oh, Jesus.*

His gaze swept over bare arms, the delicate collarbones, the lines of her shapely legs . . . and he could hardly draw in a breath. It was too much to take in. Lust careened through his system, his nostrils flaring with the effort to remain still. His fingers clutched the wooden door like a rope thrown over the side of a cliff.

"Close and lock the door," she said, her lips curving in apparent amusement.

His limbs moved automatically, doing as she asked, then he leaned against the wood. He didn't speak; instead, he ran his tongue along the back of his teeth and contemplated all the ways he'd like to ravish her. His body throbbed with need, a constant drumbeat that echoed in his groin.

"Take off your coat and your vest."

He stared at her elegant toes, her silk-covered calves, as he moved, thinking about how much he'd love those legs wrapped around his hips as he slid inside her. His coat and vest dropped to the wooden floor, and though he didn't look away from her to check, he knew his erection was tenting the front of his trousers. Had he ever been this hard? The skin of his cock was stretched tight, blood pulsing in the veins and capillaries.

Still, he didn't move.

"Now what?" he rasped.

She sat up slowly. "I want to see you. Touch you." She bit her lip and her gaze dipped lower. "Lick you."

Oh, God. She was going to kill him. He wanted that so badly, but he'd resolved himself not to push her further tonight. "We shouldn't. I'll lick you instead."

They stared into each other's eyes for a long minute. It was as if she looked straight into his soul, her brown gaze inspecting his every thought. He felt bare, exposed, like he couldn't hide how much he wanted her. How much he craved her. Finally, her lips curved and she rose gracefully. "Later. Let's do this my way first."

Heart racing, he retreated a step at her approach, but his back met the wood of the door, trapping him. He lost the ability to breathe when she stopped in front of him and lowered herself to her knees. He closed his eyes tightly in a feeble attempt to block the erotic image. "This cannot happen."

A gentle fingertip swept along his erection over the cloth, making him shiver. "Do you not want me to do this? I know it'll be clumsy, but you said yourself that I am a fast learner."

Gathering his strength, he cupped her cheek in his palm and met her gaze. "Alice, your husband should teach you about this."

"But you are my very favorite teacher."

He groaned, his head dropping against the door. Desire clawed inside him like a ravenous beast, barely restrained and struggling to break free. His skin felt too thin, too weak, to contain the depths of his need, as if he would burst open at any moment and spill all over the floor. Here was the innocent lamb, begging to be ruined, and he was too much of a bastard to refuse.

I am going to Hell.

"Fuck. All right. Unfasten my trousers." She managed it quickly, so he continued. "Suspenders next."

He helped her slide the suspenders off his shoulders, then the light wool trousers fell to his ankles. He tore off his necktie, collar and shirt, leaving him in a thin union suit that left little to the imagination. Would this repulse her or scare her away?

Slowly, she slid her palms up his thighs toward his hips. She flicked him a glance through her lashes, looking so virginal yet so sinful that his cock jumped. It was the perfect combination, like opening a traditionally wrapped gift and being surprised with something naughty inside.

"Now the undergarment," he whispered, anticipation clogging his throat.

The bulge between his legs could not be missed. He was so hard it was nearly obscene, with his balls already drawn tight and aching to be touched. Alice started near his belly button, threading the buttons through the tiny holes carefully, driving him mad with each second that passed. When she reached his cock, she didn't shy away, merely kept unbuttoning, her fingers brushing the hard ridge and making him tremble.

The sight of her, on her knees and concentrating on undressing him, was the most erotic thing he'd ever witnessed. Far more arousing than any of his other dalliances, as depraved as they might have been, because this was Alice. His very clever pupil, who over the last few weeks had blossomed into a glorious creature capable of directing a kitchen as well as seduction. The man who married her would be fortunate, indeed.

When she finished unbuttoning along his middle, the fabric parted and his cock bobbed free. The head pointed directly at her mouth, eager to find its way inside. He couldn't yet find words as he watched her examine him.

"What now?" she asked quietly.

He swallowed, his tongue thick and awkward. "Every man is different, so I'll tell you what I like. Tease me, sweetheart. Let me feel your breath and the soft pressure of your lips. Nothing too hard or too fast at first."

Bending forward, she exhaled over the crown, warm air tormenting the sensitive skin. Then she did it again along the sides, her mouth close but not coming into contact yet. He couldn't look away, couldn't blink. The tops of her breasts pushed against her corset and peeked out from her chemise, tantalizing him with each rise and fall of her chest. He fisted his hands and fought to remain still, to keep from lifting her up, throwing her down on the couch and having his wicked way with her.

Soft kisses rained along the length. Her lips were gentle, adoring every inch of his cock, and he knew he'd never forget the sight as long as he lived. She was driving him utterly insane . . . and he loved it.

When he could take no more, he told her, "Grip the base in your hand and lick the head. All around, especially underneath."

She followed his instructions perfectly, her pink tongue swirling over the head, and he had to lock his thigh muscles to keep from thrusting into her mouth. The urge to come lingered at the base of his spine, but it was embarrassingly soon, so he closed his eyes and tried to calm down. When the flat of her tongue swept over the sensitive underside, he gasped. Encouraged, she did it again.

"That's it," he crooned, his lids still closed. "Now, suck. Slide me inside that warm heaven and squeeze your hand."

He couldn't watch for fear of spending too soon, but he could feel, and the first time he coasted past her lips and onto her tongue was sheer bliss. Groaning, he pounded the door with his fist. *Do not come yet. For fuck's sake, get it together, Kit.*

She repeated the movement, bobbing up and down without him telling her to, and he knew it wouldn't be long. Without realizing it, he'd cupped the top of her head with his hand, his hips pumping slightly—until he went too far and caused her to gag.

Horrified, he pulled away. "I'm sorry," he said, panting for breath. "I lost my mind for a minute there."

"That's good, isn't it?" Her eyes were glassy and dark, her lips swollen, and she was the most beautiful creature he'd ever seen. Kit wanted to eat her alive.

"Get on the sofa," he ordered.

"Why?" Her brows pinched together. "Did you dislike what I was doing?"

"I was a second or two away from coming in your mouth, that's how much I disliked it. But I'd rather not scare you, so get on the sofa."

"It won't scare me. I'm curious to see it."

Perhaps, but he had other activities in mind at the moment. "On the sofa, Alice. Right now."

LEGS SHAKING, ALICE stood and went toward the sofa. What was Kit planning? She had quite liked sucking on his shaft like that. Never had she seen him so intense, so focused . . . so *undone*. It was thrilling to bring a man that kind of pleasure, especially a man with as much experience as Kit. He was no novice, so rattling him meant she hadn't been terrible at using her mouth.

Hands lifted her from behind. He sat on the sofa first, still in his undergarment, and brought her down on top of him, positioning her knees on either side of his hips. She felt exposed this way, the slit in her drawers revealing her sex. "What—?"

Before she could finish her question, he slammed his mouth to hers, kissing her like she was the air he needed to breathe. His hands moved to the laces on her back but she paid no attention. Her entire focus was his lips and tongue, the feel of him underneath her, the way their breath melded together as one. Threading her fingers through his hair, she held on, angling her head to get deeper. His tongue flicked hers, tangling together, their lips pulling and sucking, and she knew she'd never find a man who affected her like this one. It was like he was the match to set her ablaze every single time.

Her corset loosened and he moved his hands to the fastenings in the front. Showing a dexterity that should have frightened her but absolutely did not, he popped the metal fastenings and removed her corset. Her breasts, now free of the whalebone, were swollen, the tips fashioned into hard, needy points.

He pulled back abruptly, his eyes wild and bright as they searched her face. "I want to remove your chemise. May I?"

So polite. Was he being careful because it was her, or was he like this with all his lovers? Alice didn't wish to be handled with kid gloves. To prove it, she grabbed the edge of the cotton and dragged it over her head, leaving her bare from the waist up.

His gaze raked her torso and she bit her lip, unsure how her body would measure up against those he'd seen in the past. Yet she didn't cover herself. If he didn't like the way she looked, there was nothing she could do about it.

Gentle knuckles swept the undersides of each breast. Then he dragged a fingertip around her nipple. "God, you are lovely. Just lovely." Leaning forward, he licked the hard tip and she sucked in a breath, her hands clutching his shoulders. Then he drew her nipple into his mouth, using his tongue and teeth for pressure and a mild bite of pain, and the sweet tug echoed between her legs, a demanding pulse as more and more wetness gathered there. By the time he switched to the other breast, she was shifting her hips, desperate to ease the need rising inside her.

Strong hands cupped her backside and settled her atop his cloth-covered erection. She froze, uncertain, but he guided her, showing her how to use this part of his body for friction. And it felt incredible, the drag and sweep along her most sensitive tissues as he kept sucking on her. He grunted as she rocked, his hands sliding up to cup both her breasts. They worked together, moving and touching, panting and straining. The pleasure gathered in her belly, a rising storm just off in the distance. "Oh, Kit," she breathed, digging her nails into the muscles of his shoulders.

Releasing her nipple, he lunged for her mouth,

kissing her hard. She whimpered as he pushed his tongue inside, the hunger within her climbing, tightening, her body growing increasingly uncoordinated. The sofa bumped against the wall, but she didn't care. As if sensing her desperation, he took over, his hands at her waist, moving her rhythmically, until she broke, the pleasure overtaking her and making her quake. Her head dropped onto his shoulder, her moans disappearing into the skin of his throat. Finally she quieted and he held her, stroking her back, while her body recovered.

Under her palm, his heart raced as his chest pumped for air. His head rested on the back of the sofa, his eyes closed, a pained but pleased expression on his face. Had he . . . ?

She started to move and he caught her, holding her still. "Don't. Give me a moment."

"You haven't any idea what I was about to do."

"Doesn't matter," he gritted out. "I'm holding on to my sanity by a very thin thread. Just wait."

Ah. He was attempting to recover, to gather his wits. *This is the last time. If you want to see him unravel, this is your only chance.*

She glanced down at where their bodies rested against one another. He was still clothed, his thick erection trapped between them. Yet she could see the powerful lines, the sharp ridges and valleys, the points of his hip bones. He was beautiful, a perfect male specimen. She adored everything about him, inside and out. At least, adoration was the only emotion she'd allow herself to admit at the moment.

I hope you turn those lessons back around on him and make him beg.

She'd like that very much, actually.

They only had tonight, then she'd never see him again. And she knew what she wanted.

Everything.

The question was, would he give it to her?

Her hand crept lower and moved between them to cup his erection. He sucked in a breath and grabbed her wrist. "Alice, please. I don't want to take this further. I just need a moment."

Leaning in, she began nibbling his throat, her fingers pressing into the ridge of flesh inside his undergarment. "What if I want to take this further?"

He gave a strained laugh. "I would tell you no."

"Why?"

"You know why."

Because he didn't want to marry her. Because she was to marry someone else.

The problem was, he made it very difficult to want anyone other than him.

I have him right now, right here. Her mother returned tomorrow and with it all the expectations of her family and her class. But society wasn't stopping her from taking what she wanted at the moment. Kit was the only person standing in her way.

Had she the courage to convince him?

The Alice of a month ago couldn't have possibly demanded such things. However, the Alice who held this man's affections could do damn near anything. *I've never cared about anyone before. I care about you, Alice.*

In one sensuous move, she slid off his lap and stood. Relief flickered over his expression until her hands went to the strings at her waist. When she untied her drawers, he sat up straight. "What are you doing?"

She pushed the cotton over her hips and down her thighs, then stepped out of the garment. Then she stripped off each stocking, bending over slowly, enjoying the way his hot stare followed her every move. Now completely nude, she lifted her chin. "Take off your undergarment."

He started shaking his head before she even got the words out. "Oh, God. Don't even suggest it, Alice. I'm dying over here."

His plea emboldened her. Kit was being careful . . . but the time for care had passed. The clock was ticking and there was one more thing she needed for him to show her.

She crawled onto his lap, keeping her expression innocent while inwardly she plotted. His chest heaved and he kept his hands at his sides. One after another, she undid the buttons of his undergarment. "I want it to be you, Christopher. I don't want another man to teach me how to do this. It has to be you."

"Fucking hell," he said on a groan, and dropped his head onto the back of the sofa. "Alice, I shouldn't. I can't. You will soon have a husband and he'll be furious that you allowed me to be first."

"Wrong." She pressed a kiss to his jaw, the evening whiskers rough against her lips. "He'll be grateful that I learned such wonderful technique from a master."

He pinched the bridge of his nose between his thumb and forefinger. "No, he definitely will not. Even if I appreciate your attempt at stroking my vanity, trust me—he'll be livid."

She slid her lips to his and kissed him. "Or he'll never know. Not every woman is a virgin on her wedding night, and I bet most grooms never notice."

"Alice," he said on a long breath, almost a whine. "I don't want to ruin your life."

She squeezed her fingers around his erection, giving him a rough stroke. "Impossible. Everything in my life has been infinitely better since I met you."

He brought his hands to the sides of her face, holding her as he stared into her eyes. The tenderness and desire reflected in the dim gaslight sank inside her, deep down to the bone and sinew, and she knew this was the right decision. She felt it in every part of her body.

His voice was affectionate and soft, as if she completely baffled him. "What am I going to do with you?"

"You are going to take off your undergarment and make love to me."

He grimaced. "Alice, sweetheart. I . . ."

He was still hesitating. She could see the indecision in his expression. Had she not been clear enough? Or was it the word *love* that had thrown him off? *Stupid, stupid Alice.* That was the last reminder he needed at the moment, that she might fall in love with him. That this might be more than just lessons between friends.

"Wait," she said, placing a finger atop his lips. "What I meant to say is that you should take your undergarment off and fuck me."

Chapter Twenty-Two

The words had the desired effect.

As soon as the crude term left her mouth, Kit leapt on her, his arms crushing her to him as he devoured her with a scorching kiss. Alice melted into him, holding on as the flood of wanting built back up inside her belly at a feverish pace. He was all she needed in this moment, the world distilled to his hands and his mouth, his strong body beneath her.

He pressed hot, openmouthed kisses down the sensitive column of her throat. "You want me to fuck you?"

She nodded, unable to speak as he dragged his teeth over her flesh.

"Then help me."

He started to take off his undergarment, trying to free his arms first, but the remaining closed buttons over his stomach hindered the process. With a rip, he tore the garment open and she pushed the cloth over his strong arms. His chest was wide and sculpted, with a light dusting of dark hair in the middle. Before she could explore, he kissed her once more, and she felt him rise up to push the undergarment under his hips.

Everywhere they touched she was met with warm skin and crisp body hair. The difference in texture thrilled her. Where she was soft, he was hard. Secure. Solid and real. Never had she imagined it would feel this good.

His fingers slipped between her legs and caressed her, exploring gently. "You are slippery and swollen. Sheer perfection." After teasing the bundle of nerves atop her sex, he circled her entrance. Amid kisses to her throat, he whispered, "You must be ready to take me. I do not want to hurt you, sweetheart."

The endearment relaxed her and she rocked her hips slightly, bringing the tip of his finger inside. He swept his palm over her spine, as if calming her. "That's it. Let me in."

Soon the finger was all the way inside, and she marveled at the fullness. Was this what it would feel like to have his penis inside her? It was delicious, a pressure that wasn't quite enough to sate the burning hunger inside her belly. She shifted, and he stayed her hip with his palm. "Just wait. Kiss me."

He gave her dizzying kisses, sucking and biting at her lips, until she began squirming, looking for more. His hand withdrew and then she felt greater pressure as he worked his way inside again. Was that another finger? The stretch confirmed it as her walls opened for him. She whimpered into his mouth, the sensation overwhelming her. It was like nothing she could have imagined, but it felt necessary. Essential. She didn't wish for him to stop.

With his thumb, he circled her clitoris, not moving the fingers inside her. Just letting her adjust as he built up her pleasure. Except it wasn't like before when they were rubbing together. This was stronger, more intense, from the thickness inside her. Thighs shaking, she broke off from his mouth to drag air into her lungs.

"One more, I think." Drawing back again, he fed a third finger inside her, though it was a tight squeeze. This pinched slightly, as if her body resented the invasion, but he was patient, giving her time to adapt. When all three fingers were seated, he held them there and worked her clitoris some more. "Touch me, Alice."

Her hands glided over his rough skin, loving the way he was so different from her. Goose bumps emerged in the wake of her touch, and she relished the outward reaction of how she affected him. Lower she went, over his nipples, along his stomach, until she reached his erection. It was long and thick, resting against his belly, the head flushed dark red. She gripped him lightly, testing the feel of his soft skin stretched over rigid flesh. Fascinating.

"Pump your hand, squeeze hard."

She fisted her hand and dragged it along his length until she reached the head. A pearly drop of moisture emerged from the slit. "Again," he told her.

This time, when she pumped her hand, he did the same, dragging his fingers almost all of the way out of her channel, then sliding them back.

She closed her eyes as streaks of white heat shot through her limbs. They did it again, working in tandem, each using a hand to pleasure the other. His breathing was as erratic as hers, their skin coated in a fine sheen as the inferno between them raged.

"Lie back," he rasped. Not taking his fingers out of her, he used his other hand to support her shoulders as she maneuvered down on the sofa. Then he came up on his knees between her thighs, his hooded gaze traveling down the length of her body underneath him. "You are gorgeous. Just fucking gorgeous."

She could say the same of him, with his wide shoulders, narrow hips and flat stomach. The long shaft that jutted proudly from a nest of dark hair, the twin weights of his testicles hanging below. He was a fascinating contrast of lean, hard muscle that rippled as he moved, and her fingertips itched with the desire to explore every inch.

Curling over her, he kissed her breasts, teased her nipples, still pumping his fingers in and out of her, until she writhed, a mindless creature of unfulfilled need. It was too much to bear. "Please, Kit." She clutched at his head and pulled him up to see his face. "Please."

He rose up and slowly drew his fingers out of her core, watching the entire time. Then he used that hand along his shaft, smearing her wetness over his skin. "I always use a rubber shield, if it eases your mind."

"What?" She was distracted by the mesmerizing sight of his fist sliding along his erection and his words didn't make sense.

"A condom. They're at home, though. But do not worry, I won't spend inside you."

She appreciated his concern, as she hadn't once considered consequences. "Right."

He must have heard something in her voice because he frowned. "I apologize. I tend to be too practical about these things. Have I put you off? We need not do this."

"Kit." She came up on an elbow, desperate to get closer. Trailing her fingers down his chest, she kept going until she brushed the tops of the fingers still gripping his shaft. "I want to do this. I want you to show me."

Groaning, he released himself. "Then put me inside you."

She took him in hand, not nearly as nervous as she expected. *He's making sure I know what is happening, that I learn how we fit together.* Tugging, she guided him to her entrance, both of them watching as the reddish crown bumped against her flesh. He shifted forward, pressing, until the tip of his shaft disappeared in her channel. She fell back on the sofa and watched his face, which was tight with agony.

A few seconds later, he seemed in better control of himself. Lids opening, he stroked her thigh. "All right?"

She nodded. "Are you all right?"

He hissed through his teeth. "You are so tight and hot I think I've died and gone to Hell."

"You mean Heaven?"

"No, this pleasure is pure torture, sent from the Devil himself."

She couldn't help it. A tiny giggle escaped. Kit

smiled, though it was labored. "I am glad you are amused. At least that means I'm not hurting you."

"Is there more, then?"

A strangled laugh that sounded more like a groan emerged from his throat. He dragged a hand down his face, then glanced at where they were joined. "Yes, Alice. I'd say there's quite a bit more. Ready?"

"I am ready."

Holding the base of his erection, he began to advance and the pressure increased, her body slowly giving way to allow him inside. As he gained new ground, he withdrew slightly, then came back, rocking his hips gently while his thumb brushed over her clitoris. She felt lovingly conquered, as if he was taking the utmost care while bringing her pleasure, instead of overwhelming her.

Suddenly, it pinched, no longer a sweet invasion but a tight squeeze. Her eyes flew to his face and found him watching her closely. "Breathe," he told her. "You are tensing up. Just relax."

Angling down, he rested on an elbow, their bodies now flush. The weight of him was marvelous, like he surrounded her, protected her . . . *adored* her. He dipped his face toward hers and sealed their mouths together, kissing her sweetly, telling her without words that this was perfect, that *she* was perfect. Gradually, her muscles loosened and he gave a small thrust of his hips and he was fully seated. No pain, just fullness.

"There we go," he whispered against her cheek. "My God, Alice. I never dreamed you would feel this good."

She was curious about what he was experiencing,

if it was as glorious for him, too. "What does it feel like for you?"

"Like you're squeezing the very life from me." He kissed her. "Like I could happily die here." Another kiss. "Like I am the most fortunate man on the entire planet."

She kissed him back, feeling quite fortunate herself. Her hips tilted of their own volition, bringing him deeper, and they both moaned. Goodness, the pleasure rippled from her middle out through every part of her. He moved then, his pelvis rocking, his thick shaft sliding along her inner walls. With each drag inside her, the sensation built, multiplied, until it wasn't enough. She was hovering in delirium, suspended in lust, as he pumped above her, propped up on his elbows, his body working to maximize their pleasure. Sakes alive, how much more could she take?

As if sensing her frustration, he pressed up on his arms, still inside her. "Rub yourself," he panted. "Like you do when you're alone."

Her eyes widened. *Do that, in front of him?*

"Please, Alice. I want you to find your peak before I do." He thrust once, hard. He threw his head back and gasped. "And I won't last much longer."

Her hand drifted between their bodies and he came onto his knees, his hands spreading her thighs wide. When she touched her clitoris, he sawed in and out of her body, wild dark eyes locked on her fingers. She circled the tight bud and blissful streaks of electricity raced through her, like a switch had been flipped. They both began moving faster, Kit offering praise as she continued to work herself, telling her how beautiful, how arousing, he found her, until the world exploded, her orgasm rushing up from her toes to lift her up and scatter her to the heavens. She pulsed and panted, her head thrown back and eyes closed as it went on and on.

Kit jerked out of her, his body pulling away, and he fisted his shaft, faster this time, his shoulders hunched in apparent pain . . . and then his fingers tightened on her thigh as pulses of white heat erupted from the tip of his penis. The spend landed on her stomach, his face twisted in gratified agony, yet still beautiful. He shouted at the ceiling, a deep rumble of satisfaction that she'd never forget.

When he finished, he slumped and gave her the most adorably contented smile. He looked young and happy, without the cynicism that sometimes haunted his expression. *I love this man.*

She knew it deep in her bones. There would never be another like him in her life, not even her future husband. Kit was everything she wanted and needed . . . except the willingness to meet her at the altar. Sadness swamped her chest, a thousand pinpricks of everything she'd never have again. Her friends had tried to warn her, but she hadn't listened and she would pay the price until she drew her last breath.

And yet.

She would not beg. He had made his position clear, and her life marched onward. For years she had shoved down her own happiness, her own desires, and she could easily do so again. It would not break her.

Know your worth.

Indeed, she did—partially thanks to this man,

ironically. He'd helped her to discover her strength, her resiliency, and she would use both to walk away from him for the last time tonight. A strand of thorns wrapped around her heart, penetrating and poking, slashing her insides, but she needed to marry a man who wanted her. Who *loved* her. Or had the potential for love, anyway.

Pining for Kit was not an option. No matter how badly it hurt.

His brows lowered as he examined her, as if he was trying to see inside her mind. "Alice?"

A tear slipped out of the side of her eye and she brushed it away quickly. "That was perfect," she said, looking away as she struggled to sit up.

"Wait." He reached for his undergarment and used it to clean off her stomach. "Are you sore? Shall I fetch a warm cloth from the washroom?"

"No." She swung her legs toward the floor and sat up, wincing slightly at the tenderness between her legs. "I'll take a hot bath back at the hotel."

"Are you certain?" His hands flopped at his sides, gaze darting around the room. He appeared adorably flustered. "Why were you crying just now?"

"Kit." She reached to stroke his jaw. "I'm fine."

They dressed in silence, and she couldn't tell what he was thinking. Considering she was hardly eager to share her own thoughts, she didn't dare ask him. She needed the walls between them, a tiny bit of distance to keep the disappointment at bay. Otherwise, she might start bawling for real.

It took much longer to put her clothes on than it had to take them off. He helped her with a competency that depressed her further. There had been

many women before her in Kit's life and there
would be many women after, as well. He would
never suffer for "companionship," as he'd once
called it. She would become a distant memory, one
of the faceless women he'd bedded.

He deserved more than meaningless affairs. He
deserved to be loved and cherished, as she did.
Perhaps someday he would seek it out and allow
a woman to reach his heart. Alice would have
moved on long before then, however.

Taking her hand in his, he led her out of the
office and through the club. The room was eerily
quiet, the jocularity of earlier like a fever dream.
Yet it had happened. She and Mrs. Henry and Mrs.
Henry's children had prepared Franconi's food
and dazzled this room full of New York's crème de
la crème. Pride filled her, and she would not allow
her sadness over losing Kit to rob her of such joy.

He peeked out the door, then closed it. "John is
waiting for you out front. I . . ." Shoving his hands
in his pockets, he grimaced, not meeting her eyes.
"Alice, I don't know how to thank you for tonight.
For dinner and for . . ."

Afterward.

"Don't thank me. It was my pleasure." A lump
formed in her throat and she forced it down. "Both
were my pleasure, actually."

The edges of his lips twitched. "Good. I'm glad."

They stood there, awkwardly, until she couldn't
take it any longer. Knowing this was the last
time was like a dagger in her heart, and prolong-
ing it was only making it worse. She sucked in a
deep breath and let it out slowly. Stepping in, she
pressed a kiss to his cheek. He froze, not respond-

ing in the least, and that made her heart break a little bit more.

She edged away. "Be happy, Christopher Ward. You are so much more than you give yourself credit for. Don't let anyone ever convince you otherwise."

When he didn't react or speak, she deflated. Why wasn't he trying to make this easier? Reassure her with false smiles and his infamous charm? She hardly knew this cold and withdrawn man.

If this was what men acted like after intercourse, then Alice was in no rush to repeat it.

Lifting her chin, she reached for the knob and went out the door. Ready to leave the past and present behind.

The future awaited.

Chapter Twenty-Three

❧

Light flooded her room, jarring Alice from a deep sleep. Hadn't she just closed her eyes? "What's happened?"

Mary, her maid, was there, looking worried. "Miss, your mother's returned. Said I must wake you up right quick. I don't know what's happened but I hope she hasn't found out that I left you unattended."

"No, no." Alice pushed up to a seated position—and gasped. She was sore *everywhere*. Swallowing against the pain, she said, "That is our secret. The only way she'd find out is if one of us told her."

"I'll never tell, miss. You have my word. She'd fire me straightaway, if she knew."

She'd also commit Alice to a convent. Or an asylum.

"I'll never allow that to happen," Alice promised. "Where is she?"

"In her room. Said to send you over when you were dressed."

"What time is it?"

"Just after ten, miss."

Goodness, that late? She'd arrived home around one o'clock and hadn't fallen asleep until after three. The excitement over the night—overseeing her first kitchen, the thrill of watching the guests enjoy her food, making love with Kit afterward—had taken a long time to wear off. "Just pick out a dress while I am in the washroom. Best not to keep her waiting."

Alice gave herself no opportunity to think about Kit while she cleaned her teeth and used the facilities. She had no regrets and, like Nellie said, she intended to live as if each day was her last. No more putting off her responsibilities and wishing for things that could never happen.

When she was dressed and presentable, she knocked on her mother's door. Mama's maid answered and let Alice in, where she found her mother poring over the society talk in the newspaper. "Hello, Mama. How was your trip?"

"Sit down, Alice."

Nerves jumping, Alice lowered herself into a plush armchair. She pressed her lips together, silent. Had Mama discovered Alice's sneaking out this week? Worse, had Mama learned about Kit?

Impossible. Stop worrying. No one will ever know.

"I hear you left the hotel while I was away."

Alice's stomach plummeted to her toes. Her mouth dried out, like a meringue that had been left in the oven too long. "I . . ."

"Tell me how this happened. I hadn't realized you were so friendly with His Grace."

His Grace?

Oh. Her drive with Lockwood.

She relaxed, slumping in the chair as the relief nearly made her giddy. "Well, I—"

"Sit up straight. The duke will never want you if you slouch."

Wasn't her mother getting a bit ahead of herself? "Mama, it was one drive. We went around the park and he brought me right back. We were in public the entire time."

"I am aware. I saw His Grace this morning and he informed me of that fact. Obviously I am unhappy you went anywhere unchaperoned. However, if you must allow yourself to be ruined, best to be ruined by a duke. Now, His Grace has asked us to dine with him this evening, so let's discuss what you are going to wear."

Wait, what? "Tonight?"

Mama sighed, eyes closing as if dealing with Alice was more than she could bear. "Listen to me for once, you stupid child. Dinner, this evening. With the Duke of Lockwood. Please, do not jeopardize this, Alice. You must know what is riding on your impressing him at every turn."

"Of course, Mama."

"Yes, here it is!" Her mother pointed to a section of newsprint. "Indeed, it's right for everyone in the city to see."

Alice peered at the newspaper. "What is it?"

"A mention of your outing with Lockwood. I didn't see it in Boston, but everyone in New York will have learned of it by now." Mama's mouth twisted with dark amusement. "They all thought that Webster girl would snag him, but it turns out your dowry has lured him in."

Of course it couldn't have been Alice herself. "It's hardly settled, Mother."

"The duke won't be able to refuse such a large sum, believe me. In fact, I'll write to your father and ask him to sweeten the pot a little. Surely there is a piece of property or two that the duke has his eye on."

No, this was exactly what Alice didn't want to happen. She did not want Daddy to buy her a fiancé. "Shouldn't we wait to gauge the duke's interest before we start offering him a treasure chest full of gold and jewels?"

"Alice, this is how these matters are handled. It is a business transaction, and we must entice His Grace into taking you off our hands. As you know, you are hardly a great beauty."

Alice wilted . . . until she thought of Kit and the adoration on his face last night.

You are gorgeous. Just fucking gorgeous.

She was not a charity case. Lockwood could choose almost any unmarried woman in New York, like the Vanderbilt daughter whose dowry put Alice's to shame. Furthermore, Maddie hadn't offered up as large a dowry and Lockwood had wanted to marry *her*.

No, if Lockwood was interested in Alice, then it must be real . . . regardless of her mother's harsh words.

Mama was still talking. "Now, I think the cream Worth dress with the pale pink flowers for you tonight. You haven't worn it yet since it arrived from Paris. The other girls will be positively green with envy."

The other mothers, too? Alice didn't dare ask it, however. The comment would only anger her mother, and Mama was worse when she was angry. "Of course," she murmured as she stood. "I'll let Mary know and she can begin steaming it."

"Good. For once, you've done something right. Let's not give the duke any reason to reconsider."

THE BED WAS rocking. And not in the good way.

Kit groaned but didn't open his eyes. The spinning would stop eventually. He hoped.

"Damn it, Kit. Wake up."

The deep voice penetrated his brain. He swallowed and forced moisture into his dry mouth. "Who?"

"Kit. I need you." A rough hand on his shoulder shook him. "Now. Wake up."

He took a deep breath, his stomach roiling as he turned over. Why had he drunk so much last night? Or rather, a few hours ago. Dash it, what time was it?

Peeling his lids open, he found Preston standing by his bed. It was pitch-black out. "What are you doing here?" He closed his eyes again, but Preston pushed on his shoulder.

"Do not go back to sleep, goddamn it. I—"

It was the anguish in Preston's voice that startled Kit. Blinking, he lifted his head. "What is it?"

Preston crossed his arms over his chest and studied the wall. His throat worked, as if he couldn't speak, and it was then that Kit noted how terrible his friend looked. Hair scattered atop his head, whiskers coating his jaw. Dark circles under his eyes. Concern had Kit raising up on his elbows.

"I . . ." Preston swallowed. "I need you to come

with me. He's been found. And I—" He broke off, his voice trembling.

Oh, Christ. "Forrest?"

Preston nodded. "They say he was found on the tracks. He's . . ."

Kit's lungs collapsed, unable to draw in air. He stared at Preston, willing his friend to take the words back. To wake up and discover this was a bad dream. Anything that would prevent this from being a reality. "Jesus," he finally whispered.

"I have to go to the morgue and identify him. His parents won't go and I can't let—"

Can't let him be tossed aside like garbage.

Kit couldn't allow that, either. Their friend deserved better.

Oh, my God. Forrest is dead.

"We have to tell Harrison," he said stupidly.

"He's on his honeymoon. I'm not telling him until he returns." Preston turned and picked Kit's trousers up off the floor. "Here. Get dressed. You smell like whiskey."

Numb, Kit crawled out of bed and began to put himself together. It had been four nights since he'd last seen Alice. Kit had spent most of that time drinking, waiting for the memories to fade. For the heartache to ease. He knew from his mother's death that the pain of loss would dissipate over time. It took hours and days and weeks, then suddenly it has been months and years, and one could begin to find hints of joy now and again.

But the early stages were absolute hell.

And now his friend had died, too.

His stomach lurched, the organ suddenly undeniably angry, and Kit rushed to the washroom. Half of the whiskey he'd consumed a few hours ago came right back up.

"I hope you feel better now," Preston said dryly from the doorway. "Because what we're likely to see at the morgue won't exactly be soothing."

"Oh, Christ," Kit gasped, gripping the sink as he tried to rinse his mouth out. "Just give me a moment."

Ten minutes later, the two strode out of Kit's town house and loaded into Preston's carriage. The church bell on the corner chimed three o'clock. Kit opened the small window for fresh air, hoping to keep himself from vomiting again.

"When was the last time you ate?" Preston asked from the opposite seat.

"No idea. Yesterday?"

"You look fucking terrible."

"I know." He'd caught a glimpse of himself in the washroom mirror. "I'll be fine."

"I hope so, because I can't watch another one of my best friends drink himself to death."

Shit, that made him feel worse. Kit leaned his head against the side of the carriage. "How did you hear?"

"The Pinkertons roused me out of bed. They're fairly certain it's him, but the body was taken to the morgue before they could confirm it. I rang Bellevue and they're expecting us."

"Have you ever . . ." Kit couldn't finish it, to ask if Preston had ever identified a body before.

"No, I haven't. And, God willing, I never have to again."

"Did the Pinkertons say what happened?"

Preston smoothed his trousers, his lips pressed tight. "He was hit by a train. The rest I can surmise."

"Fuck," Kit said, and closed his eyes again. "I don't understand it. I just saw him."

"They say he left that boardinghouse on the west side and ended up on Misery Lane."

It was the stretch on East Twenty-Sixth Street near the river, where the poorest and the sickest congregated. Where people went when they'd given up. The potter's field was nearby on Hart's Island, which Bellevue used for those unable to afford proper burial. It went without saying that Kit and Preston would not allow Forrest to end up there.

They didn't speak the rest of the way. Kit was too wrapped up in his thoughts of Forrest to be of any use to a conversation. Why hadn't he tried harder to help his friend? Why hadn't he taken Forrest from his room that day, instead of offering to come back the next? If he had, Forrest might still be alive.

Because he'd been too busy with Alice and the supper club. Selfishness and lust had consumed him, and he'd abandoned his friend. Forrest had been in the city, alone, miserable and hurting, and Kit had been trying to get under Alice's skirts. How would he ever live with himself?

In all fairness, he hadn't meant to sleep with Alice. But this beautiful creature with big eyes and a big heart had looked at him—*him*—as if he could do anything. As if he had the ability to shift heavens or rearrange oceans. He didn't deserve that adoration . . . and he certainly hadn't deserved her innocence. To have been the first man inside her. But he'd been wild for her. Absolutely stark-raving mad to fuck her. He'd tried to be gentle, not to scare her with his inappropriate lust, but she'd driven him over the edge of reason.

I want to do this. I want you to show me.

And he'd given in, unable to resist her when she played the part of willing pupil. God, he was so stupid. She would regret it eventually. How could she not? He knew it with unshakable certainty. She would have a husband—perhaps even Lockwood—who would make her feel cheap and small for taking a lover outside of wedlock, though nearly every man did the same. He could not bear being the source of her shame.

She'd cried, too. A single tear, but it had gutted him nonetheless. He hated the thought of upsetting her. Had she been overcome by the act itself . . . or had it been something more? Had he disappointed her somehow?

There would be no more encounters. That had been clear in her manner when she left, with her parting words and stiff smile. The threshold of acceptable behavior had been crossed and now they must each retreat, try to carry on separately, on different paths. He was about to thumb his nose at all of society with his supper club, and Alice would marry and begin her life as a proper wife. Those two futures were like oil and water.

If only he didn't miss her so damn much.

They pulled up outside the morgue, which sat behind Bellevue Hospital and near the pier. Kit descended and started for the entrance. An ambulance was parked out front, the horses and driver at the ready in a grim reminder of the death that stalked them at every turn in this city.

Inside, the attendant pointed them downstairs, where the viewing rooms were located. The air smelled like strong chemicals, and his stomach pitched. He dragged in deep breaths through his mouth.

They stopped at the desk and Preston slid a few bills to the attendant. "We are here to see the man found on the railroad tracks earlier tonight. We think he might be our friend."

The attendant checked his sheet. "Third window on the left."

Kit shoved his hands in his pockets as they walked along the white-tiled corridor. There were eight windows in total, four on the left and four on the right, all lit up brightly. Death on morbid display. "I very much hope the Pinkertons were wrong," he murmured to Preston as they walked.

"Except they rarely are, so brace yourself."

They arrived at the window and found a small body on a table, covered in a sheet. Then Kit noticed it wasn't small. It was *half*. "Oh, fuck."

Preston knocked on the glass to get the attention of the man inside. The attendant, clad in a white medical coat, turned and nodded once before lifting the top of the sheet.

Kit's heart sank.

It was Forrest. Pale and sunken, but unmistakable.

Preston seemed frozen, not even blinking, so Kit motioned to the attendant and the sheet was lowered. Still Preston didn't move, almost as if he couldn't believe what his eyes had seen. But there were many unpleasant tasks ahead of them, and Kit had to remain practical.

Swallowing hard, he went to the desk at the end of the hall, needing to inquire as to how they could get their friend released for a proper burial.

Chapter Twenty-Four

✦

The church was nearly empty. Rows and rows of vacant pews stretched out before Alice as she slipped into the back. Surprising that there weren't more people here. The story of Forrest Ripley's death, only son of the prominent Ripley family, had been front-page news. The poor man had fallen in front of a train and been killed instantly.

So, why weren't there more mourners?

The service had already started, so she kept her steps whisper-soft on the hard tile, creeping closer. She hadn't seen Kit in over a week, but of course he would be here. Forrest had been his friend and Kit was loyal. Her intention had been to sit in the back among the crowd and pay her respects out of love for Kit. She hadn't wanted to speak to him or pressure him to see her once more. This hadn't been about them; this had been about condolences for the dead.

But there was no crowd, which meant she couldn't hide.

The reverend's voice echoed in the cavernous

space, his message about shepherds and pastures resonating off the rafters. Alice moved toward the figures in the front pews. There were two people sitting on the right side of the church, and she recognized the back of Preston's head. The woman next to him leaned in and spoke softly in his ear, then he kissed her gloved hand. Was this his mistress, Arabella?

Across the aisle sat one lone man. Kit.

There was no one else in the whole space, save the reverend. Kit's shoulders were stiff, his eyes forward. Her heart squeezed at the sight of him by himself, bearing all that grief with no one by his side. It was hardly fair for a man so well liked wherever he went. Where were his other friends? The ladies with whom he would "companionship"?

Well, she would not let him sit alone. He might not love her, but she loved him and it was an awful thing to witness his solitary sadness. If she could ease his sorrow for a second, then it was worth whatever awkwardness or heartache arose later on.

Moving into the center aisle, she walked toward the altar, toward a black casket adorned with lilies. Preston glanced over his shoulder at her approach and she noted the surprise on his face when he recognized her. Then he gave her a nod.

She didn't respond. Instead, she slipped into Kit's row and sat directly beside him, her thigh touching his. He didn't move or speak or acknowledge her in any way, so she reached and took his hand. His grip remained limp. Undeterred, she sat there, holding his hand, not leaving his side as the reverend continued the service.

After five minutes or so, Kit let out a long shuddering breath, as if he'd been holding it a long time. His fingers tightened on her gloved hand, clutching her as if his life depended on it. It was then she knew coming to sit here had been the right thing to do. No one should have to suffer alone.

The reverend finished up with a final blessing, then crossed to the side of the altar and disappeared. Clothes rustled, and Alice watched out of the corner of her eye as Preston helped the woman out of the pew and started down the aisle, leaving. Kit remained perfectly still, his unseeing gaze fixed on the stained-glass window behind the altar.

They sat in silence. Alice didn't speak or move. No one entered the church, the dust motes their only company in the midday light.

Finally, he spoke, his voice a tortured rasp. "It was my fault, you know. I was the last to see him."

The words and the agony underlying them shredded her heart. "No, Kit. The newspaper said it was an accident. That he had been drinking." Reportedly inebriated, Mr. Ripley fell on the tracks and hadn't been able to get out of the way of an oncoming train. Sadly, it happened frequently in the city, at least two or three times a week.

Kit shook his head. "He looked terrible. I should have tried to help. I should have done something—" He bit off the last word.

"No, do not think that." She gripped his arm with her free hand and shook him slightly. "You are not responsible."

He swallowed hard. Then he moved away slightly, pulling his hand from hers, and she started to worry—until he stretched out on the pew, put his head in her lap and closed his eyes. A deep ache settled in her chest as she stroked his hair.

"The wheels cut his body clean in two," he said after several minutes. "Pres and I had to identify him at the morgue."

Lord, that must have been awful. "Oh, Kit. I'm so sorry."

"No one else came. All the friends he made over the years, all the people he knew. His family . . . no one came today. Not even his parents."

She could tell this bothered him, so she repeated, "I'm sorry."

"Maybe I should have hired some professional mourners. Then it wouldn't have seemed so empty in here."

That almost sounded worse, paying people to mourn at a funeral, but she didn't say it. Unable to help herself, she removed her glove and caressed his head. His hair was soft, and she enjoyed touching him again, even if it was for an awful reason. "Are you sleeping?" she asked quietly. "You look tired."

"Can't. When I do, I either dream of Forrest or—" He pressed his lips together.

"What?"

"You. I dream about *you*, Alice."

She blinked down at him, but his expression didn't change. "Oh."

"That came out wrong. It's not that I dislike dreaming about you. It's the waking-up part that is like a kick in the teeth." His lids lifted and deep brown eyes stared up at her. "I miss you. Very much."

Her heart cracked, tiny fractures of misery that

threatened to crumble her foundation. She pushed a lock of hair off his forehead. "I miss you, as well."

"Do you?"

"Of course. Why would I lie about such a thing?"

"I read the papers. I know you have been busy with Lockwood."

"One dinner and one drive in the park hardly qualifies as busy."

"Two drives in total, then. The Fifth Avenue drawing rooms must be abuzz with engagement speculation."

They were, but Alice tried not to pay any attention. It was hard to drum up the proper enthusiasm when her soul cried out for another man, the stubborn one currently lying in her lap. Fortunately, her mother was excited enough for the both of them. "I thought you didn't care about society gossip."

"I don't, except when it pertains to you, apparently. Is he insufferably boring?"

"Not at all. He's kind and smart."

Kit grunted, a noise that hinted at both disbelief and displeasure. "He won't let you near a kitchen, you know. A duchess who cooks? It would scandalize all of England."

"It's a good match for me, Kit. Excellent, actually." And it wasn't as if she had any other prospects.

"Of course it is. I'm sorry, Alice."

It wasn't what she'd wished for him to say. A small part of her had hoped he would jump up and declare his intentions. Drag the reverend out from wherever he was hiding so he could marry them here on the spot. Anything but wish her well with another man.

I am a scoundrel, dear Alice. That is why I haven't married.

Why was she hoping he would change? He wouldn't, and wishing for it was an exercise in futility.

All the hurt from the other night came rushing back, cramping in her gut. She couldn't help but mourn the conversations they'd never have, the moments they'd never share. The smiles they'd never exchange. The inside of her chest was raw, like someone had taken a bread knife to the sensitive skin, and her lids began to burn with unshed tears.

I need to leave.

She lifted him and began to edge to the side. "Kit, I must go. My mother is expecting me."

"Oh." He sat up, his weary gaze studying her face. "Thank you for coming. It means more than I can ever say. Forrest would have really liked you."

Drawing in a breath, she squeezed his hand. "I didn't come for him. I came for you. Goodbye, Kit." She stepped into the aisle, anxious to disappear.

"Alice, wait."

She paused and looked over her shoulder. Kit was thin and pale, anguish etched in the beautiful lines of his face. "You'll . . . come to see me before you leave for England, won't you?"

Everything in her longed to go back and throw herself in his arms, declare her feelings and lay herself bare at his feet. To beg him for scraps of time and attention between his other conquests. Two months ago, she probably would have done it without blinking. But she was not that woman any longer. She needed to do what was best for herself, no matter how much it hurt.

"I'm sorry, but I can't. I think it's best if we never see each other again." She walked away, her boot heels loud on the old tile.

Shoes slapped behind her and Kit caught her arm. His eyes were panicked, a little wild, as he searched her face. "Just like that? You don't want to ever see me again? Are we not friends?"

Was he truly this dense? She retreated a step, putting distance between them. "Kit, you shouldn't ask it of me. It's unfair. Can you not see? I wish for more than friendship from you and you are incapable of it, which hurts."

He put up his hands. "Alice, I warned you. I never lied. If I led you on in any way, then I apologize—"

"Stop. I never expected you to feel something deeper for me. You've made your thoughts on marriage perfectly clear. But I must have it. For many reasons. And so, we arrive at an impasse. You have your companionship every night, and I need something more permanent. While I do not wish you any harm, please, do not make this more difficult for me." A tear spilled out from behind her eyelid, and he watched it roll down her cheek.

"I care about you, I do. However, I am incapable of anything more. I'll always be a scoundrel, a bounder."

"Balderdash. That is an excuse. Everyone is capable of love. But some people"—she pointed at the casket—"prefer to push it away."

His face fell, hurt flashing in his expression. "I am nothing like him."

"For your sake, I hope you are right. Goodbye, Kit."

She walked out of the church and this time he did not stop her.

KIT STOMPED INTO the foyer of his town house. A terrible headache lingered behind his eyes, the pain his constant companion since the night of Forrest's death. It had receded temporarily when Alice rubbed his head after the service, but now the pounding in his skull was back.

I wish for more than friendship from you and you are incapable of it, which hurts.

He hadn't wanted to hurt her, ever. Was that why she cried the other night in his office? At the time, he attributed it to the emotion of her first experience with a man. Now he suspected the tear may have signaled something else. Something deeper.

Everyone is capable of love, but some people prefer to push it away.

The words pricked at him. Yes, Forrest had pushed everyone away, his demons too powerful to overcome, but that was not Kit. He had countless friends and acquaintances, a party wherever he went. The only person he'd pushed away had been his father, but that conniving bastard deserved it.

Granted, he didn't see his brother or sister often. Both were still angry that Kit had retained his vast trust fund, while their funds had been bamboozled by dear old Dad. Perhaps he should make more of an effort to mend fences with his siblings. After all, they had a hatred for their father in common.

His gaze swept the empty entryway, the quiet rooms, and he stifled a sigh. Sitting alone at the funeral had been harder than he'd imagined. Arabella had come to comfort Preston, but there hadn't been a soul to offer Kit comfort or share his grief . . . until Alice arrived. She hadn't kept her distance or waited for permission, either. Instead, she saw him in the pew and came right up to hold his hand.

Christ, he missed her.

The front bell clanged, startling him. Wasn't the entire city aware that he was in mourning? Who the hell would be calling today of all days?

Without waiting on his butler, Kit yanked open the door. His anger dissipated when he found Nellie Young standing there, a bag in her hands.

"You are an idiot." She pushed by him and came inside, not even caring that he hadn't invited her.

"Not keen on callers today, Nellie," he said, still holding on to the door.

"Don't care, Kit," she said over her shoulder on the way into the salon. "I'm here to toast your friend and leave you to your misery."

He flung the door shut, which closed with a satisfying snap. She was pulling a bottle and two glasses out of her bag when he threw himself into an armchair. "Not keen on drinking today, either."

"Yes, your friend died in a drunken accident, I am aware." She poured a small amount of clear liquid into each glass. "But you will do this."

He accepted the glass from her and sniffed it. The vapor nearly melted his lungs. "What is it?"

"Poitín. It's Irish and it'll burn like the fires of

Hell going down. Ready?" She lifted her glass. "Death leaves a heartache no one can heal; Love leaves a memory no one can steal. To Forrest."

He lifted his glass. "To Forrest." Together, they tossed the liquid in their mouths and swallowed. His throat went up in flames and he was certain his stomach had combusted. Leaning forward, he wheezed and gasped for breath.

By the time he gained control of his lungs, Nellie was already packing up. "Wait," he said. "Give me a minute. I need you to explain."

"My mother was Irish." She pointed to her fiery red hair. "When she died, some of her family held a wake in the house. I remember hearing the songs and the prayers. It was filled with sorrow, but joy, too. I always thought it was a nice way to remember people. So, I never go to funerals, but I like wakes."

"Where do you get that stuff?" He tilted his chin toward the bag where she'd stashed the liquor.

"Some boys over in Hell's Kitchen. Any other questions before I go downstairs to say hello to Mrs. Henry?"

"Yes. Why did you call me an idiot when you first walked in?"

"Because you're letting Alice marry the duke."

His jaw fell open. "I am not *letting* her do anything. If she chooses to marry Lockwood, then that is her decision."

"Kit. She is in love with *you*. Unfortunately, you won't marry her, so what other choice has she?"

"I never lied to her. I never made promises or whispered sweet nothings in her ear."

"Bully for you. Tell me, how many of the women

you've slept with over the years came to the funeral today to hold your hand?"

His brows shot up. "How did you know?"

"You'd be surprised at what I know. And that is not an answer."

"None."

"Exactly. And how many other women came to your rescue and cooked a five-course dinner for fifty people?" She paused but he didn't bother answering because the question was clearly rhetorical. "You think this devil-may-care, I-cannot-be-tied-down attitude is appealing, but I'll tell you the truth. It's not. Because we all know what this façade is hiding: fear."

Irritation swept over him like a rash. "What about you? You are unmarried and flout society every chance you get. How am I any different?"

She rolled her eyes. "I am a *woman*. Marriage is a death sentence for me, not salvation. You're a man. You get everything upon marriage—a constant bed partner, money, property, someone to feed you and look after you. Worse, you already have a loving, caring, wonderful woman who would trade anything to marry you, and you are too selfish to see it."

"I am not afraid of marrying Alice."

Smirking, she relaxed in the chair. "Tell me, then. Why won't you marry her? Because I know you are wild about her."

"I didn't even know until today that she was interested in marrying me."

"Again, not an answer—and I am skeptical that it's never crossed your mind before. But let's not quibble. Why won't you marry her?"

This conversation was making his head hurt worse. "Fine. Let's see. First off, I am opening a supper club, which is hardly a respectable business. Her parents would never approve."

"Sounds like you are *afraid* that her parents would refuse your suit. What's next?"

He gritted his teeth. "With my lack of standing in society, any wife of mine would practically be an outcast."

"So you're afraid the mean old matrons of Fifth Avenue will hurt your wife's feelings?"

"I am beginning to truly regret opening the door to you today."

"I bet. In tennis terms, I believe it is thirty–love in my favor. Tell me your next reason. No, let me guess! How could a man like you ever be faithful to just one woman?"

Crossing his arms, he glared at her. Yes, that had certainly crossed his mind.

"What?" She cupped her hand to her ear. "What did you say? That I'm right again? Forty–love, Mr. Ward."

"The reason for your spinsterhood is becoming glaringly apparent."

She threw her head back and laughed. "You make it so hard to be cross with you. All right, let's get down to the brass tacks. Just say it, Kit. Just tell me the real reason and then it can be out in the open."

Shooting to his feet, he crossed to the window and clasped his hands behind his back. He didn't want to say anything more. She would mock him for whatever insecurities came out of his mouth. "You wouldn't understand."

"Would I not? I know the whispers inside your head, the ones that make us doubt ourselves. The voices in the dark that tell us we are not worthy. You and I, we are kindred spirits. Which is how I *know.*"

He rubbed the back of his neck. How had she guessed that he still had his father's voice in his head? That he feared the old man was right about him.

Worse, that he feared he was just like Franklin Ward. The charmer, the confidence man. Incapable of fidelity. One foot out the door at all times.

He did not *want* to be that man . . . but what if he was? What if it was deep in his blood, waiting for an unsuspecting woman to bring it out of him? He couldn't risk it.

Alice deserves better.

"Perhaps," Nellie said, making him realize he'd spoken aloud. "But feelings never bother with what one deserves."

The tone had him turning. "You sound as if you are speaking from experience."

"Immaterial. She wants you but is settling for a duke. The question is, what do *you* want? Because if it's Alice, then you must act quickly. And it's worth noting, her mother won't risk Alice being compromised. So do not think to do as your friend Harrison did. You'll have to woo her the old-fashioned way."

He gave a dry laugh that held no humor whatsoever. "I wouldn't even know how."

"I suggest you figure it out, then." Nellie picked up her bag. "Unless, of course, you are ready to lose the best woman you will ever meet to another man."

The idea of Alice and Lockwood sat in his stomach like a stone, more painful than the poitín. *She wants you but is settling for a duke.* Was it true? Alice had said she'd wished for more from Kit, but he'd told her time and time again that he wouldn't marry her.

"I will pop down and say hello to Mrs. Henry. Think about what I said, Kit."

"I will. Thank you, Nellie."

She crossed the floor but then paused at the door. "Oh, and one more thing. Alice is my friend. If you are not prepared to crawl through fire to win her, then I won't let you have her. Enjoy your afternoon."

Chapter Twenty-Five

❧

$\mathcal{M}$ary placed a huge flower bouquet—lilies of the valley and gardenias—on the tea table in Alice's suite. "These just arrived for you, miss."

Flowers? Alice put down her ladies' magazine and reached for the card tucked into the bouquet. Had Lockwood sent these? Her heart, which should have raced at the idea, gave a mere thump. It was becoming more difficult to muster excitement for a match.

He's a duke, for goodness' sake. She had no other choice and Lockwood would make a fine husband. Alice should be positively thrilled.

She tore open the card. The crisp writing was short and to the point:

> *Fondly,*
> *Mr. Christopher Ward*

These flowers were from Kit? Her lips twisted into a broad smile. Then it fell. Why was he sending her flowers? And *these* flowers, in particular?

Lilies of the valley were used to signify purity, either of person or intent. Gardenias represented sincerity in a promising new relationship, though Kit couldn't possibly know that. She could not imagine that he followed such silly floriography.

Still, they were lovely. Perhaps this was his way of thanking her for coming to the funeral yesterday.

"Is there a vase?" she asked her maid. "If not in here, there might be one in my mother's room."

Mary went through the adjoining door into the other suite while Alice admired the beautiful bouquet. She had cried for most of the afternoon after leaving the church. For Kit, for herself. For what would never be. She loved him, but she would not give up her future because of him.

When Mary returned, she was not alone. "I hear you received flowers from the duke," her mother said, wide eyes on the bouquet. Before Alice could hide the card, Mama snatched it out of her hand. "Christopher Ward? That scapegrace from the house party? Why on earth is he sending you flowers?"

"I haven't any idea," she lied. "But they certainly are pretty."

Her mother pointed to the flowers. "Mary, dispose of those this instant. We must take care not to scare off the duke."

"No, please. I'll put them in my room." Alice lunged for the box but she was too late.

In a flash, her mother gathered the flowers and handed them off to Mary, along with the card. "They will be disposed of and that is the end of that." As if seeing Alice for the first time, Mama gave her a once-over. "Now, what are you wearing this afternoon?"

"This afternoon? Have we plans?"

"Alice, there is a tea at the Van Allens' home. I told you this morning at breakfast. Do you never listen?"

Alice had hardly been paying attention, her mind stuck on memories of Kit. The idea of a society event today, with small talk and uncomfortable stares, sounded like absolute torture. "Must I go?"

Mama's eyes widened. "Of course you must go. You are about to become a duchess, so we must show you off. The lilac dress, I think, Mary," she called out to Alice's maid.

The bell rang. Mama perked up and rushed to take a seat opposite Alice. She arranged her skirts and motioned for Mary to hurry. The maid answered the door and the duke's smooth voice filled the space. "The Duke of Lockwood here to see Miss Lusk."

Mary bobbed a curtsy. "Come in, Your Grace."

Mama rose, doing her best at a welcoming smile. "Your Grace. How lovely of you to call this morning."

Lockwood entered and promptly bowed. "Mrs. Lusk, Miss Lusk." He looked dashing in a blue suit, his hair swept off his face. Freshly shaven, as if he'd just come from the barber shop downstairs in the hotel. Alice waited for some reaction, a zing of lust or attraction, but it never came. While she appreciated Lockwood's appearance and personality, he didn't set her heart aflame.

Only one man managed to do that.

You must stop thinking about him.

"Hello, Your Grace," she said, and retook her seat.

"Good morning. I am wondering if you have dinner plans this evening. I realize it is last minute, but I would love to dine with you both in the hotel dining room."

"I am not certain I feel up to dinner tonight," her mother said, coughing delicately into her hand. "But Alice would love to go. Wouldn't you, Alice?"

Not feeling up to dinner? That meant Alice would dine alone with the duke. Granted, they would be surrounded by a roomful of people, but still. What was her mother doing? "Uh, yes. Of course. I would love to, Your Grace."

"Excellent. Eight o'clock? I'll come by and escort you down."

"I shall look forward to it."

After a few minutes of small talk about the weather and his plans for the afternoon, he departed. Mama's eyes were ablaze with satisfaction as she turned to Alice. "This is very good news. If he brings up the subject of marriage, try to look surprised."

"Mama, he isn't going to do that, not over dinner in a public dining room. And why aren't you coming with us? You aren't ill."

"This is the perfect opportunity to give you both time alone while still remaining in public. As I said, act surprised if he floats the idea of a marriage between you."

"I'll try," she muttered.

Her mother's gaze narrowed until her lids were tiny, angry slits, and she folded her arms across her middle. "It wouldn't kill you to appear even the tiniest bit happy at this development. Against all odds, you have a duke honoring you with his attentions. I expect you to smile and be agreeable tonight."

"I will, Mama."

"Now, I must write to the Van Allens and cancel for this afternoon."

They weren't attending the afternoon tea? "Wait, why?"

"Because you have a dinner to prepare for. We want you looking your best. Perhaps a nap first, then you may bathe and Mary can arrange your hair."

The day stretched out in front of Alice like a military field march, during which she'd endure her mother's heavy surveillance until she could escape to the hotel dining room. "Yes, Mama."

"Also, you should eat something small so there is no need to eat during dinner tonight. There is nothing more off-putting to a man than watching a woman shovel food in her mouth."

Alice knew this advice to be complete rubbish. She thought back to Kit's lesson in the kitchen in Newport.

Anything that calls attention to a woman's mouth has the potential to drive men wild.

And he had shown her exactly why in the club, which was that men loved to have their members sucked. She had loved it, as well, driving him wild with soft kisses and warm breaths, listening to his growls and grunts as she moved. Knowing she would never have another opportunity to see him like that made her want to weep. Again.

Her heart aching, she went into her bedchamber. Returning to her bed sounded like a fine idea at the moment. Then she spotted a small piece of vellum on her pillow. *The card from Kit's flowers.* Her pulse leapt. Mary must have saved it for her.

Lying down on the bed, Alice gazed at the paper, the neat writing. It was her last flower arrangement from Kit, so she hated to part with the card, even if it made her seem like a silly lovesick fool.

She lifted it to her nose and inhaled. The scent of gardenias still clung to the paper and she closed her eyes, missing him with a ferociousness that scared her. Would this terrible pain ever go away?

KIT SLAMMED THROUGH the door of the supper club, the early-evening quiet only serving to amplify his loneliness. That had been a complete waste of an entire dashed afternoon.

Using Preston's connections, Kit had secured an invitation to the Van Allens' garden tea today because Alice had been on the guest list. Except her mother canceled at the last minute, which left Kit hobnobbing with Knickerbocker snobs for the better part of three hours. Granted, he was very good at hobnobbing, but he hated that High Society crowd, with their judgmental stares and whispered gossip.

In those elite circles, the Wards were nothing more than a tragic example of marrying outside their class. His blue-blooded mother had married for love, after all, choosing a working-class man instead, and then he took her money and deserted her. All afternoon, the women at the tea party had looked down their noses at him over oolong and macarons, setting his teeth on edge at every turn. It had been a miserable day.

You'll have to woo her the old-fashioned way.

Thus far, he'd tried flowers and one failed society party. Not off to an encouraging start. He needed to do better to prove to Alice that he was serious about her. About them. About marriage.

Dragging a hand through his hair, he strode toward the bar. After all that tea, he was looking forward to a stiff drink. He poured a neat whiskey and then checked his pocket watch. His appointment should arrive at any moment.

His eyes drifted toward the office door. Heat and longing rushed through him, an ache that hadn't dissipated since the night of the preview. Nellie was right. He wasn't willing to let her marry another man, and his reasons for rejecting marriage had been based in fear. Once he'd admitted it, the barriers hadn't seemed so great, so insurmountable. Because while they might share blood, he and his father were nothing alike. Kit had a firm handle on the concept of right and wrong. His father could not say the same.

Nor was he like Forrest, self-destructive and isolating. Kit didn't want that future. No, he needed Alice by his side—not just at funerals and in the kitchen, but every morning. Every night. Every moment in between. He would never tire of her or want anyone else. The question was how to make her believe it. He'd spent more than a month telling her the exact opposite . . . and time was running out.

The bell sounded and Kit put down his drink. At the door was a man in a dark brown suit. He struck out his hand. "Mr. Ward?"

"Indeed, and you must be Mr. Littleton." They

shook and Kit brought the man into the main room. "May I offer you a drink?"

"No, thank you. I'll take a few notes and be on my way. Nice place." Littleton glanced around. "Mr. Hearst said it was quite a night."

Littleton worked for the *New York Journal*, Hearst's paper in the city. The newspaper magnate had asked to do a feature on Kit's club, which would only boost its popularity. Needless to say, Kit had readily agreed. "Shall we sit?" He gestured to a table.

The reporter lowered himself into a chair and flipped through a tiny journal. For the first few minutes, they chatted easily about Kit's and Preston's backgrounds and their decision to open the supper club. Then Littleton turned to the night of the preview. "Madame Durham, a well-known Black opera singer, was an inspired choice for entertainment. Have you seen her perform before?"

"I have," Kit answered. "At Carnegie Hall a few years ago. She's the best there is, in my opinion. We plan on hiring performers—actresses, dancers, singers—of every color and background, much as Mr. Carnegie does, but in a more intimate setting."

"And you used Chef Franconi's recipes, cooked by one of his apprentices. A Chef Lucciola."

"Yes, that's correct. Franconi was gracious enough to allow us both the use of his recipes and his apprentice."

Littleton continued to scribble on the paper. "And this chef? We heard rumors it was a woman."

Kit stopped breathing. He'd sworn the waiters and kitchen staff to secrecy, and none of the guests had seen Alice. So how had Littleton learned of this information? He forced his body to relax. "Ludicrous. Who told you such a thing?"

"I have two sources."

"Who must not have attended that night."

Littleton didn't confirm or deny it, instead changed tack. "Unusual to hire a woman as a head chef. Were you concerned that a woman in the kitchen here would scare off potential customers?"

"Are you implying that a woman cannot cook? Because hundreds of years of history have proven otherwise."

"But not in fine dining. There are no women in any of the hotel kitchens or restaurants. Women work in home kitchens."

Though Kit wanted to defend Alice's brilliance, he could not reveal her identity as Chef Lucciola. To do so would ruin her standing in society. Mrs. Lusk would ship her daughter off to a convent in Europe if that happened. Furthermore, it would sink the supper club. As Littleton pointed out, women did not work in fine dining kitchens. "Chef Lucciola is an apprentice of Franconi. If you speak to anyone who ate here that night, they will tell you the food was superb."

"Indeed, I have heard many accounts of the meal that was served. My question is whether Chef Lucciola is a man or a woman."

"I have already answered that question."

"Not really. You called the question"—he checked his notes—"ludicrous. But that is not an answer."

"Does Hearst know you are pursuing this angle?"

"It was his idea, sir."

Goddamn it. Kit should have known better than to trust Hearst. The man was out for sensationalism, to sell as many newspapers as possible. "What if I refuse to answer any more questions?"

"That is your prerogative, of course, but I should warn you that I already have a name for the woman posing as Lucciola."

Time ground to a halt as Kit's heart ceased to beat. He stared at Littleton, hoping the reporter hadn't discovered Alice's identity. "Who?"

Littleton's eyes studied Kit's face—watching for a reaction, no doubt. "Miss Alice Lusk of Boston. She and her mother are staying at the Fifth Avenue Hotel, which is where Franconi happens to work."

Holy fuck. How on earth had this come to light? It was now imperative to throw the reporter off the scent—or both he and Alice would be ruined. She'd never forgive him, either. Any hopes of marrying her would be dashed.

He tilted his head back and laughed. "A debutante? Here? If I were to hire any woman, I'd use the cook from my own household, who is more than competent in the kitchen. I can promise you, Lucciola was not Miss Lusk. I'd be ruined if that were true."

"It did sound strange, I have to admit."

"Of course, because you are a logical human being. How would a debutante like Miss Lusk learn to cook like Chef Franconi, one of the greatest chefs in the world? It doesn't make any sense."

"Well." He scratched his head with the tip of his pencil. "Franconi did work for the Lusks in Boston for a number of years. It could be that she was friendly with the chef . . ."

"And? Keep going." He leaned back and smirked. "I cannot wait to hear the rest of it."

"I know," Littleton chuckled, appearing slightly sheepish. "I hardly believed it myself."

"The idea of Franconi teaching this young girl to cook . . . and her mother allowing it? No, no. Whoever gave you that information clearly has never met a society mother. Such a thing would never be condoned, and no girl would have the freedom to come here and cook for three days."

Littleton nodded. "That makes sense. Yet, these sources are very compelling."

"You may believe me, Mr. Littleton. And I sincerely hope you do not pursue this further and ruin a young woman's reputation."

Littleton closed his journal. "Well, I should get going. I have to type this up for tomorrow's edition."

They both stood and Kit led Littleton to the door. As he pulled open the wooden panel, a sense of unease prickled the back of Kit's neck. "I assume we have put this Lucciola business to bed?"

"As long as I am able to confirm the man's existence, yes. Good evening, Mr. Ward."

Watching the reporter head toward Broadway, Kit began to sweat under his suit. This was bad. Very bad. He must warn Alice immediately. They had to find someone in Franconi's kitchen willing to pose as Lucciola to fool Hearst and his reporters.

Because if they didn't, everything would be ruined—especially Alice.

Chapter Twenty-Six

※

Alice stared at the Duke of Lockwood over the rim of her water glass. He was perfectly turned out in a black evening suit with white vest and bow tie, his handsomeness and aristocratic bearing drawing nearly every eye in the room. The tables around them were full, as they were on most nights, and Alice tried not to fidget under the increased attention.

This is what you wanted. A man who likes you, a man you might grow to love.

Why, then, was she so forlorn? So dead inside? It could not be because of Kit, as she had decided to put him firmly out of her mind for good. Flowers or not, Kit was headed down a different path. Alice had to marry to escape the insufferable presence of her mother, to start a life in her own home with her own kitchen. And with a man who wanted her by his side. She was not a rebellious upstart, willing to throw away her chance at security and happiness on a man who refused to claim her publicly.

In her head she knew this was the right decision,

but her heart was not operating on logic. No, that particular organ followed a completely separate set of rules, and it was devastated at the moment, yearning for the man who'd stolen a chunk of it the other night.

It will heal. The hurt will go away.

She had to keep telling herself as much. Otherwise, she might crumple into a ball under the bedclothes and never emerge.

"What do you recommend?" the duke asked as he studied the menu. "I hear the lobster thermidor is excellent."

Her throat closed up with memories of the other night, of Kit and his mind-numbing kisses. "Yes," she finally managed. "It is delicious."

"Excuse me, sir. Miss." Their waiter interrupted by setting down a plate of clam fritters. "Chef has sent this for you to enjoy. He said it is one of the lady's favorites."

"Please give Chef my thanks," Alice said, and the waiter left. She gestured to the plate. "Try one. His clam fritters are heaven on a plate."

"I don't see those on the menu." Lockwood put down his menu and cocked his head. "How did Chef Franconi know?"

Because I spend at least four nights a week in his kitchen, watching and tasting. Learning.

"He used to work for my parents in Boston. I've known him since I was a young girl."

Instead of exhibiting ducal horror at the commingling of classes, Lockwood appeared fascinated. "You are like an onion, Miss Lusk. So many interesting layers. Did you spend a lot of time in the kitchen, then?"

"More than my mother liked, actually. She was forever chasing me out of there."

"You must have a love of food, I would imagine."

"I do, though it's not something I often discuss. Girls are supposed to sew and learn how to manage a household. Be the perfect hostess."

"Why must it be one or the other? My mother spent quite a lot of time meal planning and working with our cook."

Yes, but Alice's interest was not in the planning of a meal, as such, but rather the preparation and improvement. However, she couldn't tell that to Lockwood. She was willing to be honest about most things, but not that—not yet, anyway.

They had just started on the clam fritters when there was a disruption behind her. People were staring at something over her shoulder, so she glanced in that direction—and froze. Kit was in the dining room, headed straight for her.

His gaze, dark and troubled, did not leave her face. Why on earth was he here? How had he known she was in the dining room?

"What is Ward doing?" Lockwood murmured, but she couldn't answer because Kit was coming closer, almost alongside their table. She couldn't breathe, couldn't blink, as she drank in the sight of his tall, gorgeous form eating up the ground with his long legs, fierce determination stamped in the set of his jaw.

Her head tilted as he arrived, his body nearly vibrating with tension. Without preamble, he said, "May I speak with you? Privately?"

She cast a nervous glance at the duke, who was frowning at Kit. Clearing her throat, she said, "Mr.

Ward, you remember His Grace, the Duke of Lock-wood."

"Lockwood," Kit said with barely a nod in the other man's direction. "Alice, now." He reached for her arm to help her up, and the duke came to his feet.

"Ward, what is this about?"

"A bit of an emergency," Kit said, guiding Alice toward the kitchen. "I'll return her in a few moments, I promise."

"Miss Lusk," Lockwood said, confusion evident in his voice. "Are you all right with this?"

Alarmed by Kit's behavior, Alice nodded. She had to find out what was behind his strange interruption. "I shall return in a moment, Your Grace. Go ahead and order dinner."

Kit nearly dragged her away from the table, his fingers firm on her arm. She leaned in and spoke sharply under her breath. "Kit, what are you doing? Why are you dragging me into the kitchen?"

"We have a problem, but we cannot discuss it out in the open like this. Follow me." He pushed open the swinging door that led to the busy kitchen. The sous chefs and waiters looked up, but relaxed when they saw her. She waved as Kit tugged her to the tiny table Franconi kept along the wall. "You might want to sit down for this."

"Kit, you are scaring me." She lowered herself into a chair. "What is it?"

He dragged his fingers though his hair, disheveling the strands, and began pacing in the cramped space. "I invited both Hearst and Pulitzer to the preview in the hopes of gaining press for the supper club. Which it has, but it's the wrong sort. Do you understand? It's the wrong sort of attention. For me." He gave her a pointed look. "And for you."

Oh. Her hand wrapped around her throat, horror sinking into her veins like a cold fog. "What do you mean?"

"I mean," he said as he sat in the empty chair opposite her, "that this reporter has not only learned that I hired a woman chef, he's also learned said woman was *you*."

"That's impossible. The waiters and kitchen staff were sworn to secrecy. They all personally promised me."

"Who knows what Hearst did to get someone to go back on his word? He could have blackmail material on one of the waiters. I just . . . I don't know. But we have to figure out what to do. The reporter is going to come looking for Chef Lucciola. If we cannot produce him, then we are both ruined."

"Oh, God." She dropped her head in her hands and closed her eyes. Her reputation. Her mother. *Lockwood.* "Oh, God," she repeated.

"Alice." He touched her hand gently. "I am so sorry. If I had any idea it would turn out like this, I would never have allowed you to help me."

"You tried to talk me out of it. Repeatedly. No, I only have myself to blame." If the story was published, what would she do? Return to Boston with Mama? Live out the rest of her days in humiliation and misery? No one would marry her. She would end up a spinster, unloved and a burden. Tears burned the backs of her lids. "Oh, God."

"I know." Kit squeezed her fingers, his voice full of sympathy. "We can fix this. We just need someone to pose as—"

"Indeed, this is interesting." A man in a dark suit stood aside the table, smirking at Kit.

Alice frowned up at him. "Who are you?"

The man inclined his head. "Mr. Littleton. And who are you, Miss . . . ?"

"Do not answer that," Kit snapped. "Littleton, what are you doing here?"

The man hooked a thumb over his shoulder. "Came to speak with Franconi. See if I can't get to the bottom of this little mystery."

Alice stifled a gasp. Was this the reporter working on Mr. Hearst's story?

Waiters continued to go in and out of the swinging door, the kitchen in constant motion. Which meant Alice was unprepared to hear Lockwood's voice suddenly beside her. "Miss Lusk, is everything all right?"

The reporter's eyes widened and he grinned. "Miss Lusk, is it? This certainly is a coincidence to find you here with Mr. Ward. Did he tell you that I just left his club?"

"I don't know what you're talking about," she lied.

"Is this man bothering you?" Lockwood asked her, pointing at the reporter. "If so, I can fetch the maître d'hôtel."

"Everyone calm down," Kit said, putting his palms out as he stood. "Littleton, this is not the time or the place. You may call on me at another arranged time to get answers, but you will stay away from Miss Lusk."

"Lucciola, my dear. What is happening here?" Chef Franconi arrived into their circle, unhappiness at having his domain overrun evident on his face. He concentrated on Alice. "Are you being harassed?"

"Lucciola?" Littleton's smirk grew wider. "I see. If you all will excuse me, I believe my work here is done."

"Wait," Kit called, not a little desperately. "We can work something out."

"I answer to a man more powerful than any of you. I apologize, Mr. Ward. Good night." The reporter disappeared out the back of the kitchen, toward the alley.

Alice couldn't move. All that she'd feared had just come to pass in the last two minutes. Why hadn't she and Kit gone outside? Why had she agreed to help his supper club in the first place? Why hadn't she waited to pursue her dream of cooking until after she was married?

There were no good answers to those questions, except that she lost all her sense and reason around this man.

"I believe I will lock the back door," Angelo said, and followed the path the reporter had taken out of the kitchen.

"Shit!" Kit slapped a palm on the white-tiled wall.

"Ward," the duke barked. "There are ladies present."

"This doesn't concern you, Lockwood. Go back to your table."

"I will stay as long as Miss Lusk is here."

Kit took a menacing step forward. "I said, go back to your table. Now."

The edges of Lockwood's mouth tightened. "Or?"

Alice's head throbbed and the tension between the two men certainly wasn't helping. Ignoring them, she stared at the wall. What on earth was she going to do?

FURIOUS WITH HIMSELF and the reporter, Kit was happy to transfer some of that anger onto the duke. Moving in, he snarled, "I said, go back to your table. Now."

Lockwood had the nerve to lift a brow. "Or?"

"Or I'll put my fist in your face. You are upsetting her." He pointed at Alice, who was as pale as snow.

"*I* am upsetting her?" Lockwood's voice rose in outrage. "Fairly certain you have done a fine job of that on your own. And why was a newspaperman here? What was he talking about?"

"None of your concern." If it was the last thing Kit did, he would stop that story from running. Who did he know at the *Journal*? There must be a favor he or Preston could call in . . .

He would not let this ruin Alice's life.

Speaking of Alice, she was worrying him. As still as death, she merely stared at the wall in front of her. He knelt at her side and gentled his voice. "Alice, I will find a way to make this right, I swear."

A hand jerked him upright, away from her. Lockwood. The duke got in Kit's face and had the gall to snarl, "Get back. You've clearly done enough."

Rage tightened Kit's muscles, and he shoved Lockwood with both hands. "You don't know what the hell you are talking about. Furthermore, you have no right whatsoever to keep me away from her."

"As her escort tonight, her welfare is my responsibility. Therefore, I have every right." Lockwood stepped forward, rolling his shoulders like a bare-knuckled fighter in the ring.

Oh, so that was it, then? In a blink, Kit shrugged out of his coat and tossed it on the wooden table in front of a too-quiet Alice. If Lockwood wanted a fight, Kit would be more than happy to give him one. "Hardly, you pompous, overprivileged, stick-up-your-arse—"

Lockwood lunged and threw a punch, but Kit blocked it and offered up one of his own. Unfortunately, Lockwood twisted out of the way so Kit's fist glanced off his ribs instead of inflicting damage.

"Stop it!" Alice put her hands between them, and soon Franconi was there, too, pushing the men apart. Tugging on Kit's sleeve, she dragged him away from the duke. "Stop, both of you. Just stop!"

She was breathing hard and her eyes were wet, and the anger instantly left Kit's body. He hated seeing her upset. "Forgive me, Alice. For everything. I am so sorry. I will find a way to keep that story from running, I swear."

"What on earth is going on in here?" a voice shrieked.

Alice stiffened and grew paler. "Oh, God, no," she whispered as she shut her eyes. "Please, no."

Mrs. Lusk rushed into the kitchen, her expression awash in horror and disapproval. Her gaze swept over Kit and Lockwood, then settled on Alice. "What on earth are you doing in here? When they told me you were hiding in the kitchen, I nearly didn't believe it. Have you lost your mind, Alice? Get out in that dining room at once."

"Signora, how nice to see you again." Franconi greeted Alice's mother like a long-lost cousin, kissing her on both cheeks. "You look well."

"Hello, Chef Franconi. I do apologize for my daughter's rude behavior. I will get her out of your kitchen at once." Mrs. Lusk gripped her daughter's arm, and Alice winced. "Your Grace, I'll have her settled at your table presently."

Tears started leaking from Alice's eyes and Kit's chest twisted, like a fist was squeezing his lungs. "I do not think continuing dinner is in Miss Lusk's best interest at the moment, ma'am."

"I will decide what is in my daughter's best interest, thank you very much. Which, incidentally, does not include any more floral deliveries from a worthless scoundrel like you."

"You sent her *flowers*?" Lockwood peered at Kit, then his face cleared. Nodding, he gave a deprecating, humorless laugh. "I see. It's nearly happened again, hasn't it? Astoundingly poor luck on my part."

"I apologize," Kit said. No use pretending he didn't know what Lockwood was talking about, and he wouldn't deny his feelings toward Alice. "It's nothing personal."

"Really? Between you and your friend Archer, it feels quite personal. However, I won't dig in my heels this time." Straightening his vest, he inclined his head toward Alice. "Miss Lusk, I wish you the very best of luck."

"Your Grace," Alice rushed out. "I am deeply sorry for all of this. It was never my intent to harm you or embroil you in another scandal. Yet it seems I've done both."

The edge of Lockwood's mouth hitched. "One thing I will say about this country: it is never boring. Good evening to you all."

When the duke started to leave, Mrs. Lusk's eyes went wide. "Wait, do not leave yet. She is normally well behaved. She won't give Your Grace a lick of trouble."

Lockwood paused at the door. "It's not the trouble that is the problem, madam. Good evening."

Mrs. Lusk whirled in Kit's direction, her lips pressed tight. "This is *your* doing, you complete imbecile. You have ruined my daughter's chances at becoming a duchess. Ruined her chances at happiness. How *dare* you?"

"Madam, if you would just listen—"

"I do not need to listen to you, Mr. Ward. You are a lazy, shiftless, idiotic man who takes whatever he wants without thought to the consequences. You've drawn Alice in with your false flattery and—"

"Mama," Alice shouted, the word reverberating off the tile. "Stop saying those horrible things to Mr. Ward and to me. To everyone. *Just stop being so horrible.*"

All the waiters and kitchen staff froze at the outburst, the room still except for the sizzle of food on the range. Mrs. Lusk's mouth fell open, then she narrowed her gaze. "How dare you speak to me that way? I am your mother, and everything I have done has been for you."

"No, it's been for *you*. Please do not pretend otherwise. If you cared about my happiness at all, you would not act like this, as if I am a constant embarrassment to you."

"You stupid girl. I have tried to make you a better person, which has clearly failed. Tonight, you have run off the best marriage prospect in the last three seasons. Now what will you do? Who will marry you now?"

"I am going to marry her." The words were out of Kit's mouth before he could stop them.

Instead of expressing relief, Alice seemed to shrink, withdrawing into herself. "You don't mean that."

"Indeed, I do." More tears fell from her lashes, her lips pink and puffy from crying, and she was still beautiful. He'd never tire of looking at her, at discovering every little thing about her. "I want to marry you."

"As if Mr. Lusk or I would ever consent. Give our only child over to you? Absurd," Mrs. Lusk said derisively. "Her dowry could buy her another duke or a European prince."

"I don't want to buy a husband, Mother." Alice swiped at the tears on her cheeks. "I want to marry for love."

"That is ridiculous. No one of our station marries for love." Her mother glanced around, as if just noticing that they were attracting attention in the kitchen. "This is unseemly, Alice. Come along. We shall continue this upstairs."

"Wait," Kit said, a little desperately. He had the strangest feeling that if Alice left the kitchen, he'd never see her again. He'd already lost one person dear to him; he couldn't stand to lose her, too. "Let me explain, Alice."

Mrs. Lusk gasped at his use of her daughter's given name, but he didn't look away from Alice. She was shaking her head but hadn't yet moved, her feet rooted to the floor. Before she could react, however, her mother grabbed her arm. "Upstairs, Alice. Now."

The touch jolted Alice out of her thoughts. She yanked her arm from her mother's grip and stepped back. "No, Mama. You return upstairs. I need a minute with Mr. Ward."

"Alone? Absolutely not."

Alice's chest rose as she drew in a deep breath. "I am staying to talk with him. Here, in full view of the kitchen staff. Your presence is not required, so go upstairs."

"I don't think—"

"Now, Mother," Alice ordered loudly, her voice hard and sharp.

Mrs. Lusk blinked, as if she couldn't believe Alice had dared speak to her in such a manner. "We will discuss this impertinence when you return to your room." She spun on her heel and stomped out of the kitchen, nearly colliding with a waiter in the process. "Get out of my way," she snapped, and pushed through the swinging door.

Alice exhaled, her shoulders drooping, and Kit lowered his voice. "I meant what I said. I want to marry you, Alice."

A fresh tear slipped from the corner of her eye, slowly rolling down her face. "No, you don't. You feel sorry for me and you feel guilty. I'd rather have a husband who wants me only for my dowry."

"You're wrong. I care about you. I would be honored to marry you." That only made her cry harder, so he rushed to explain. "Alice, I need you. In my life, at my side. Day and night."

"Please, Kit. Just leave me alone. We have done

enough damage to each other. There's no need to make things worse. By tomorrow, I'll be the laughingstock of the entire city—"

Her voice broke and she pushed by him, running from the kitchen and toward the back stairs. Defeat crashed through him, hurt and anger burning his throat. He'd ruined everything by not telling her sooner. Just as he suspected, she didn't believe him . . . and thanks to Hearst and his newspaperman, she never would.

He stood there for a long moment, his mind reeling. "Was that your idea of a proposal, signore?" Franconi leaned against the wall and wiped his hands on his apron. "Because that was depressing."

"What do you mean?"

The chef shook his head. "You have to speak from here." He poked Kit in the chest. "Tell her you love her. So, do you love her?"

There it was—the tug deep in his chest when he thought of Alice. Overflowing happiness, so much so that he feared his chest might crack open with the force of it. Yet panic lurked not far behind, like storm clouds on a sunny day. There was every possibility he'd ruined his chance with her for good. He might never see her again.

Was love a combination of such tenderness and fear? A bone-deep affection haunted with the worry it could all disappear in an instant, mixed with a desperation to never leave her side? If so, then he was drowning in love for her.

"I do."

"Then why are you standing here?"

Chapter Twenty-Seven

❧

Chest heaving, Alice hurried up the staff stairs. Everything had gone so horribly, horribly wrong. The entire city would be laughing at her in a matter of hours. Posing as a chef, cooking in a supper club, chasing off a duke . . . she was positively ruined.

Her throat closed. Oh, God. What had she done?

Unable to take another step, she collapsed against the wall somewhere between the third and fourth floors. Being ruined wasn't even the worst part. No, the look in Kit's eyes, the pity and guilt, had shredded her heart like strips of paper. He didn't wish to marry her. He merely wished to *save* her—and she would never marry a man for those reasons.

Years and years with her mother, as joyless as the white, unadorned walls of this stairwell, stretched out in front of her. There would always be the snide comments about Lockwood, the probing questions about Kit. The reminders of her failings to find a husband. Alice would never escape.

This is your doing. You have no one to blame but yourself.

That was true. She had gone to Kit in Newport, hoping to change her life—and she had. Except in the end, it had changed for the worse, not the better.

She rested her forehead against the smooth plaster as more tears slid down her cheeks. Despite everything, though she was ruined, she could not regret those moments with Kit. Their encounters had been wonderful, with more passion than she'd dreamed possible. Those memories would carry her through the dark days ahead, when she was back in Boston with her parents and hiding inside their home.

Lord, that prospect was depressing. She stared at her shoes. Perhaps she'd stay here all night. Better this than facing her mother's anger.

You can withstand it. You'll not let her make you feel small and stupid, not again.

No, she wouldn't, would she? Not after what had been said in the kitchen. Alice felt relief at putting her mother in her place. It had been a long time coming. Now they would forge a new relationship, one where Alice voiced her opinions more often. Starting tonight.

Or perhaps they would sever their relationship altogether. Cut off the rotten branches so that the tree might thrive, as Nellie had suggested.

No better time like the present. Alice had nothing to lose. Literally nothing. No marriage prospects, no reputation, no Kit. By morning, she'd be the laughingstock of the city. Her mother held no sway over Alice's future because there *was* no future. Let them send her off to a convent or an asylum. She no longer cared.

Resolve settled in her veins, a steely determination she'd never experienced before, but one she knew was here to stay. A new chapter had begun in Alice Lusk's future, and whatever happened would be without her mother's criticisms. Straightening off the wall, she marched up the remaining stairs.

She didn't bother going to her own suite. Instead, she walked directly inside her mother's room. Mama was pacing, giving orders to her maid about packing their things. When Alice came in, her mother stopped and glared, her hands on her hips. "I hope you are happy, young lady."

"I am not happy, no. In fact, I've never been happy—except for when I am away from you."

"A mother's role is not to make you happy but to ensure you are raised properly. To see that you make a good match. Which is now impossible thanks to what just happened in the dining room. You are a disgrace!"

"No, I am not." Alice's body shook with anger and words poured out of her mouth. "I am many things you would not begin to understand, but none of them are bad. I am a kind person who cares about other people. I love cooking and serving food. I like wine and flowers and being in a kitchen. Furthermore, I fell in love with Christopher Ward. He made me very, very happy, Mama."

Her mother's eyes bulged. "Has he ruined you? I swear, I will—"

"You will do nothing. Whatever happened between Mr. Ward and myself is private. I won't have anyone forced to marry me, be it for my reputation or my dowry. And if you try and push it, I will leave and you will never see me again."

The lines on her mother's face hardened at the threat. "After all your father and I have done for you? I cannot believe how ungrateful you are being."

Ungrateful? Alice dashed away a rogue tear. "Should I have been grateful, Mama, when you called me stupid? Or when you ripped food out of my hands? Or made me dance with the old men with fetid breath because, as you put it, how could I expect better in a husband? You have spent my whole life telling me how little I matter to you and everyone else. So do not lecture me about gratitude."

"I said those things to toughen you up. The world is a cruel place for women. You must be practical, Alice."

"I didn't need toughening up. I needed your unconditional love. I needed someone to listen to me, to make me feel like I matter. You never did that." But Kit had. A sharp lance of pain went through Alice's chest, but she pushed it aside for later. "You didn't even want me to have friends my own age. I've been drowning for years in loneliness and insecurity, but I am done. I don't care what happens to me anymore. I'll go live abroad, find work in someone's kitchen. A restaurant. Anywhere, if it means getting away from you."

"You are hysterical," her mother said, but there was worry in her eyes, as if she feared Alice might mean it. "And your father will never allow any of that."

"Daddy loves me, far more than you ever did. Who do you think called you home to Boston for three days? Daddy did that for me because I asked him to. Because he knows how impossible it is to be around you."

Every angle on her mother's face sharpened. "The two of you conspired against me? I should have known something was amiss. I suppose this was when Mr. Ward seduced you."

"He did not seduce me—I seduced him." It was quite gratifying to watch her mother's face lose all its color. "Yes, I seduced him, Mother, and I am now ruined. Furthermore, it was the best experience of my life!"

Her mother gasped. "You . . . you . . ."

"Do not dare call me a single nasty name, not ever again."

They stared at each other for a long moment. Finally, her mother said, "Pack your things. We leave for Boston first thing. Your father will be heartbroken to learn what you've done."

Doubtful, but Alice would rather explain to Daddy and take her punishment than spend another minute under her mother's thumb. "We shall see, won't we? Until morning, Mother."

Heart pounding, Alice yanked open the door and escaped into the corridor. Her skin was hot with anger and frustration, the pent-up fury boiling in her veins like water on a range.

In the corridor, a familiar figure leaned against the wall in front of her room.

Kit.

She wiped any hint of expression off her face and tried to appear calm, though every part of her longed to feel his arms wrapped around her just once more before she returned to Boston. But she had to look out for herself now. Silly crushes on men uninterested in marriage were out of the question. "Why are you here? I said all that needed to be said in the kitchen."

"Yes, but I didn't. May I come into your room?"

"You are wasting your time."

"No second spent in your presence is ever wasted. Please, let me talk to you."

"I'd like to be alone, Kit. And you should be chasing that reporter, not me. That story will ruin your supper club before it even opens."

"You come first, Alice. Always. Do you not yet understand? I am besotted beyond measure. You've stolen my heart from the moment we met in Newport."

Her own heart squeezed, soaking in the words like a dried-out sponge. But was it real . . . or pity?

Perhaps privacy would be better. She opened the door to her room and he followed her inside. Instead of sitting, she crossed to the opposite side of the room, putting as much distance as possible between them. "You are telling me what you think I wish to hear, just so I will let you rescue me. But I won't marry someone who pities me, who feels sorry for me. I won't marry you to assuage your guilt. We would only make each other miserable." Like when Kit took a mistress in a few years and stopped coming to her bed. That would kill her slowly, like a thousand tiny cuts to her heart.

"I don't need to rescue you. I decided to win you before this all happened."

She narrowed her gaze, studying each of his

familiar features, from the dark eyes and perfect nose, to the high cheekbones and sharp jawline. He appeared sincere, but she was skeptical. "Kit, there is no need to lie—"

"I have never lied to you, not once, and I never will." His mouth hitched and he shoved his hands into his trouser pockets. "Why do you think I sent you the flowers? I even went to that terrible Van Allen tea party to see you."

Alice's jaw fell open. "What? You went to a tea party?"

"I heard you were attending, so yes. I had Preston wrangle an invitation for me, and God only knows what I'll owe him in exchange for that favor. Anyway, I suffered through an afternoon of hideous small talk and disapproving stares all for naught because you weren't even there."

"My mother canceled at the last minute because of Lockwood's dinner invite." Kit had gone to a society event—and he hated society events. None of this made sense. "I don't understand. Why flowers and tea parties? That's not like you."

"Believe me, I know. Nellie told me I needed to woo you the old-fashioned way. That was what I thought she meant."

Alice couldn't help it—she laughed. "You took advice from Nellie?"

"It made sense at the time. Regardless, my efforts to convince you to marry me were already underway before that reporter showed up."

It seemed astounding, but she was beginning to believe him. "You were adamantly against marriage. And now you have changed your mind? Why?"

He sighed and shook his head. "I don't know. A combination of things, I think. Losing Forrest, realizing I could lose you to Lockwood. Nellie made me admit that I was afraid of treating my wife as my father treated my mother. That I feared I would treat you the same."

"Oh, Kit. You are not your father. You are honest and loyal to a fault. Smart and honorable, too. How could you ever doubt it?"

His smile was soft and tender, not the practiced version he gave everyone else. No, this smile was hers and hers alone, and it made her stomach flutter. "That is what makes you so special," he said, "that you see me in such a way. No one else thinks of me in flattering terms like that."

"They would if they knew you like I do."

"Don't you see? That is why I love you, why I need to marry you. Why I want you by my side for the rest of our lives."

Surprise lodged in her throat, making it hard to breathe. Love? He loved her? It seemed too good to be true. A man like Kit, in love with a plain and boring woman like Alice?

When she didn't immediately say anything, he stared at his toes. "I heard what you told your mother."

"You did?" Goodness, would the mortification never end?

"To be fair, I think the entire floor heard." That soft smile was back, and her insides melted. "I am so proud of you, sweetheart."

Swallowing, she folded her hands. "I probably should have done that years ago."

"In any case, you stood up for yourself and put

her in her place. I nearly applauded." He quirked a brow. "I also heard you say that you fell in love with me."

"That can hardly come as any great surprise, considering. Lord knows I've been making a fool of myself over you since the moment we met."

"The same is most definitely true for me."

"Really?"

In four steps, he reached her and cradled her jaw in his hands, his forehead pressed to hers. "There's no one else for me but you, Alice. And I swear, I will dedicate myself every day to making you happy. I'll buy you a restaurant, if you wish."

"You would let your wife be a restaurateur?"

"Of course. I won't ever stop you from doing what you love. Did you think I wanted a proper society wife? You would hate it and so would I."

"Yes, but I'm worried . . ." Emotions and thoughts tangled in her mind like strands of spaghetti. How could she put this into words?

He searched her gaze. "You are worried, what?"

"That I won't be enough. That you'll soon realize your mistake but it will be too late."

"You think I am lying to you."

"No, I think you are . . . overcome. By Forrest's death, by the article, by Lockwood. I don't wish to make any rash decisions regarding my future—or yours."

"I see."

He dropped his hands and stepped back. Her stomach plummeted to the carpet, until he grinned. "You wish for proof. I must prove to you that I am serious about marrying you. That I won't change my mind in a day or two."

"I don't want you to regret this. After you've had time to think about it, you'll see that it would never work between us."

"You're wrong, but challenge accepted." He bowed with a flourish. "Until tomorrow, Miss Lusk."

Chapter Twenty-Eight

❧

The massive French-style mansion sat on the corner of Commonwealth Avenue in the heart of Boston's exclusive Back Bay neighborhood. The mansard roof was dotted with chimneys, and large windows overlooked the thoroughfare. There were more than fifty rooms, complete with secret passages, and sky-lights designed by John La Farge. Alice loved every square inch of her family home, had explored each nook and cranny while growing up here.

As she exited the carriage, however, the sight brought her no sense of comfort. This world was no longer hers. She would need to leave—and not to her own home with a husband. But to a different life, most likely in Europe, away from the gossip and her mother.

Mama hadn't spoken one word to Alice today. They missed the early train and had breakfasted separately at the hotel in New York. At least it had given Alice the chance to say goodbye to Angelo and the other hotel staff members she had grown fond of.

Her mother clearly hadn't recovered from the previous evening's events, her bitterness freezing the surroundings during their journey like a block of ice. The difference now was that Alice didn't care. She had been lonely before Kit and Nellie and Katherine . . . and she could withstand it again. So, she ignored her mother and read a cookbook Franconi had recommended, making notes in the margins of things she would like to try, ingredients to add.

Their butler, James, opened the door, and two footmen hurried down the walk to deal with the luggage. James pulled the door wide. "Madam, miss. I trust you had a nice—"

"Is he in?" her mother snapped, cutting off whatever James had been about to say.

"Yes, madam. He received your telegram and is waiting in his study."

This was news to Alice. Were they speaking of her father? "Hello, James. You are looking well."

"Hello, miss." The butler smiled down at her, a rare break of emotion for the usually stoic man. "It is nice to have you home."

Mama had already left for Daddy's study, so Alice leaned in. "You just missed my lemon poppyseed cake."

"I did," James said. "No one makes it better, miss."

The compliment thawed out a tiny piece of her battered heart. "I'll make you some this afternoon."

"But . . ." His eyes darted to where her mother had disappeared. "She won't like that."

"It doesn't matter anymore, James. It really doesn't matter."

His salt-and-pepper eyebrows flew up. "I see.

New York has certainly done you some good, then."

Her chest tightened, the pain from last night nearly sending her to her knees. But James didn't need to hear all that, not at the moment. "I should go and see Daddy before she gets him riled up."

"Your father instructed me to send you to the kitchen instead."

Daddy didn't wish to see her? And why would she go downstairs now? "I don't understand."

James lowered his voice. "He said that he and your mother had things to discuss and you should go to the kitchen until they were finished."

Alice's shoulders fell. "At least I can start on the poppyseed cake, I suppose."

"Now, don't look so glum, miss." He gave her a nod. "It'll all work itself out."

Alice tried for a smile but couldn't really muster the enthusiasm. She'd lost her reputation, her friends . . . Kit. Nothing would ever be the same. "Thank you, James."

A few minutes later, she approached the kitchen. In a booming voice, Chef Point, their French cook, was giving direction to the kitchen maids and other staff. He wasn't as keen to teach Alice, not like Angelo, but she badgered him often enough that he relented every now and again. "Bonjour, Chef," she called upon entering—and then stopped in her tracks.

Kit was in the kitchen. This kitchen, here in Boston. In her home.

And he was covered in flour.

What on earth . . . ?

She blinked, certain she was hallucinating. The

kitchen grew quiet, but she could only focus on Kit, who froze at the workbench, a pastry brush in his hand. "Damn. You're early," was all he said.

"What are you doing here?"

The side of his mouth hitched sheepishly. "Making you babka." He held up the brush and a small dish. "I was just glazing it now."

The kitchen staff trickled out of the room until only she and Kit remained. Alice drew closer to the workbench. "Yes, but why? And how?"

"I cabled Mrs. Berman and she sent instructions. Chef Point helped me locate all the ingredients."

She peeked into the bread tins. A bit flat, but otherwise two perfectly shaped loaves. "But this takes hours. How long have you been here?"

"I took the first train up from New York City. I arrived around nine-thirty."

"Does my father know you are here?"

"Yes." He didn't elaborate, and the questions multiplied inside her mind. Was this why her father had sent her downstairs upon her arrival? What had Daddy and Kit discussed?

"And my father didn't have a problem with you coming to bake in our kitchen?"

"No. He seemed quite entertained by the prospect."

She rubbed her forehead. "I still don't understand why you're here and . . . baking."

He set the brush down. "You once said that food makes memories. That it's like love on a plate. And I believe it because I remember this bread, that particular evening, as the moment I fell in love with you. I saw you in a completely different light, as this competent and bossy—and incredibly alluring—woman. I've never wanted anyone more than when you sucked sugar off your finger. I tried to run, tried to deny what was happening, but that was the instant I was gone for you, Alice Lusk."

She gripped the thick wooden top of the table, her mouth dry. Words eluded her. "Kit . . ."

For a brief second, he appeared insecure, a smile that didn't reach his eyes. A chink in his rakish armor. "So what better way to prove I love you than to make this bread for you?" He slid one of the tins forward. "Why don't you cut a slice?"

"It's too hot. It needs to cool for at least twenty minutes."

"I really can't wait that long." Holding the tin with a cloth, he tipped the hot loaf onto the tabletop and reached for the bread knife.

"Wait." She came around to his side of the workbench and put a hand out to stop him. "You'll ruin that bread if you cut it now."

He sighed and placed the knife down. "Alice, there's something in the bread."

"I don't understand. What do you mean?"

"There's *something* in the bread."

"Repeating the words doesn't make the meaning any clearer, unfortunately."

"Oh, for God's sake." He glanced at the ceiling. "My mother's ring is in the bread, Alice."

A . . . ring? Was he serious? One peek at his somber and—dare she say it?—terrified eyes gave her the answer. Kit was indeed serious.

Taking the cloth to protect his hands, he lifted the entire loaf into his palms and dropped to one knee. "Alice, I love you madly. Will you do me the honor of becoming my wife?"

It was even better than she'd dreamed. Kit loved her and wanted to marry her. He'd baked for her. Fresh tears welled and panic crossed Kit's face as he watched them fall. He asked, "Are those happy tears . . . or rejection tears?"

"Happy. Definitely happy." She leaned down and kissed him briefly on the mouth. "Yes, I will marry you."

Standing, he crushed her to him with one arm and took her mouth in a deep kiss. She kissed him back eagerly, her fingers digging into his coat to pull him closer while her mind spun. She would never tire of this, their undeniable connection. They had an effect on the other that defied logic, that would confuse most anyone else. But not her. She understood him and the same could be said in reverse. He had helped her to discover so much about herself . . . and they weren't done yet, apparently.

She felt as if he deserved a warning, though. There was every chance her parents would not approve. She broke off and tried to catch her breath. "We may need to elope."

"No, we won't. Your father gave me his blessing this morning."

"He did? What did you tell him?"

Kit stroked his knuckles across her cheek. "I told him the truth. That I fell in love with you and would find a way to marry you, whether he approved or not. I think it was baking you bread that sealed the deal, though."

"What about your supper club?"

"I was able to postpone the story until tomorrow morning. Whatever happens, we'll face it together."

She liked the sound of that. She wiped a smudge of flour off his cheek. "The club will be successful. You'll find a way, Kit."

"Would you like to be our head chef?"

Was he drunk again? "What about the scandal? People won't take the club seriously with a female chef."

"First, I like scandal. And second, the only person who takes me seriously is you. So let them underestimate us, my love. It'll be that much sweeter when we become wildly popular. You deserve this, Alice. With your talent, you could work in any kitchen in the country, but I'd be honored if you chose mine."

It was everything she'd ever wanted. Her own kitchen, a loving husband. She felt like the luckiest woman in America. "Then yes, I would love to be the head chef."

He dragged her flush to his frame, where she could feel every hard bit of him against her body. "Good, because I believe we will be spending a lot of time in my office going over *details*."

Desire unwound in her belly at his husky promise, and she shivered as she thought about all the things he had left to teach her.

"Are you cold?" he asked, drawing away slightly.

"Not in the least. Just considering how we will fill all those long nights ahead, Professor Ward."

His grin turned positively predatory. "I'm certain we'll come up with something. You always were a very diligent student."

Rising up on her toes, she wrapped her arms around his neck. "I do like to impress the teacher."

Chapter Twenty-Nine

❦

Gotham Supper Club
One Year Later

Kit pushed through the swinging door that led into his wife's domain. In other words, the kitchen. He found her at the range, sprinkling something green into a cream sauce. "My love, the ladies are growing restless. I am slightly afraid to go back out there."

Alice's mouth curved. "They adore you."

"And who could blame them? However, they do get quite rowdy when they are hungry."

Each month, Alice cooked a five-course luncheon for ladies only. This was the single day of the month when just women were allowed in the supper club, and Alice invited various groups to come and dine. Suffragettes, radicals, political wives and actresses, women of every color and social status, all sitting side by side to enjoy Alice's cooking. His wife often said that nothing could bring people together better than food.

He loved to watch her work in here, in total command and so very smart. Thanks to her innovation and talent, the supper club had sold all its memberships, despite some early grumblings about a woman chef. Kit hadn't paid them any attention. Alice's food spoke for itself and, as he predicted, the brouhaha died down once people tasted her creations. There wasn't an empty seat to be had in the dining room when the place was open.

"Where are you with plating?" Alice asked over her shoulder.

Her first assistant and Mrs. Henry's daughter, Opal, was busy preparing the tiny plates of oyster vol-au-vent. "Nearly ready, Mère Ward."

Kit hid his grin. The title of mère was used in France for female professional cooks, and Alice's staff had adopted it because she refused to let them call her "chef."

"Kit, darling. As much as I like you hovering under normal circumstances, you are in my way at the moment." Alice gently moved him aside and transferred the heavy pan from the range onto the counter. She and Opal began spooning the oyster mixture into the pastry cups, while Alice continued to give instructions to the rest of the kitchen staff. Good thing she'd been training Opal to run the kitchen, because she would soon be unavailable.

After summoning the waiters to deliver the food, Kit leaned over and whispered, "I'll leave you alone for now. But you are mine after everyone leaves."

Alice bit her lip and shook her head. "Do not distract me. I need to concentrate."

Raising his hands in surrender, he left the kitchen and went to his office. He'd wait there while looking through paperwork. When he burst through the door, he came to an abrupt halt. Preston was seated in Kit's chair, feet up on the desk, while Harrison lounged in an armchair. Both were smoking cigars and looking quite at home. "Have I missed an invitation?"

"No," Harrison said. "You never invite us here, though I haven't the faintest idea why."

"Exactly," Preston agreed. "And I am part owner, for Christ's sake."

"Because the club requires paying members with cachet." Kit went over and lifted a fresh cigar out of the holder on the desk. "Neither of you qualify."

"I have plenty of cachet." Preston tossed Kit a lighter. "Or have you forgotten who ultimately convinced Hearst to kill that story about your wife?"

"Yes, fine. You have cachet. This one"—he pointed at Harrison—"is only accepted at social events because his wife is a minor sporting celebrity."

"A sporting celebrity who is never home," Harrison grumbled as he checked his pocket watch. "I'm leaving in two hours for Cincinnati where I'll finally meet up with her."

"Then why are you here?"

Preston lifted his considerable legs and put his feet on the ground. "We're here to toast him. It's been a year."

"Oh, shit," Kit said, and dragged a hand through his hair. "A year already. Jesus."

Forrest had been dead a year. It hardly seemed real sometimes.

Harrison poured clear liquid from a familiar-shaped bottle into three tiny glasses. Kit grimaced. "Is that what I think it is?"

Preston shrugged and stamped out his cigar in the ashtray. "I liked your story about the Irish and their wakes. I asked Nellie where she got the poitín."

Harrison smelled it. "Christ, that's strong. Am I going to regret this?"

"Most definitely." Kit raised his glass. "To Forrest."

"To Forrest," the other two men echoed, and they all touched glasses before throwing the liquor down their throats.

Kit was prepared for the inferno that blazed in his mouth and stomach, but Harrison wheezed for a full five minutes. Preston laughed and shook his head. "You're growing soft in your old age, Archer."

"Fuck. You," Harrison gasped.

"Kit," Preston said. "Profits are way up, the club is doing well. Congratulations."

"Thank you. Alice gets most of the credit, however."

"I know, which is why I am worried about what happens in a month."

"It'll be fine." Kit crossed his arms over his chest, not about to back down. "She won't be gone long."

"So you say, but I know how these things go . . ."

"She deserves it, after how hard she's worked."

Preston's expression hinted that he wasn't convinced, but he turned to Harrison, who'd finally caught his breath. "Shall we leave Kit to it? Then we may all go off and grieve in our own ways."

"Sleeping with your women, you mean," Harrison said. "You two will be consoled and coddled while I'm on a train headed west."

"No one cares about your celibacy, Harrison." Preston clapped him on the shoulder. "It's not my fault you fell in love with a woman who travels more than a Pullman porter."

Harrison shook Kit's hand. "Good luck. I'll see you when I return, hopefully."

Preston was next. "Tell Alice I am twice as fond of her as I am of you."

"She knows that already. Get out of here."

He cleaned up after his friends departed and got to work. There were performers to secure, orders to be placed, members to bill and many more menial tasks he'd never imagined. Preston kept after him to hire a manager, and Kit thought the time may have arrived. He was not meant to tally ledgers and argue with suppliers. Besides, they could well afford it now.

An hour and a half later the door swung open. Alice had removed her apron and repinned her hair, but she still had a smudge of chocolate on her cheek. With a wan smile, she dropped onto the sofa. "I don't know why, but these ladies' luncheons take it out of me. Much more so than a regular dinner service."

"Because you were up late last night." He came to sit next to her on the sofa.

"And whose fault was that?"

"Guilty." Leaning in, he kissed the chocolate off from her skin. "Delicious, as always."

She sighed and dropped her head onto his shoulder. "Charmer."

"I have a question for you."

Snuggling closer, she said, "All right."

"Do you want your anniversary present now or on the actual day?"

She pulled back, her eyes wide. "You bought me an anniversary present? I didn't know . . . that is, I haven't yet had time to get you anything."

"There is no need for you to buy me anything. I wanted to surprise you, to do something nice for you considering how happy you've made me."

"You've made me happy, as well." She moved in to kiss his mouth. "Very happy, indeed."

"I'm glad, sweetheart. So, tell me your answer."

"Now." She grinned, practically bouncing in her seat. "I definitely want it now."

He knew she'd say that. Going over to his desk, he retrieved the tickets from the top drawer. He brought them over and sat down. "Here."

She took the pieces of paper and studied them. "You've booked passage to . . . Plymouth, England. Oh, that's lovely. I've never been to England."

"We are going to Plymouth, but we aren't stopping there."

"We aren't?"

"From there we'll continue on to Paris."

"Paris?" At his nod, her jaw fell open. "Is this real? You are taking me to Paris?"

"We leave in three weeks."

"Oh, my God." She threw herself against him and squeezed tight. "This is so exciting. I have always wanted to go."

He was aware. However, she didn't even know the best part yet. "Wait, there's more."

"More?" She drew back and searched his face. "Are we going somewhere else, too?"

"No, just Paris. You see, with Chef Franconi's help, I've secured a week-long private training for you with Chef Mourier at—"

She pounced on him, pushing him down onto the couch, where his head smacked against the armrest. "Ow," he murmured as pain spread through his skull.

His wife was too giddy to notice his discomfort as she stared down at him. "Chef Mourier has agreed to meet with me. The Chef Mourier from Maison Maire?"

"Yes, Alice. That Chef Mourier. He said he is excited to meet this protégé of Franconi's."

"I cannot believe it. Kit, this is the very best present I've ever received. Thank you hardly seems enough, but thank you. I'm beyond grateful." She rained kisses all over his face.

He chuckled and wrapped his arms around her tightly. "You are welcome. Happy anniversary, sweetheart." He rose up to kiss her mouth.

"I love you," she whispered when they broke apart. "How will I ever give you anything as meaningful? You've chosen the perfect gift for me."

"I don't need gifts. Just my willing pupil by my side."

She kissed him briefly, then traced his jaw with her fingers. "Speaking of, Nellie told me of some very nontraditional uses for a wooden spoon. Are you interested in hearing them?"

Based on his wife's adorable blush, he had a very good idea of what they were. "I most definitely do."

She pushed to her feet and gave him a saucy smile. "Why don't I retrieve one from the kitchen? Then I can teach you a thing or two."

Acknowledgments

❧

The first example of a supper club I could find was the Vaudeville Club from 1893. A group of society gentlemen, including Stanford White, founded a private supper club inside New York City's Metropolitan Opera House while it was being renovated after a fire. This club would later transform into the Metropolitan Opera Club, which still operates today.

Madame Durham is based on several Black opera singers and performers of the Gilded Age, including Matilda Sissieretta Joyner Jones and Marie Selika Williams. The first African American to sing at Carnegie Hall (then called the Music Hall in New York), Jones was the highest paid Black performer of her day, and she ended up performing for four American presidents as well as British royalty. Williams was the first Black artist to perform in the White House, and while in Europe she performed for Queen Victoria in 1883.

There are so many people I would like to thank here, but space constraints are a real thing. So to all the romance readers, bloggers, booksellers and librarians—you make writing a pleasurable endeavor when life gets very difficult. I am incredibly thankful for all of you! Your clever tweets and beautiful bookstagram posts never fail to make me smile.

I love, love, love to work on these stories with my editor, Tessa Woodward. She is as much a fan of the Gilded Age as I am, and she helps me fine-tune these crazy historical plots and characters into something that (hopefully!) makes sense. So thank you, Tessa! Also, my heartfelt thanks to everyone at HarperCollins/Avon for all their hard work on my books, including Elle Keck, Jes Lyons, Sam Glatt, Alivia Lopez, Angela Craft, Guido Caroti and the rest of the folks behind the scenes.

Where would I be without the friends who help pick me up whenever I need it? Diana Quincy deserves some sort of medal for putting up with me, as do Sarah MacLean and Sophie Jordan (whose brilliant mind suggested a kissing lessons book!). I am beyond grateful for the wit, wisdom and support of these three ladies. Thank you also to Lenora Bell, Eva Leigh, Nisha Sharma (keep those book recs coming!) and the other writer friends who make me laugh and smile every day (you know who you are!).

I have to give a special shout-out to my softball partner-in-crime Damita (aka TeamBossBabe), who will never see this but deserves my gratitude all the same. Without her help in managing our daughters' crazy softball schedules, I would legit never finish a book.

Lastly, thanks to my mom, who reads all my

stories first, and the rest of my family for their support. Also, I could never do this without the husband who gladly makes dinner, does laundry, cleans and deals with everything else in equal measure, giving me time to write when I need it. Indeed, I am the lady who got lucky.

Want to make babka? It's very easy and so delicious! My absolute go-to recipe for chocolate babka is here, courtesy of Lisa Kaminski: tasteofhome .com/article/how-to-make-babka. (Tag me if you try it!)